The story of Josephine Cox is as extraordinary as anything in her novels. Born in a cotton-mill house in Blackburn, she was one of ten children. Her parents, she says, brought out the worst in each other, and life was full of tragedy and hardship – but not without love and laughter. At the age of sixteen, Josephine met and married 'a caring and wonderful man', and had two sons. When the boys started school, she decided to go to college and eventually gained a place at Cambridge University, though was unable to take this up as it would have meant living away from home. However, she did go into teaching, while at the same time helping to renovate the derelict council house that was their home, coping with the problems caused by her mother's unhappy home life – and writing her first full-length novel. Not surprisingly, she then won the 'Superwoman of Great Britain' Award, for which her family had secretly entered her, and this coincided with the acceptance of her novel for publication.

Josephine gave up teaching in order to write full time. She says 'I love writing, both recreating scenes and characters from my past, together with new storylines which mingle naturally with the old. I could never imagine a single day without writing, and it's been that way since as far back as I can remember.' Her previous novels of North Country life are all available from Headline and are immensely popular.

'Bestselling author Josephine Cox has penned another winner' *Bookshelf*

'Hailed quite rightly as a gifted writer in the tradition of Catherine Cookson' *Manchester Evening News*

'Guaranteed to tug at the heartstrings of all hopeless romantics' *Sunday Post*

JOSEPHINE COX

Somewhere, Someday

headline

First published in hardback in 1999 by
HEADLINE BOOK PUBLISHING

First published in paperback in 2000 by
HEADLINE BOOK PUBLISHING

This edition published in paperback in 2006 by
HEADLINE BOOK PUBLISHING

16

ISBN 978-0-7472-5757-8

Typeset in Baskerville by Palimpsest Book Production Limited,
Polmont, Stirlingshire
Printed and bound in Great Britain by
Clays Ltd, St Ives plc

Headline's policy is to use papers that are natural, renewable and
recyclable products and made from wood grown in sustainable forests.
The logging and manufacturing processes are expected to conform to
the environmental regulations of the country of origin.

HEADLINE BOOK PUBLISHING
A division of Hodder Headline
338 Euston Road
London NW1 3BH

www.headline.co.uk
www.hodderheadline.com

DEDICATION

I want to tell you about two dear friends by the names of Roger and Janet.

Those of you who live in the Blackburn area and know 'The Corporation' public house will probably have seen these two 'genuine' articles. You can't miss Roger – he's the one with the microphone in his mouth, singing to every dewy-eyed woman in the place.

His wife, Janet, simply looks on and smiles. She's patient and tolerant and all those things us women have to be for the sake of peace and quiet. She's seen it all before . . . all the singing and flirting, and carrying on. He's asking for trouble, I can tell you that, but, as far as I know, Janet has never been known to smack him in public. (Mind you, I don't know what they get up to in private, but that's their business, and I wouldn't dream of asking!!!)

Thank you, Roger, for all the things you do, and Janet, for letting him do it!

Looking forward to seeing you soon.

CONTENTS

PART ONE

SUNSHINE AFTER RAIN

Chapter One

Bedford town, 1909

IN THE DARK, between the cool, soft sheets, she clung to him, her loving gaze uplifted to his face as he lay sleeping.

For what seemed an age she lay still, her mind in turmoil, thinking about yesterday, *fearing tomorrow*.

When at last she turned away, he moved closer, awake now and, like Kelly, unsure of the future. 'I'll always love you,' he murmured. 'Don't ever forget that.'

'I won't,' she promised. In that moment, Kelly could not let him know how much she loved him. It wouldn't change anything. His decision was made and she must abide by it.

Closing her eyes, she pushed away the heartache and let the tide of sleep envelop her.

But he didn't sleep. Torn between his instinct and this woman whom he loved more than he had ever

3

thought possible, he could find no peace. He knew that in the end, whichever way he turned, there would be a price to pay.

——————<>——————

AWAKE EARLY, KELLY climbed out of bed and hurried down to make breakfast.

'Everything as normal,' she told herself as she busied about. 'Mustn't make him feel guilty.' She had always known this day would come, but knowing didn't make it any easier.

A short time later, when Barney made an appearance, she smiled as always and hid the ache in her heart.

Seated across the table from him she observed this man who would soon walk out of her life. Grateful for the time they had spent together, she counted herself luckier than most. It would have been cruel not to wish him well, for this gentle, darling man had given her so much.

Barney was not strikingly handsome; he wasn't the cleverest person in the world, nor was he wealthy. To anyone but her, he was just an ordinary, unassuming bloke, with twinkling eyes and a gift of bringing laughter where before there was none. In the five years during which he had been her friend and lover, Kelly had learned to trust again. She had dared to love and, most of all, she had learned not to be afraid.

Since coming to live in Bedford town, Kelly had been

more content. The demons that haunted her were quieter now . . . not gone for ever, because they never could be, but they were no longer destructive and that was because of him – like the ache in her heart now was because of him. Yet she understood.

'I don't blame you,' she murmured. 'You warned me from the start . . . but I just kept hoping you might change your mind.'

Anxiety rose in her. When he walked out of that door, she would be all alone again.

Concerned, he left his chair and came to where she sat. Gazing down at her for a moment, at that gentle, familiar face, he loathed himself. He saw how his decision to go had brought the sorrow back to those sincere brown eyes, and it pained him. But what could he do? If he stayed now, it would only postpone the day when he must go yet if he left now, would she be strong enough to keep the bad memories at bay?

How could he be sure?

He loved her more than he had loved *any* woman, but was Kelly's happiness more important than his? Should he sacrifice his own dream for her? More importantly, would she thank him for it in the end?

For what seemed an age he continued to look on her, remembering how good it was between them. Filled with emotion, he couldn't bring himself to speak, or tear himself away from those soulful eyes that gazed up at him with such understanding.

Her voice gentled its way into his mind. 'It's all right,' she breathed. 'I *do* understand.'

Her words struck deep. Reaching down, he drew her to him, not tenderly as usual, but savagely, with a kind of desperation. 'Oh, Kelly!' Feeling her in his arms like this, with her hair brushing his face and the wetness of her tears on his skin, he wanted to stay . . . to be with her always.

But he couldn't.

Already he had stayed too long.

Easing herself from his embrace, Kelly stood up, crossed to the dresser and reached into the cupboard. Taking out a small, worn portmanteau, she brought it to him. 'I got this ready a week ago,' she explained. 'In here, you'll find clean clothes and toiletries. And a small sum of money.'

He couldn't believe it. 'You've had this ready for a week!' How could she have known? 'But . . . I never said—'

'You didn't have to,' she stopped him. 'It was there in the way you looked at me, with that faraway longing in your eyes. Lately, I'd wake up in the early hours and you'd be standing at the window, gazing out at the night like a lost soul.' Her voice broke. 'I knew *then*,' she confessed, 'but I thought . . . *hoped*, it wouldn't be this soon.'

'It doesn't mean I don't love you, or that we'll never see each other again.'

'I know.'

'What will you do?'

'I haven't thought about it.'

Troubled now, she dropped her gaze, trying not to show him how much she needed him to stay. His question echoed in her mind; it was the same one she had asked herself time and again. When he was gone, what *would* she do?

She had no plans. All these years she had lived from day to day. Always afraid. *Always looking over her shoulder*. Barney had helped her forget, but now he was going and she felt lost.

'Kelly?'

Hesitantly, she raised her eyes, but said nothing.

Stepping closer, he put his hands on her shoulders. 'Promise me that you'll take care of yourself.'

Kelly nodded.

'You know what I mean,' he urged. 'Don't let the past overwhelm you. What happened was not *your* doing. You must never forget that.'

'Barney!' She didn't want him to think she would fall apart the minute he was gone, nor did she intend to. 'Don't worry about me,' she told him kindly. 'I know things were bad when we met, but I'm stronger now.'

Torn, he gazed at her for a moment. 'I need to believe you,' he whispered. 'These past years you've put it all behind you, and if I thought my going would bring it all back, I'd stay. Whatever it took, I swear to God . . .'

'Ssh!' Kelly put her finger to his lips. 'I *want* you to go,' she lied.

His eyes widened. 'You *want* me to go?'

Smiling, she reassured him, 'The sooner you go, the sooner you'll be back.'

His eyes clouded over. 'You know I can't promise that.'

'I remember . . . "No promises".' It was what he had said that very first night.

'Five years,' he murmured incredulously. 'Who would have thought it?'

'And now it's time to go.' The arrival of this single, agonising moment had always been the one certainty in her otherwise uncertain life. For so long she had dreaded its coming. Yet now the moment was here she felt calm . . . almost relieved. She loved this man, and always would. But his roving soul had never really belonged to her.

Confidently, she walked him to the door. They kissed and held each other, and soon it was time. 'Away with you now,' she told him, her smile as bright as the day.

As he walked down the street, she watched with a heavy heart. When he turned to wave, she waved back.

For a time, the clatter of his boots echoed along the flagstones. A few moments later the silence told her he was gone, perhaps for good. 'Goodbye, Barney,' she murmured. 'God go with you.'

As she turned towards the front door, a familiar voice made her swing round. 'Morning, dear,' it said, and she groaned inwardly.

'Morning, Molly,' she answered resignedly. Molly

Tamworth was a busybody, but harmless enough. Widowed these past ten years and childless, she didn't have much of a life, so she eagerly followed everyone else's, much to their annoyance. 'Did you know Jack Pally at number three has been carrying on again?' she asked in a lowered voice.

Kelly was in no mood for gossip. 'I'm sorry, Molly,' she said, 'but I can't stop just now.'

Molly appeared not to hear. 'Shocking business if you ask me! His missus caught the two of 'em red-handed. She came home from church on Sunday, found the two of 'em *in her bed*, if you please!' Tutting loudly, she rolled her eyes skywards. 'It doesn't take a genius to know what the buggers were up to . . .'

She might have gone on, but something in Kelly's manner silenced her; only for a moment, though, until her quick little mind put two and two together. 'All right are you, dear?' Bursting with curiosity she edged closer. 'Summat troubling you, is there?'

'No, I'm fine, thank you Molly.' Longing to get away, Kelly gave her short shrift. 'Must go, though. I've got things to do.'

'Only, well . . . I saw your Barney going down the street just now,' Molly blatantly persisted. 'You haven't broke up, have yer? Oh, I hope not. He's such a nice man.'

'Look, I really have to get on!'

Kelly needed to be alone with her thoughts. There were plans to be made and much to do.

Before the other woman could protest, Kelly hurried into the house and closed the door. 'Nosy old devil!' She couldn't help a wry little smile. 'You have to feel sorry for her though. I expect she's lonely . . . like me.'

The reality was only now beginning to hit home.

For the rest of the day Kelly busied herself, trying to postpone the minute when she must contemplate a future without Barney. It wouldn't be easy, she knew. For five long years her life had revolved around him, and now she had only herself to worry about. Would she stay here, or would she go? And, if she did leave, *where* would she go?

Madly cleaning the house from top to bottom, she shut the important things from her mind. She didn't want to think about them, at least not until she had to.

It was five o'clock when Kelly finally fell into a chair, exhausted. For a long time, she sat there, her face heated from the warmth of a newly lit fire, and her aching legs stretched out in front of her. 'What now?' she asked herself, and as though it had been brewing in her subconscious, the answer was suddenly stark in her mind.

'*Go home, Kelly.*' Surprising her, the words tumbled out: '*It's time to lay the ghosts.*'

Restless, she took a box from the dresser and set it down on the table. It was an old shoe-box. At one time it had held new boots, but now it was stuffed with memories . . . both good and bad.

Seating herself before the box, she was still for a

while, curiously gazing at it; knowing what was inside yet afraid to open it in case the memories escaped and were lost for ever.

Gingerly now, she removed the blue ribbon that held the tattered lid to the box. Laying the ribbon down she lifted the lid and put it aside. Another moment and she had the entire contents of the box spread out before her.

Kelly knew them all by heart. Every article – each damning word and picture – was etched in her memory for all time.

Trembling, she set them out in order.

First came the yellowing newspaper cuttings. These were the oldest and the most chilling of all, chronicling the tragedy as it unfolded . . . the brutal killing of 'a good man'; the events leading up to it and the consequences that followed.

It was all there, too harrowing to read.

There were also two letters. The first one, dated four years before, was a brief outpouring from Kelly's brother, Michael; the other, dated only months earlier than Michael's, was a long and seemingly sincere letter from her mother. Both had been hidden away, out of sight but not out of mind.

Hesitantly, Kelly re-read the letters.

As always when she read Michael's letter, her emotions were a mingling of love and disgust, for though she loved him still, she had seen a weak and cowardly side to his character that she never knew existed.

Her mother's letter, while dealing with the same issue, was of a different nature. Sure and repentant, it betrayed the deeper feelings of a woman who had suffered and was suffering still.

Neither letter had ever been answered by Kelly.

As she read now, the tears flowed down her face. The pain had not gone away. It never would.

Dear Kelly,

I'm glad you did not change your name. Even so, it took me a long time to track you down.

As you may or may not know, your brother did change his name, and was even more difficult to find. But then he was always weak, while you were strong. Changing his name was his way of hiding from what happened, and who can blame him for that?

My sources tell me that you and Michael have gone your separate ways and have not been in touch for some long time. Though I find that very sad, I do understand, especially as I, too, chose to isolate myself from those I love.

I have known your whereabouts for some time now. You see, for my own peace of mind I needed to watch you both from a distance – to know you were safe.

These past years have not been easy for any of us, but we were right to put the miles between us. I have not regretted that decision, even though there were times when I desperately needed you. However, common-sense prevailed and I kept away.

Now, though, in my sixty-fifth year, I feel the need to let you both know how much I love you. In case I might cross your mind now and then, you should be aware that I am well and financially secure.

Like you, I have many regrets, but I refuse to let the past destroy me. I pray that you too have put all the bad things behind you.

The future is all that matters.

Neither of you have anything to be afraid of . . . or to be ashamed of. Always remember that.

Remember, too, that you are in no danger. I am watching over you.

I know this letter will come as a shock, and I am aware that you might not thank me for reminding you of a time you would rather forget. But I need you to know that I love you still, and always will . . .

The letter ended . . .

. . . I have enclosed my lawyer's address. I do not expect you will want to contact me but, as I have said, I am fortunate enough to want for nothing so if there is anything you need – anything at all – please, Kelly, let him know and he will tend to it.

He has instructions and will carry them out to the letter. You have my word that your privacy and your past are protected.

Goodbye, Kelly. I'm always thinking of you,

Love from your mother.

When the letter was finished, Kelly sat quite still, eyes closed, for a long time. Then she folded the letter and laid it aside.

There was a photograph, too, taken in the autumn of 1876, when Kelly was ten years old and her brother twenty. The picture portrayed a family much like any other: mother, father, and two children, dressed in their Sunday best and standing stiffly to attention.

A very ordinary picture, betraying nothing of the extraordinary events destined to happen a short time later; *on a day when all their lives would change for ever*.

Now, as the memories all became too much to bear, Kelly began to pack everything away, making the same bitter comment that she had so many times before: 'It's not much to show for four lives.'

Yet, though her 'life' had been bleak for a very long time, it had not ended there, because now she had other, kinder things to remember, all to do with Barney and the last five years.

In the shoe-box was a photographic portrait of Barney, showing his lopsided grin, and some of her, shy and happy as he trained the camera-lens on her. There were others of the two of them, laughing in the sunshine, obviously delighting in each other's company.

Remembering, she traced the outline of his face with the tip of her finger. 'I'll miss you,' she murmured, 'but I don't blame you. With your wandering, gypsy soul, I never expected you to stay for so long ... neither of us did.'

Holding his picture to her heart, she went on: 'I don't suppose I'll ever see you again, will I?' Yet she knew that if he wanted to find her, she could move to the other end of the world and Barney would track her down. It was a comforting thought.

With great care, she replaced the final pieces of her life into the shoe-box and tied up the lid with the same blue ribbon that had kept it secure these many long years.

Returning the box to the dresser, she closed the door on it. 'I won't open it again . . . not for a while anyway,' she mused. It was too painful, and anyway, if all went well, after today her time and energy would be taken up in a new direction; a direction which, strangely enough, would take her *back*, almost to the beginning. Because only then could she begin to go forward.

'"Going home",' she breathed. 'Oh Kelly . . . just think of it!' And suddenly her heart was full.

A short time later, she locked up the house, put the guard in front of the fire and went to bed. But she didn't sleep. Instead, she lay wide awake, looking out of the window at the stars and making plans.

The more she thought about it, the more she began to look forward. It wouldn't be easy, she knew that, but, 'Tomorrow will be the first step. After that, we'll see.'

Folding her hands together, she said a little prayer: 'Dear Lord, help me to be strong. Help me, and others, to forgive.'

So much to forgive and half a lifetime already gone. That was *another* sin. Yet, even now, there was still time to make amends. But where to start? How to find the courage?

'There has to be a way,' she whispered.

After a while, she closed her eyes and went to sleep, feeling calmer than she had done in a very long time.

———◆———

IT WAS THE loud knocking that woke Kelly. 'What? Who's that?' Hoisting herself up on her elbows, she cast sleepy eyes round the room. When the knocking persisted, she scrambled out of bed and ran to the window, a smile creasing her face when she saw it was old Ned, the knocker-upper.

The old man looked up. 'Morning, miss.' His tooth-less grin made her chuckle. 'It's five o'clock. Time to get yer pretty little arse outta bed.'

'Thank you, Ned!' Giving him a wave, she groaned to herself, 'I forgot all about Ned.'

The five o'clock call was for Barney. Kelly herself didn't usually rise until ten minutes before he went off to work, at about six-thirty. 'Ah, well, as Ned so rightly says, it's time to get my "arse" out of bed . . . though I'm not sure about the "pretty" bit.'

Drawing her nightgown tighter, she scrutinised her round, homely figure in the mirror. 'Not bad for forty-three. Oh, but there *was* a time when I recall being slimmer and more fetching,' she mused, 'but them days are long gone – more's the pity.' These days she had more important things on her mind than her fading looks.

Kelly had no illusions about herself. She was no beauty and never had been. There was nothing exceptional about her. She had good legs and a passable figure – strong, thick hair, and eyes that Barney called, 'brown and warm as nutmeg'. Nothing special; nothing to be conceited about. But Barney had loved her, and that was enough.

Impatient with herself, she snatched up her robe and went down to get the house warm. 'October!' She shivered. 'The worst month of the year!' It was the end of summer and the onset of winter, an 'in-between' month. A 'nothing' month.

A moment later, on her knees before the grate, Kelly was piling kindling on top of the crumpled paper when she suddenly realised something very curious. 'My God! Why did I never see it before?' Leaning back on her haunches, she shook her head. 'Every big change in my life has been in the month of *October*!'

She recounted the major episodes. 'When the family was split up . . . when I met Barney . . . and now he's gone and here I am about to embark on the loneliest journey of my life. Every time my life changes direction, it's always in October!'

She wondered if it meant anything in particular, but in the end decided it was just one of those peculiar coincidences. 'When all's said and done, it's just another ordinary month,' she declared philosophically and, pushing the observation aside, got on with the task in hand.

In no time at all she had the fire crackling away, the tea brewed and her brown earthenware mug standing at the ready. Set out on the table was a piping hot breakfast – two fried eggs, a slice of bacon, and a chunk of bread on a side plate, to mop up any fatty juices. 'Just what the doctor ordered,' she chuckled, settling down to the feast. The smell of the sizzling bacon and familiar aroma of freshly brewed tea had sharpened her appetite.

Later, when the last drop of tea was drunk and every morsel of food enjoyed, Kelly lost no time in organising herself for the day ahead. Fond of making lists, she made one now:

(1) Finish the dress for Mrs Cooper and take it back.
(2) Let all the customers know I shall be closed for business from today.
(3) Close up the house, give a week's notice to the landlord, and talk to Jack Denby about shifting the furniture.
(4) Take all my savings with me – enough for a deposit on a house, and enough to keep me going until I get work.

When the list was complete, she leaned back in the chair and thought about what she was doing. 'You're taking a big step, Kelly, lass,' she told herself, 'but Barney's gone, and however much you might wish it different, it's not likely he'll be back.'

Barney had set out on his own adventure. Now it was her turn. 'If you don't do it now,' she decided, 'you never will.'

Excited yet apprehensive about her decision to confront the past, Kelly swiftly put her plan into action before she had a chance to change her mind.

By ten o'clock she had cleared and washed her breakfast things, dusted round and, using the sheets off the beds, covered all the soft furnishings. The curtains were left half-drawn, and the fire allowed to die right down; even so she put the guard in front.

'Can't be too careful,' she murmured. 'There were rogues and thieves even here.'

She then washed and dressed, choosing an ankle-length black skirt, with a brown woollen cardigan over her blouse, and strong, laced boots over thick dark stockings.

Next, she packed a small portmanteau, taking only the basic things – several changes of undergarments; toiletries and a warm jumper, her silver-backed mirror and hairbrush, and two pairs of serviceable, warm stockings. 'That should be enough for the few days I'll be away,' she observed. After that, she hoped to put the final part of her plan into action, but for the moment she was stepping into the unknown. 'God help me,' she muttered. 'If this is to work, I must burn all my bridges behind me, once and for all.'

Checking the portmanteau one final time, she closed the lid, clicked shut the hinges and carried it down to the front door.

Standing it on the mat, she lingered a while, staring down at the familiar, small brown case, recalling the day she had carried it over this very threshold. 'Today is the first time in five years that case has seen daylight,' she reflected.

Mentally shaking away the cobwebs, she returned to the parlour where she collected Mrs Cooper's finished dress. It was a beautiful thing, a gown of emerald green, with cream lace at the wrists and neck. 'I've done a right good job with this dress, even if I do say so myself,' she declared proudly. Laying the dress into a fold of paper, she covered it with the leftover material and draped it carefully over the back of a chair, ready to take with her.

All that remained to do now was to check through the house once more, and ensure that she had all her savings intact. These were kept in a small cash tin behind the horse-hair settee.

She counted the money out. 'Six pounds in all.' It was a respectable amount, painstakingly earned from her dressmaking skills, but, 'What with moving all my things and paying rent in advance, it won't last long if I don't get work fairly soon.'

At the front door, she gave one last glance round. 'Well, Kelly, my girl, you've taken the first step, but it won't be the hardest one.' A shiver of apprehension rippled through her. 'You've made a start though, and come rain or shine, there'll be no turning back now!'

The hearty chuckle made her swing round. 'Talking to yourself is the first sign of madness, did yer know that?' It was Molly Tamworth. 'I heard you mumbling to yerself,' she went on, 'but I couldn't quite hear what you were saying.' Slightly deaf, she cupped her hand round her ear, obviously expecting Kelly to enlighten her.

Instead, Kelly gave her a smile. 'Morning, Molly.'

Ever alert, Molly's quick eyes spotted the portmanteau. 'Off on a holiday, are yer?'

'Not a holiday, but yes, I expect to be away for a few days.' Or if things took a turn for the better, she might not come back at all.

'That's nice, dearie. I expect yer meeting that fella o' yourn?'

Kelly thought it best to play along. 'There's not much you miss, is there, Molly?'

'I'm a nosy old bugger, that's why. I ain't got nowt else to do with me time.'

There was something very sad about the poor thing, and Kelly was moved to offer, 'Would you like to earn a shilling?'

'All depends what I'm asked to do for it.'

'Keep an eye on the house while I'm gone?'

Molly's eyes lit up. 'Money in advance?'

'If you like.'

'Done! Give us yer shilling then.'

Digging into her purse, Kelly gave her the shilling. 'I'll be gone a few days . . . a week at the most.'

Pocketing the money, Molly held out her hand again. 'I'll want the key.' Her eyes glittered with anticipation. There was nothing she liked more than rooting about amongst other folk's things, whenever she got the chance, that was.

'You'll not need the key,' Kelly assured her. 'Everything is secured, I just want you to see who comes and goes and to frighten anyone away that you don't like the look of.'

'Oh, I'll do that all right, don't you worry!'

Thanking her, Kelly said goodbye.

Walking down the street she had to smile. 'I can rest assured that the house will be in safe hands anyway,' she chuckled. 'What! Even a *pigeon* won't be able to settle on that roof without her knowing it.'

Her first call was to Mrs Cooper, a rather large, well-endowed lady of ample fortune. 'Oh, it's beautiful!' She was so thrilled with the dress that she gave Kelly an extra two shillings; though her smile dropped when Kelly informed her she would need to find someone else to make and mend her clothes in future.

All Kelly could do was apologise. Mrs Cooper had been one of her best customers.

Apologies over, she made her way to the local grocery store where she paid to have a message pinned on the noticeboard. 'Are you going away for good then?' Mr Noble was a dear old soul. 'Only the notice says you won't be dressmaking any more.' His old eyes spotted what she was carrying. 'And I see you've got your case packed for off.'

Having no heart for explanations, Kelly bade him farewell. 'I expect I'll see you in a few days,' she said, and quickly made her getaway.

The next stop was her landlord's office. A lumbering giant of a man, he spent his days in a dingy back-room office. The place smelled of camphor and linseed. 'State your business!' Impatient and busy, he hardly ever looked up at his visitors.

Kelly's voice rang out loud and clear. 'I've come to give notice.'

He shuffled aside his papers and peered at her through tiny rimless spectacles. 'You've what?' Shaken by her announcement, he left his mouth hanging open. It was not a pretty sight.

'I've been very comfortable in Albert Street all these years,' she admitted graciously, 'but now I'm obliged to give a week's notice.' There! It was said, and it seemed like a weight off her mind.

'Why?' Like a great spreading thing, his enormous body crept forward until the desk was smothered beneath him.

'My circumstances have changed.'

For what seemed an age he stared at her, his nose wrinkling as though he might sneeze and his huge, flabby hands fidgeting with a scroll of paper which, in minutes, was reduced to shreds. 'You say you're obliged to give a week's notice?'

'Yes, sir.'

'You've got it wrong!'

'No, I haven't.'

Grinning wickedly he told her, 'I have the agreement to hand, and it says you are required to give a *month's* notice.'

Kelly did not argue. Instead, she opened her bag and took out a copy of the same agreement. 'I've got it here,' she advised him, 'and it says, quite clearly, in your own hand, "The tenant, Miss Kelly Wilson . . . will be obliged to tender one week's rent, and one week's notice, on vacating the said premises."'

Holding the document out, she invited, 'Would you like to see for yourself?'

Knowing he was rumbled, he leaned forward, completely covering the desk top. 'I see you're a woman of learning?'

'I like to think so.'

'Very well. I accept your week's notice.'

'As from today.' Realising how far she had come in her plan already, Kelly could only pray it would all work out.

'Don't have much choice, do I?'

Handing him a written paper, she told him, 'This

is to say I have one week's grace from today, in which to have my furniture and such removed from the premises.'

'Why would I want this?' Scornfully, he threw the paper on to the desk.

'Would you please sign it?'

He laughed aloud and the whole room seemed to shake. 'You don't trust me, is that it?'

'Just a precaution, sir.'

Giving an almighty sigh, he adjusted his spectacles and scanned the letter. Snatching up a pen, he signed the document and, skimming it across the desk to her, demanded sullenly, 'Now – one week's rent in lieu, if you please!'

Expectantly holding out his hand he was lost for words when Kelly quietly informed him, 'You will have your week in lieu, and another week's rent on my return, sir. I expect to be away only a few days, a week maybe, but no longer.'

Shaking with temper he took a moment to compose himself. 'Then, my dear, you will return to find your furniture gone and a new tenant settled in!'

'And *you*, sir, will find yourself in all manner of trouble.'

'What the devil d'you mean?'

'When I tell the neighbours how you've been charging them a much higher rate than you charged me *and* that you've sold off the factory at the end of the street for a slaughterhouse.'

His fist slammed down on the desk. 'What! You're a damned liar!'

'Maybe so. But who do you think they'll believe – you, or me?'

'I don't give a stuff *who* they believe! If they cause any trouble I'll have them out on the street before they know what day it is. I'll soon put in new tenants. There are plenty of folk out there looking for decent housing.'

'Hmh!' Kelly stared him out. 'Let me see now, there are twenty-eight houses down Albert Street. Think you can fill them all, do you?'

'Twice over, damn you!'

But Kelly had her teeth in him now, and wouldn't let go. 'I don't think so,' she said coolly. 'Especially after they're told how you've earned a sly reputation for putting up the rent the minute they've signed on the dotted line . . . and how, if they have the misfortune to miss just *one* week's rent, you send in the bailiffs, who seize whatever they can lay their hands on. Oh, and what about the slaughterhouse? No self-respecting person will live near the smell and noise of such a hellish place, however desperate they might be. I'm sure they'd rather take their chances under a railway bridge.'

'You spread one malicious lie about me and my business, and I swear to you now I will have you thrown in jail and flogged until the skin hangs from your back! I can do it too. Don't think I can't.'

Kelly shook her head determinedly. 'Oh, I'm sure

you could arrange all that,' she agreed. 'The pity of it is, the harsher you treat me, the more of a monster you become, and the more all good folks will steer clear of you.'

Seeing she was winning the argument, she went on, 'No, sir. If you empty those houses, they'll *stay* empty. Oh, but then again, you might get a few undesirable tenants willing to take them on – ruffians and the like – who'll make your life a misery.'

'GET OUT!' Every flabby fold of skin was shivering. 'Get out, you witch! Before I strangle you with my own hands!'

Unperturbed, Kelly remarked, 'I take it we're agreed, then? I will expect to report here in a week's time, carrying my due rent and the keys. Until then, I bid you good day, sir.'

With that, she quietly departed; behind her she could hear his booming voice yelling threats after her. Then came the thud of what sounded like a heavy object being thrown at the door.

'Tut, tut.' Kelly glanced back in disdain. 'What a frightful temper, I must say!' Farther down the corridor, she fell against the wall and collapsed in a fit of giggles. 'The poor old bugger!' she laughed. 'And as for *you*, Kelly Wilson . . . well!' She rolled her eyes to the ceiling. 'Barney would have been proud of you!'

The final stop was Amy Street. Here she found the blacksmith at his forge. 'Well, you're a pretty sight, Miss Wilson.' In his late forties, a happily-married man with four handsome daughters, mild-mannered Jack Denby was well-respected in Bedford town. 'What can I do for you?'

'Morning, Mr Denby.' Kelly wondered at being called 'pretty' for the second time that morning. Happen others could see what she couldn't see herself. 'I have a mind to move North,' she informed him. 'I know you do house-moving and such in between your blacksmithing, but, well, I'm not sure if the North might be a bit far for you to travel . . .'

He stopped her. 'Away with yer,' he smiled. 'The further it is, the more I earn – unless you've a mind to ask me if I'll do it for nothing, in which case the answer has to be no. I've five hungry mouths to feed . . . not counting my own, o' course.'

Kelly assured him that she wouldn't dream of asking him to do such a journey for nothing. 'No, I have the means to pay you,' she assured him. 'If you'll tell me now how much it is, I'll put the sum aside.'

He scratched his chin while thinking. 'North, you say.'

'Blackburn town.'

'A fair way then?'

'Can you do it?'

'Aye, I can do it right enough, but it'll cost yer summat in the region of . . .' he blew out his cheeks and sent the words rushing out in a burst of air, 'near enough a guinea, I'd say.'

'That's too much!' Kelly was horrified.

'Away with you, it's no such thing!' He began counting on his fingers. 'First of all there's the nag's feed *and* the shoeing. He's not about to walk all that way without needing new shoes, is he? Then there's wear and tear on the wagon, not to mention my time and labour when I could be smithying.' He regarded her with interest. 'I suppose you'll be wanting me to shift it on my own, will you?'

'Well, *I* can't help – except for the small things.'

'Right, well, that'll mean I might have to get a lad for shifting the heavier stuff. That's happen a few shilling more.'

'All right then. One guinea, and I'll pay half right now if you say the job's agreed.'

'Agreed!' They shook hands on it. 'And when is it to be done?'

'I can't give you a definite day or time, or even an address yet. But I'll be back in a few days and hope to have all the information then.'

As she paid over the ten shillings and sixpence, he wrote out a receipt and promised, 'I'll be here and waiting, you can count on me.'

The bargain was sealed.

'I'll be back within the week,' Kelly advised him, and with all the loose ends neatly tied, she went on her way.

At the railway station she bought a return ticket to Blackburn town. 'Visiting kith and kin, are you?' The ticket-master was a chatty soul.

'You could say that,' Kelly replied. Under her breath she murmured, '"Kith and kin" . . . and all they left behind.'

As she boarded the train, she glanced back at Bedford town and all she had known – the rows of little houses and the bridge in the far distance. In her mind's eye she could see the curve of river and the swans gliding there. 'I'll miss you when I'm gone for good,' she whispered.

Even now she wasn't sure she had made the right decision. As the train chugged away, she caught sight of the river, and the trees, and her heart turned somersaults. 'Dear God, don't let me live to regret what I'm doing,' she prayed.

Especially not now, when she had burned all her bridges behind her.

Chapter Two

IT WAS MANY hours later when the train drew into Blackburn main station. Kelly couldn't wait to disembark and put her feet on firm ground.

It had been a long, tiring journey. The constant swaying motion of the train had caused her stomach to churn. Then, when it seemed the ordeal would soon be over, the train was kept waiting outside of Preston while they cleared a blockage on the line. It had seemed to take an age and now, being so close to the town where she had been born and bred, and where the tragic sequence of events had begun, her courage was ebbing. 'Come on, Kelly!' she chided herself wearily. 'You've come this far . . . you can do it.'

Squaring her shoulders, she climbed down from the train, the only passenger to disembark at this stop. Like a lost soul she stood in the middle of the platform, glancing about, searching for the exit.

'Take your bag, ma'am?' A kindly porter came to her

rescue. Without waiting for a reply, he relieved her of the portmanteau and placed it on his trolley. Thanking him, she let him lead the way out.

In the main foyer, she tipped him for his trouble. 'I need a taxi-cab,' she told him. 'Where will I find one?'

'Straight through there,' he told her, and pointed to the main doors. 'You'll see a line of cabbies waiting by the kerb.' With a friendly wink he warned her, 'Watch out for the big fat fella . . . he'll get you where you're going all right, but he'll take you twice round the gasworks first, and charge you double for his trouble.'

Kelly thanked him. 'I don't suppose you could direct me to a respectable boarding house, one with reasonable rates?'

'Well now, you really *have* come to the right fella!' Puffing out his chest, he informed her with pride, 'My sister Fran keeps a clean boarding house on Park Street. I swear, on me old mam's grave, you'll not find more respectable and reasonable premises in the whole of Blackburn town.'

Hopefully peering about, he raised his voice in case anyone else might be searching for bed and board. 'Freshly laundered sheets on the beds, and good wholesome food on the table,' he stoutly declared. 'She takes care of her boarders, does our Fran! Now, you tell the cabbie to take you straight to Park View boarding house, halfway along Park Street, off Preston New Road. He'll know it, I'm sure.'

Kelly congratulated herself on having found such a

gem. 'You've warned me about the big fella and I'm grateful for that,' she said, 'but I was just wondering . . . I don't suppose you could advise me which cabbie I *should* hire?'

Leaning forward, the porter confided, 'Providing he's not already out on a fare, you won't do better than look for a man with a dark 'tash, and a grey horse, with his cab painted the colour of mulled wine.' His face beamed with pride. 'That's my brother, Ted,' he revealed, 'the best cabbie in town.'

Kelly chuckled. 'Thank you,' she said. 'You and your family are a little industry all on your own.'

'Well, we have to look after our own, isn't that the truth?' he said, and gave her a wink.

Kelly nodded, but his words of wisdom made her think of her own family.

So much love. So much pain.

'Goodbye,' she said gratefully, at the same time taking her portmanteau. 'I've no doubt we'll meet again.'

'Oh, I'm sure, ma'am.' And he went away whistling a merry tune.

Outside, Kelly scanned the long line of cabs, each with their owner sitting atop. Sure enough, the first one to approach her was the big fat fella. 'Where to, ma'am?' Boldly assuming she had already given him the fare, he jumped down to take her luggage.

Kelly stretched her gaze beyond, to the smaller, shabbier cab parked immediately behind the fat fella's. She recalled the porter's description. Yes, this was the one. 'Thank you,' she told the man, 'but I've already made my choice.'

Seeing how the little man with the 'tash was looking in her direction, she gave him a nod.

When he quickly scrambled from his seat to open the cab door, she made her way over to him; much to the indignation of the big fella. 'Hey! I was first.' Glaring from Kelly to the other man, then back again, he grew red in the face. 'You take the first cab in line, and that's *me*! It's the way we do things round these parts.'

'Well, it isn't the way *I* do things.' Kelly smiled knowingly. 'Besides, being the first doesn't always make you the best.'

'Hold on there, missus!' Now he was insulted. 'I've never been questioned afore, and neither has the arrangement . . . first cab gets first fare. It's allus been that way.'

'Don't you think that's a bit unfair? I mean, you and the other cabbies are free to agree any arrangement you see fit. But it's *me* who's paying the fare, and with due respect, I've already made my choice and it isn't you.'

When he seemed shocked, she wisely added, 'But you're very kind to offer, thank you all the same.' It was no use antagonising him, she thought.

In a moment she was across the cobbles and climbing into the second cab. Without a backward glance they set off at a respectable trot to the boarding house on Park Street.

For Kelly, the ride through town and on to Preston

New Road was more of an ordeal than she'd feared. As they passed familiar landmarks, it was like the whole of her life flashing by; that grand, proud Town Hall, and the beautiful museum with its fine façade and thick stone walls; the familiar picture-house at the corner of the main street; the sweet shop with its bull's-eye windows; the big stone arches leading into Corporation Park . . . nothing had changed. Nothing ever would, not in her mind's eye anyway.

The cabbie's voice interrupted her thoughts. 'Here we are, miss.' Jumping down, he opened the door for her.

When Kelly stepped on to the pavement, he looked towards the house and waved his arm in an extravagant gesture. 'This is Fran Docherty's boarding house . . . and you won't do no better than this, if you don't mind me saying. You see, she's my own sister, and that's how I know.'

Kelly took a moment to look at the house. It was one of those places that had long ago seen its best, but was impressive all the same. Big and sprawling, with clusters of thin chimneys and long, narrow windows, it had tall gable-ends interspersed with thick dark timbers, a wide, winding path to the front door, and an ornate iron gate leading from the pavement. Despite its air of faded grandeur, it was a proud, commanding house.

'Good woman, bad marriage,' the cabbie's voice confided softly in her ear. 'He left my sister with nothing but this place . . . the only thing to stand between her and the workhouse. But she made good, God bless her, and while you're here, our Fran'll see to it that you're as snug as a bug in a rug.'

'It's a lovely house.' Surprised that he should tell her about his sister's downfall, Kelly changed the subject. 'I'm sure I'll be fine here.' She gazed a moment longer at the house. There was an air of contentment about it that made her feel she had come to the right place.

Fran Docherty, too, was a delight. A big, bustling mound of a woman, she had a soft, squashy smile that reminded Kelly of a newly stuffed eiderdown. 'Come in! Come in!' Grabbing Kelly's portmanteau, she ushered her into the hallway. 'How far have you travelled, lass?' she enquired kindly, at the same time noting Kelly's tired face. 'My word, you look out on yer feet, so yer do.'

Leading her to a comfortable armchair she sat Kelly down. 'You just settle yerself there,' she said, 'an' I'll fetch yer a tray of summat. Now then, what would yer like?' Before Kelly could answer, she wagged a finger. 'A toasted teacake and a pot of tea, that allus does the trick.'

As she sailed grandly out, she gave the cabbie his instructions. 'Now then, Ted, you don't want to waste time here, losing fares and all. Come into the kitchen and I'll find you summat hot and tasty to send you on your way.' As she hurried off, he dutifully followed . . . like a little lad after his mammy.

Having caught her breath, Kelly settled into the chair. 'I can see there'll be no arguing with *her*,' she chuckled. All the same, she liked Fran right from the start. 'I've a feeling me and this Fran will get on just fine,' she murmured. 'She says what she thinks – a woman after my own heart.'

Looking round the room, she saw how painstakingly it had been furnished: long, flowery curtains hung at the windows, the furniture had been lovingly polished and adorned with all manner of pretty ornaments, the rugs seemed to grow round your feet as you walked on them, and the warm, safe walls enclosed you. That 'good' feeling Kelly had experienced outside grew stronger.

On the mantelpiece was a row of miniature photographs. Curious, she went to take a closer look: 'All children!' The cabbie had said nothing about his sister having children. 'Good woman, bad marriage', that was what he'd said.

Kelly was intrigued. Four children, eh? Three girls and a boy, all very handsome, and none of them with a look of the big woman.

Hearing someone approach, Kelly returned to her chair. It was Ted. 'You'll be well looked after here,' he told her, and in a minute, was gone.

'I suppose you know Ted's my brother?' Entering the room with a tray the size of a single bed, Fran laid it on the small table between them.

Kelly nodded. 'Your other brother told me – the porter.'

Fran laughed aloud. 'I had an idea Wilf had sent you.' While she talked she poured the tea. 'I went through a bad patch some time ago, and they've taken it on themselves to look after me.'

Kelly thought of her own brother. 'You're very lucky.'

Something in Kelly's voice told Fran that here was another casualty of life. 'Here you are, lass.' Handing her a cup of tea, she waited until Kelly had taken a sip and placed the teacup on the table, before saying kindly, 'Have you any brothers?'

'Just the one.' The way things were, Kelly thought she might as well not have any at all.

'Sisters?' Handing her a small plate containing the teacake, she warned, 'Mind yourself, lass, it's piping hot.'

Kelly shook her head. 'No sisters.' Taking a bite of the teacake, she gasped with delight. 'This is wonderful,' she said, licking the butter from her lips. 'Did you bake it yourself?'

Beaming with pleasure, Fran told her, 'I bake *everything* meself. There was a time when the muffin man used to call, but not any more.' She chuckled. 'Except when he runs short and wants me to bake him a batch.'

'And do you?' Kelly couldn't believe she was talking to this woman as if she had known her all her life. But it felt natural; Fran was such an easy person to talk to.

'Now and then,' Fran replied. 'I've learned the value of money, see, and every penny helps.' The smile slipped and her eyes clouded with sadness. 'Sometimes life can be so cruel. You never know what's waiting for you round the corner.'

'I understand what you're saying.' Kelly knew all about life's nasty surprises.

Glancing at her new guest's face, Fran suspected she might have touched her on the raw. Quickly changing her mood, she declared: 'Cleanliness and good food, that's my motto. Clean sheets weekly and towels changed every morning – and as far as food is concerned, I like my guests to have everything new on the day. I've got chickens out the back for fresh eggs, and a vegetable patch where I grow all my own produce.' She grinned broadly, showing a good set of teeth. 'I bet you never expected that, did you, eh? Not in such a posh street as this.'

'From what I've seen of you already, nothing would surprise me,' Kelly joked.

Fran laughed aloud. 'Come as a shock to you, have I?'

'Like a breath of fresh air,' Kelly chuckled.

There was a moment as each woman quietly observed the other, and liked what she saw.

Fran was the first to speak. 'Eat up,' she said, 'then I'll show you to your room.'

A few moments later they were on their way upstairs. 'This house is all I have,' Fran confided. 'At first it was like a millstone round my neck. But then I realised it were a damn sight more than many another poor sod could call their own, so I stopped feeling sorry for myself and got down to work.' Looking sideways at Kelly, she said gruffly, 'It wasn't easy. Many a time I thought I'd lose my sanity.'

Suddenly she was smiling, slightly embarrassed. 'Will you listen to me!' she tut-tutted. 'Telling you my life story, when all you want is to freshen up and rest after your journey.'

'That's all right,' Kelly assured her. 'There's time enough.'

In fact, in those few moments when Fran had lowered her guard, Kelly found herself drawn to her in friendship; something she had never experienced before. Self-conscious and full of secret guilt, she had kept her distance from other people, scared lest they might come too close. Except for Barney, of course ... He was different.

Thinking of Barney brought a lump to her throat. She had always known the day would come when he would follow his heart and take to the open road. She had tried so hard to prepare herself for his going, but, right now, she wished with all her heart that she could have gone with him.

Fran turned the top step and came onto the landing. 'You mustn't mind me, you know,' she commented. 'I don't usually confide in folk, but you have such a kind face, all my troubles sort of tumbled out afore I realised. You'll be wishing you hadn't been brought here now!' she said ruefully. 'I'm a silly old bugger, and I'm very sorry if I've embarrassed you.'

'You haven't,' Kelly assured her. 'Besides, we all have

our troubles. We all need to tell someone, sometime.' Kelly had told Barney everything, and he had listened without judging. She had loved him for that, and even if he was gone for ever, she would *still* love him for ever.

'Well, here we are then.' Sweeping into the room, Fran threw out her arms in a grand gesture. 'This is the best room in the whole house,' she declared, adding with a wry little grin, 'it's even better than mine.'

The bedroom was surprisingly large. The two long windows made it very light and open, and the high ceiling lent a feeling of spaciousness. It was simply furnished, but spotlessly clean.

Rushing to the window, Kelly looked out; from her vantage point she could see almost the whole of Corporation Park . . . so painfully familiar. She gazed at the long sweeping lawns and the lake in the distance, and her heart was that of a child again. So choked with emotion that she couldn't speak, she merely roved her eyes over the place where she had known so much joy.

The longer she looked, the more she remembered . . . how she and her family would often walk in the park; the way the ducks chased them for food; she and her brother Michael, running up and down the banks, laughing and happy. Ordinary, innocent children without a care in the world, until . . . 'Oh, dear God!' Kelly didn't even realise she had uttered the words aloud.

'Are you all right?' Concerned, Fran came to her side. Misreading the situation, she offered, 'It's not my busiest time right now. I can find you another room if you don't like this one.'

Suppressing the awful pictures in her mind, Kelly muttered, 'I'm sorry, I was miles away.' *Years away!* 'This is a lovely room.' How could she explain?

Fran saw the tears; she felt the pain and could do nothing. 'If you're sure then?'

Kelly nodded gratefully. 'I am,' she said. 'Thank you.'

'Then I'll leave you to yourself.' Albeit frank and open-hearted, Fran could be discreet when the occasion demanded. 'When you're ready, we can go through the usual things – breakfast times and such. Oh, and if you're wondering, this room is the same rate as the others – two shilling a night including breakfast and dinner.'

'That sounds very fair to me.' Kelly was glad she had come to this place, and this woman. She had feared strangers, but somehow Fran didn't feel like a stranger.

Before she left the room, Fran looked at Kelly in a meaningful way. 'Would you be offended if I confided something to you . . . *again*?' She smiled self-consciously. 'Only I think it might help us both.'

Intrigued, Kelly shook her head. 'No, I wouldn't mind,' she answered quietly. 'Please . . . go on.'

'Do you recall what I told you before, about this house and my circumstances, and how there were times when I feared I might lose my sanity?'

'Yes, I remember.'

'I came from a broken home, married young, had

four children in as many years. My husband Jonas was a quarry owner, filthy rich . . . though you wouldn't have known it to look at me and the kids. He was one of those people who wouldn't spend a halfpenny where a farthing would do. He was also an arrogant, spiteful man in his nature – bad through and through. Being young and trusting, I didn't realise until it was too late.'

The plump woman paused for a second. 'When things started to go wrong, I always blamed myself . . . *he* did that to me. He had a way of making me feel worthless. In the end, he ran off with some woman – I don't know who she was, and don't want to. God only knows, I was glad to see the back of him! I only hope he treats her better than he treated me and the kids.'

Kelly was shocked. 'He ran off and left you alone with four children?'

'Like I said, Jonas is bad right through. But he left me this house . . . all written out legally, thank God! He said it was more than enough. But there was to be no money.'

She looked at Kelly for a long moment, before finishing in a sombre voice: 'I don't mind telling you that to get where I am now was a long, hard struggle. With four children to raise and no other income, I had to knuckle down and do the best with what I'd got.'

'From what I can see, you've done yourself proud.' Kelly was filled with admiration.

Fran looked round the room and her eyes shone with

pride. 'Time and again, I could have sold this house and bought a smaller one, but what would that have solved? The money would never have lasted long enough to see us through. The children were young, so I could hardly go out to find work. The "friends" we had when my husband and I were together . . . they all vanished like the wind when things got tough. I managed without them though, just like I managed without *him*. I started taking in laundry, looking after other folk's bairns, anything to earn a bob or two.'

She shrugged, a look of sadness clouding her eyes. 'In the end it was all for nothing, because as soon as they were old enough, my kids took off and sided with their father. I haven't seen them since. There I go again,' she said softly, her head bowed. 'Burdening you with my troubles.'

Kelly was intrigued. 'Why are you telling me all this?' She knew there was a deeper message.

Fran smiled; a soft, knowing smile that touched Kelly's heart. 'I saw you at the window just now,' she said gently, 'and I can tell you've been hurt somehow. I wanted to tell you that I know all about pain and family, and I know how things can easily destroy you. But, you see, when things were at their worst, I learned something very precious. I learned about faith and strength, and how, when it comes down to it, you must believe in *yourself*, because there is no one else. Learn to trust your own instincts and you'll soon realise that nothing is so bad you can't rise above it.'

Departing the room she closed the door behind her, leaving Kelly wondering about herself. A rush of guilt swept over her. Maybe I'm not as strong as you, but I will try, she thought. Oh yes, she would try!

After all, she had not come all this way to fail.

With renewed determination, she set about unpacking her portmanteau. When that was done, she washed in the hot water Fran had brought up, and laid down on the bed.

She was soon in a deep sleep, her worries temporarily forgotten.

⟫•⟪

LATER THAT EVENING, Kelly went downstairs to the dining room, where a number of fellow guests were enjoying supper: a young couple, probably newly wed, judging by the way they hung on to each other, two women of middle age, and an elderly gentleman who had his eye on Kelly from the moment she entered the room. 'That's Mr Sanderson,' Fran explained with a knowing smile. 'He fancies himself as a Jack the Lad.'

Curiously stealing a glance at the old fellow, Kelly noted how distinguished he seemed, with his silver-headed walking-stick and long, grey handlebar moustache; he had a halo of white, fluffy hair and a round shiny bald patch on top, and even from where she was sitting, Kelly could see the long, straggling hairs growing from his nose.

Suddenly he turned and winked at her. 'How old is he?' she asked, trying not to giggle.

'Eighty-four and proud of it!' Fran chuckled. 'He's harmless enough,' she promised. 'He would if he could but he can't. Got the urge but not the get up and go . . . if you know what I mean!' She giggled girlishly. 'The old devil's tekken a fancy to you!'

When he winked again, this time with a toothless grin, it was all Kelly could do not to laugh aloud; especially when one of the middle-aged women told him sternly, 'If you can't behave, Mr Sanderson, you'd better go to your room and stay there!'

Stifling her laughter, Kelly concentrated on her meal. She ate a good helping of hot-pot, and afterwards had a slice of apple pie. 'That was a wonderful meal,' she told Fran as she passed her in the hallway. 'I'm away to sleep it off now. I've a busy day tomorrow.'

Fran was disappointed. She went through the breakfast times again. 'If you could make it nine o'clock, you and me can have our breakfast together,' she suggested. 'Only, it's their last day tomorrow, this lot, so they'll be having breakfast early. By quarter to nine, they'll all be gone and there'll be only the two of us. It's rare that I get guests at this time of year, at least until the Christmas period. I'm always busy then.'

'Breakfast with you?' Kelly warmed to the idea. 'Yes, thank you, Fran. I'd like that very much.'

And, from the look on her face, so would Fran.

W HETHER IT WAS because she had taken a nap earlier, or because tomorrow was the day when she would see the old house again after all these years, Kelly didn't know. Whatever the reason, she slept badly, dreaming a lot and waking in a cold sweat.

Even now, standing at the window looking out over that beautiful park in the morning light, Kelly could not rid herself of the awful knowledge she had carried all these years.

In her mind's eye she could see her father's lifeless body, lying twisted and bleeding, draped over the settee like a rag doll.

She could see the face of his killer as it turned towards her; so guilty. *And oh, such terror etched on its face.* That image was the worst of all, a secret kept between them, to haunt and cripple over the years. *Mother said there was no other way.*

The tap on the door startled her. 'Who's there?' Swinging round she instinctively pressed herself against the wall, her voice trembling. 'What do you want?'

'It's only me,' Fran called. 'I came to tell you they've all gone and I'm about to cook breakfast for the two of us – bacon and egg, with a helping of mushroom, unless you prefer something else?'

Flustered, Kelly rushed to put on her robe before going to the door and peeping out. 'Just toast for me,' she said gratefully. 'I can't face anything else this morning.'

Fran observed the dark hollows beneath Kelly's eyes.

'Look, lass, if you'd rather stay in bed a while longer, don't let me bully you into coming down.'

Kelly reassured her. 'I'll be with you in half an hour.'

Fran's homely face broke into a smile. 'It's been a long time since I sat down to breakfast with someone else. It'll be a treat.'

With Fran gone, Kelly soon pushed the bad thoughts to the back of her mind. She splashed her face with cold water to erase the night's ravages. Then she washed, dressed and brushed her hair until it shone.

Half an hour later she breezed into the dining-room where Fran was already serving their breakfast. Greeting Fran with a brightness that belied the turmoil beneath, Kelly observed, 'My! You do set a pretty table.' The table was covered with a freshly laundered blue and white check table-cloth; there were muffins and honey and, in the centre of the table, a huge brown earthenware teapot, steaming from the spout.

'Why, thank you!' Fran beamed with pleasure. 'I do me best.'

Seating herself opposite the other woman, Kelly told her, 'Really, you needn't have worried about me.' Thinking she sounded ungracious, she quickly added, 'But it all smells so wonderful, I'll probably eat you out of house and home.'

While Kelly chatted, Fran bustled about and soon the table was complete; now there was a rack of toast, and in front of Kelly, a bowl of steaming porridge, the thick, warm aroma wafting up and stirring her appetite.

Just as she'd described, Fran had a plate of eggs, bacon and mushrooms. 'I heard you in the night,' she revealed, stuffing a forkful of bacon into her mouth. 'My room is right next door, you see. I heard you cry out a couple of times. Weren't sure whether I should come in and see if you were all right.' She peered at Kelly curiously. 'You *are* all right, ain't yer, lass?'

Kelly swallowed a spoonful of porridge. 'Oh dear, I am sorry,' she apologised. 'I hadn't realised. I'm prone to nightmares, you see, always have been.'

Not always, she corrected herself inwardly. *The nightmares only started after the killing.*

Fran took a sip of her tea. 'Must have been a bad nightmare,' she commented quietly.

Looking up at the other woman, Kelly asked, 'Do you remember what you told me . . . that when it comes down to it, there is no one but yourself?'

Fran nodded.

'You were right,' Kelly admitted. 'I know that now. The nightmares won't go away until I can face them in daylight.'

Fran smiled knowingly. 'I understand. And if you need someone to talk to, I'll be here.'

'You're very kind.' Kelly liked this woman, but knew she could never confide in her.

The truth was too shocking.

Taking a final spoonful of porridge, she laid down her

napkin. 'I have to go now,' she said, 'things to do.' With that, she left the table and hurried away to get ready.

Upstairs, Kelly took a moment to compose herself. The idea of going back, actually walking down that same street where it all began, was already sapping her courage. 'If you don't do it now,' she told herself sternly, 'you never will!'

She went to the mirror and brushed her hair for the second time; anything to delay the inevitable. A moment later she put on her coat and scarf and stood by the window, quietly contemplating the ordeal ahead. 'Don't be afraid,' she whispered. 'The sooner you start, the sooner it will end.'

She smiled wistfully. 'Face the nightmares in the daylight,' she reminded herself. 'Isn't that what you said?'

<hr />

A SHORT TIME later, Fran heard the front door being closed. Curious, she hurriedly slurped down her tea and went over to the window, where she watched Kelly walk away, shoulders stooped as if they carried the weight of the world. 'There goes a woman with a secret,' Fran murmured thoughtfully. 'Haunted she is, the poor little bugger!'

Shaking her head, she lowered the curtain and returned to her breakfast. 'Life is a devil,' she mused. 'But I can't help her if she won't tell.' She slapped a spoon of honey over the top of a muffin. When it ran off the plate and stuck to her pretty table-cloth, she scooped it up with her spoon and sucked it clean, a look of contentment on her face.

⟶◦⟵

THE WALK TO Johnson Street only took twenty minutes, but it was the longest walk of Kelly's life.

At the bottom of Park Street she turned left, across Montague Street and along Preston New Road. The houses to her right were exactly as she remembered; set back high from the pavement, with deep windows and tall chimneys. This was where the better-off raised their families and entertained other well-to-do folk.

To her left were houses of similar style, but on a lower level and with smaller gardens. Built in blocks of eight or more, they were set between the many streets which cut steeply down towards the factories.

These narrow cobbled streets, flanked by narrow little houses, seemed a world away from their high-born neighbours. Inhabited by ordinary, God-fearing folk, they were small and cosy, often crammed with large families and ringing with down-to-earth chatter about everyday matters. In times of good and bad, these close-knit communities looked out for each other. Every family knew every other family, and every mother looked out for every child.

Hardly daring to glance at them as she passed, Kelly

hurried by. Afraid to linger should the memories come flooding back, she pressed quickly on towards Johnson Street; the street where she was born.

At long last, she was going home, and the nearer she got the more she remembered . . . the nightmare, the fear and uncertainty that followed, and then the awful loneliness.

But that was before she found Barney, and a better life.

'Johnson Street.' The words issued from her lips almost without her knowing. It was hard to believe she was actually only a few steps away from standing on that street, near *that* house. And she had travelled so far, over so many miles. *Through a lifetime.*

The nearer she got, the faster her heart began to beat. 'Almost there,' she told herself. 'Keep strong.' And she did, though it wouldn't have taken much for her to turn around and leave this town for ever.

When the moment came, and she was standing at the top of Johnson Street, Kelly was filled with a strange kind of calm, as though it wasn't her standing there, but someone else. Someone she didn't even know.

Mesmerised, she gazed at each house in turn; *all but one.*

Deliberately, she turned her back to it – the house where she and her brother had lived with their parents; the house she had loved, the house she had feared. If she were to stretch out her arm now, she could touch it, and she would. She *must*! But, fearing her own emotions, she prolonged the inevitable.

Like an old friend, or enemy, it called to her, daring her to turn and see. She so wanted to look at the house, at the small, significant things. She hoped the words her brother had scratched into the windowsill had lasted the test of time. *Michael and Kelly for ever* – he had written it with their mother's kitchen knife. No one had noticed; no one knew except she and her brother. Was it still there? Dare she look?

She remembered the door too, solid and permanent, as if it might be left standing long after the house and everyone in it had fallen away. She needed to see if the door was the same one that her father had put in after the old one warped with the weather; the door with the big, dark keyhole and a letter-box that sang in the wind. The door through which she and her loved ones had passed time and again.

It was stark in her mind now, that wonderfully familiar door made of dark, solid wood, with four panels and a small brass knocker in the shape of a crown. Oh yes, she longed to look on it, but try as she might, she did not quite *dare*.

Instead, she roved her eyes over other familiar things: grubby, stone-framed windows; paving flags in long straight lines like little soldiers, some more worn than others; lampposts with stiff, inviting arms; and a road filled with plump, misshapen cobblestones that resembled new-baked loaves. Little had changed.

Choking back a well of emotion, Kelly devoured it all. She had forgotten how it felt. Until now, she had not realised how much it meant to her.

After a moment, she raised her gaze and looked beyond the street to the distant view. As she did so, her heart turned somersaults.

Kelly had always thought this to be the most wonderful view in the world. Even though she had been a long time away, it had stayed in her mind's eye, etched on her soul for ever.

Now, in this unforgettable moment, she drank it in, her soul crying out with excitement. Almost as though she was being lifted from the ground, she felt herself fly, soaring with the view, down and away, over the heart of Blackburn town and beyond, to the hills. She saw the church spires and the towering cotton-mills, the endless, shifting sky spreading its fluttering wings over all below, and her quiet eyes knew it all.

This was what she remembered . . . grimy, smoky Blackburn town; so beautiful, it took her breath away. 'How I've missed you,' she sighed, and her heart was broken.

In that special moment, she had left behind all the terrible, frightening things . . . the pain and fear of yesteryear. For now, she wanted only the good memories, the ones that had for too long been buried deep. The ones she had thought were gone for ever. Now, she knew they had always been there. They were there now, and the moment was unbearable.

A child cried out and the wonderful moment passed.

Kelly's attention was brought to a place halfway down the street, where a mother was spanking her child. 'What have I told yer, yer little sod?' she demanded. 'Yer not to wander off like that. There's all manner o' weird folk about . . . they'll snatch yer up and make off with yer, an' it'll serve yer right!' Another slap or two, and the child was inconsolable. Still chiding her, the woman dragged the child inside, and silence reigned.

But only for a time.

'I *never* want kids!' The woman seemed to come out of nowhere. Tall and willowy, she had striking green eyes and long, shiny brown hair tied back with a brown velvet ribbon. 'More bloody trouble than they're worth.' Pausing a moment, she boldly looked Kelly up and down. 'Can't say as I've seen you round here before!'

'That's because I haven't *been* round here – not for some time anyway.' Kelly took offence at the woman's hostile manner.

'Hmh!' For what seemed an age, the stranger scrutinised Kelly. 'Who might you be looking for?'

'No one in particular.'

Another curious, surly glance and the woman strode away.

Kelly watched as she walked into a house some way down the street. *She's* a nasty piece of work and no mistake! she thought. One thing was certain; if she did rent a house down this street, Kelly wouldn't be having much to do with that one!

'Watch out!' A small boy with a hoop came rumbling by with a dog at his heels. Barking with excitement, the dog leaped sideways, knocking Kelly off-balance. 'Sorry, missus!' Intent on whipping his hoop to great speed, the lad didn't even turn round. 'He didn't mean nuthin'.'

Startled but unharmed, Kelly smiled to herself, feeling more at ease than she had done for a long time. The street was coming alive, she thought, and with it, the more pleasant memories.

She watched the milkman as he swung into the street, then reined in his horse to serve the many customers who stood, jug in hand, each awaiting her turn. He chatted awhile, and laughingly chucked the bairns under the chin, before measuring out the milk from his churn with a ladle, dipping it in and bringing it out full to the brim, before carefully pouring it into each jug.

In her memory's eye, Kelly could see herself in that queue. A small girl carrying a jug almost as big as herself, she would dare to touch the horse's chest and pat his face when he looked down. If he kissed her for an apple, she would screech with delight. Such vivid, precious times.

Unaware that she was being watched, Kelly let the tears flow.

'You all right, lass?'

Kelly discreetly wiped her eyes. When she turned, she saw a man of about sixty years old. He had a rush of grey hair that could sweep the streets clean, and a kind face, with eyes blue as the summer skies. 'You seem to be upset about summat,' he observed in a kindly way. 'Is there owt I can do to help?' His smile was round and chubby, like that of a child.

'You're right,' Kelly admitted, 'I *was* upset, but I'm all right now.' Her smile was as bright as his own. 'You're very observant.'

'That's 'cause I've got nowt else to do but spy out the winder and see what's going on in the world,' he admitted cheerfully. When he began walking, Kelly stayed with him. 'I'm a widower,' he confided sadly. 'I had the best woman a man could wish for . . . but she passed on some ten year ago.'

When he stopped, so did Kelly. 'I'm very sorry.' She had taken an instant liking to him. Holding out her hand in friendship she said, 'My name's Kelly . . . Kelly Wilson.'

Shaking her by the hand, he replied brightly, 'The name is Charlie Porter, and I'm pleased to make yer acquaintance.' Observing her more closely he gave a naughty wink. 'By! Yer a bonny lass,' he said cheekily. 'I can't recall seeing you round these parts afore.'

'I used to live down this street.' The words tumbled out before she realised. 'But that was a lifetime ago.'

'Ah! *Now* I understand!'

Intrigued, she wanted to know, 'What do you mean?'

'Just now . . . I saw you wiping away the tears, as if you'd lost an old friend, or mebbe just found one.' He was obviously curious. 'Grew up in Johnson Street, did yer?'

When Kelly hesitated, he changed the subject. 'I don't know how long you've been standing there, and it's none of my business, but if you don't mind me saying, lass, you look frozen to the bone. I reckon a nice hot brew would put the roses back in yer cheeks. What d'yer say to that, eh?'

His offer was tempting, and he was right. Kelly *was* frozen to the bone. Up here at the top of Johnson Street, the wind could cut a body in half. 'That would be wonderful.' She even clapped her hands in appreciation. 'If it's no trouble, that is.'

'No trouble at all,' he confirmed. 'I've got all the time in the world. What's more, it's been years since I enjoyed the company of a pretty lass.'

Chuckling, he glanced down the street. 'I bet old Lizzie Edwards is peeping out the window right now, wondering who the devil you are.' His grin was impish. 'When she sees me and you go into the house, she'll be green as pea-soup . . . that bloody jealous she won't know what to do with herself!'

When Kelly followed his gaze with inquisitive eyes, he grabbed her by the arm. 'Let the old nuisance suffer.' Propelling her forward, he urged, 'Come on, lass, afore we *both* catch us death o' cold.'

Charlie's parlour was pleasant and cosy, and the chap himself was a treasure. 'Sit yersel' down,' he ordered, helping Kelly off with her coat. 'I'll get the kettle on.'

While he was in the scullery making the tea, Kelly took a moment to look around her. It was the kind of room that breathed love and welcome. The furniture was solid, dark wood, and in front of the cheery fire was a half-moon rug made up of hundreds of colourful rag-strips, each one the same length, and carefully woven into the hessian fabric beneath. The ends, too, were beautifully bound.

'My missus made that.' Charlie had come up behind Kelly without her realising. 'Night after night she'd sit where you are now.' With great care he handed her a cup and saucer and, holding his to his lap, sat down before her. 'I can see her now,' he said, 'head bent and eyes screwed in concentration. She'd spend hours, weaving and picking, snipping and fixing.' His gaze went to the rug. 'All she had were a handful of rags and an old coal sack. Yer wouldn't think anybody could make such a lovely thing out of nothing, would yer, eh?'

'She was very talented.'

Sighing from the depth of his boots, he murmured, 'She were a good lass.'

Realising he needed to talk about her, Kelly said softly, 'I can see she must have been very special.'

'Oh aye, she were! Pretty too, just like yerself.' Placing his cup and saucer by the hearth, he rose from his seat and took down a photograph from the dresser. 'There she is,' he pointed to the woman in the picture. 'That were my Lucy.'

Taking the photograph, Kelly gazed down at the woman. 'You're right,' she said, 'she's very pretty.' The woman was small and dainty, with a mass of dark hair and brown, smiling eyes. Charlie stood beside her and, in between them was a boy aged about fourteen years. 'Is this your son?'

Kelly looked up to see Charlie grinning proudly. 'Aye, that's our Luke,' he answered.

'He's very handsome.'

'Trouble is, he seems to attract the wrong kinda woman, if yer know what I mean.'

Kelly smiled. 'That's a father talking,' she commented. 'No woman would ever be good enough for your son, am I right?'

'Happen, aye, yer could be right.' Chuckling, he took up his cup and saucer and sat down to finish his drink. 'Luke's a fine young man, though I say so meself. I don't know what I'd have done without him. Since his mam was took, he's been my right arm.'

Tenderly, he glanced round the room. 'If it hadn't been for Luke, I might have lost this house. I were ill, d'yer see, an' couldn't pay the rent. But he put it all to rights. He gave up his own house in the next street and moved in here with me. He pays board and lodgings, though I say it don't seem fair. He never makes me feel like I owe him anything, an' he's allus telling me, "This is *your* house, Dad. One day I'll buy it for you, and hand you the deeds on a plate".'

Quietly smiling, he dwelt on that a moment while Kelly sipped her tea. Suddenly he looked at her. '"You're dreaming, lad," that's what I told him. Whoever heard of owning your own house, eh? Nobody *I* know of, and that's for sure.'

'He obviously thinks you're worth it.'

'D'yer know, it wouldn't surprise me if he walked through that door one fine day and handed me the keys to this house, just like he promised. By! That'd be summat, wouldn't it, eh?' He laughed aloud. 'Charlie Porter owning his own house . . . it don't bear thinking about!' His eyes lit up at the prospect. 'He'll do it if he can, I know that. Since he were a lad he's kept every promise he's ever made.' Suddenly, his old eyes clouded over. 'But he shouldn't be thinking of me. He's had a rough time of it these past few years, what with *her* and all!' Anger coloured his voice. 'She's been a bugger to him, an' still is whenever she gets the chance.'

Sensing his bitterness, Kelly thought it best to hold her tongue. Whoever *she* was, it seemed there was bad blood between her and this kindly old fella.

'I reckon the worst day of his life were the day he clapped eyes on that hellcat!'

'Is your son married?'

His own curiosity getting the better of him, Charlie replied with a question: 'You said yer name were Wilson?'

Kelly nodded. 'That's right,' she confirmed, 'Kelly Wilson. I used to live round here as a child.'

His curiosity finally overwhelmed him. 'An' did yer live in that house on yon corner?'

Again Kelly nodded, sure now that he had guessed. 'The one with the boarded-up windows?'

'I don't know – I haven't looked.'

The old man paled. 'By! I should have realised.'

Fear gave way to relief. 'You know, don't you?' Somehow, his knowing made it all that much easier.

'It were *you*, weren't it? That night, when all hell were let loose ... it were *you* as came running to this very house, straight into my arms, trembling and crying and full o' terror.' Shocked by his own vivid recollections, he shook his head slowly from side to side. 'What in God's name brings yer back, after all this time?'

'I *had* to come back.'

'Aye, lass, I reckon yer did.' Deep down inside, he understood.

'You were kind to me that night.' Kelly had not recognised him at first, but she knew him now. 'I thought you would have been long gone from these parts by now.'

'Not me!' There was a deep pride in his voice. 'I were born in this street. I got wed from here, raised my only son here. I've grown old in this little house o' mine and I've never regretted a minute of it.'

'I envy you.'

'You mustn't envy me, lass,' he cautioned. 'One way or another, somewhere, someday when we least expect it, we all get our little share of Paradise, even if it's only fleeting.'

'That's a lovely thing to say.'

He sighed contentedly. 'I wouldn't mind a shilling for every cobble I've walked on down this very street.'

Kelly observed the old man and thought how content he seemed.

'It's all I've ever wanted, too,' she told him. 'A family around me . . . to be able to make a home in one place and never want, or need to move.'

Charlie nodded knowingly. 'Aye, lass, I've been lucky, there's no denying that.' Sensing her deeper emotions, he gave her a moment before going on softly, 'I can imagine it's been a bit of a nightmare for you. Torn from your roots like that, and none of it your fault.' Gently he probed, 'Something like that . . . it *must* have turned yer life upside down, lass?'

'Oh, it did.' And was still doing so, she thought. Otherwise why had she travelled all this way? Why couldn't she let it rest and make a new life? Why would she need to rent a house in this same street, to experience the old familiar things, to walk over the same cobbles and tread the same path she had trodden as a child?

The answer was the same as before: to lay the ghosts, to go back before she could go forward with a new, braver heart. That was why, and however painful, she would not flinch from it.

Charlie had been watching her, admiring her, only able to imagine the trauma she must have suffered. He knew this particular journey could not have been easy for her. 'Move far away, did yer?' he asked. 'After . . . well, you know what I mean, after it were all over?' To his mind Kelly's mother was lucky not to have been hanged for what she did. And he wasn't the only one to feel that way.

Kelly nodded. 'My brother moved South and took me with him.' She was astonished to find herself talking so freely with this old man, who in spite of comforting her on that shocking night, was almost a stranger. Before now she had only ever spoken about it to Barney, and even then it had taken her a long time to confide in him.

'If I remember rightly, weren't yer brother studying to be a teacher or summat?'

Kelly was impressed. 'You've got a good memory, Mr Porter.'

'Hey! Tha' needn't be so formal, young 'un!' he complained with a wag of his finger. 'The name's Charlie, if yer please.'

Kelly didn't argue. He was such a darling, and she found him so easy to be with. 'Sorry, Charlie,' she apologised, suddenly giggling like a shy young girl. 'And I'm not such a young 'un neither.'

He wouldn't have it. 'Away with yer! How old are yer now, eh? Thirty-eight, thirty-nine, mebbe?'

Sighing for all the lost years, Kelly told him, 'I'm the wrong side of forty, have been these past three years.'

'Well, I never!' All the same, he was adamant. 'Yer ain't got the cradle marks off yer arse yet!'

The more she talked with him, the better Kelly felt. And there was something else. 'How old did you say your son was?'

'I didn't say, but he's about your age.'

Kelly wondered about that. 'It's strange,' she commented thoughtfully, 'I can't seem to recall him, but I do remember you, and I have a vague recollection of your wife.'

'Aye, well, it's not surprising yer can't recall our Luke,' he explained. 'The lad didn't come to live in this street until after you and your brother were gone.' Flushing a deep shade of crimson, he went on in a sober voice, 'Afore I met my lovely wife, I were a bit of a Jack the Lad.' He laughed self-consciously. 'Yer wouldn't think that *now*, would yer? Not with all me muscles gone to fat an' all me proud looks lost in wrinkles.'

'You're still a handsome man,' Kelly gave him back his pride, 'and you're wrong, because I *can* imagine you being a Jack the Lad.' Charlie still had that look of mischief, and a certain flirtatious way with him that was very pleasing.

'Aye, well, there's been a lot o' water under the bridge since then.' Charlie's eyes twinkled. 'But, like I were saying, lass, I had my fling like any other red-blooded young man, but there were one particular lass who meant a bit more than the others, if yer know what I mean.'

The twinkle in his eye began to fade. 'I got her in the family way, d'yer see? Her father were raging mad!' Rolling his eyes to heaven, he visibly shook. 'The bugger wanted to kill me there and then. He might have done so too, if it weren't for the lass coming between us. Anyway, he stood over the pair of us while we took our vows, but

I didn't mind that, even though by this time I'd come to realise I weren't as serious about her as I thought. But the lass were in trouble 'cause of me, and I'd have wed her anyway. I were never one to shirk my duties.'

Seeing the determined look on his face, Kelly did not doubt his sincerity.

'Me an' the lass were content enough when all were said and done,' he told Kelly. 'Her father had property and a bit o' money to set us up, but we wanted to do it our way.'

Filled with a sense of pride, he went on, 'We lived in one of her dad's terraced houses along Craig Street, but I made sure we paid the rent every Friday without fail. I didn't want to give him a chance to say I weren't providing proper for his only daughter. Oh aye! Watched me like a hawk he did, but we showed him . . . we made that little house into a home, fit for *anybody* it were. I worked long hours in the foundry, and we never went short of anything.'

Kelly smiled. 'It sounds idyllic.'

He paused, seeming to struggle with his memories. 'The night she started with the bairn were terrible. A man feels so helpless and guilty.' Looking up at her, he bared his emotions. 'A woman doesn't realise that, does she? An' yer can't tell her, 'cause you don't want to add to her burden. Do yer know what I'm saying, lass?'

Kelly's heart went out to him. 'Yes, I think I do,' she answered, 'but you could be asking the wrong person. You see, I never married, never had a family.' Not even the family she was born into, because the night her father was murdered, everything fell apart.

Slipping into his own troublesome thoughts, Charlie went on, 'When the bairn came early, things started to go wrong.'

Bowing his head, he took a moment to compose himself. 'It were a bad time for my wife. She were only a little thing, d'yer see? Two days and nights we sat, me an' her mam and dad. All we could do were pray she'd come through . . .' He gave a heart-wrenching shudder. 'But we lost her all the same.'

Deeply moved, Kelly didn't really know what to say. 'I'm sorry' seemed so futile, but she said it anyway, with as much feeling as she knew how. 'It must have been hard,' she said, 'raising a child on your own?'

His voice hardened. 'Never got a chance! *They* med bloody sure o' that! They blamed me for what happened. Oh, and I blamed myself too. Time and again I wished to God things might have been different. In a way, I could understand how they felt. The mother weren't so hard on me. But the *father* . . .' He blew out his cheeks in exasperation. 'Like a mad thing he were . . . wild with grief, wouldn't listen to reason. Took agin me he did . . . wanted to put me under the ground with his lass. He had money an' power an' he used them to fight me off. By! He were a right, awful bas—'

Holding himself in check, he swallowed hard before going on in a gentler tone, 'It were a cruel thing, the lass being taken like that. Oh, but she left a wonderful legacy.

She gave birth to a beautiful little lad.' Clearing his throat, he spoke with immense pride. 'She allus said if it were a lad, she wanted him to be called Luke. The christening took place a week after his mammy's funeral.'

'Oh Charlie, I'm so sorry.' What a dreadful thing to happen.

Charlie gave a sad, lonely little smile. Forcing himself to go on, he revealed, 'Her parents took the lad from me the same day. I never stood a chance against their might. The upshot of it all was that I didn't get to see him again until he were twelve year old, and only then because they went down with tuberculosis and never recovered from it.'

'So he lost his mother, father, and then his grand-parents who no doubt loved him, in spite of what they did to you?'

'Sometimes life can be so cruel.' Charlie had taken to Kelly in a way he rarely took to others. 'But then you'd know all about that, wouldn't yer lass, eh?'

Kelly smiled wryly. 'I'm glad you have your son back.'

'He's worth all the heartache.' Charlie's eyes lit up whenever he talked about Luke. 'I only wish things had been different – with his grandparents, I mean – though I've an idea they might have been sorry about the way they treated me, because they left instructions with their lawyer that the lad was to be sent on to me, his daddy. Soon after that, the lawyer turned up here in a horse and carriage.'

Blowing out his cheeks again he sighed, as though wearied by it all.

'It were an end and a beginning all at once,' he said. 'The lawyer was a hard-faced old bugger who treated me as if I were summat to wipe off the sole of his shoe, but it didn't matter. All that mattered was that he had my son with him. Right from the first, it were made plain that neither he nor I were to get a penny from his grandparents' wealth . . . not that it bothered me at all, but I would have thought they might have provided for the lad's future. With all their money and power, they could have done him so much good. Instead, they sent him on his way, with little more than the clothes on his back.'

'Money isn't everything,' Kelly reminded him.

'You're right, lass.' Now, when he smiled, his eyes glittered with tears. 'They sent him to me, an' I couldn't have wished for nothing better. Me an' the lad hit it off right away. At first, considering what happened with his own mam and all, I thought he might bear some malice towards my wife, but I needn't have worried, 'cause the lad didn't have no malice in him whatsoever. My dear wife struck up a wonderful relationship with him straight off. She took him under her wing and raised him as her own. Oh, but we were a real family, the three of us. The lad settled in as if he'd been here all his young life, an' grew to love us, just like we loved him.'

He glanced round the room. 'There's been a great deal of happiness in this little house,' he sighed, a deep, weary sigh that told its own tale. 'I don't mind telling yer . . . it would break my heart to leave it.'

'There's no reason why you should, is there?'

'Not with our Luke taking care of things, no.' Brighter now and better for having talked it all out, Charlie wondered, 'And what about you, lass? Have yer just come for a visit, or d'yer have a mind to move back to these parts?'

Kelly gave the question some thought. 'I had thought to move back, for a while at least.' She hardly dared to ask. 'What happened to the old house? Why is it all boarded up?'

'It's been empty a long while, lass.'

'Not all this time, surely.' Kelly was amazed. 'Not since we went away, you don't mean?'

'Oh no, lass. There's plenty o' folk have moved in, but soonever they find out a man were murdered there, they pack their bags and move on. They do say as how the landlord is at his wit's end. Well, I ask yer, what use is a property like that to a landlord, eh?'

All manner of questions ran through Kelly's mind, but one in particular would not be quietened. 'Why doesn't he sell it?'

''Cause nobody wants the bugger, that's why!'

'He could always make it an attractive proposition by dropping the price.'

Charlie laughed out loud. 'He's tried that an' all. There was one time when he came close to getting rid of it. This big Irish docker from Rosamund Street rented it for a fortnight after his own home burned to the ground when a paraffin stove overturned. He'd come into a bit o' money, so he were looking for a place to buy. It seems he took a liking to your old house, so he and the landlord came to an understanding on price. He were on the verge of signing papers an' all.'

'What happened?' It was obvious something had gone wrong with the signing.

Charlie confirmed it. 'His wife started having nightmares and things, claimed she'd seen a ghost in the back parlour.' Suddenly, he caught his breath, his face falling in dismay. 'Oh, lass! I am sorry. Me an' me big mouth!'

Realising he'd put his foot in it, he was full of apologies. 'I'm a silly old bugger, letting me tongue run away with me like that. Whatever were I thinking of?'

Reaching out to touch his hand, Kelly assured him, 'It's all right. Go on, Charlie. Please.'

Relaxing, Charlie took a breath and went on, 'Well, as it turns out, the Irish fella knew all about what happened in that house, but chose not to tell his missus until the place were signed and sealed.'

'I expect she found out anyway.' Strange, she thought, how it seemed as if they were talking about some other house, some other happening, and none of it anything to do with her.

'It were Bert Chandler as told her. He's an odd-jobber round these parts – turns his hand to anything as long as it pays a bob or two. Anyroad, when she asked him to sweep the flu, he refused. "I aint stepping foot in that house," he told her. "Some say it's haunted, others say it's cursed. You'll not get nobody to come there, missus," he said, and put the fear o' God in her! Well, o' course she put an end to the signing there and then. "It's me or this place," she told her husband. "You stay if yer like, but I'm off!" And the pair of 'em were gone that same night. There's been no interest in it since.'

'Is there a way I could see inside it, do you think?' Something had taken hold of Kelly and wouldn't let go, and for some inexplicable reason she felt she could not leave the street without setting foot in that house.

Charlie was taken aback. 'Are yer sure that's what yer want, lass?' he asked cautiously. 'I mean, it's bound to bring it all back.'

Knowing it was so, Kelly felt her heart sink but, 'It's never really gone away,' she answered sadly. 'And, like I said, coming back to this street, going inside that house . . . it's something I really *need* to do.'

Charlie had an explanation. 'Some time back there were an old fella lived along the canal. He had this gangrenous leg, d'yer see? Finally, the doctors gave him a choice. "Have the leg cut off, or lose yer life," that's what they told him. He let them cut off his leg, an' d'yer know, the old bugger lived to be eighty-six year old.'

Kelly saw what Charlie was getting at. 'You're saying, what happened to my father . . . everything . . . that it's like that man's leg, filling me with poison and destroying my life?' It seemed so simple, and yet it wasn't.

'Aye, lass, that's what I'm saying. You've carried that burden long enough, and now yer have to cut it out of yer life and give yerself a chance to recover.' Struggling out of the deep, squashy armchair, he told her, 'If yer serious about wanting to see inside that house, you've come to the right fella.'

His face creased into a grin. 'The landlord left me a key. Said if I were to find him a tenant, there'd be a bob or two in it for me.'

'And did you find him a tenant?' Now she knew he had a key and could let her in, Kelly was not sure whether her courage would allow her to enter the house.

'Not so you'd notice,' he confessed. 'But I did earn tuppence once, when I let a tramp sleep there.'

'Only once?' Kelly couldn't suppress a smile.

'Well, happen a couple o' times.' Taking a key from behind the clock on the mantelpiece, he chuckled mischievously. 'One night the bugger brought his mates along, so I charged 'em tuppence each.' He gave a wink. 'I never did tell the landlord,' he said. 'Must 'a slipped me mind. He'll not miss it though. That tight-fisted bugger's got more money than I'll *ever* have!'

Apprehensive deep-down, Kelly followed him to his front door and then down the street. 'You're an old rogue, Charlie,' she teased.

'So they tell me,' he laughed. 'So they tell me.'

Chapter Three

WHILE CHARLIE FIDDLED with the rusting lock, Kelly stood by, her heart in her mouth and all manner of disturbing thoughts rampaging through her mind. What in God's name would she find inside? And how would she feel, walking into that house again, after what had happened?

Suddenly she was trembling. The Irishwoman had claimed to see a ghost. Maybe it wasn't a 'ghost'. Maybe it was the 'badness'. Did the badness still linger? Would the atmosphere be unbearable in this house of memories? Would coming here be the worst mistake she could ever make? Would it resurrect the terror she had felt and the awful sights she had seen? Would her nightmares return to drive her insane?

Or would it be a healing experience, as she hoped?

She shrugged inwardly. Whatever the outcome she was here now; too close, and unwilling to turn away.

'Right, lass!' With one almighty thrust, Charlie flung

open the door. Straight away the stench enveloped them. 'God Almighty!'

Covering his nose with one hand, he told Kelly to leave the door open, then he fled down the passage and into the scullery, where he crashed open the back door to let the air rush through. 'It's the last time I let them stinking buggers in 'ere!' he gasped. 'Gawd knows what they got up to. Using the place as a bloody shit-house, I shouldn't wonder.'

Charlie was angry, and when he was angry he said what he felt, made no bones about it. 'Dirty sods! They'll get the toe of my boot up their arse if they show their faces round 'ere again, I can tell yer that!'

Kelly's attention was elsewhere. She stood by the parlour door, peering through the gloom, her heart turning. For a long, anxious moment she didn't say anything, nor did she move.

Concerned, Charlie asked, 'All right are yer, lass?'

When she still didn't answer, he discreetly made himself scarce; going out of the scullery door, he went down the yard steps and checked the cellar. 'Poor little sod,' he muttered. 'She should never have come back.'

Oblivious to all but her immediate surroundings, Kelly moved slowly into the parlour. Her disbelieving eyes swept all corners of the room. 'My God,' she gasped, 'it's all still here, just as if it was only yesterday!'

Nothing had changed. And yet it *had* changed. Seeing it all again was like standing outside a mirror looking in. The image was familiar, and yet somehow it was a stranger looking back. As though she was not part of it all, and never had been.

It was a weird, unnerving, yet exhilarating experience.

The sound of a closing door shattered the silence, and suddenly Charlie was back. 'They've had some kind of carry-on in the cellar,' he told her. 'There's candles an' blankets an' empty beer bottles.' Shaking his fist in the air he cursed, 'The buggers lied to me all along! I told 'em straight . . . just the two of you, I said, an' the landlord will have my guts for garters if he finds out I've let you in. The sods! Soonever my back were turned, they opened the doors to all and sundry. Took money for it an' all, I shouldn't wonder.'

Suddenly aware that Kelly had her mind on other things, he came to her side. 'If it's too much for yer, being in here like, we can allus leave,' he suggested kindly. 'If yer want to, that is?'

Kelly said nothing, but quietly shook her head, smiling. Her mind was whirling. Deluged by so many memories, she was surprised to discover that not all of them were bad.

'It's a bit gloomy in here.' Leaving Kelly to her thoughts, Charlie crossed the room and threw back the curtains; holey and worn, they disintegrated in his hands. 'I'm buggered if the whole place ain't falling apart,' he complained. 'If that landlord doesn't spend money on it soon, there'll be nowt left standing to save!'

No sooner had he said that than his foot went through

a floorboard. 'See what I mean?' he declared, rubbing his ankle. 'Rotten right through.'

In the rush of daylight, Kelly saw how everything had deteriorated. The walls were streaked with damp, and the parlour door hung loosely on its hinges. Even as she stood there, Kelly felt the destructive passage of time.

It was so sad, she thought. Once, long ago, this parlour had been the hubbub of domestic life; a small room with a long oven range and cupboards either side of the fireplace, it had been an ordinary room, housing an ordinary family. It was where she had known love and happiness, and she had believed these stalwart walls would protect her from life and its pitfalls. How wrong she had been.

Now the place was cold and derelict, unloved and unwanted, and it was hard for Kelly to come to terms with its demise. The image of how it used to be danced in front of her dazzled eyes; her mam quietly singing from the scullery, a crackling fire burning in the grate, with herself and Michael as children, lying at its hearth, arguing over the jigsaw puzzle, and rolling about in a mock-fight.

Ironically, the same rug they had played on as children was still there, but like everything else, it was filthy and fit only for a bonfire. Dark, spreading stains covered the brown and blue pattern, and the whole thing was peppered with burn-holes, probably made by falling cinders and casually dropped cigarettes.

The big oak sideboard, which had been her mother's pride and joy, was a sorry sight; one drawer was missing, no doubt used for firewood, and the whole surface was marked and scarred by years of misuse. There was a wide, ugly split down one door, as though someone had swung an axe to it, and with one leg collapsed it leaned to the side like a drunken man.

The two armchairs were sagging and misshapen, and springs were pushing through the sofa in every direction. The cushions her mother had made were gone, and there was a long rip in one of the arms.

'It's a sorry mess,' she murmured. Yet strangely enough the longer she stood there the easier she began to feel.

Surprisingly, though smoke-stained and lopsided, her mother's two drawings were still on the wall. One showed a group of children fishing from a jetty, the other drawing was of a boat in a pretty little harbour, with cottages on the bank and people walking along the quayside. 'One day I'll live in a place like that,' her mother used to say, all dreamy-eyed. And, in childhood innocence, Kelly believed her. Tears rained down her face; tears of regret, and oddly enough a peculiar kind of relief. Since she had taken the decision to return here, to this place she had fled from as a child, Kelly had dreaded it. Now that the actual moment had arrived, however, she felt a quiet sense of peace. And yet . . .

Somewhere a dark, secret voice whispered a warning.

Pushing the bad thoughts aside, Kelly soaked it all in: the things she had known as a child, the things she had remembered and kept in her mind's eye. But though she looked at each one in turn, her eye was always drawn back to that one place: the sofa where her father was found.

She was there and had seen it all; the lifeless form, spread out in a growing pool of blood, and the *other one* . . . still holding the knife, looking up with huge eyes, bright with horror. Try as she might, she could not forget that terrified face. She never would.

Unable to look any longer, she covered her face, her breathing slow and heavy and her legs like jelly beneath her.

'Aw, lass, you're torturing yerself. Come away.' When she felt the touch of his hand on her shoulder she flinched, crying out, filled with terror.

'It's all right.' Gently, Charlie led her out of the room. 'Come away from here,' he coaxed. And she did. But only as far as the scullery. Then on, upstairs, to each of the three bedrooms.

Everywhere was in a state of neglect and pitiful ruin. 'It's not good for you to see it like this,' Charlie complained, but as Kelly went from room to room an idea grew in her mind until she could not put it aside.

Outside the house, she told Charlie of her plan. He was mortified.

'What!' He stared at her as though she'd lost her mind. 'You can't be right in the head to think o' doing such a thing! Sleep on it . . . don't mek any decisions until you've given it a deal more thought.'

But Kelly's mind was made up. 'I don't need to sleep on it. If I can muster enough money for the deposit, I mean to buy the house, Charlie,' she told him. 'If you'll give me the landlord's name and address, I'll go round there now.'

In spite of his misgivings, Charlie had to admire her. 'You're a stubborn little sod, I'll give yer that,' he sighed, nodding his head reluctantly. 'If yer sure?'

Kelly's brown eyes shone with determination. 'I'm sure.'

Tutting disapprovingly, he conceded, 'You'd best come inside an' I'll get it for yer.'

A short time later, Kelly prepared to leave. 'What will yer do if yer can't afford what he's asking?' Charlie wanted to know. 'He's a canny bugger. Soonever he knows yer interested enough, he'll push the price up.'

'It won't do him any good,' Kelly assured him. 'If he tries pushing up the price, I'll just walk away.'

But she hoped it wouldn't come to that. 'He's got more to lose than I have,' she said. Although that wasn't altogether true because, now she had her heart set on it, she wouldn't rest until the key was in her hand and her name on the deeds.

'Wish me luck, Charlie?' She was so glad to have found a friend.

Charlie laughed. 'I reckon it'll be *him* as needs the luck.'

'What kind of man is he?'

'He's a nasty, sly sort, I can tell yer that. Goes by the name of John Harvey. Mid-forties, fancies himself with the ladies. Some years back he inherited a thriving property business from his father.' Snorting, he added contemptuously, '*He* were a tight-fisted bastard an' all!'

'Well at least I know what I'm up against.' Kelly was in fighting mood. It would take heaven and earth to shift her from her purpose.

'God go with yer, lass.'

'Thank you, Charlie.'

'Happen I'll see yer afore too long, eh?' Although he wanted her to succeed, Charlie wondered if it might not be better for her to leave this place here and now.

'I'll be back sooner than you think,' she promised. And astonishing him with a fond kiss on the cheek, Kelly bade him cheerio.

As she hurried away, she began to wonder about her decision. 'Barney always said I was impetuous,' she mused. 'It seems he was right after all.'

Remembering Barney sobered her thoughts. 'Where are you now?' she wondered aloud. 'Roaming the highways and byways, I expect . . . free as the wind, and not a care in the world.' One thing was certain. 'It's just as well you don't know what *I'm* up to,' she chuckled. 'I've no work, no prospects, and not too much money in my pocket. Yet I'm prepared to spend every penny I've got, and even borrow if I have to!'

A great withering sigh forced her eyes to heaven. 'Dear God, let me be doing the right thing.' For a moment she slowed her steps, her mind in turmoil. But somehow, despite the doubts, her deeper instincts remained strong. She knew she was taking a risk, but she couldn't walk away. For too long the past had controlled her. Now she was facing it head on and it felt good. A strange blush of contentment came over her.

'I'm doing the right thing,' she told herself.

<hr>

WHILE KELLY TURNED out of the street at one end, Luke Porter turned in at the other. Tall and confident, with coal-black eyes and rich brown hair, he made a striking figure. 'Kissing strange women now is it, you old devil!'

Intent on watching Kelly as she walked away, Charlie was both startled and delighted by Luke's arrival. 'You're back early!' As always, his old eyes lit up at the sight of his son.

'It's been the devil of a day,' Luke explained wearily. 'First thing this morning the job was stopped when the surveyor was late. At two o'clock this afternoon I was pacing the floor at the Infirmary after one of the tilers fell off the roof and broke his hand in two places.'

'Don't tell me,' Charlie groaned. 'Jack Monaghue!'

'Worried out of his mind he was,' Luke confirmed. 'What with that big family and no other money coming in, he's every right to be worried.'

'Is there nowt yer can do for him?'

Luke's face broke into a grin. 'Don't worry.' He and Charlie had known and respected Jack for many years. 'As luck would have it, we've just secured the contract for renovating that big old warehouse down Kenton Street. Jack's one of the best men we've got. He'll work till he drops. It would be a sin and a shame to have him sitting at home, especially when he could be stripping down the warehouse ready for us to move in. Like I said to the boss, it would benefit all round because if Jack didn't do it, we'd only have to take a man off the job we're on now.'

'And what did he say?'

'He said as how Jack might turn out to be a liability. Anyway, it took some doing but I managed to persuade him that Jack Monaghue with one hand was as good as any man with two! In the end he agreed. Jack has to sign a paper first saying as how the boss won't be held responsible if he hurts himself. He'll be all right though. "Take it at a steady pace," I told him. "We'll not be ready to move in for a few week yet".'

'You're a good man, son.' Charlie's eyes shone with pride. 'You know how to look after your own.'

'All part of the foreman's job.'

'You're too modest, son.' Charlie was immensely proud of Luke's achievements. 'It's no wonder you've been put in charge. It's just a pity the bugger doesn't pay you what you're worth!'

'Don't give it another thought, Dad,' Luke told him. 'You know I've got an eye to starting up my own business before too long. Meanwhile, I've got regular work and a wage coming in. That's more than some.'

'All the same, I shan't be sorry when you break out on your own!'

Wisely changing the subject, Luke gestured in the direction Kelly had taken. 'Who's the looker then?'

Charlie was surprised. 'I didn't know you'd seen her.'

'I saw her kiss you, if that's what you mean?' When he winked, his eyes twinkled, rather like Charlie's.

Blushing a deep pink, Charlie burst out laughing. 'The days of a young lady kissing me for pleasure are long gone, I'm sorry to say.'

'So! Who was she?'

Something about Kelly's smile and the way she had reached up on tiptoe to kiss his father had made an indelible impression on Luke's mind.

Charlie lapsed into a brief moment of thought before answering. 'Her name's Kelly. I knew the lass when she lived with her family . . . here, on this very street. She were just a bairn then, an' caught up in a terrible thing.' He shook his head soulfully, the whole episode flooding back. 'It were a long time ago, son. I never thought I'd see her again, but as yer can see, she's back – and filled with ideas that can only bring heartache, if yer ask me.'

His old eyes crinkled with pleasure. 'She's such a nice lass,' he said, but his smile was short-lived. 'And I'm worried about her.'

Observing his father's downcast face, Luke wondered about this pretty newcomer. 'Let's go inside,' he suggested, 'then you can tell me all about it.'

Charlie seemed not to be listening. Instead, he was murmuring to himself, 'It might have been better if she'd never come back.'

Luke loved and respected his father and it concerned him to see how upset he was. 'Come on,' he urged. 'Come inside.'

At the same moment that Charlie turned towards the house to follow Luke inside, a slim, dark-haired woman came chasing up the street, a look of pure hatred on her face: 'You cheating bastard!' she screamed at Luke. Wild with jealousy, she flung herself at him. 'Carrying on behind my back now, is it? And don't deny it! I saw her with my own eyes, looking as if butter wouldn't melt in her mouth. Well, it won't last, I can promise you that! I'll warn her off, just like I've warned off all the others who thought you were footloose and fancy-free!'

Enraged, Luke grabbed her by the arms. 'You don't know what you're saying!' His quiet, dignified voice belied the anger inside. 'I've no idea who she was,' he stated, 'but I'll tell you this . . . even if I did, and we *were* seeing each other, it would be none of your business!'

'Is that so!' Her dark eyes narrowing, she hissed a warning: 'I think you might have forgotten one small thing, Luke Porter. For better or worse, you and me are still *wed*!' Her smile hideous to see, she spat out the word 'wed' with such force that it might have been clogging her throat.

'Forget that I married *you*?' he replied bitterly. 'You couldn't be more wrong.'

'You'd better tell that hussy to bugger off back to where she came from!' Laughing in his face, she revealed, 'I spoke to her earlier, you know – asked her what she wanted. Well, of course she wouldn't tell *me* that she was looking for you, would she, eh? The cunning little cow probably guessed I was your wife and thought it best to keep her trap shut.'

This time it was Charlie who answered. 'Why don't you clear off and leave him alone, yer bloody lunatic!'

Rounding on him, she screamed like a banshee, 'This has nothing to do with you, old man!' Lunging forward she raised her arm to hit him, but Luke's reaction was quick.

'That's enough!' Swinging her round, his dark angry eyes met hers. In a quiet, trembling voice, he told her, 'You've done all the damage you're going to do to this family.' He had put up with a lot from this vindictive woman; attacking *him* was one thing, attacking his father was another matter altogether. 'Your argument is with me, not with my father.'

'Then you had better tell the old sod to keep his nose out of it!' Filled with hatred, her green eyes flashed on Charlie, but the hatred was mutual and it was a terrible sight to see.

Tossing her head, she returned her gaze to Luke. 'He needs to learn that whether he likes it or not, I'm wearing your ring.' Holding out her hand, she triumphantly displayed the thin gold band he had put on her finger some years before. 'You're my husband, and there ain't nothing he can do to change it.'

There followed a long, heart-searching moment when Luke looked deep into her eyes and wondered how he could ever have seen beauty in such wickedness. Through her trickery, this woman had taken too much of his life. It was time now, to be rid of her.

Quietly addressing his father, he advised, 'Go inside, Dad. I'll be along in a minute.' He waited for Charlie to leave before returning his attention to the woman, whose sly, satisfied smile only served to fire his anger all the more.

'You're right,' he conceded, 'we *are* wed. And no, there is nothing my father can do to change that.'

With his next words, her smile slipped away. 'But what he can't change, *I* can. God only knows why I've let things go on the way they are. Maybe I was hoping you'd change, or maybe I've been too busy to even think about it.' His face hardened. 'I can see now I've been a bloody fool! When we were together you gave me no peace. And now, even though it's finally over between us, you still won't let go.'

'You'd better get used to it,' she whispered, 'because I'll *never* let you go!'

'Oh, but you will.' Drawing back, he looked at her with disgust. 'Because now I see that the only way to get you off my back once and for all, is to finish this farce of a marriage between us.'

'What do you mean?' Fear sounded in her voice.

'I intend seeing a lawyer, as soon as I can.'

Realising she had pushed him too far, she cunningly changed tack. 'Please Luke, don't be hasty. We can make it work, you'll see. We haven't given it a real chance.'

Stony-faced, he shook his head. 'You've had every chance, Stella,' he said, '*years* of chances. We tried and it failed. Our marriage was a shocking mistake and we both know it. Now, for both our sakes, we have to put an end to it.'

'It's *her*, isn't it?' With startling speed she was on him, pummelling her fists against his chest. 'She won't have you, I'll see to that!'

Struggling to hold her off, Luke pressed her back towards the wall; all the while she was screaming, out of control, out of her mind with jealousy. 'All right, *don't* tell me. I'll find out who she is, and when I do, she won't look so pretty!'

In that split second Luke realised what she was about to do, but she acted so quickly that he was power-less to stop her. Swinging her fist through the air, she smashed it into the stone wall behind them. With a cry of pain, she crumpled in his arms then thrust him away when he tried to help her. 'NO!' Holding out her damaged fist, she laughed through her tears. '*That's* what her face will look like if she tries to take you from me.'

Lowering his gaze to her hand, Luke was shocked. A mangled mess of skin and blood, it seemed that every knuckle was broken. Her voice trembled in his face. 'She won't be so pretty then, will she, eh?' Riddled with pain, she began shivering uncontrollably. 'Tell her,' she cried. 'You tell her to keep away!'

Sickened by such madness, Luke took hold of her. Gently, he calmed her. 'For God's sake, Stella, be still.' Ripping away the sleeve of his shirt he wound it round her hand. 'We have to get you to the Infirmary.'

'You! Get away from her!' Embittered by life and having driven away anyone who might have befriended her, Stella's mother was a formidable woman, whose life centred round her only child.

'For God's sake, can't you see she's hurt?'

'You leave my lass alone!' Grabbing Stella by the arm, she drew her away. 'We don't need no help from the likes of *you*.'

With that, she hurried away, Stella clinging to her, quietly whimpering; but not so hurt that she couldn't look back with a meaningful smile. Her eyes remained fixed on Luke until in the end it was he who turned away.

CHARLIE WAS SHOCKED. 'She *what*?'

Seated at the table, Luke looked up at his father. 'She must be crazy,' he said, 'to smash her fist into the wall like that. Whatever came over her to do such a thing?'

Shoving two mugs of piping hot tea on the table, Charlie sat himself down. 'What drove her to it?'

Taking a moment to think and sip his tea, Luke revealed, 'Stella's got it into her head that me and this Kelly of yours are having some sort of affair.'

'The woman's mad as a hatter.' Charlie never minced his words.

'She means to harm her.'

'Does she now?' Raising his mug of tea, Charlie took a long scalding gulp.

'You were right all along,' Luke conceded. 'I should have found time to end the marriage sooner.'

'Better late than never.'

'Where did I go wrong?'

Making a sound that could have been either a laugh or a sigh, Charlie told him, 'It weren't *you* as went wrong, son.'

'I wish I were as sure as you.'

Banging his mug so hard on the table that the tea splashed all over the cloth, Charlie stared Luke in the face. 'Stella is a charmer and a liar! First, she waltzes into the street and pretends to be the wide-eyed innocent.

Then she plays on your goodness by claiming she was beaten raw as a child – another lie as it turned out! Then, when she's got you up the aisle, it's wanting this and that, and spending your wages even afore you've got through the door.' His face flushed with anger, he concluded: 'She's a bad lot, son. You're well shot of her.'

Luke glanced at him, but said nothing.

Charlie, though, had more to say, and did so. 'And as if that weren't enough, she went and stole all the money you'd been saving to buy that old house on Victoria Street. "I'll do it up and sell it for a profit," you said. "I'll be my own boss at last." Hmmh! She put paid to that an' all, didn't she, eh?'

When Luke still gave no reply, he leaned forward, lowering his voice. 'Don't ever feel guilty where that one's concerned,' he said kindly.

'I don't.' But it was a lie, because Luke did feel guilty – about so many things.

'Don't forget how her own mother took pleasure in telling you, soon after you were wed, that Stella were carrying another man's child. My God! Any other man would have kicked her out there and then, but not you, oh no! You've often said you'd love kids, and so here she was, offering you a chance to raise the bairn as your own. Then, just as you were looking forward to being a father, making plans and getting the nursery ready and all, she snuck off to that old witch on Duckworth Street and had the poor little bugger done away with.'

Luke didn't need reminding. The horror and the

guilt of it all had been with him ever since. 'You don't have to worry,' he murmured, 'I have no feelings left for her.' He gave a small, bitter laugh. 'To tell the truth, I don't even know if I ever *did* have any feelings for her. It all happened too quickly. One minute she was crying on my shoulder . . . the next minute we were wed.'

'Aye, well, you're not the first man to be caught like that and you'll not be the last,' Charlie replied knowingly. 'She's a clever, scheming woman, who knows how to play the game.'

'Well, the game's over.' Sighing deeply, Luke felt a great surge of relief. 'I can't get things moving fast enough now.'

'I'm glad to hear it, son.'

Getting out of his chair, Luke stood over his father for a minute, before saying quietly, 'You'll have to warn your new friend.'

'What? Kelly, you mean?'

'Warn her that she's made a bad enemy.'

Charlie answered slowly, as if turning the matter over in his mind. 'Crazy as she is, she's got more sense than to hurt the lass.' He looked up with anxious eyes. 'She wouldn't, would she?'

'Like you said . . . she's mad as a hatter.'

Charlie thought again. 'Naw,' he muttered, 'Stella's all mouth when it comes right down to it. Besides, she likes her freedom too much to risk being jailed. Threats, that's all they were. Empty, jealous threats.' Still, like Luke, he wasn't altogether sure.

'Tell me more about the newcomer.'

Charlie's face broke into a slow smile. 'She's a lovely lass, but a bit wilful.'

'In what way?'

'That boarded-up house at the end of the street used to belong to her family.'

Luke's eyes widened with astonishment. 'What! You mean number twelve – the one where the murder took place?'

Confirming it with a nod, Charlie confided, 'The murdered man was her father.'

'Good God!'

'She came back to lay a few ghosts, I reckon. But now she intends buying the house to live in.' He shook his head. 'I tried to change her mind, but she'd have none of it.'

Looking at Luke with big sorry eyes, he begged, 'Warn her off, son. Tell her she'll be making a big mistake, coming back here after all this time. It can only bring unhappiness.'

'What makes you think she'll listen to me?'

'She might not.'

'But you want me to try all the same?'

Charlie nodded.

'All right, I'll have a word with her, if I get the chance,' Luke agreed. 'It's as well to put her on her guard.'

'You don't really think Stella will harm the lass, do yer?'

'Not if I can help it.' All the same, Luke was never more sure that Stella was unhinged. 'It wouldn't be right not to warn her though,' he said. 'I expect you're hoping it might even change her mind about moving back into that house.'

Recalling the determined look in Kelly's eye as she left to see the land-agent, Charlie gave a chuckle. 'I wouldn't count on it, son,' he said. 'What's more, if Stella was foolish enough to take her on, she might find she's met her match.'

In his mind, Luke could see Kelly stretching up on tiptoe to kiss his father. It brought a smile to his face. 'There's not much of her though, is there?'

'Not much of an armful, I'll grant you that,' Charlie admitted. 'But she's a brave little bugger. Yer wouldn't catch *me* moving into that house, not for a gold clock, yer wouldn't!'

'You say she was on her way to see John Harvey?'

'I couldn't stop her.'

'And did you tell her what a slimy bastard he is?'

'Didn't mek no difference.' He laughed. 'Still, if John Harvey reckons he can take her for a fool, he's got another thought coming. 'Cause if yer ask me, he won't even know what's hit him.'

'She's made quite an impression on you, hasn't she?' Luke had never seen his father so taken by anyone.

'Aye, and when yer meet her, you'll understand why.'

Luke recalled again the tender image of Kelly reaching up on tiptoes, her hands on Charlie's shoulders as she planted that kiss on him. Then her smiling, pretty face as she bade him goodbye.

It was a pleasing image, bringing a glow to his heart that took him by surprise.

Chapter Four

JOHN HARVEY saw her coming. From his window on the first floor, he watched her pause outside his office, his interest aroused. 'New face,' he muttered, leaning forward to get a better look. 'Pretty too.'

Unaware that she was being observed, Kelly straightened her shoulders, took a deep breath and glanced up; as she did so, John Harvey quickly drew back. Only momentarily though, because once Kelly had looked away, he returned to the window, his face peering out, his avaricious eyes following her every movement.

'Well, it's now or never!' Running her hands over her skirt, Kelly mounted the steps to the front door. Her stomach was churning and her hands were sweaty; only now did she begin to wonder whether she was up to this fellow, John Harvey. There was only one way to find out, and that was to face him head on. 'I hope I'm not biting off more than I can chew,' she muttered, closing the door behind her.

Once inside the office, enclosed in that small, musty space, with the smell of old paper and stale tobacco, Kelly felt overwhelmed by the task ahead.

Talking to Charlie, she had been brimming with confidence. Now, as she tapped on the clerk's window, her hands trembled. 'I'd like to see Mr John Harvey,' she said, addressing the thin, sallow-skinned creature with a brave smile.

'He's busy,' came the young woman's churlish reply. 'Do you have an appointment?'

Kelly shook her head. 'I'm afraid not,' she apologised, 'but I'm here on a very important matter, and if you could explain to him how it might be of more benefit to him than to me, I'm sure he'd find time to see me.'

Regarding Kelly as though she were something that had just crawled out from under a stone, the clerk took her time, chewing on her pencil and leaning back in her chair.

Riled by her attitude, Kelly stretched herself up to her full height. 'Didn't you hear what I just said?' she demanded. 'My visit might be of benefit to him.'

'So?' The clerk shrugged her shoulders. 'He *still* won't see nobody without an appointment.'

At the top of the narrow stairway, the man himself watched the scene unfold beneath him. He liked the look of Kelly, with her pleasantly curved figure and pretty, expressive eyes. She was like a breath of fresh air; not in the first flush of youth, yet with a certain presence and brightness that seemed to light up a room.

Forgetting that he too was also not in the first flush of youth, John Harvey leaped down the steps two at a time, almost cracking his ankle when his leg gave way. To the watching women below, however, he was suave and smiling as he hurried towards them betraying nothing of his excruciating pain.

The clerk sprang to attention. 'Mr Harvey! I were just saying, you don't see nobody without an appointment.'

'There's always the exception, Miss Burke,' he answered, bowing oddly when Kelly charmed him with a smile.

'I'm sorry to burst in like this,' Kelly said, 'but I'm interested in buying a property and was given your name.'

His eyebrows shot up. '"Buying" a property, did you say?'

'Yes, that is what I said.'

'Most people rent.' Stepping forward, he was like a cat after a mouse.

'You *are* a land-agent, are you not?'

'The very best.'

'And you *do* sell premises as well as let them?'

'We most certainly do.' He looked her up and down. 'It's just more usual for people to be looking for rented property,' he repeated slyly. 'Especially a woman on her own.'

'I see.' Kelly had taken an instant dislike to him. 'And you'd rather not sell to a "woman on her own", is that it?'

'I didn't say that.' His smile was curiously disarming.

'So I have come to the right place after all, then?'

'Indeed you have, Miss . . . ? Mrs . . . ?' He was hopeful, having noticed she was not wearing a wedding ring; not that he would have been deterred by such a minor complication.

Kelly put him out of his misery. 'It's *Miss*,' she answered, offering her hand in friendship. 'Kelly Wilson.'

'Ah!' In that moment, as he smiled down on her, she thought he was not such a bad-looking fellow; with his clear blue eyes and mop of fair hair, he seemed very boyish. 'Kelly Wilson. Lovely name, if I may say so.'

'Thank you.' Remembering how Charlie had warned her against this man, she proceeded with caution. 'I'm looking for a property,' she informed him, 'preferably not too far from Corporation Park.'

'Corporation Park area, eh?' He could hardly conceal his excitement. 'Well now, you really *are* in luck.'

Taking her by the elbow he propelled her towards the stairs. 'As it happens, I do have a delightful little house, situated at the top of Johnson Street. Number twelve.'

Feigning ignorance, Kelly played him at his own game. 'Johnson Street?' Mounting the stairs, she paused to look him in the eye. 'I'm not interested in buying *that* side,' she said, moving forwards again. 'I was thinking more towards town . . .'

'It's a good buy,' he argued. 'Besides, there's very lit-tle towards town . . . big houses, big prices, I'm afraid.'

Pausing halfway up the stairs, Kelly turned. 'I'm sorry,' she lied, 'it seems I'm wasting your time. If all you have to offer is the house on Johnson Street, I might be better trying the other land-agents.'

'Oh no!' Wide-eyed and frantic, he told her, 'I do have other properties that might suit.' Urging her forward again, he assured her, 'It'll only take a minute to look at what's available. I'm certain we can fix you up with a suitable property.' In fact, he had precious little on his books; apart from that damned house on Johnson Street, there were only a few shops and a rundown warehouse.

Kelly allowed herself to be ushered into his office, a surprisingly spacious room, with a smell of shoe-polish and a grimy window looking out over Blackburn rooftops. Curious, she glanced at his shoes: dark brogues, shone to a mirror-finish. It made her smile.

Throwing open the window, he invited her to sit at the desk. 'The house on Johnson Street is in very good condition,' he began. 'You really should give it some consideration.'

Kelly shook her head. 'I've already told you, Mr Harvey, I'm *not* interested.' Gesturing to his filing cabinet, she curtly reminded him, 'I thought you said you had other properties?'

'Of course!' Hurrying to the cabinet he flung open the drawer. 'We've had a very busy time,' he lied.

'Everyone seems to be on the move.' Delving into the drawer, he returned to the previous year's files, when business was brisker.

Taking out two sheaves of paper, he discreetly removed the SOLD labels, and the prices.

'Here you are.' Handing them to her, he pointed to the details. 'Is this the kind of thing you're looking for?'

'Hmh!' Skimming through the details, Kelly pretended to be interested. 'They might be, but I can't see any prices.'

'Ah, well!' Smiling down on her, he oozed charm. 'The main details will be downstairs with my partner. In fact, I'm not really sure whether these two properties are still available.' He was a glib liar, well-practised. 'I know he had interested parties only this morning, and as I've been out and about, I don't know what the outcome was.'

Hurrying to the door, he explained, 'I'll have a word with him. It'll only take a minute, his office is directly beneath us.' When he smiled he was decidedly handsome. 'Meanwhile, please make yourself comfortable.'

Fancying herself in the hand-mirror, the clerk applied a tiny smudge of rouge and gently rubbed it in with her fingertips. Hearing the ominous footsteps coming down the stairs, she quickly put away her compact, leaped out of her seat and stood stiffly to attention. 'Mr Harvey!' Shifting her gaze to the stairway, she was surprised to see that he was on his own.

She was even more surprised when he grabbed her

by the shoulders and gave her a good shaking. 'Don't think I didn't hear you, you little baggage! Haven't I told you before ... you're here to treat the customers with respect!'

'Sorry, Mr Harvey.' The more he shook her the more her voice trembled.

'The next time I find you being rude to the customers, you'll be sacked on the spot! Without pay. Do you hear me?'

'Yes, Mr Harvey.'

'Good!' Thrusting her away he ordered her to be seated.

Dutifully she sat down, her eyes looking up and her fingers nervously intertwining. He leaned forward and, fearing that she was about to be clapped round the head, she instinctively put up her arms to protect herself, crying out when he took hold of her wrists and wrenched them aside. *'Shut up, you little fool!'* he hissed.

The clerk quickly shut up, and Harvey leaned over again, his voice falling to a whisper. 'Johnson Street ... the house we had to board up. You know the one?'

'Yes, Mr Harvey.'

'Do you recall who we got to board it up?'

Grimacing in concentration, she gave him a name: 'Tom Brewster, I think.'

'Ah! So it was. Right, well, as soon as our visitor leaves, I want you to get round Tom Brewster's place and tell him I need it *un*boarded and I want it done tonight. I also want him to go inside and spruce the place up – open the windows, dust everything in sight. Leave nothing out. Tell him to get on his knees and scrub the floors if he has to; and make sure the lavvy's fit to look at.' He glanced up the stairs. 'This one will probably want to inspect everything first-hand.'

'I'll do it right away, sir, soonever she leaves.'

His blue eyes twinkled. 'Tell him I might have a buyer for it at long last, and if I make a sale there'll be a few shillings in it for him.'

Staring at him as if he'd gone mad, the clerk's voice came out in a croak. 'Oh, Mr Harvey! She's never buying *that* house, is she?' Instinctively she looked behind her. 'Some folks say it's haunted.'

This time, much to her astonishment, the girl *was* clapped round the head. 'I'll haunt *you* if you don't learn to keep your mouth shut!'

Under her breath, Helen Burke swore to herself that one of these days she'd up and go. But she'd been saying that for two years and was still here. 'A glutton for punishment', that's what her mam called her.

The truth was, she fancied Mr Harvey something rotten. And the more he chastised her, the more she wanted to bring him to heel; to wear his ring on her finger; to lie in bed beside him of a night. Her mother didn't understand. Nobody did. And she would never tell. While she loved him like she did, she would stay with Mr Harvey whatever anyone said; even if he *was* a monster who ran roughshod over her feelings.

Oblivious to her tender emotions, John Harvey

turned on her yet again. 'Oh, and when I come down, I want you to make a point of telling me that my partner, Mr Osmond, has had to go out again.'

'But you haven't got a partner, Mr Harvey.'

'I know that, you brainless idiot!' he sighed impatiently. 'But that's for us to know, and her to find out. Now, don't forget: as soon as she leaves, get round to Tom Brewster. Tell him what I said, and also say that if it's not done tonight, he'll get no more work from me.'

'Yes, Mr Harvey.' Her heart sank. Why couldn't he be nice? Oh, *why* couldn't he be nice?

At that moment the tables turned and it was Kelly who stood at the top of the stairs, longing to box his ears, like he'd boxed that young girl's who, rude though she was, did not deserve to be maltreated like that. 'Well, Mr Harvey?' she said coolly, raising her voice. 'Are the properties sold or what?' As if she didn't know already.

Shocked to the core, he swung round. 'Oh! Miss Wilson! I . . . um . . . well, as a matter of fact they are.'

Swiftly composing himself, he walked to the stairway and held out his hand for her to come down. 'I'm afraid properties like that do go very quickly. We only took those two houses on a week ago and already they've been snapped up – as will the one on Johnson Street, I'm sure.'

Shrugging her shoulders, Kelly thanked him again for his time. 'I'm sure something else will come on the market,' she said. 'Fortunately, I'm not in all that much of a hurry.'

'Look, I'll tell you what.' He did not intend letting

her go, and that was exactly what Kelly had counted on. 'Take a look at the house,' he urged. 'It's very similar to the ones that have been sold. If you like it, I daresay we can strike a deal.'

'I've already told you, I'm not interested in that area.' Sweeping past him, Kelly opened the door to leave. 'So if you've nothing else, I'll be on my way.'

From behind the desk came the voice of the nervous and confused clerk. 'I'm sorry, Mr Harvey, but your partner has just left.'

Under his poisonous look, she lapsed into a dark silence.

Just then, Kelly found herself almost lifted from her feet by the force of the door being flung open. 'WHERE IS HE, THE HEARTLESS BASTARD?'

The young woman was thin and waiflike, with copper-coloured hair tied back and a child at each side of her; in fact, she seemed little more than a child herself. 'You never give up, do you, you sly, grasping bugger!' Her angry eyes sought the land-agent out.

'What the devil d'you mean, bursting in here like this!' From the safety of the corner Harvey ordered her out.

The woman was too enraged to listen. 'One of these days you'll get your come-uppance, you see if you don't!' Making straight for him, she shook her fist in his face. 'You'll be glad to know they've been round. Oh yes! They've done your dirty work for you, because you're not man enough to do it yourself!'

With an anger to match her own, he grabbed her arm and propelled her to the door, the children scrambling after them. 'I'm man enough to see you off my premises,' he told her. 'And if you show your face here again, I'll be man enough to call the authorities. Now be off with you!' With that, he manhandled her to the door and threw her on to the pavement.

Even after he shut the door, her screams and abuse carried on the wind: 'John Harvey, you're a *rat*!' she yelled. 'I've given you every bleedin' penny I've got, and still it ain't enough. You ain't heard the last of me yet, not by a bleedin' long chalk, you ain't!'

Snatching the tail of the door-blind he thrust it down. 'Dreadful woman,' he told Kelly. 'Hasn't paid her rent for months on end, then screams blue murder when I have to send in the bailiffs.'

Kelly's sympathies were with the woman. 'That seems a drastic action,' she accused. 'The poor creature's obviously desperate.'

'Poor creature indeed!'

Switching on the charm again, he pleaded with her. 'You're obviously a very intelligent woman . . . unlike *that* little tramp. I'm sorry, but there are times when harsh decisions have to be made, even though it might go against the better instinct. I'm a businessman, but I wouldn't stay in business for long if I allowed people to stay rent-free in my properties, however "desperate" they were.'

Much as she wanted to secure the house on Johnson

Street, Kelly was made to wonder whether she really wished to do business with this man; at the same time another daring plan was already forming in her mind.

Opening the door, she let herself out. 'Thank you for your time,' she told him. 'I'm sorry we couldn't do business.'

'What about the Johnson Street house?'

Turning away, Kelly smiled. He was hooked good and proper, she thought.

'Look, I'm prepared to lower the asking price.' Stepping on to the pavement he pursued her down the street. 'There's no harm in you taking a look,' he argued. 'It's number twelve. See it first, then make up your mind.'

Pausing, Kelly looked him in the eye. 'Like I said, I have other agents to see, but if I find the time in between, I'll make my way there tomorrow morning . . . about eleven.'

He could hardly contain his delight. 'Wonderful! You won't regret it, I promise.'

'Just a look,' she told him. 'And only if I find the time.'

'Find the time, and I'll make it worth your while.'

Seemingly uninterested, Kelly made no comment and left him standing there.

<hr/>

A S SHE WALKED away, they were both feeling satisfied; one because he believed he was about to unload a property that had been like a millstone round his neck; the other because she knew she had him in the palm of her hand. 'By teatime tomorrow, the deal will be done,' she promised herself. 'And it won't be *me* who gets taken for a ride.'

Having seen which way the distraught woman had gone, Kelly rushed to catch up with her. As she turned the corner, she saw her, stooped down with her two arms round the children, her head buried in their faces. The soft sound of her crying tore at Kelly's heart.

'Hello.' Coming up on the young woman, Kelly glanced at the children: a boy with an unruly mop of dark curls, and a fair-haired girl with the largest brown eyes Kelly had ever seen. 'What beautiful children.' They wore grubby rags and had no shoes on their feet, but they were exquisite.

Embarrassed at being seen to cry, the woman dried her eyes. 'This is Tom,' she said, introducing the boy. 'He'll be seven next Friday.' Patting the girl's long, fair hair, she said, 'And this is Sally, who's just five.'

'Hello, you two.' Kelly had always wanted children, but the circumstances had never been right, and now she thought her chance had gone for ever. 'My name's Kelly.'

Holding out her hand, she was overcome with emotion when the girl slid her tiny fingers into hers. 'Our Amy's crying,' she said, her big brown eyes filled with tears.

'Go away!' The boy glared at Kelly, his bottom lip

trembling and his fists clenched tight. 'You're *his* friend. I saw you!'

'No, Tom!' The young woman drew him to her. 'The lady was a customer.' Looking at Kelly, she grew suspicious. 'That's right, ain't it?'

'Yes, that's right,' Kelly confirmed. 'John Harvey is no friend of mine and never could be.'

'See, I told you.' The young woman ruffled the boy's hair. 'She don't like him any more than we do.'

'What was she doing in there, then?'

'*Business*, that's what! Now behave yourself. I've had enough trouble for one day.'

Ignoring the woman he asked Kelly, '*What* business?'

Kelly laughed out loud, but not too loud in case he was offended. 'The truth is, I've recently moved to this area and I haven't got a place to live. John Harvey sells houses and I want to buy one.'

'Hmh!' The boy wasn't impressed. 'If you don't pay your rent, he'll throw you out on the street, like he did us.'

The other woman chuckled. 'You don't pay rent if you buy a house,' she said. 'You *own* it.'

He considered that for a moment, before asking Kelly, 'Are you a landlord?'

'No. You're only a landlord if you let other people live in a house and they pay rent to you.'

'Are you a rich lady?'

With a laugh, Kelly shook her head. 'It would make life easier if I was.'

The young woman wagged a finger at him. 'Stop asking questions,' she chided. 'We've got a lot to do . . . get summat to eat, find somewhere to sleep.' Tugging at the children, she apologised to Kelly. 'I'm sorry, we've got to go now.'

The boy's curiosity was still not satisfied. 'How much do you need to buy a house, lady?' He set his mouth determinedly. 'When I'm rich, I'll buy *her* a house and everything what she wants.' He looked up at the young woman and love shone from his face.

Kelly's heart turned over. 'I'm sure you will,' she said humbly, 'but your mammy's right. You must be hungry. Are you?' She glanced from the boy to the girl.

The boy looked sulky, and the girl stared at her in an odd way, making Kelly realise she had said something wrong. 'Are *you* hungry?' she asked lamely.

Glancing up at the young woman, the girl answered, 'She's not our mammy.'

Confused, Kelly apologised. 'I'm sorry,' she told the young woman. 'I just thought . . .'

The woman shrugged her shoulders. 'It don't matter.'

Sensing that she didn't want to talk about it, Kelly changed the subject. 'I know it's none of my business,' she said, 'but have you really nowhere to sleep tonight?'

'Nowhere to sleep tonight, nor any other night after that – unless it's under the canal bridge.' Beneath her breath she muttered something that made Kelly go cold. 'Happen we'd do better to jump off it!'

Touching her hand in friendship, Kelly murmured softly, 'Please . . . don't say that.'

The young woman looked at her. A great sadness filled her brown eyes, and Kelly thought she had never seen anyone so beautiful. Glancing down at the children, Kelly suggested, 'If it's all right with your . . .'

Stopping herself, she looked at the woman, who told her, 'Amy, that's my name.'

'Well,' she addressed the children once more, 'if it's all right with Amy, I think we should all go and get something to eat. I don't know about you two, but I'm starving.'

This time, the girl nodded, but the boy remained stiff-lipped and hostile.

'He's angry,' Amy explained with a sorry smile. 'Angry against the world and too small to do anything about it.'

Kelly touched the boy's hair, drawing away when he flinched. 'I know how you feel, Tom,' she said softly. 'And it's all right to be angry sometimes. But not if it makes you unhappy.'

'You don't know nuthin!'

'I know what it's like to be hungry,' she persisted. 'And I know there's a fish and chip shop down the street.' She sniffed the air. 'I think I can even smell it from here.'

'Don't want no fish and chips. Don't want nuthin!'

'That's all right.' Winking at Amy, Kelly began walking away. 'I'll have to go now, before they sell out of fish. They might even have some potato dabs, all crispy and crunchy, and covered with thick juicy batter . . .'

'He's a *bad* man!' The boy swung round to look at her, his big dark eyes moist with tears. 'He sent men to throw us out, and now we ain't got nowhere to go.'

Kelly felt he was willing to confide in her. 'If you come with me, we can sit in the parlour at the back of the fish and chip shop,' she promised, 'and you can tell me all about it.'

The boy looked up at Amy, and when she nodded, he smiled from ear to ear. 'All right, lady,' he told Kelly, 'but only if I can have some of them potato dabs.'

'You can have as many as you like,' Kelly told him, and he followed her like a lamb.

———◆———

AMY HAD SAID little on the way to the shop, and she was quiet now as they filed up to the counter. 'Fish and chips four times,' Kelly announced, hardly able to see over the tall counter, 'and a potato dab in each one please.'

The assistant was tall and lean, with an upside-down smile and a tuft of hair on the top of her head that waved from side to side as she moved. 'In or out?' she asked, popping a hot chip in her mouth.

'Sorry, what was that you said?'

The girl patted her mouth with her hand, puffing

and blowing as the chip burnt her tongue. 'Are you eating in or out?' Discreetly catching the hot chip in a piece of newspaper, she grabbed a tumbler of water from behind the counter and gulped it down. 'It's extra if you eat in,' she said, blowing her nose on her pinnie.

Even though the girl's actions put her off the food, Kelly couldn't help but laugh to herself, and when she turned round, her companions were doing the same. 'Dirty cow!' Amy whispered as the girl turned to scoop out the chips. 'Look at that! She's spilling dewdrops on the plate!'

'I ain't having no plate.' The boy was adamant.

'We'll have them in the newspaper,' Kelly told the girl, and was relieved when the food was handed over and they were able to retire to the back parlour, where they laughed until their sides ached.

'Ssh!' Putting her finger to her lips to silence the children, Kelly said they should eat up and maybe she'd have enough money in her purse to buy them a jar of sarsaparilla each afterwards.

Amy quietly regarded this kindly older woman, with her pretty face and bright sparkling eyes. 'Who are you?' she asked. 'And why are you being so kind to us? I mean, you don't even know us.'

Kelly had been enjoying her potato dab, but now she put it down and licked her lips. 'I heard you tell John Harvey that you had given him every penny you had,' she replied quietly, 'yet he still turned you out of your home.' Reaching out, she clasped her hand round the other woman's fist. 'That tells me all I need to know.'

'Aren't you curious about me, and the children?'

'I'd be a liar if I said I wasn't.'

Amy regarded her companion with interest. It had been a long time since she had found somebody she might confide in, and this stranger had such a warm, honest nature. It only took a moment for her to decide. 'I'm in charge of the children,' she said, 'but as Sally rightly said, I'm not their mammy.'

'I understand.' Kelly thought she had it all figured out.

'But I love them as much as any mother could.'

'I can tell that.'

For a while they continued with their meal. The boy finished first. 'That salt made me thirsty,' he said, looking hopefully at Kelly.

'Me too!' Clambering from her seat, Sally stood beside her brother. 'The chip burnt my tongue . . . see?' Opening her mouth she showed Kelly her tonsils.

Feigning horror, Kelly tutted, 'Goodness me! I think you need a sarsaparilla to cool it down, don't you?'

'Ooh, yes please.'

'You'd best ask Amy if it's all right first.' Reaching into her purse, she waited for Amy to give the nod.

When she said yes, they ran off to the counter, their excitement undimmed when they were told to stand in the queue with everyone else.

Enchanted, Kelly watched them chatting to the customers. 'They're lovely children, Amy.'

Amy glanced up. 'None better.' Now, as she bent her head, Kelly suspected she was crying.

Kelly's heart went out to her. 'You don't have to talk about it if you don't want to,' she said, 'but you know what they say – a trouble shared is a trouble halved.' She liked Amy from the start. 'Besides, I'm a stranger here. I need a friend too.'

'You can't mean you want *me* as a friend?' Amy raised her face and through the tears came a look of astonishment.

'And why wouldn't I want you as a friend?'

'Because you're . . . different.'

Kelly shook her head. 'You're wrong, Amy. I might have clean clothes and a good pair of boots on my feet but inside, we're alike. Oh, I know you have the children, but at the end of the day when they're fast asleep, you're all alone, just like me. We neither of us have any real friends, and in different ways we've both known hardship at one time or another.'

'You don't *look* like you've known hardship.'

'And you don't look like you've just been thrown out of house and home.' She beamed. 'You certainly don't look like someone who would burst into John Harvey's office and frighten the living daylights out of him!'

Amy chuckled. 'Do you really think I frightened him?'

'You frightened *me*, never mind him!'

They laughed at the way John Harvey had thrown her out, and at the way she'd stood her ground and called him a rat. By the time they'd finished talking, the chips were cold and the batter on the fish had gone soggy. 'You make me feel good,' Amy told her. 'I haven't laughed like that in a long time.'

'Me neither,' Kelly admitted. 'I think we're good for each other.'

Again, Amy fell silent, and Kelly left her to her thoughts. She suspected Amy had things she needed to tell, but wasn't yet ready. All in good time.

The children came back with their drinks, and when they had finished, the little entourage left the chippie and made their way down the street. With the children in front, the two women sauntered along, neither of them wanting the encounter to end. 'Where will you go?' Kelly broke the silence.

'Don't you worry about us,' Amy answered with a hesitant smile. 'We'll find somewhere.'

'Will you let me help?'

'What do you mean?'

'I can ask Fran to take you in until you find some-where,' she offered.

'Who's Fran?'

'She's a big-hearted lady who keeps a guest-house. I'm sure she'd find a room for you.'

'I ain't got no money.'

'You're not to worry about that.'

'I ain't asking for no charity!' Amy was on the

defensive. 'I only let you treat us to fish and chips 'cause the kids were hungry.'

'I'm not offering charity,' Kelly protested. 'Anyway, the offer is for one week's board and lodgings, that's all! You can pay me back when you make good, or it can be a gift from one friend to another; that's up to you. But there *are* conditions.'

'What conditions?'

'That the children go to school for an education and you get yourself some work.'

'There *ain't* no work! Don't you think I've tried?'

Kelly paused and Amy followed suit, while the children skipped ahead. 'I've got a plan,' Kelly said slowly. 'What if I could find a proper home for you and the young 'uns . . . and offer you work into the bargain?'

Amy was taken aback. 'Oh! If you could do that, it would be like a dream come true!'

'And would you send the children to school?'

Indignant, Amy told her, 'I'd like nothing better than for them to get an education.'

They walked a little further talking awhile, and Kelly informed Amy of the plan she had begun forming in her mind. 'I was in John Harvey's office, like I said, to buy a house. Only I want a particular house, for a particular reason.'

'What house?' Amy asked, curious.

'You wouldn't know it.'

Like Amy, she had things to tell, but wasn't ready yet. 'I'll know tomorrow whether it's mine or not,' she went on. 'All I need to know for now is, will you let me ask Fran if she has a room for a week. It'll take at least that long for me to sort myself out.'

As from the start, Amy found herself trusting her. 'All right,' she said, 'but I don't want it for nothing. Soonever I start earning, I'll pay you back every penny. That's *my* condition.'

'It's a deal!'

They shook hands, hugging and laughing, and the friendship was sealed.

'I'm not going to no school!' Tom had been eavesdropping.

'You'll go to school and learn,' Amy told him severely, 'and so will your sister. If you want to be summat special in life, you have to learn.'

'I want to be a chip-shop lady!' Young as she was, Sally had her future all mapped out.

Tom too. 'I want to be a tram-driver,' he declared proudly.

'That's what I mean.' Like Kelly, Amy was trying to keep a straight face. 'You'll both make your fortunes and make your mammy proud.'

On Amy's impulsive remark, all three of them grew quiet. Sally began crying and Amy picked her up. 'It's all right,' she soothed, holding her close. 'We're all together now, and I'll never leave you.'

Made curious by the turn of events, Kelly felt a small hand slide into hers. When she looked down it was to see Tom staring up with sorrowful eyes.

Deeply moved, she squeezed his hand and smiled. 'Come on, sweetheart,' she murmured. 'Let's go home.'

Where, just as Kelly had imagined, Fran welcomed them with open arms.

Chapter Five

FRAN FINISHED HER breakfast and leaned back in the chair. 'I'll be sorry to see you go,' she said, taking Sally on to her lap. 'Still, it'll be nice for you to have your own front-door key, and I daresay you wouldn't mind if I popped in to see you from time to time?' It was more of a question than a statement.

'You're welcome any time.' Kelly began clearing away the dishes. 'You already know that.'

While Kelly chatted with Fran, Amy took the children to one side. 'You two go and get washed,' she told them. 'We've a lot to do.'

'When can we go to school?' Tom wanted to know.

'As soon as I can arrange it,' he was told. 'Anyway, you've soon changed your tune, haven't you? One minute you don't want to go and now you can't wait.'

'That's because I don't want to be stupid all my life.'

'You're *not* stupid,' she answered, giving him a hug.

'You're a clever little chap and they'll soon find that out, I dare say.'

Reassured, he turned his mind to the new home. 'Will I have a room all to myself?' he asked hopefully.

Amy wagged a finger. 'You know what Kelly told you,' she reminded him. 'There are only three bedrooms . . . one for me, one for Kelly, and you and Sally will have to share the other. We're going to divide it by a curtain down the middle, remember.'

'I don't want to share!'

Drawing him aside, Amy spoke sternly. 'Don't be ungrateful, Tom,' she whispered. 'It's very good of Kelly to let us into her home, especially as I won't be able to pay rent for some time.'

'I had my own room at the other house.'

'Yes, but that was different,' she chided. 'Besides, we were thrown out of that house because I couldn't pay the rent. If it wasn't for Kelly, we'd be walking the streets and sleeping rough under a hedge somewhere. Don't forget that.'

He glanced at Kelly, who was scraping leftover bacon scraps into the bucket. She had been so nice to them, he thought. 'I'm sorry, Amy.' Shame coloured his face.

'So I won't hear any more about you and Sally having to share . . . *will* I, Tom?'

Looking dejected, he shook his head slowly.

'That's all right then.' Hugging him again, she urged, 'Go and get ready. And take Sally with you.'

When the children were out of the room, Amy

helped the other two women to clear away. 'I heard what Tom said,' Kelly admitted, 'about not wanting to share with Sally.'

Amy was mortified. 'I'm sorry,' she said, 'I was hoping you hadn't heard.'

'I've been thinking,' Kelly mused. 'There might be a way for Tom to have a room of his own. That bedroom is the largest of them all. I was just wondering . . . what if we could knock another door in from the landing? I've already looked and there's enough space.'

'No. I won't even hear of it.'

Brushing Amy's protest aside, Kelly outlined her idea. 'We could divide the room with a kind of solid partition – wood panels or something. Then Sally and Tom would have their own little rooms.' The idea had been growing over the last few days. 'What do you think?'

'I think it's too much to ask.' Amy was adamant. 'I'm just grateful that you've offered us a roof over our heads until I find something of our own.'

'Yes, but while you're with me I'd like to do my best for you.' In fact, Kelly was looking forward to having them with her. The idea that they might not be there for too long was unsettling. 'Once he starts school, it would be good for Tom to have his own room.'

Amy shook her head. 'Things like that cost money and I know you've stretched yourself to the limit just to put down a deposit on the house. I mean, only last week you went back down South to sell lots of your bits and pieces, and now here you are, with next to nothing, and having to start again. You shouldn't be worrying about Tom having his own room. Don't you think you've got enough on your plate?'

'I suppose you're right,' Kelly admitted. 'But I won't give up on him. If I find a way to get the lad his own room, he shall have it!' Once Kelly got hold of an idea, she was like a dog with a bone.

⟶◆⟵

C HARLIE WAS SEATED on the front doorstep smoking his pipe when he saw them coming down the street; a comical little sight they were and all, he thought.

Kelly and Amy were in front, and Fran coming up behind with the two bairns. Between them they carried mops and buckets and all manner of paraphernalia.

'Here come the workers!' Scrambling up, Charlie waved a cheery hello. Delighted as always to see him, Kelly waved back.

'Yer look as if yer mean business,' he chuckled. 'Yer make a man feel ashamed, so yer do.' Knocking out his pipe against the wall, he squared his shoulders and presented himself for work. 'Right then! What would yer like me to do?'

Kelly regarded him for a minute. 'What are you like at plumbing?'

'Terrible!'

'Carpentry?'

'Worse.'

'What about brickwork? The chimney's falling down.'

He shook his head. 'If I started messing about with that kind o' thing, the whole bloomin' house would likely fall down round yer ears.'

'Can you put shelves up in the scullery?'

'If yer like, but they'll fall right back down again.'

'Best forget that then, eh?' Ignoring the sniggering from the others, she told him, 'Happen it might be best if you tell me what you *can* do?'

Grinning from ear to ear he advised her of his talents. 'I can strip walls and scrub floors and make the best brew in Blackburn town.'

'Can you paint?'

'What, yer mean windows and doors and such?'

'Something like that.' The old bugger's hard work, Kelly thought with amusement. 'But before you can paint them afresh, the old stuff has to come off. I reckon they're buried in umpteen coats of paint.'

Charlie gave her a confident wink. 'Nuthin' to it,' he said, 'I'm yer man.' And without further ado, he followed her into the house.

Everyone knew their jobs. Fran was to pull down the ragged curtains and burn them in the yard. Amy had volunteered to scrub and varnish the stairs and banister. Amid protests and aggravation, the children had been dressed in Fran's old pinnies and scarves, and even some odd gloves she'd found in the stair-hole cupboard. Tom had complained that he looked 'like a scarecrow'.

'It doesn't matter what you look like!' Kelly told him.

'You're not being let loose on that old fire-range unless you're covered up, and there's an end to it.' So, armed with cleaning cloths, tins of thick, sticky black-lead, and looking like Eskimos, the little ones set to.

Kelly's workload was tenfold. Apart from co-ordinating the whole operation, she was to clean and disinfect the lavatory in the coal cellar. After that she would tackle the scullery sink and clear out the drains, which were clogged with all manner of debris. When that was done, her next assignment was to throw out and burn the filth that had accumulated in the alcove cupboards, whose insides would then need scrubbing to rid them of the rank smell.

Afterwards, she would tear up the linoleum and scrub away the stains from the floorboards beneath. There was also that pretty Victorian fireplace in the front parlour that was so grimed up with dirt and smoke, you could hardly see the flowers and fruit adorning the ironwork. Then there were windows to clean and curtains to hang, and so much more it was impossible to do it all in a hurry, much as she was desperate to move in and make it a home again.

'You'll have to be patient,' she told herself. 'Everything will be ready in its own good time.'

Softly singing, she boiled the kettle on the gas ring and filled her bucket. Next, she mixed a good measure of Jeyes fluid into the water, before making her way through the scullery and down to the yard. The lavatory was situated just inside the coal cellar.

The smell was sickening. 'Even animals wouldn't leave it like this,' she muttered in disgust. But it had to be done, and it was her place to do it so, tying a scarf round her mouth, she rolled up her sleeves and went to war.

Three times she returned to the scullery, boiling the kettle and refilling her bucket. 'You'll run the tap dry,' Charlie said, and was glad he hadn't been asked to do that filthy job; though he would not have refused all the same.

With grim determination, Kelly scrubbed and rinsed and wiped until the sweat dripped from her face. After what seemed an age, she stood back to admire her handiwork, and then it all seemed worthwhile. The lavatory bowl sparkled as it had not done since new, and when Kelly put the wooden seat down, it was four shades lighter than when she had started. The walls, brushed free of cobwebs, were fresh with two new coats of whitewash, and the red tiled floor had been transformed by the application of hot water, soda crystals and a big helping of elbow grease.

She then cut out numerous newspaper squares and hung them from a piece of string on the wall. 'At last there'll be a clean and civilised lavatory should anyone need it,' she said, and even as she spoke, Tom was rushing Sally down the steps. 'Quick,' he shouted, 'she needs the lavvy!' Whereupon he left her at the foot of the steps and ran back up, tripping over Fran's old pinnie as he went.

Covered in black-lead and with smut on her face, Sally looked a picture. 'I reckon I got it done just in time,' Kelly chuckled, though desperate as she was, Sally wouldn't have cared one way or the other.

A few moments later, the little girl climbed the steps, and Kelly was left alone with her memories. Strange, she thought, how many times I came down them same steps and climbed back up again. She gazed at the scullery window. And how often I looked out of that window to watch our mam hanging out the washing in this little yard.

Glancing round the yard, she only now realised how the tall brick walls made it so dark and uninviting. I'll have to brighten it up, she promised herself, but as yet, had no real idea of how to go about it.

For now, she was in no hurry to go back inside the house. Feeling as if she needed a moment to herself, Kelly decided to take a well-earned breather. 'They'll be working that hard, they won't even miss me.' She hoped she hadn't set them too demanding a task. But they'd all volunteered to help and, from what she had seen when she popped her head round the scullery door a while ago, they were having the time of their lives.

Swilling the contents of her bucket down the drain, she sat on a half-filled coal sack and took stock of her situation. 'Whoever thought I'd come back here to live?' she asked herself, still amazed by the recent turn of events.

Yet here she was, and here she would stay, until all the demons were gone.

Startled by a sound above her, she looked up and saw Luke standing there; he was a fine figure of a man, and just for one split second, she imagined it was her Barney. But Barney was not so tall, nor his hair so thick and dark. 'Don't look at me,' she pleaded as Luke made his way down the steps. 'I must look a frightful sight.'

Luke didn't think so. Sitting on the coal sack, with her hair blown by the breeze and her mop and bucket beside her, she looked delightfully vulnerable. 'You look like someone who needs a hot drink.'

In fact she was gasping. 'You've saved my life,' she beamed. The sight of a mug of tea in his hand made her lick her lips in anticipation.

'They've all stopped for a break. Dad's in the scullery brewing tea, and Fran's gone down to the corner shop for a chocolate cake.' His smile was wonderful. 'They seem to be having the time of their lives up there.'

When he passed her the mug, she cupped her hands round it. 'I don't know what I would have done without them.'

'They all care for you,' he said. 'Dad never stops talking about you.'

'Charlie's lovely,' she replied with a smile. 'They're *all* lovely! I'm lucky to have found such good friends.'

He looked at her and thought how lovely she was too. According to what Charlie had told him, he knew she was in her early forties, but there was a charm and innocence about Kelly that made her seem much younger. 'Pity, we didn't really get a chance to talk, did we,' he said, 'when you came round to the house the other Saturday.' Being close to her like this was so good. It seemed an age since he had felt comfortable in a woman's presence. The disastrous experience with Stella had sapped his confidence.

'What would we have talked about?' Little did he know the effect his nearness was having on Kelly. She felt like a young girl, shy and trembling.

'We could have talked about you.'

Embarrassed, she buried her face in her mug. 'You wouldn't have found me very interesting.' Her past maybe, but not her.

'It would have been nice just to talk, don't you think? Much like we're doing now.'

'What? With me looking like a skivvy and smelling of God knows what.'

'I hadn't noticed.' He *had* noticed her bright, honest eyes and attractive smile, though.

Suddenly a starling hopped on to the wall, its head cocked to one side, a vibrant song trilling from its beak. 'Oh, look!' Almost afraid to breathe, she watched the bird peering down on them.

Its abrupt appearance took Kelly back to a glorious summer's day when she was just a child. Her mother found an abandoned chick in the cellar and brought it to the steps where Kelly was sitting. 'Poor little thing,' she told Kelly, 'its mammy's gone and left it.' When the chick died in her hand, they both cried.

Now her own mammy was gone, and here she was, back in that same yard, almost as if she had never been away.

'How's it going then?'

Startled out of her reverie, Kelly apologised. 'Sorry, I was miles away.' As she looked up, the bird flew off, and for one awful minute she felt incredibly lonely.

'The work,' he repeated. 'How's it going?'

'We're getting there, I think.' Warmed by his nearness, she felt curiously safe. 'All I need now is a plumber and someone to get the gas working properly. The gas ring splutters and spits every time you turn it on, and the other night when me and Amy were washing down the pantry walls, the lights went out without any warning.'

'Leave it to me.'

'What? You mean *you* can fix it?' Just now, when she looked into his eyes, she felt a strange sensation. This was only the second time she had met Luke, and both times he had made her feel strangely unsettled.

'I can't exactly *fix* it, no.' Squeezing himself on to the sack beside her, he explained, 'In our work we have to be ready for anything. There have been the odd emergencies when we've needed to call out a gas-fitter. One bloke in particular comes to mind,' he said. 'I'll get him to come over and check it out, if you like?'

Kelly was thrilled. 'You don't happen to know any good carpenters and plumbers as well, do you?'

'As a matter of fact I do know a good plumber. As for a carpenter, you're looking at one.'

'What, *you*? Charlie never told me you were a carpenter.'

'That's because he'd rather boast about me being promoted to foreman. But I'm a carpenter by trade, so here I am, at your service.' His eyes twinkled mischievously. 'Just tell me what you need.'

'Charlie said you work such long hours, you never have a minute to yourself.'

He smiled. 'What does my old dad know?'

Kelly laughed. Now she felt she was beginning to know him. 'All right then,' she said. 'I need new shelves in the scullery, and the alcove cupboards in the back bedroom need new doors. The old ones are rotten right through.'

'Consider it done.'

There was something else, but as yet she hadn't spoken about it to anyone.

Sensing a problem, he asked softly, 'What else do you have in mind?'

It was a moment before she found the courage to answer. 'In the front bedroom, there's a sort of cupboard. It runs all along one wall.'

'We've got one the same,' he revealed. 'It's more a space than a cupboard, isn't it? It's where the rafters slope in. It creates a channel right along the wall.' While he spoke he gesticulated with his hands to explain what he meant. 'Usually there's a door at one end. I expect it's gone rotten, has it? Well, no matter. I can soon replace that as well.'

'I don't want a new one.'

He could hear her voice tremble, sense her fear. 'What is it you want then?'

'I want it boarded up.' Now her voice was filled with hatred. 'I don't want anyone to know there was ever a cupboard there.' She could never erase the memories, nor the fearful cries that haunted her dreams. But she could, and *would*, destroy that door, so she never had to look on it again.

Wanting to ask but knowing he shouldn't, Luke stole a glance at her face; Kelly had turned away, head down, and seemed totally preoccupied. Now, when she turned to look at him, he saw how pale and nervous she seemed. 'Can you do that for me?' she asked. 'Soon?' She seemed desperate that he should do this one particular job.

He wondered about the dark secrets this house held. 'I'll have it done by tomorrow night, if you like.'

Visibly relaxing, she thanked him. 'I saw a big second-hand wardrobe in town yesterday,' she said. 'I'll buy that and put it over where the door used to be.' No one will ever know the door was even there, she thought. Except her. Every time she went into that room, *she* would know.

Thankfully, she would hardly ever have to go into that room. She had given Amy the choice of rooms and Amy had chosen the front one, 'So's I can see what's going on outside,' she joked. 'I'm a nosy bugger, me.'

Kelly was happy to take the back bedroom. From here

she could see into the yard, where her mam used to beat the rugs and sweep the flagstones.

'A plumber and a gas-fitter,' Luke reiterated. 'Is there anything else you need?'

She shook her head. 'Thanks anyway.' She daren't bring herself to look into those dark, brooding eyes.

'Kelly?'

'Yes?'

'Are you all right?'

Still she kept her gaze averted. 'Why do you ask?'

'I just get the feeling you need to talk, that's all.'

'No. I need to work, *that's* what I need to do.' Forcing a laugh, she said, 'I'll have the others on my back if I don't do my share.'

As she stood up he caught hold of her hand. '*Look* at me.'

When she hesitated, he asked again, 'Please, Kelly . . . look at me.'

Slowly she turned her head. 'I'm all right,' she murmured, 'really I am.' Until now she hadn't realised how handsome he was.

'I hope you don't mind, but Dad told me everything,' he confessed. 'So I know it can't be easy for you . . . coming back here. I meant what I said just now. If you need anything at all, I'm never far away.'

He found himself inexplicably drawn to her. She was so different from Stella. So wonderfully, refreshingly different. Now, more than ever, he was glad that Stella would not be his wife for much longer.

'Thank you, I'll remember that.' It was good to know he was there if she needed him.

'Right then.' Springing from the hard, lumpy seat, he shook the coal-dust from his jacket. 'I'll go and check the job out.' Giving her a curious look he asked, 'Are you sure about wanting that doorway boarded up?'

Kelly had no doubts. 'I'm sure.'

Taking a step away he told her softly, 'I enjoyed our little talk. Did anyone ever tell you – you're good company?'

'I might say the same about you.' He had such a warm, easy manner, Kelly felt as though she'd known him for ever.

'We should do it again sometime.'

Suddenly thinking of Barney, she felt guilty. 'Let me know how much the work will cost.'

He looked at her and shook his head. 'Shame on you.'

'Why?'

'Are you paying the others to help you out?'

Dropping her gaze, she answered, 'I did offer but they wouldn't let me.'

'I'm not letting you either. I have plenty of spare wood, so I do the work for nothing, or I don't do it at all.' Reaching out, he thrilled her by cupping his hand under her chin and raising her face to his. 'All right?'

'If you say so.'

'I do.' The touch of her skin against his fingers was like velvet. 'Right then.' Reluctantly, he turned away. 'I'd best leave you to it.' He didn't want the encounter to end, and neither did Kelly.

From the window, Charlie had seen them together, and his old heart was gladdened. When Kelly mounted the stairs to the scullery a short time later, he stood in the doorway. 'You and our Luke go well together,' he remarked thoughtfully.

And though she made no comment other than a smile, Kelly knew exactly what he meant.

⊰⊱⊰●⊱⊰

THE HOURS FLEW by.

'My God, look at the time!' Pausing for a minute, Fran had taken the pocket-watch from her apron, and gasped aloud at how late it was. 'It's half-past four!' Untying her apron she threw it aside. 'If I don't get back, there'll be no dinner for the guests and then what will they say?' To Fran's surprise, a party of ten visiting Methodists had booked all of her available rooms two days before.

Kelly was filled with remorse. 'Leave what you're doing and go.' Putting her paintbrush down, she wiped her hands on the cloth and dug into her purse. She hurried across the room and held a silver coin out to Fran. 'You'll get a cab at the bottom of the street,' she explained. 'I'll come and see you off.' She felt responsible when all was said and done.

Fran was adamant. 'You'll do no such thing!' Folding the coin into Kelly's fist she told her kindly, 'You've more urgent things to be spending that money on, lass. Besides, I don't need no cab. *And* I can find my own way to the tram stop without you leaving your work.'

Kelly opened her mouth to argue, but stopped when Fran gave her a hug. 'I'll not hear another word!' she declared soundly. 'Now then, finish what you have to do, and I'll see you when you're ready.' She added a stern warning, 'And don't go buying fish and chips 'cause I'll have a thick, meaty hot-pot bubbling on the stove by the time you get back.'

The mention of hot-pot set everybody's stomachs rumbling. 'I'm hungry *now*!' Sally wailed. And Tom did the same.

'Hey! Stop meithering, you two.' On her knees by the fireside, Amy was up to her elbows in suds and water; the children had made a good job of the fire-range, but half the black-lead had spattered over the quarry-tiled hearth. 'You'll have to wait,' she said, waving her scrubbing brush. 'We won't be finished for a while yet.'

Fran had an idea. 'I'll take them home with me, if you like.' She donned her coat, ready for the off. 'By the time you and Kelly get back, the children will be fed and washed, ready for bed.'

Even if Amy had protested, which she was not about to do, the children gave her little choice. Running across the room they flung their scrawny arms round her neck, so excited at the prospect of a hot meal and a warm fireside that Amy felt obliged to let them go. 'Now don't give Fran any trouble on the way,' she warned, 'or I'll tan your arses good and proper.'

'We won't!' they cried in unison.

Kelly got their coats. 'Hands and face washed first,' she ordered. 'We don't want the tram-conductor thinking you're a pair of vagabonds, or he might refuse to let you on.'

It took barely a minute to run a wet flannel over the two of them then she threw their coats over their shoulders. 'Be off with you now,' she urged, and so's not to miss the five o'clock tram, Fran took them down the street at a run.

Amy and Kelly watched from the front parlour window. 'Look at their little legs go,' Kelly remarked with a grin.

'It's their *bellies* that're going,' Amy said. 'And it's Fran's hot-pot that's doing it.'

It was a comical sight all the same; Fran pushing along, as quickly as her ample figure would let her, and the two bairns trotting alongside.

'I'm looking forward to some of that hot-pot myself,' Amy admitted, and Kelly felt the same.

'We shouldn't be too long behind.' She turned to view the room and was thrilled. 'It's amazing,' she said, 'what we've all done in such a short time.' The fire-range stood proud and shiny, just as she recalled from her childhood. A bright fire had been lit in the fireplace. The floorboards, though still damp from the onslaught of water and scrubbing, were like brand new timbers. Every wall was stripped and washed, ready for painting, and the windows were so clean she could see her own reflection in them. 'You've done me proud,' she told Amy. 'You've *all* done me proud.'

Amy argued it had been more fun than she could have imagined. 'It's a pity we can't get rid of that smell though.'

A shiver went down Kelly's back. 'What smell?'

'You mean you haven't noticed it?'

Kelly shook her head. 'No.'

'You're the only one who *hasn't*,' Amy said doubtfully.

Banishing foolish imaginings, Kelly thought perhaps she *could* detect something rising above the carbolic and soda crystals. 'Where do you think it's coming from?'

'Can't tell.' Amy shrugged her shoulders. 'Fran even went down the cellar to see if it was coming up from there, but it wasn't.'

Like two bloodhounds they got to their knees and edged their way over the floor. 'It's stronger here,' Amy said, pointing to the floorboards beneath her. Bending her head she put her nose to an open knothole. 'Phew! Smells like summat's gone rotten down there.'

Kelly thought so too. 'I can't understand why I didn't notice it before.' Resting back on her haunches and trying to ignore her feelings of reluctance, she suggested they should pull up a floorboard and peer inside. 'I'll get something to use as a lever,' she said, and in no time at all, was on her way back from the scullery with Charlie's big screwdriver. 'This should do it.'

Inserting the tool into the small slit between the floorboards, Kelly put all her strength behind it, until slowly, the floorboards began to separate. 'Quick!' she called to Amy who was watching her every move. 'Get the broom! Wait until I've got the floorboard far enough out, then shove the broom in to hold it.'

Three times they got it far enough out, only to have the broom snap and the board spring back into place, almost taking their fingers with it. 'It's no good!' Breathless, they took a moment to think. 'We'll have to get something stronger to hold the floorboard long enough for us to take it out.'

Amy held her nose. 'The stench *is* coming from under there,' she declared. It was so strong they could almost taste it.

They both had the idea at the same time, but it was Amy who voiced it: 'The poker! That should do it.' The poker was not a real poker but a long thick coach-bolt, left by the previous tenants.

With the right tool, it took just a few minutes. 'I'll do it, Amy. You stand back.' Kelly thought this was something she had to do herself.

Enveloped in the stench and feeling sick to her stomach, Amy didn't argue.

Taking off her apron, Kelly tied it round her mouth and nose. 'Blimey! You look like a bank robber,' Amy joked.

Kelly laughed too. 'Behave yourself,' she said, and leaning forward peered down into the darkness. 'God

Almighty!' Even through the crumpled layers of cloth, the smell of corruption was overpowering.

Amy also leaned forward, but not too close. 'What have you found, gal?' she asked.

Kelly blew away the dust. 'I'm not sure,' she said in a tremulous voice. Taking the broken broom-handle she began poking about inside. 'I think I've found the culprit.' Reaching in deeper she made several attempts to hook it on the broom-handle.

'It ain't a dead body, is it?' Amy's eyes were big and curious as she looked over Kelly's shoulder.

'Watch out!' As Kelly swung the broom-handle up, a dark shape dropped off the end and wrapped itself round Amy's ankle. 'It's got me!' she cried, and set off at a run, her screams rising to a crescendo as she went. With the shape caught on her bootlace, the faster she ran, the more it bounced and bobbed about. 'Jesus, Mary and Joseph! It's still after me!' she screeched. 'Gerrit orf! For Gawd's sake, gerrit orf!'

Kelly chased after her. 'Stand still!' she cried. 'It's *not* after you. It's caught on your bootlace.'

Shivering with fear, Amy stopped and squashed herself against the wall, eyes closed as Kelly took the rat by the tail and flung it aside. 'The bugger's dead.'

Amy felt foolish. 'You could have told me.'

'If you'd have stopped screaming long enough to listen, I *would* have!'

Still shaking, Amy stared at Kelly in disgust. 'It was *awful*.'

In her mind, Kelly could still see Amy running round in circles and, try as she might, she couldn't keep a straight face. 'You should have seen yourself,' she chuckled, 'leaping round the room with a dead rat swinging from your bootlace.' Mimicking Amy she made her laugh too. 'It's after me . . . gerrit orf!'

'You bugger!' Amy was still shaking, but this time with laughter. 'I bet you did it on purpose.'

Protesting her innocence, Kelly said she would never do such a thing. Amy knew it, and laughed at herself. 'I'm glad the kids weren't here,' she said, 'or I'd never hear the last of it.'

'I won't tell,' Kelly promised, and Amy knew she was safe.

But it was the highlight of the day and Amy said so. 'I never laughed so much until I met you,' she said. 'You're an absolute tonic, so you are.'

After all the excitement, Kelly thought a cup of tea was called for. 'Put the floorboard back or make the tea,' she told Amy. 'It's your choice.'

'I'll make the tea.' Amy didn't fancy going anywhere near that hole.

'Strong and sweet then,' Kelly said, 'with plenty of milk. Oh, and if there's a ginger biscuit, *that* might go down well an' all.' Fran's homemade gingernuts were wonderful – crisp, buttery and full of flavour.

Her mouth watering at the prospect, Amy went to put the kettle on. What she discovered in the scullery dashed both their hopes. 'Charlie ain't left much tea and there's no sugar at all,' she informed Kelly. 'Shall I go and ask him for a borrow?'

'No, we'll manage.' Kelly answered. 'Use what there is.'

'And there ain't no biscuits left neither,' she wailed. 'Some greedy bugger's ate the lot!'

Kelly smiled. 'That Charlie's got some answering to do tomorrow,' she said; there was no doubt in her mind who had stolen the last crumb of food.

While Amy pottered about in the scullery, Kelly set about putting the rat outside. Scooping it up in a dustpan, she dropped it through the parlour window to the yard below. 'It's getting dark,' she told Amy. 'I don't fancy messing about down there tonight. I'll shift it in the morning.'

Engrossed in counting out the tea-leaves, Amy took no notice.

'Right!' Kelly left the dustpan on the windowsill. 'Now we've got rid of the smell, I'd best put this floorboard back afore somebody falls down the hole.'

As it was beginning to get dark, she rolled up a piece of newspaper. Taking a light from the fire, she lit the lamp with the flame and, before it could burn her fingers, threw the paper on to the embers. 'It's getting cold in here now,' she muttered. 'Shan't be long afore we go home.' Funny, she thought, how she had come to call Fran's house 'home', when, as she had come to realise, this place had always been her home and now would be so once again.

She was about to drop the floorboard into place when, out of the corner of her eye, she saw something gleaming. Curious, she got down to her knees and, leaning over the hole, she peered in. The light from the lamp had caught a shape, small and square, with an oddly familiar, brilliant clasp. Intrigued, Kelly took a closer look.

Leaning further forward, she blew away the dust and there it was. At first she refused to believe what she was seeing. But then, as her mind fled back over the years, she had no doubt. 'Oh, dear God!' She remembered the day the tiny box had gone missing . . . that day of awful violence.

As the memory grew stronger, the old hatred came flooding back.

Carefully she drew the object out. For a long, traumatic moment she held it in her hands, her eyes and heart coveting the box, all manner of emotions overwhelming her. Placing her fingers over the clasp, she began to open it. Suddenly afraid, she took her fingers away. It was a moment before she tried again, then stopped, reluctant to see what was inside. Cradling the box like a mother might cradle her child, she softly wept.

Unaware, Amy came through the door. 'It'll taste bloody awful!' she said. 'There ain't no sugar and hardly any milk. But it's wet and warm, so that'll have to do . . .' She would have gone on chatting, but something about the way Kelly was sitting hunched and quiet on the floor made her pause. 'Kelly, gal, what's up?' She came nearer. 'Don't tell me you've found another dead rat.'

When Kelly looked up, tears rolling down her sorry face, Amy knew there was something very wrong. Quickly setting the cups on the hearth, she hurried forward. 'What is it, gal?' she asked, kneeling down beside her. 'What's the matter?' Her anxious eyes were drawn to the object in Kelly's arms. 'What have you got there?'

Not yet ready to tell, Kelly bowed her head and looked away. Gently, Amy closed her two arms about her. 'What's upset you, eh?' Laying her face on Kelly's head, she murmured, 'We're friends, ain't we? You can tell me.'

A moment passed. Warm and safe in Amy's arms, Kelly sobbed quietly. In that instant a deep and special friendship was formed. Instinctively, the two women knew that for the rest of their lives, they would always be there for each other. 'It's my mother's.' Kelly's knuckles were strained and white where she had clasped the box to her heart.

Amy glanced at the box. It was a small, beautiful thing, figured on top and inlaid with mother-of-pearl. The clasp was in the shape of a rose. 'It's lovely,' she breathed, her curiosity heightened. 'Did you find it under the floorboards?' She couldn't imagine how anyone could put such a delicate thing in such a horrible place . . . unless it was to hide it.

Kelly's attention was so taken with the box, and the way it had come to be hidden, that she didn't hear Amy's questions.

'Come on, gal.' Easing her up, Amy took Kelly across

the room and sat her in the one chair. 'My God! You're freezing cold.' She poked the fire to liven it. 'Here, drink this.' Handing Kelly a mug of tea, she sat on the edge of the chair. 'We'll get warm, then make our way home, shall we?'

With the box on her lap, Kelly gratefully sipped the tea. When she was warmed through, she put the cup down on the fender and undid the clasp. 'It was my mother's jewellery box,' she told Amy. 'The last time I saw it I was just a little girl.'

'It's a beautiful thing.' Amy was mesmerised. 'But what was it doing under the floorboards?'

'Before that it was my grandmother's. I remember her saying it was to be handed down through the generations of girls.' She smiled sadly. 'It was to be mine next.'

'Do you know what's inside?' Amy was aching to see the contents.

'My mother only wore these things on special occasions. "I'm looking after them for *you*," that's what she used to say.'

'Your mother sounds a lovely person.'

'She was . . . *is*.' Kelly's mind flew back to the letter her mother had sent. 'She went away.' Her voice fell to a whisper. 'I haven't seen her for several years.'

Amy felt guilty. 'I'm sorry, gal.'

Looking up, Kelly told her, 'Just now, this minute, I'd give everything I have just to be with her.'

'Don't you know where she is?'

'I'm not sure.' Kelly had often wondered if she had moved on since sending the letter.

Then, slowly, she took the items out of the box one by one. There was a small jewelled brooch in the shape of a fish, a string of pearls and two rings, one plain, the other fashioned in emeralds.

Amy had never seen such precious things. 'Oh my Gawd!' Her eyes widened in wonder. 'I wouldn't dare wear 'em,' she gasped. 'I've come across rogues who'd cut your throat for less.'

'They're not mine to wear,' Kelly said.

''Course not, gal . . . not if your mam's still alive.' Amy didn't fully understand the situation, but she felt there was something bad in Kelly's background.

Tracing the tip of her finger over the fish brooch, Kelly remembered as if it was yesterday. 'She wore this on my birthday.'

'Can I hold it?'

Tenderly, Kelly laid it in the palm of Amy's hand.

'I ain't never seen nuthin' like it afore.' Amy lovingly stroked the brooch. 'Except in shop winders, o' course.' Persistent but kind, she said, 'I can't understand how your mam could leave them behind. D'yer think she hid 'em under the floorboards and then forgot all about 'em?'

'She would *never* do that.' Kelly began to see the whole picture now. 'It must have been him,' she said bitterly. '*He* hid them under the floorboards.'

'Who?'

'My father.'

147

Seeing the look on Amy's face, Kelly told her, 'He was a wicked, devious man. He ruined all our lives . . . even after he was dead.' She raised her eyes to see Amy's reaction, but there was only kindness and understanding in her face.

Sensing that Kelly needed to talk, Amy urged, 'Go on, gal, it's all right.'

Grateful, Kelly let the past wash over her. It was a good feeling. Sitting there in the lamplight, with the dying fire casting a reassuring glow into the room, she felt safer than she had in a long time. With Amy beside her, she felt she could tell everything. She had often spoken to Barney about her past, and he was wonderful. But he was a man and could never see it from a woman's point of view.

'He used to beat her,' she began, 'beat her until her body was raw.' She paused, the tears welling in her eyes but not falling. Taking a deep breath, she continued, 'When it got too bad, I would cry and shout for him to leave her alone.' A small, wistful smile crossed her features. 'I wanted to kill him with my bare hands, only the bedroom door would be locked and I couldn't get in.'

Amy thought it was just as well, or she might not be here to tell the tale.

'One time, he flung open the door and grabbed me.' Turning her head, Kelly lifted the ends of her hair to reveal a deep, ugly scar across the back of her neck. 'He whipped me bad,' she said. 'He told me the next time, he would lash the head off my shoulders.'

Horrified, Amy looked at the scar and wondered at

the man who could do such a thing. Reaching out, she took hold of Kelly's hand. There was no need of words.

'After that, my mam was always afraid for me,' Kelly revealed. 'She told my brother Michael that when it got really bad, he was to take me down to the coal cellar – you couldn't hear anything down there. We'd huddle together in the dark and he'd tell me stories of little people with wings and pointed feet, and how they lived in the cellar and hid whenever we went down.' She smiled. 'He said that if you believed in them, they would grant a wish. I believed it all, and wished for my dad to go away and never come back.' The quiet smile melted beneath the sadness. 'But the beating went on, and I stopped believing.'

It was painful for Kelly to recall it now. 'After a while, we'd go back upstairs, when *he* had gone down to the pub and his cronies. Our mam would hug us and say how everything was all right . . . that we weren't to be frightened, but I'd see the marks on her face and neck, and hate him more than ever.'

'What about your brother?'

'Oh, my dad never hit Michael because he knew he would never challenge him. Not like me.' Kelly resented that. There had been times when she hated her brother almost as much as she hated her father, but it was a short, angry hatred, soon burned out. She came to realise it was her father who had made him that way.

'Michael used to tell our mam, "When I'm a man I'll beat him, like he beats you". But I knew he wouldn't.

Michael was a coward – I knew that. But he couldn't seem to help it. And I loved him all the same.'

'What happened to your brother?'

'He went away. We had to, you see . . . after it happened.'

'What happened, Kelly? Tell me.'

'It was my tenth birthday. Mam had made me a wonderful party,' Kelly began. 'Mam baked the cake and dressed it with candles, and all the neighbours came.' Her voice broke with emotion. '*He* said I wasn't to have a party, that it was a bloody nuisance.'

She smiled, a sad, childish smile. 'They fought for days . . . like they fought about everything she wanted to do.'

Her eyes widened in surprise. 'Somehow she managed to persuade him. He didn't stay, though. He went to the pub. "I won't be back till it's over!" he said, and to be truthful, I didn't want him there. He always spoiled things.'

'At least you got yer party.' Poor as her childhood was, Amy thanked the Lord she had never suffered in the way Kelly had suffered.

'It was the best party ever,' Kelly said softly. 'We laughed and played, and everyone was having a wonderful time. Mam lit the candles on my cake and I couldn't blow them all out at once.' She chuckled then. 'Lenny Parker got excited and blew them all out instead. I didn't really mind, but his mam clouted him round the ear and threatened to take him home if he didn't behave himself.'

A change of mood came over her as she recalled what happened next.

'*He* came back early, drunk as a lord. "I want this lot out of here," he yelled, and began throwing things about. The children were crying and everyone knew he was out for trouble. In minutes they were all gone; except me and our mam.'

'What about your brother?'

Kelly sighed. 'Michael hid in the scullery as usual.' Reliving the day, she described it in every detail. 'When he began swiping things off the table and smashing them against the wall, Mam shouted for Michael to take me out.' In her mind's eye it was as real as the day it happened, over thirty years ago. 'As we ran through the scullery door, I saw him! He grabbed our mam by the hair and fought her to the ground. I screamed for Michael to help her, but he seemed to be frozen.'

Pausing to take a breath, Kelly wondered if she could go on. It was too real, too alive in her mind.

She heard Amy's voice, soft and persuasive. 'Don't keep it inside,' she said. 'There's just you and me here, no one else.'

Knowing she could trust her, Kelly went on. 'It had been raining all day, and was still coming down heavy,' she said. 'The yard and cellar were flooded ankle-high as always. Anyway, Michael took me down the steps as far as we could go, and there we sat.' She shivered. 'It was cold, too. The rain soaked us to the skin, but we couldn't go back inside. We daren't.' Closing her eyes, she could hear it all. 'My father was like a crazy thing. We could hear him shouting, things being thrown about, and our mam . . . oh, dear God, she sounded terrified. We could hear her cries, "Don't . . . please don't".' Here Kelly's voice broke. 'I tried to break away from Michael, but he held me fast, so all I could do was call out to my father. "Leave her alone!" I yelled, over and over. But he took no notice.'

When she faltered, Amy urged, 'Go on, Kelly.'

'Suddenly it all went quiet. We heard the key click in the back door, then a sound from inside, like furniture being shuffled about. I remember Michael telling me to stay where I was, and not to move until he came for me.' Frowning, she momentarily closed her eyes, reading the pictures in her mind. 'He went to the top step and stood on tiptoes, looking through the window. I heard him shout out, then he was banging his fists on the door. "Open this door! Let me in or I'll break it down!" I'd never seen him so agitated. Suddenly the door gave beneath his weight and he was in. "Stay where you are, Kelly!" he yelled. Because I was afraid and confused, I did as I was told.' Putting her hands over her ears, she said, 'I sat very still, with my eyes closed and my hands like this, and I waited.'

'Your brother was very brave.' Amy remembered what Kelly had said about him being a coward.

'Yes, he was brave.' Sighing deeply, Kelly revealed the full horror of what had happened. 'He found our mam lying on the floor, blood seeping from her temple and her face white as death. I heard him shout, "You bastard! You've killed her!" There was a terrible fight. I heard Michael cry out in pain, and my father threaten to kill him as well. I knew he would and I was terrified. I wanted my mam . . . I called out to her but she didn't answer. Only Michael. "*Run, Kelly!*" he yelled. "*Get help!*" Then he made a noise like a scream and there was a thud – I thought it was the furniture falling over. I should have gone for help. Instead, I ran up the steps and into the parlour and I saw her . . . she was pulling herself up by the table, groaning, covered in blood.' Kelly hid her face in her hands, her voice falling away in a sob. 'I wanted to go to her but I couldn't move . . . Oh God, I couldn't move . . .'

Holding her close, Amy let her take her time.

'She got to Michael and tried to take the knife out of his hand; it was gripped so tightly in his fist, she had to hit him so he would let it loose.' Looking up with eyes full of horror she whispered, '*Michael* killed him. *It wasn't our mam who did it!*'

Stunned by the whole revelation, Amy listened silently as Kelly told her in hushed tones, 'When the authorities came, our mam said it was *her* who killed him. They took her away and put her in jail for manslaughter for a long time.'

'Did Michael never confess?'

'She told him not to. In prison, she would only see us once, then wouldn't let us go any more.'

'Why was that?'

'She said it would be best if Michael took me far away. And that when she got out, we were never to try and contact her. She wanted us to make a new life and forget all about what happened. People round here would never forget though, that's what she said. We were to move somewhere else, where folks didn't know about us.'

'It must have been really hard for you.'

'Michael took me South and looked after me. We never talked about what he did.' Her voice hardened. 'It took me a long time to forgive him for letting our mam go to prison for a murder she never committed.'

'How did the jewellery box come to be under the floorboards? You said your mother was wearing the brooch, and yet here it is.'

'I've been thinking about that,' Kelly answered. 'I think he must have torn it off her in the fight, then, when she was knocked out, he hid it all under the floorboards ... maybe to sell it later. Or maybe he wanted to hurt her even more. He knew it contained her most cherished possessions and that she would never willingly part with it.'

'Is your mother still alive?'

'As far as I know.' Please God that she hadn't died since her letter.

'Did Michael ever try to contact your mother?'

'He never even spoke about her.' Kelly gave a tearful smile.

'Where is he now?'

'I don't know.'

'Do you *want* to know?'

Kelly gave it a moment's thought before answering. 'It's too late now. We're strangers . . . all of us.'

'I'm sorry, gal.' There was little Amy could say to comfort her.

'So am I.'

She didn't tell Amy of the letter her mother had written, nor how she was sorely tempted to seek her out and tell her how much she loved her. Michael too. Sometimes she would lie awake at night and wonder about him, and her heart would break.

'Let's go home,' she said, and Amy agreed it was time.

Suddenly there was a knock on the door. 'Hello! Are you in there?'

Recognising Luke's voice, Kelly composed herself. 'Come in, Luke,' she called out, and was pleased to see his smiling face appear round the door. 'We're just about to pack up,' she told him. 'The fire's out and we're both tired anyway.'

Just then the lamplight flickered and danced. 'Looks like you're almost out of paraffin too,' he said. 'I'll nip back and get some if you like.'

Kelly was grateful and told him so, but added, 'We're about finished for today. We'll make an early start in the morning.'

Luke insisted on walking them to the tram-stop. 'You never know who's hanging about at this time of night,' he warned. 'I wouldn't rest if I didn't see you safely on the tram.'

Kelly had her mother's jewellery box safe under her coat. From now on, she wouldn't let it out of her sight.

At the tram-stop, Luke watched them climb aboard. 'See you tomorrow.' His dark eyes rested on Kelly's quiet face, and he knew tomorrow night would not come quickly enough.

'I reckon he'd have you for his sweetheart if you let him.' Amy had seen the way Luke smiled on Kelly, and though she would never admit it, her own hopes were dashed by it. She had fallen for Luke the first minute she saw him, but judging from the way he had looked at Kelly just now, he would never give *her* a second glance.

'I already have a sweetheart.'

Amy was surprised. 'Where is he then, this sweetheart of yours?'

Kelly thought of Barney, and her heart warmed. 'On the other side of the world for all I know.'

'Why do you say that?'

'Because he's a wanderer, never happier than when he's sleeping under the stars or heading for pastures new.'

'What's his name?'

'Barney.'

'When will you see him again?'

'Who knows?' Kelly hoped she would see him again, for life was not the same without him. 'Have *you* never had a sweetheart?' She was curious about Amy.

'Never had a chance.'

'Why not?'

Just then the conductor came to collect their fares. 'Where to, me beauties?'

'Bottom of Argyle Street.' Kelly handed him a florin and he gave her the change. 'You look like you've been up the chimneys,' he told them and went away whistling.

'Cheeky bugger!' Amy chuckled. 'I didn't know we were that grubby.'

'You were saying you never had a sweetheart?'

'Thanks to me mam and dad, I never got the chance,' Amy confessed. 'It was four years ago, when I was thirteen. There was what you might call a parting of the ways. Me dad went one way with a lass half his age, and me mam went the other way on the arm of a sailor.' Shrugging her shoulders, she said, 'I ain't seen hide nor hair of 'em since, and don't want to neither.'

'And you were left with the children?'

'Sally was just a year old. It's not been easy,' she admitted, 'but it's been worth it.'

'I always wanted children,' Kelly said wistfully, 'but it wasn't to be.'

'It's never too late,' Amy told her, 'especially when you've got a handsome fella like Luke Porter making eyes at yer.'

Brushing her comment aside, Kelly replied, 'I'm not ready for that kind of relationship.' Not with Barney always on her mind she wasn't. 'Besides, I'm not as young as I was.'

Amy told her not to be so silly. 'What age are you anyway – thirty-four . . . thirty-five?'

Kelly was flattered. 'You're a few years out, I can tell you that!'

'You should be proud o' yerself!' Amy chided. 'Thirty or forty – it don't matter. You're a good-looking woman, with exciting dreams and the will to make them come true. *That's* all as matters.'

Thanking her lucky stars that she and Amy had met, Kelly told her softly, 'I'm glad we're friends, Amy.'

'So am I,' Amy answered.

She owed Kelly a lot. More than Kelly would ever know.

❦

A S THEY CLAMBERED off the tram, the cab followed the two women up Park Street. The driver parked discreetly some distance away, then waited until they had gone into Fran Docherty's.

Inside the vehicle, a small, sharp-eyed man took out his notebook and made an entry. That done, he replaced the book in his waistcoat pocket and tapped on the window. 'The railway station,' he told the driver. 'As quick as you can.'

PART TWO

MEMORIES

Chapter Six

TAKING A MOMENT to enjoy his meat pie and cider, Michael perched himself on the deep window-ledge; from here he could see the lay of the land before him . . . acres upon acres of good pasture, each blade of grass kissed by the rain and sparkling like jewels.

He loved it here in Harrow. Since fleeing his native Blackburn, he and his sister, Kelly, had lived in dark corners, always moving, always afraid. Now, thank God, he had found a way of life that afforded him the privacy and quiet he craved.

Some time after he and Kelly parted company, he changed his surname from Wilson to Wills and made a brand new start. Apart from the unexpected and unnerving letter he had received from his mother some time ago, he had had no visitations from the past. No stranger knew who he was, or the dreadful thing he had done, and if Michael Wills had his way, no one ever would.

But even though he felt protected from his background, Michael was not without anxiety of a kind. Having married in haste, he now bitterly regretted it, for his wife Joyce was greedy and selfish. Not only that – she was a constant source of worry to him. Six years ago, when he was at his lowest ebb, Michael had made the mistake of confiding in her. At first she shrank from him in horror; until she saw how to turn his shocking secret to her own advantage.

From that day on, he was at her mercy.

While he worked all the hours God sent, she frittered away every penny he earned, never missing an opportunity to belittle him in front of others, or to goad him about the fact that he had never made a great success of his life.

Joyce was a woman who turned heads; attractive and immaculately dressed, she was ten years younger than him, and never failed to remind him of that. Strong-minded, sharp-tongued and always looking for faults, she was totally without compassion, or a shred of love for him.

Consequently, over the years his feelings for her were eroded, until now there was nothing left except routine and familiarity, and very occasionally some small measure of companionship, when it suited her purpose. He could no longer love her as he did when first they wed.

Nor could he hate her. He had learned at a young age how hatred was a terrifying and dangerous thing.

He had only ever hated one person, and that was his father.

Even then, because of what happened, the hatred was mingled with shame and guilt.

He glanced at the skies. Spiked with fingers of twilight, they had a kind of magnificence. 'Never two skies the same,' he murmured. 'Mysterious . . . like life.' He had come to cherish nature's wonders.

Reminding himself he had work to do, he thirstily finished off the last drop of his cider and packed away the empty jar. I need to get that door hung before dark, he thought, and his heart sank at the prospect of going home to Joyce.

Thrusting his wife from his mind he concentrated on his work. First he positioned the big iron hinges, then he measured the heavy oak door against the frame and skilfully planed the wood where it didn't fit snugly. He had made the door and shaped the hinges himself, and the pride he felt in his work was evident in his face as he toiled for perfection. Working up a sweat he threw off his coat and fashioned the door until it was a thing of beauty, his hands moving lovingly over the wood.

Deeply engrossed in his task, he didn't hear her approach. 'Michael?' The voice was soft and kind. He recognised it and his heart soared.

Securing the door on the trestle, he went to meet her. The sight of this lovely lady always lifted his heart. 'Kathleen!' A widow these past six years, Kathleen was the mistress of this beautiful place.

'I brought you some food,' she said. These days she used any excuse to be near him. Dipping into the wicker basket she took out a parcel wrapped in muslin. 'A meat pie and some muffins,' she explained. 'And here . . .' Taking out a small earthenware jug, she handed it to him. 'I know how fond you are of sarsaparilla.'

'Thank you,' he said. 'You're very thoughtful.'

'I saw you from the upstairs window,' she said, 'and as it's such a lovely afternoon I thought it would be nice to bring the food myself rather than send Polly.' Polly was her trusted servant.

'Well, it's much appreciated.' Michael always felt shy in her company; shy and privileged. He felt foolish too. Here he was, a man in his fifties and she a woman not much younger, and his heart fluttered like that of a lovesick boy whenever she was near.

'Go on then,' she gestured to the food. 'Tuck in. Don't mind me, I'll make my way back now.'

He didn't want her to go. 'Won't you sit with me?' he asked hopefully. 'I'm sure you'd like to see what I've been doing with my time.' She took an interest in what he did; not like Joyce, who shrugged aside his work as if it was nothing.

She smiled and her face was like a summer's day. 'Are you sure you don't mind?'

'I'd be glad of your company, Kathleen.' Gesturing to a fallen tree some short distance away, he told her, 'This is a good spot. From here you can see down to the rooftops of Harrow.'

When she stepped in front of him, he followed, his heart singing. Tall and elegant, with short fair hair and soft grey eyes, Kathleen had a way of making a man feel special.

'You shouldn't have come across the field,' he chided. 'The rain's made it soft and muddy underfoot.'

Raising a foot she chuckled. 'All the trouble I went to, and you haven't even noticed.'

Glancing at her boot-clad feet he laughed. 'Ah! I see you've taken my advice at last, and bought yourself some sturdy boots.' The dark, heavy boots were suitable for all terrain, and she wore them well.

'They're not very ladylike, are they?' she said.

'A lady is a lady,' he answered soberly, 'no matter *what* she wears.'

Kathleen blushed. 'I'm glad I bought them anyway.' Seating herself on a log, she folded the hem of her skirt over her knees so that it wouldn't drape on the ground. 'Now it won't matter whether it's wet or dry, I'll be able to walk over the fields at any time.'

'You really love this land, don't you?' He felt the same way. It was a kind of bond between them.

She had been stretching her gaze towards the town of Harrow, but at his words she turned to look at him, her grey eyes soft and thoughtful. 'Yes,' she confessed, 'I do love this land . . . almost as much as you do.'

Embarrassed, he concentrated on taking the cork out of the jar. 'I have no right to love this land,' he answered.

'What do you mean?'

'I mean, it isn't mine to love.' The land was like a

soul, never owned, always free. 'I'm just a caretaker.' Taking a deep swig from the jar he satisfied his still-raging thirst.

Kathleen kept her eyes on his face. Such a strong face, she thought – not handsome, but with sincere dark eyes that were too often sad. 'How can you say that?' she demanded, a little angry. 'You have *every* right to love this land! My father and his father before him worked it with their own two hands. They tended every blade of grass, every clump of soil, and all their lives never knew anything else.' Her eyes shone with admiration. 'But I swear I've never met anyone who understands and respects the ways of nature like you do.'

'It wasn't always like that.' His memories took him back to a place he didn't want to revisit. 'I was born and raised in a cotton-mill town – back-to-back houses, and cobbles from one end of the street to the other. The only countryside I ever saw were the lawns in Corporation Park.'

Taken aback, she stared at him for a moment. 'Michael! Do you know, that's the first and only time I've ever heard you speak of your past?' Kathleen had long suspected he was hiding something.

Mortified, he didn't know what to say. He had already said too much. 'I'd better get on.' Tipping his hat as always when she was near, he excused himself. 'Will you be all right going back on your own?' he asked nervously. 'Or will you want me to walk you back?'

She shook her head and he was relieved. The longer

he was in her company, the less guarded he seemed to be.

'Michael?' Stepping close, she asked quietly, 'Have I offended you?'

'Of course not.' She was too close now, *much* too close.

'Because if I have, I didn't mean to.' She felt instinctively it was something to do with his past.

'Believe me, you haven't done anything to upset me.' His senses reeling, he stepped away. 'I really must get on though, or I'll not have this door secured before dark.'

'I'll make my way back then,' she said, and hurried away.

He stood there, disillusioned and angry with himself. 'You bloody fool, Michael!' The world was an empty place all of a sudden. 'She would have stayed, and you let her go!'

With a heavy heart he finished his work and afterwards, made his way across the fields.

Kathleen was in the garden, raking up the leaves. When she saw him pass by, she paused, her neck stretched to see him over the hedge. 'What is it about you?' she wondered aloud. 'What makes you so sad?'

As he strode down the lane and out of sight, the twilight deepened and soon it was difficult to see far. All the same, she continued to gaze at the spot where he had turned from the gateway. 'I wonder what you would say, Michael Wills,' she whispered, 'if only you knew how much I love you?'

B UT MICHAEL COULD not hear her.

Unaware, he wended his way home. His thoughts lingered with Kathleen. He had no way of knowing how she felt: he only knew how *he* felt – that he would have given years of his life just to be with her.

The further he travelled, the heavier his heart grew. He was going home to someone else; someone he wished to God he had never set eyes on.

Chapter Seven

KELLY COULDN'T SIT still. So excited that her furniture was on its way at last, she had been waiting at the house in Johnson Street since breakfast-time and now it was coming up for noon. She paced back and forth at the window, waiting for Jack Denby's wagon to come round the corner. 'For Gawd's sake, gal!' Amy was fussing with the curtains when Kelly rushed by her yet again. 'You're gonna wear the bleedin' floor out!'

'Where the devil is he?' Peeking at the mantel-piece clock, a house-warming present from Fran, Kelly groaned. 'He was supposed to be here an hour ago.'

'Happen it ain't his fault.' Amy came to peer through the window beside her. 'What if he's got caught up in traffic? Yer know what it's like on that main street of a Saturday morning.' Giving Kelly a little shake, she told her, 'Calm yerself down. He'll be here any minute, you see if he's not.'

'It's not like him,' Kelly fretted. 'Jack Denby takes a

pride in being on time. When we made the arrangements last week, he told me he'd be here at eleven o'clock, and here it is almost midday.'

'Look, he's along the road somewhere between Bedford and here.' Amy sympathised with her but thought it best to cheer her up. 'Whether he's late or early, you said yerself the man won't let you down. It's on its way, that's all you need to know.' Kelly couldn't bear to think of all her precious furniture and things, strapped on the back of that wagon in the middle of nowhere. 'What if it rains?' she wanted to know. 'It'll all be ruined!'

'I'm sure he'll have sheeted it down,' Amy argued. 'Sure to Gawd he wouldn't leave it open to the elements.'

'How do we know?' Though she had great respect for Jack, Kelly had her doubts. 'He's a man, isn't he? And men don't put the same value on furniture and bric-à-brac as we women do.'

'Come away from that window,' Amy urged. When Kelly remained glued to the spot, she tried another tack. 'Damn! Will yer look at that!' Drawing Kelly's attention to the curtains, she wailed, 'They *still* ain't hanging right, gal. What am I doing wrong? Look!' Irritated, she snatched at them. 'They're up and down like the high seas, and I'm buggered if I know what to do next.'

If her ploy was to take Kelly's mind off the arrival of her furniture, then it worked like a charm. Climbing up on a chair, Kelly examined the curtains from the top. 'Here's your trouble,' she told Amy. 'Some of the stitching's come undone at the top, and it's letting the curtains dip every now and then.' Untying the string from the nail, she slid the curtains off it and handed them down to Amy. 'I'm not happy about using string,' she sighed, 'but at the minute I can't afford much else.'

'It'll all come right for you, gal.' Amy had no doubts. 'With your dressmaking skills, the folks'll soon be flocking to yer door.' Pointing to the curtains, she commented, 'Look at the wonderful job you've done with these. I'm only sorry yer let me loose on the hemming of this pair, and what a right pig's ear I've made out of 'em too.'

'Not your fault, Amy.' Kelly was just grateful for all the hard work Amy had put in. 'There's nothing wrong with this stitching,' she said. She examined it closer. 'It looks like the draper sold me a reel of old thread.'

It wasn't true, but it put the smile back on Amy's face all the same. 'Right! Give them 'ere and I'll have another go.'

Handing Amy the curtains, Kelly clambered down from the chair and gave Amy a brand new reel of thread from the sewing-box. 'You mend that curtain,' she said, dividing the pair between them, 'and I'll mend this one.' And while she settled in the chair, Amy sat beside her on the floor.

As they sewed, they talked about this and that, but mostly about the house, and their new lives. 'I can't believe my luck in meeting you,' Amy remarked. 'I thought me and the bairns would end up sleeping on the streets like three vagabonds.'

'Not you,' Kelly answered. 'You would have found a way.'

Amy laughed aloud. 'What? Marry a rich old man on his last legs?'

After a spate of light-hearted banter, Kelly's mood grew serious. 'I haven't forgotten what Charlie said, about folks not wanting to buy this house. And what about the Irishwoman saying the place was haunted?'

'Well, even if it is, it don't worry me.' Amy's big eyes roved suspiciously round the room.

'I'm worried folks won't come here for the dress-making.'

Amy was confident. 'They'll come,' she said reassuringly. 'Once word gets out about how good you are, they'll be here in droves.'

'Not if they've heard tales about the house.'

'Aw, it'll be all right, gal. Besides, we're living proof there ain't nuthin' here to harm 'em. Two women, two bairns, and not a man between us.' Her face broke into a mischievous grin. 'More's the pity.'

Kelly's spirits lifted. 'I didn't think I could ever live here again,' she admitted, 'but now that I'm so close to moving back in, I'm beginning to look forward to it.'

'There yer are then, gal. Look forward, instead o' backward. That's the idea.'

Looking up from her sewing, Kelly realised what a true friend she had stumbled across in Amy. 'What would I do without you, eh?'

'Wait till we've lived under the same roof afore yer

say that, gal,' Amy warned. 'With two lively bairns under your feet and another woman scruffing up yer kitchen, yer might wish you'd never clapped eyes on me.'

'Amy . . . do you really think I'm doing the right thing?'

'What – letting me loose in yer kitchen?'

Kelly shook her head. 'No, silly! I mean, coming to Blackburn. Moving into this house. There's an old saying . . . "Never go back".'

'Sometimes you *can't* go back, and that's worse.' Amy often wished things were like they used to be, before their mam and dad went away. 'What *made* yer come back, after all this time?'

'Just a feeling.' Kelly wasn't altogether sure why. 'I was only a bairn when it all happened. Before I knew it, Michael whisked me away. Mam told us never to contact her, and it was like my whole world had fallen apart. Afterwards, me and Michael moved so often I can't even recall where we went. When I was old enough, I set out on my own, wandering from place to place until I settled in Bedford. But I was never *really* settled, not until I met Barney.' A contented smile lifted the corners of her mouth. 'He made me laugh . . . made me feel alive. Oh Amy, he was the best thing that ever happened to me. He chased the shadows away, and I loved him for it.'

The smile dropped, her voice shaking as she spoke. 'Then he left. But I can't blame him for that. He never deceived me about his intentions. From that first meeting, I always knew there would come a day when he might walk out of my life; for a day, a week, maybe even for ever.'

'What made him want to go?'

'I don't really know, but I was surprised he stayed so long. You see, Barney was a man without roots . . . a free soul. In winter he used to pace the floor like a lion in a cage. In summer he would walk the hills and dales and often he wouldn't come back until dark. It was as though he couldn't breathe unless he was outside.'

'Was he a gypsy?'

Kelly sighed. 'I always said he had a gypsy soul, but to be honest I don't know what made him the way he was. All I do know is that after he'd gone, I was lost. It was a terrifying feeling, just like when our mam was taken. I was ten years old again, snatched away from everything I relied on.'

Collecting her feelings, she paused. 'I began thinking about Blackburn and everything, and it was as though I'd left something behind.' She gave a small, bitter laugh. 'It's hard to explain, but it was my *life*.' Angry tears filled her eyes. 'And they took it away.'

Amy sensed her distress. 'So yer came back to pick up where yer left off?'

'It had been in the back of my mind for a long time,' Kelly confessed, 'but I was always afraid to take that first step. It was Barney going that triggered it all off.' Looking up, she wondered aloud again, 'Have I made a mistake, Amy?'

Her friend gave a small, reassuring smile. 'Mistake

or not, I would have done the very same. Besides, you've already told me, it weren't all bad, what happened in this house. Cling to that, and you'll be fine.'

Relieved, Kelly hugged her. 'You're right.' The smile returned to her eyes. 'I expect I'm just feeling sorry for myself because Jack hasn't arrived with my things.' Suddenly, they were more important than she'd realised, because they were *her* things. Hers and Barney's. Another life. Another time.

'This time tomorrow you'll have all your bits and bobs about you, all set out and looking grand.'

Glancing round the room, Kelly explained, 'The house seems really strange without any furniture, but I had to get rid of it and start afresh. Too many memories. Mind, I was surprised it was in such reasonable condition, after more than thirty years. Even more surprised that John Harvey didn't flog it while he had the chance.'

'Yes, after we'd polished up the two wardrobes and that hall table and the few other bits, they came up lovely. And you got good money for it. Like you said yerself, every penny helps.' Amy chuckled. 'I felt sorry for that poor man though. Once you started haggling over the price, the poor devil didn't know which way to turn. You played him like a fiddle, so yer did.' Her chuckling grew until it became a roar of laughter. 'Honest to Gawd, Kelly! I reckon he paid up just so he could make good his escape.'

'The swindler! If he'd had his way, I'd have only got *half* what it was worth.' Though Kelly felt the teeniest bit sorry for him too. 'I bet nobody's ever stood up to him before,' she said. 'He went down that path like a scalded cat.'

'Serves him right.'

'Still, I'm glad it's all gone; except for the rug where me and Michael used to play. I needed to keep that,' she murmured, her heart aching, 'for old times' sake, if you know what I mean?'

'I never thought you'd get the stains out.' Always practical, was Amy.

Kelly ran her fingers along the back of the chair. 'And this chair. I remember how Michael would drag it to the window. Hour after hour he'd sit here, watching the children playing on the cobbles. He was so quiet and shy, he never had the knack for making friends.'

Amy saw the look of longing in Kelly's eyes and couldn't even begin to imagine the trauma behind them. 'D'yer know what?' she said. 'I reckon you've come home because you *belong* here.'

Kelly thought about that. And the more she thought about it, the more she realised it was the truth. Home because she belonged. Yes. It had a good ring to it.

Soon the conversation turned to the children. 'They reckon the teacher's a monster, sent to make their lives a misery,' Amy said. 'Mind you, I bet the teacher feels the same way about *them*.'

'You've done a good job with them,' Kelly said softly. 'They're such wonderful bairns, Amy.'

Amy knew what Kelly was thinking. 'Will that

Barney fella o' yourn ever turn up here, d'yer reckon?'

Kelly shook her head slowly. 'I don't know, Amy. It's up to him.'

'What about Luke?'

A faint blush spread over Kelly's face. 'What about him?'

'He fancies yer, anyone can see that.' Amy wished it was *her* he fancied.

Kelly's mood darkened. 'I've already told you. I'm keeping myself for Barney.'

'What if he don't turn up?'

Kelly didn't answer, because she didn't know what to say. Luke was here. Barney wasn't. And who knows what the future might hold.

<hr />

THE CURTAINS WERE mended and replaced. The two women polished the fire-range and gave the scullery floor another scrubbing, and still the furniture hadn't arrived. 'It's getting dark.' Kelly lit the lamp. 'You go,' she urged. 'The children will be looking for you.'

Amy was unsure. 'They'll be all right with Fran. I'll stay with you a bit longer.'

But Kelly wouldn't hear of it. 'You've been here all day,' she reminded her. 'Look, I'll hang on here for another hour or so.' Glancing at the clock she saw it was already four o'clock. 'I'll wait till seven o'clock, then call it a day. I'll pin a note on the door when I leave, and Jack can come and find me.'

When Amy began to argue, Kelly grabbed her bag and propelled her to the door. 'Tell Fran not to bother about cooking for me. I'll get a bag of hot potatoes from the barrow near the tram-stop.' Wrapping Amy's coat round her shoulders, she thrust the tapestry bag into her hands. 'Have you got enough for the fare?'

'Anybody'd think I were a snotty-nosed kid,' Amy protested light-heartedly.

'Go on with you!' A little encouragement and Amy was on her way. 'And don't talk to any strangers!' Kelly laughed at the look on Amy's face. 'Tell Fran I'll be home a bit after seven,' she promised.

She stayed at the door a moment, watching Amy hurry down the street. It was a bitter cold day, with a cutting chill that whipped up the goose-bumps and sent a shiver down the spine. One last wave to Amy, a quick glance up and down the street before, disappointed, she hurried back inside.

Taking the lamp from the sideboard, she went straight upstairs. Here she made her way from room to room, checking for the umpteenth time that everything was ready.

The bedroom had warm, brown curtains at the window and a rug to go between the children's beds. On the wall was a wood-framed picture of a dancing clown. Kelly had paid a shilling for it in the market. The children will like that, she'd thought. And they did.

Her own room was painted a soft, creamy colour. The curtains were white and flowered, and just now, in the soft glow of lamplight, it seemed a safe, cosy place.

Closing the door, she lingered a moment, unwilling to go into the front room, yet knowing she must. 'It's just a room,' she told herself. 'What harm can it do you now?' For a moment she seemed to see her mother coming out in the mornings, with her lovely long hair all tousled and that dark sadness in her eyes. Then she'd see Kelly waiting and her eyes would light up. 'Hello, sweetheart,' she'd say, and they'd hug and hold each other, and for a while the hurt would be forgotten.

Feeling apprehensive, Kelly began to make her way along the landing. 'It's over,' she told herself. 'He's gone now, and your mother's safe.' She remembered Amy's words: 'It weren't all bad, what happened in this house . . .' And it was true.

Hesitantly, she pushed open the door. Holding the lamp before her, she stood transfixed, her eyes roving the room and her mind playing tricks. Inside her head the pictures unravelled . . . her mother seated in the chair by the window, head down and her face covered in bruises; other times, her father wild-eyed, standing with his back to that small, low door, and her imprisoned mother's cries coming from inside – desolate, terrified cries that tore Kelly's soul inside out.

'Don't torture yourself!' Kelly moaned and forced herself to turn away.

With the door open, she stood outside the room, her

back to the wall, tears of anguish rolling down her face. 'Go in!' she told herself. 'If you don't go in now, you've lost and *he*'s won.'

Slowly, she made her way inside, the light going before her, creating weird patterns on the walls. Her hesitant footsteps echoed, a strange, empty sound against the bare floorboards. This was the first time she had been in the house alone, in the dark, and it was an eerie feeling. Almost instinctively, she found her way to the far wall. Here she ran her hands along the smooth, new plaster where the door used to be. 'There's no way in now, Mam,' she whispered. '*He* can't shut you inside any more.'

The sound of her own voice was oddly reassuring. Almost lovingly, she fell to her knees, her face against the cold wall and her heart pounding. Oh, but she did miss her mother! She so wanted to see her, and hold her, yet now she had the means to find her, she couldn't bring herself to do it. Deep down, the hurt was still there. 'You went away,' she murmured. 'It wasn't you who should have gone away. It was Michael.'

Anger flooded her senses. Quickly, she hurried from the room. 'It's Amy's room now,' she said, closing the door. A moment to reflect, then she made her way downstairs to wait for Jack.

There were still a few lumps of coal in the scuttle. 'I should go down and get more,' she muttered. But it was dark in the cellar and there were rats. Shivering, she emptied the scuttle on to the fire. When it was spitting and roaring, she took off her shoes and sat crosslegged on the rug. 'Come on, Jack!' she kept saying. 'Where the devil are you?' An empty house was a cold unloving house, she thought, but once her furniture was in, the whole place would feel different.

When the knock came she almost leaped out of her skin. Going along the passage, she called out, 'Is that you, Jack?'

'It's *me*!' The voice was comfortingly familiar. 'It's freezing out here, lass. Let me in.'

Relieved, Kelly swung open the door. 'Fran! What are *you* doing here?'

'I've brought you some food.' She carried a wicker basket on her arm. 'Amy said you hadn't eaten all day.'

'Where is she?' Kelly glanced down the street.

'She wanted to come and so did the bairns, but I made them stay at home where it's warm. And anyway, Amy has promised to dish up and clear away after the guests have eaten. She's a good girl, that one.'

'Didn't she tell you I meant to get hot potatoes from the barrow on the boulevard?'

'No need for that,' Fran tutted. 'Not when there's good food in the cupboards.'

Closing the door behind her, Kelly followed Fran down the passage. 'You shouldn't have come out here in the dark. Like you said, it's really cold out there.'

Setting the basket on the floor, Fran went to warm her hands. 'I've brought cheese and bread, and homemade pickle . . . oh, and there's a fat slice of fruitcake made this morning. But you don't want it, so I'd best take it back, eh?' Sneaking a glance at Kelly, who was peering slyly into the basket, she went on, a mischievous twinkle in her eye, 'I mean, if I shouldn't have come, and you'd rather have 'taters off some old barrer, well, I might as well go. Give me a minute to warm meself then I'll be off.' Turning away, she secretly smiled.

Just as she suspected, Kelly came across the room at a run. Flinging her arms round Fran's ample body, she hugged her tight. 'Oh Fran, I'm glad you're here, you don't know how much,' she admitted. 'Only, I don't like to think of you wandering about in the dark.'

'I got here all in one piece, didn't I?' Contented now that she was warmed right through, Fran pecked her on the cheek. 'I've brought fresh supplies of milk, sugar and there's a packet of tea as well.' Satisfied that she'd thought of everything, she declared with a grin, 'Right then, lass, will *you* put the kettle on or shall I?'

Kelly squashed a full kettle on to the coals. It wasn't too long before the water was boiling and the tea brewing in the pot. She joined Fran at the fireside, Fran in the chair and Kelly on the rug. 'I was meaning to come back soon,' Kelly told her, tucking into a cheese sandwich.

'Aye, well, in the meantime I'm making sure you don't starve.'

'Seven o'clock, I told Amy. I don't want Jack to come all this way and not find me here.' She glanced up at the mantelpiece clock. 'It's nearly six now. When you're ready I'll walk you to the tram, then stay a while longer. There are hours yet before the last tram home.'

Fran had made up her mind on the way there. 'If you're staying, so am I.' And there was nothing Kelly could do to persuade her otherwise.

'Has Charlie been round?'

Kelly chuckled. 'Only about ten times today,' she said. 'He's been waiting for the furniture to arrive so he can help set it out for me. The last time he popped in, it was to tell me not to try moving anything on my own, that he'd be back soon. He's gone to meet Luke from work – a bit of business, he said.' Kelly tapped her nose. 'I've an idea Luke might be looking to branch out on his own, and wants his dad's opinion about some job or other.'

'It's nice when a son respects his father,' Fran remarked, 'though I've a feeling Luke's only asking his dad to make him feel included.'

'Well, whatever the reason, Charlie was like a dog with two tails when he left here.'

'He's a lovely bloke, is Charlie.'

Something about Fran's dreamy expression made Kelly wonder. 'You really like him, don't you?'

Fran was not telling. 'Happen I do, happen I don't,' she said coyly. But there was a certain gleam in her eye that confirmed Kelly's suspicions. Wouldn't it be wonderful, she thought, if Charlie felt the same way . . . Fran's mood softened. 'He's the kindest man I've ever met,' she declared, and would say no more.

Kelly was reminded of Barney and for a time the two women were lost in pleasant thought.

Sitting there, with Kelly at her feet and the warmth from the fire making her drowsy, Fran felt quite at home. 'It's a cosy little house, lass,' she remarked, chewing on her fruitcake, 'the kind of place I mean to find when I retire.'

Having enjoyed her food, Kelly sipped at her tea. 'You're right,' she answered thoughtfully, 'it *is* a nice house.' It was her father who had created the fear in it. 'I'm up to my ears in debt because of it though,' Kelly confessed. 'Once I get going on my dress-making, I hope to start paying it off.'

'And you will, lass, I'm sure of it. Besides, Amy tells me that now the children are going to school, she means to get work in town. What with her paying board and you doing your dress-making, the money will soon roll in, you see if it don't.' Fran wished she was in a position to help, but all she had was her boarding-house and a small income. Enough to be comfortable, but never anything left over. Besides, she didn't think Kelly was the kind to take handouts. 'Amy tells me you've already put out an advert for your services,' she went on.

'I won't wait for the rush though.' Kelly's doubts would not go away.

'You're too hard on yourself, lass.' Drawing out the cushion from behind her, Fran pointed out the pretty frills and folds. 'I mean, look at the beautiful work in this,' she said. 'It wouldn't surprise me if this time next week, you were fighting off the customers.'

'Oh Fran, I hope you're right, because I've never been in debt before and it worries me sick.'

'I can believe it, lass.' And then suddenly Fran was sitting bolt upright. 'Hey up, what's that?' she said.

Stiffening, Kelly listened. 'What?'

'That noise.'

Kelly was on her feet in a minute. 'It's a wagon!' she cried, spilling tea all over her front. 'It's Jack. He's here! Oh Fran, he's here!'

Before Fran could gather herself, Kelly was up the passage and out the door, and sure enough there was the wagon, rolling down the street, with Jack on top, peering into the night to see which house it might be.

'Jack, I'm here!' Laughing and crying, Kelly ran full pelt down the street. 'You don't know how glad I am to see you.' Breathless, she scrambled up the step and on to the seat where, wrapping her arms round his neck, she hugged him till he couldn't breathe. 'Gerroff!' The blacksmith wasn't used to such high spirits from women in their forties, but he could get used to it, he thought with a cheeky grin.

Climbing down, Kelly walked back to the house, slightly out of breath. As she got to the front door she caught sight of Luke and Charlie coming the other way. 'He's here!' she called. 'Jack's here and he's brought my things.'

The two men had been deep in thought, but now

they quickened their steps to a run, though Charlie's run was more of a trot. Fran too had come out in a rush and begun off-loading the cart even before Jack had stopped. 'Hey! Be careful there, missus!' he warned. 'That wheel could chop your foot off, like a knife through butter.'

Sensibly Fran stepped back, though not before grabbing a box filled with pottery. 'I'll take it to the scullery.' Like a cat with the cream, she ambled away.

Kelly called after her, 'Put the kettle on, Fran.' Worried that Fran was doing too much, Kelly discreetly suggested, 'And I'm sure Jack here would like a taste of your fruitcake . . . and happen a cheese sandwich if there's one left.'

The ever-hospitable Fran immediately invited Jack inside. 'I should think you're tired and hungry, aren't you?' she asked. 'But never you mind. There's enough food in that basket to feed an army, and I'm sure Kelly wouldn't mind one bit if you were to sit aside the fire and put your feet up.'

After a long and weary journey, the offer was one Jack could not refuse. 'Thanks, missus,' he said, and sat down to be waited on.

For the next hour everyone worked hard. Neighbours peeped from windows, wondering if they should help with the fetching and carrying but in the end, for whatever reason, they decided not to; instead they left the work to others and returned to warm their bellies in front of the fire.

Excited as a child, Kelly ran up and down the steps,

explaining where she wanted things put: 'The sideboard against the window, please,' she told Charlie. 'And the bed goes in the big back room.'

'The other beds are coming tomorrow,' Fran told him. 'A leaving present from me to Amy.'

'That's very generous if yer don't mind me saying.' Charlie was impressed. Fran was a fine figure of a woman, and he knew from eating her snacks that she was also a wonderful cook. She had a good, kind heart too, or she wouldn't be here now, rushing about like a young 'un and eager to please.

Fran was still muttering about the beds. 'They'll do till she can afford new ones,' she explained. 'I've had them in the out-house for months.'

'All the same, you're a good lass,' he said, winking. 'I reckon somebody should be buying *you* a present.' He gazed at her for so long she burnt her fingers on the teapot.

When the cart was empty and everything set just where Kelly dreamed it would be, they gathered round the fire, drinking tea and listening to Jack tell about his journey. 'Coming across country is like an adventure,' he said. 'You wouldn't believe the things you see . . . foxes playing with their young 'uns; coloured birds of a kind I've never seen afore; and beautiful, wild creatures that you never see in the city. And when the sun comes up, it's like the whole world's turning upside down . . . wonderful! By! I've some memories to take back with me, I can tell you.'

With everyone enthralled by his tales, only Kelly noticed the fire dying down. Discreetly, she sneaked away, taking the scuttle with her. Going quietly out of the back door and down the steps to the cellar, she shivered and said aloud, 'Winter's on us now. I'd best order a dozen bags of coal.' Sorting the knobs of coal from the slack, she scooped them up and dropped them in the scuttle; intent on her task she didn't hear Luke coming across the yard. When he appeared at the doorway she recoiled in fright. Realising who it was, she clapped her hand to her heart. 'Oh, Luke! You gave me a scare.' With this yard leading on to the back alley, any vagabond might find his way in.

'I didn't mean to.' Entering the cellar, he took her by the shoulders. 'Here, let me do that.' His intention was to gentle her aside and fill the scuttle while she went back up to the warmth of the parlour. Now though, with his fingers curled round her soft, small shoulder, he couldn't let her go.

Kelly made no effort to move. Standing here so close, with those dark eyes looking down on her, was too wonderful. 'You're a lovely woman, Kelly,' he told her, and when his mouth came down on hers in the softest of kisses, she unashamedly reached up and, wrapping her arms round his neck, kissed him back.

The kisses grew longer, and more passionate, and soon he was sliding his hand inside her blouse. When he touched her nipple with the tips of his fingers, she didn't resist. Instead, she let him ease her back until she was against the wall. More fondling and kissing, and all the while he murmured tenderly in her ear. Thrilling to his touch, Kelly felt wanted; she felt herself responding in a way she had not imagined. Now, when she felt him harden against her, she was ready.

His hand crept over her thighs, drawing her to him, touching her where only Barney had touched her. She closed her eyes, answering his kisses, wanting him as much as he wanted her. When they slid on to the makeshift bed of a pile of boxes and an old rug, and he lay down on her, she whispered his name, 'Barney.' Horror filled her senses; she had called for *Barney*!

There was a moment of disbelief, before Luke stood up and backed away. 'We'd better go,' he said, shame in his voice. 'They'll wonder where we are.' He fastened her blouse and brushed away the coal-dust. Then he filled the scuttle and led the way back, through the yard, up the steps and into the house.

Not a word passed between them until he reached the parlour where he told her, 'If you're going back, I'll walk you and Fran to the tram-stop.'

'No need,' she said shyly, thanking him. 'Fran and I won't be leaving for a while yet.' Embarrassed and guilty, she searched for any excuse to avoid his company.

Inside, Jack was ready to leave. 'You keep in touch, mind,' he told Kelly, and she promised she would.

At the door, they all huddled together to see him off: Charlie and Fran in front, Luke and Kelly to one side. As Jack's little ensemble went off down the street, they said their goodnights. 'Now, are you sure you don't want to be taken to the tram-stop?' Charlie was tired but gallant.

'I'm sure.' Fran was a determined lady. 'Me and Kelly have things to do yet, but thanks all the same.'

'See you tomorrow then?'

'Quite likely.' Her smile was full of promise.

Behind them, Kelly was looking at Luke in a way that told him she felt as bad as he did. 'Goodnight, Kelly.' His voice was soft and forgiving.

'Goodnight, Luke.' Her heart was like a lead weight inside her. Without meaning to, she had done him a terrible wrong.

Suddenly he moved closer, his hand found hers and held it tight. 'It's all right,' he murmured, and she knew he understood.

Outside, though, there was another, who would neither understand nor forgive.

Across the street, skulking in the dimly lit alley, Luke's estranged wife saw it all: saw him hold her hand; saw the way he looked at Kelly. And her soul was filled with hatred.

Unable to watch any longer, Stella Porter slunk away.

———⟫•⟪———

'BARNEY BOUGHT ME this.' Holding up a small white vase patterned with pink roses, Kelly told Fran, 'It was the first anniversary of our meeting.'

Fran said it was very pretty. 'He sounds a real romantic, your Barney.'

Feeling nostalgic, Kelly replaced the vase on the sideboard. 'He was always buying me little presents,' she said. 'I never knew what he'd turn up with next.' She laughed. 'Once he brought me a china teapot . . . said he got it from a street peddlar. "A real bargain", he said. When we took it out of the box the teapot had no spout, just a big hole where it should have been.'

Fran chortled. 'Still, it sounds to me as if his heart was in the right place.'

When Kelly grew quiet, Fran wisely changed the subject. 'Where do you want this copper sieve?' Long and thin, it had a string tied to one end.

'I used to have that hanging in the fireplace,' Kelly recalled. 'Happen we'll just leave it in the hearth for now.'

It took an hour to get tidied up after all the others had left. They put the china in the display cabinet, the brass companion in the hearth, and all the crockery in its rightful place in the scullery. Then they hung the pictures from the picture-rail and laid the rugs. When everything was done, the house looked like a real home. 'It's lovely!' Fran sighed. 'Just lovely!'

Kelly thought so too. 'I think I'll be very happy here,' she murmured. Throwing out the old stuff and bringing in the new had certainly changed the atmosphere in this little house. It was a wonderful thing. Rolling down her sleeves, she told Fran, 'Jack said the bedding fell off the cart and got muddy, so I'll be coming back with you tonight if that's all right.'

Fran scalded her for being silly. 'If I had my way, I'd keep you all with me till Kingdom Come,' she said.

'I'll wash the bedding tomorrow and dry it in front of the fire.' Tired and dirty, Kelly was eager to make for the tram. Time was getting on – it was nearly nine o'clock.

Fran, too, was ready for off. 'If we leave now, there'll be time for a quick cup of cocoa, then a good night's sleep, ready for tomorrow.' Sliding on her coat she told Kelly, 'I'll give the boarders their breakfast early. That way I can come over on the nine o'clock tram with you and Amy.'

'There's not a lot to do,' Kelly reminded her. 'We've broken the back of it now.'

'You'd be surprised, lass,' Fran replied. 'There's your bedding to wash and Amy's beds to be made up; then there's the fire-grate to be cleaned out and all the linen to be stacked in the cupboards. There's the larder to stock, and God knows what you might be short of, once you've checked.'

Kelly had an idea. 'We'll make a trip into Blackburn town,' she said, 'you, me and Amy. And we'll call in at the Larder for pie and mushy peas.'

Fran thought it was a great idea. 'We shall have to get back in time for Amy to fetch the childer from school,' she said, winking. 'I've got a little surprise for you all.'

Intrigued, Kelly asked, 'What surprise?'

'Huh! It wouldn't be a surprise if I told you!' Still chuckling, she led the way out and stood on the step, waiting for Kelly to lock the door. 'Oh, the childer will love it,' she said, clapping her hands together in delight. 'You and Amy an' all.'

'Brr!' Pulling up the collar of her coat, Kelly shivered. 'I can't believe how cold it's got.'

'Hold on to me, and we'll keep each other warm.' Linking arms, they hurried down the street. 'Can I ask you summat?' Fran slowed her steps.

Forced to Fran's pace, Kelly nodded, 'Ask away.'

'I'm just being a nosy old bugger, but did you know that Luke never took his eyes off you all night?'

'Really?' Kelly was glad it was dark, so Fran couldn't see her face burning red.

Fran tutted. 'Don't you be coy with me, lass,' she reprimanded light-heartedly. 'You couldn't keep your eyes off *him* neither!'

'I won't deny I find him attractive.' There was no use lying to Fran. She had a way of knowing.

'And it's plain he likes you, so d'you think you'll get together soon?'

'I'm not sure.'

'What about your Barney?'

'I might never see him again.'

'Then it seems to me you might be forced to make a choice.' Squeezing Kelly's arm, she pointed to Luke's house as they passed. 'Charlie's a good man,' she sighed. 'I don't mind telling you, I like him a lot.'

'I know.'

'Hmph!' Giggling like a schoolgirl, Fran said, 'It seems like we've been watching each other, while they've been watching us.' And the idea was so funny, that the two women couldn't help but laugh.

About to turn the corner at the bottom of the street, they were deep in conversation, when suddenly, out of nowhere, a figure leaped from the alley. 'Jesus, Mary and Joseph!' Clinging to Kelly, Fran clutched at her heart. 'Who the devil are you?'

'*She* knows!' The figure advanced. Wild, manic eyes fixed themselves on Kelly, the voice low and shivering, as though every word caused immense pain. 'Ask her. Go on! Ask her why she's set her sights on another woman's husband.'

Kelly knew then. She had met the woman once before, and had since been warned about her by Charlie. 'Stella!' Taking stock of the other woman she noticed the madness in her eyes, and the long thick wedge of wood she carried; sharp and jagged, it might have been a broken chair-leg. 'I have no quarrel with you,' Kelly said coldly. 'Please . . . move aside!'

The other woman's laughter was eerie. 'Luke is *mine*.' Lunging forward she thrust the weapon under Kelly's chin, at the same time grabbing her hair with her free hand, making Kelly cry out in pain. 'You're pretty, I'll give you that.' Tracing a finger over Kelly's fine features, she whispered, 'You won't be so pretty when I've finished with you!'

'GET OFF HER, YOU BITCH!' Fran tried to put herself between them.

'Stay back, you old hag!' Kicking out, Stella sent Fran sprawling. 'Unless you want the same treatment.'

When Kelly struggled to get free of her, Stella yanked her hair hard, making her bend her head back until she could hardly breathe. 'Don't!' One word, but it was heavy with malice. 'Or I might decide to break your neck right now.' Raising the sharp edge of the truncheon, she scraped it along Kelly's chin. 'It's sharp, don't you think? Took me a long time to get just the right edge to it – see?' Twisting it against Kelly's neck, she drew blood. 'You have to twist it a certain way to do the worst damage . . . press it hard enough and it will split the skin wide open.'

She didn't finish the sentence, however, because Fran was at her back, pulling at her coat, her scream echoing through the air. 'YOU LEAVE HER ALONE, D'YOU HEAR?!'

Enraged, the other woman swung her arm in a vicious blow, while at the same time keeping a fierce grip on Kelly, who was desperately struggling to be free of her. The mighty blow sent Fran hurtling against the wall; there was an odd, scraping sound and then silence. Through shocked eyes Kelly saw the blood oozing down the wall, and Fran's upturned face, deathly white in the lamplight. The sight of her friend in trouble gave her the strength she needed. 'YOU BITCH! SHE'S DONE YOU NO HARM!' Kicking out, she knocked her assailant off-balance. Grabbing her chance, she ran to Fran, who lay unmoving, one arm flung sideways, the fingers still gripping her basket. 'Oh, Fran!' Kneeling down, she saw how serious it was. 'HELP!' Her scream sailed through the air. 'SOMEBODY PLEASE . . .'

She heard a rushing sound. Looking up, she saw the thick wedge of wood coming down on her, and there was nothing she could do. The blow was savage, meant to kill. Then another, and the echo of running feet on the cobbles.

———⟫•०•⟪———

INSIDE THE HOUSE, Luke leaped to his feet. 'Ssh a minute, Dad.' They had been talking about Kelly and Fran; and how the arrival of both women had touched their lives.

'What's wrong, son?' Curious, Charlie followed him along the passage to the front door.

'Just now . . . somebody cried out, I'm sure of it.' Flinging open the door he looked up and down the street. It took a minute, he wasn't sure, but then he was running down the street. In the garish glow from the street lamp he saw the blood down the wall, then the bodies beneath, crumpled and twisted. 'Hurry! Get help!' He sent Charlie away at a run. 'They're hurt bad.'

It was only when he fell to his knees beside them that he recognised Kelly and Fran. 'Oh, no! Oh, dear God!' Tenderly he held Kelly in his arms, his mind frantic.

Suddenly it was all clear. And he knew in his heart who had done this terrible thing.

With all the shouting and noise, neighbours began to gather. 'Poor buggers . . . looks like they're goners to me.' Bill Turner knew a bit about first aid, but this was beyond his capabilities.

Somebody wondered if they'd been robbed, but Fran's basket and Kelly's bag lay untouched. 'There's some wicked swines walking the streets!' one man said. 'I wouldn't mind getting my hands on 'em – I'd mek 'em suffer, I can tell you!'

Down the street, an old woman inched open the door and peered out. Terrified by what she saw and heard, she softly closed the door. 'You've done it this time.' Shaking her head in disbelief, her eyes stricken with fear, she told the cowering woman, 'You'd best find somewhere else to hide. I want nothing to do with murder.'

'Mind what you're saying, you old cow!' Lunging at her, the younger woman took her by the throat. 'You know what I'm like, Mam,' she hissed. 'Anybody hurts me, I hurt them. Now, you keep your mouth shut!' Pressing her fingers into the leathery skin, she whispered madly, 'One word, that's all. And I'll cut your tongue out!'

The old woman didn't argue, nor did she struggle. She knew only too well what shocking deeds the other was capable of.

Chapter Eight

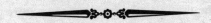

IN THE WEEK following the attack, the whole of Blackburn was buzzing with the news. The papers carried the story daily: *A brutal murder*, they said. *And the police still haven't caught the culprit.*

Johnson Street had been a hive of activity for days; every house was searched, every able body questioned, but no one knew anything. 'It was a vagabond,' they said. 'He saw the two women and planned to rob them, then got frightened off when Luke came running down the street.'

They had no way of knowing the truth. Kelly was still very ill and had not been able to talk to the police. Luke voiced his suspicions and they searched the house but found no sign of Stella. 'She was gone from here *days* afore the attack,' her mother claimed, and as none of the neighbours had seen hide nor hair of her for some time, they found no reason to disbelieve her.

But the old woman knew her daughter was guilty; she

knew her whereabouts too. And every day was a living night-mare.

In those first few days, Kelly's life hung in the balance. Amy and Luke spent days and nights at the Infirmary, seated by her bedside, softly talking to her, praying she could hear, and that somehow she would find the strength to come back to them.

On the third day their prayers were answered.

Exhausted from their long vigil, Amy and Luke had fallen asleep. Amy was curled up in the chair; Luke was slumped forward across the bed, one arm towards Kelly, his hand covering hers. In his dreams he saw her smile, heard her voice, and his heart was content. In that void between sleeping and waking he felt her hand move in his and knew it was no dream.

'Hello, you.' Kelly's brown eyes had been closed these many days, and now they were smiling at him, and he couldn't hold back the tears. 'Oh, thank God!' Shaking with emotion, he stroked her hair and kissed her, and told her how afraid he had been.

Waking, Amy saw her and was overjoyed. Running for the nurse, she gave vent to her own emotions and, as she careered into the office, was so overcome she could hardly explain what had happened.

Realising the urgency, the nurse hurried to Kelly's side, summoning a doctor as she went. To the delight of everyone, including the other patients who had given up their own prayers for her, it was soon clear that Kelly was on the mend at last.

After that Kelly went from strength to strength. 'When will she be strong enough to be told about Fran?' Luke had asked the doctor the same question time and again, and always the answer was the same: 'Not yet. It might prove to be too much of a shock.'

Today though, the doctor hesitated. 'She will have to know, sometime, and she's doing so well I was thinking she might be allowed home quite soon. She's a remarkable woman, I must say. She had a determination that will serve her well. As I've already mentioned, it's fortunate that the force of the blows didn't crack her skull. Even so she sustained injuries that will take time to heal, and the scar on her temple, though it will fade with the passage of time, may never completely go away.'

'You're right.' Luke's admiration for Kelly was ten-fold. 'She *is* a remarkable woman. That's why I'm convinced she can handle the truth – about Fran, I mean.'

'I understand what you're saying, and though I can mend the physical, I'm not qualified to know what goes on in a patient's mind. It's my duty to be cautious in these circumstances.' The doctor had seen it all before; the patient begins to recover, then for some reason there's a setback. A shock could easily do that. 'I don't know . . .'

'*I* know.' Luke was sure of Kelly's strength. 'She keeps asking after Fran,' he said. 'She knows I'm hiding something, and it's playing on her mind. Won't the danger of her *not* knowing cause more damage than if she was told?'

In the end, the doctor saw the sense of his argument. 'Tell her gently,' he warned. 'And the other friend – Amy Slater, isn't it? I think it might be wise if she were there when you told her.' He also commissioned a nurse to be in the room at the time.

Thanking him, Luke said he would leave it for another day. 'I'll break it to her tomorrow,' he decided. 'In the morning, when she's had a good night's sleep.'

The following day was Saturday. Desperately saddened by recent events, Charlie promised to take care of the bairns. 'I've watched over 'em this past week,' he reminded Amy, 'and they ain't come to no harm yet.'

Knowing how deeply he was affected by all that had happened, Amy asked, 'Are you all right, Charlie?'

His smile was half-hearted, betraying something of what he was suffering. 'I'd rather have the bairns here than be on my own,' he said. 'Tell Kelly I'm thinking of her.' When she hesitated, he urged, 'Go on, lass. We'll be fine.'

Amy thanked him for what he'd done. He had taken Tom and Sally to their school and fetched them afterwards, and never a word of complaint. Fran's murder had been a terrible shock to him but, like an old soldier, he kept his feelings hidden.

'Don't let them bully you.' Amy gave a small laugh. 'They can be right little buggers when they want.'

'Naw.' Charlie would hear nothing against them. 'These little darlings have been the saving of me.'

'Be good,' she told the children. 'Look after Charlie now.'

A moment later, eager to get to Kelly, Luke came running down the stairs. 'Ready, Amy?'

'Aye, she is,' Charlie answered for her. 'You tell Kelly I'm not fond o' visiting the Infirmary, so she's to be quick an' come home.'

A short time later, Amy and Luke left the house.

While the children played on the rug with some old dominoes he'd found, Charlie took a broom from the scullery. 'Now then, you two, I'll nobbut be a minute. I've been meaning to sweep the slack together in the cellar. There's too much waste, but it all costs money and when all's said and done, the slack burns every bit as well as the big stuff.'

Tom offered to help. 'I used to help when we had our own house,' he said proudly. 'I'm big enough to use a broom, I can show you if you like.'

'I bet you can.' Charlie thanked him for the offer, but said, 'You stay here, lad, an' look after yer sister. Like I say . . . I'll nobbut be a minute.'

'That's important too, isn't it?'

'What, looking after yer sister? I'll say it is. The most important job in the world.'

Closing the door behind him, Charlie made his way down to the cellar. He didn't sweep the slack. Instead, he went to the far side of the cellar where he sat on the low window-sill and sobbed his heart out. 'Oh, Fran,' he cried, 'I was just beginning to love you. Now, I'll never see you again.' The idea of Fran lying in the mortuary broke his heart. He had felt the stirrings of love and knew she felt the same. In his mind her mischievous eyes smiled at him, and the pain was unbearable.

'I HOPE WE'RE doing the right thing, Amy.' Sitting beside her on the tram, Luke voiced his concern. 'Do you think I've done wrong in persuading the doctor that she should be told?'

'No.' Touching her hand against his, Amy sought to comfort and reassure him. 'You did right.' She tried not to show how her love had deepened for him over the past week. 'Kelly never stops asking after Fran,' she whispered. 'We can't avoid the truth any longer . . . and Kelly wouldn't want us to.'

Squeezing her hand, he raised it to his mouth; pressing his lips against her flesh he told her softly, 'You're such a good friend, Amy. I'm not surprised Kelly thinks the world of you.'

As he turned away, he could not have known the turmoil he had created in Amy's heart. But she had nothing to cling to, except his gratitude. That's all he felt for her, and maybe friendship. But not love, not of the kind she craved. That was reserved only for Kelly, and God knew she needed it, for her friend had been through so much, and it still wasn't over.

Doubts began to set in. 'She'll be all right, won't she,

Luke?' Amy asked tremulously. 'I mean, she's bound to take it real bad. What if . . .' Ashamed of herself she turned aside.

Luke, too, had concerns, but he was determined not to keep Kelly in the dark any longer. 'She knows something isn't right,' he answered thoughtfully. 'Kelly deserves to be told the truth but,' and he prayed it would not have to be this way, 'if you really think it's a mistake, we can always leave it for a while longer.'

After a brief consideration, Amy's fleeting doubts melted. 'No. The sooner it's done the better.'

Disembarking from the tram, they hurried to the Infirmary entrance. Once inside, he took her by the shoulders. 'Can I ask you something, Amy?'

'Ask away.'

'Has Kelly ever said anything to you . . . about me?'

'In what way?'

He felt foolish, but had to know. 'Has she ever said . . . whether she likes me?' He couldn't bring himself to spell it out, not with Amy's blue eyes searching his like that.

Amy gave her brightest smile. 'Well, o' course! She likes you a lot!'

He swallowed hard. 'Enough to marry me, do you think?'

Taken aback, the young woman took a moment to answer. 'I don't know,' she murmured. 'That's summat you'll have to ask Kelly.'

Filled with shame, he apologised. 'It wasn't fair of me to ask you,' he declared. 'And it isn't fair of me to ask Kelly . . . not yet anyway.'

Suddenly, for some inexplicable reason, he felt oddly uncomfortable in Amy's presence.

For a moment there, beneath Amy's tortured gaze, he wasn't even sure of his feelings any more.

<hr />

K NOWING HER FRIENDS were due to visit, Kelly had lain there, watching the clock. 'Don't worry, they'll be here soon, I'm sure.' The nurse was a small, busy creature with a happy disposition. 'Look!' Pointing to the doors, she said, 'Talk of the devil, sure to appear.' And just as she had promised, there was Amy and Luke, hurrying down the ward.

As they approached, the nurse stepped away to a discreet position close by. The doctor had warned her, and she was ready.

After the initial hugging and kissing, they sat beside her bed and dreaded the moment she would have to be told about Fran.

'It's wonderful to see you sitting up,' Luke said, and Amy told her, 'Oh Kelly, you look lovely.'

Kelly tutted. 'I'm sure!' she chuckled. 'With half my hair cut away and bruises all over my face, I think I look more like a street boxer.' But she was grateful all the same. 'It's so good to see you,' and then, to their astonishment, she told them: 'This time you're not leaving until you've told me about Fran.'

When an awkward silence descended, Kelly knew her suspicions were founded. For a moment she couldn't bring herself to say it, but then, in a harsh, painful whisper, she asked, 'Fran's dead, isn't she?'

Amy looked to Luke for support, and he didn't let her down. Taking Kelly's two hands in his, he murmured, 'I'm sorry, Kelly. But we can take some small comfort from knowing she didn't suffer. They say the moment she went down, it was already too late.'

'Oh, dear God, no . . .' Shaking her head Kelly stared from one to the other, as if expecting them to say it was all a mistake after all, and Fran would be along any minute to see her.

Through stricken eyes she stared at Luke. 'It should have been me . . . not her.' Though she had half-expected it, Kelly still wasn't prepared for such devastating news.

She tried so hard not to break down in front of them, but the emotions were so overwhelming she could hardly breathe. Now, when she started sobbing, she couldn't stop. It was as if she had opened a dam and it poured out, carrying her along, taking her strength. 'I knew,' she choked. 'I *knew* you were keeping it from me, and oh, I was so afraid.' Visions of that homely face and the dear, funny smile ran through her mind; she thought about their conversation as they walked towards the tramstop that night. Poor Fran, poor Charlie.

Luke took her in his arms. 'It was Stella, wasn't it?' He was tender in his questioning. 'She was the one who did this, wasn't she?'

Kelly closed her eyes, reliving the attack and trembling with horror at the memory. 'I've only ever seen her once but yes, I'm almost sure it was her.'

Seeing how distressed she was, the nurse stepped forward. 'You should go now,' she told them. 'Miss Wilson needs her rest.'

Kelly protested. 'Please, nurse, just a few more minutes. There are things I need to know.'

'All right, a few minutes, then I'll be back.' Her warning was clear.

'She's right.' Seeing how pale she was and how her hands trembled and twitched at the bedcovers, Luke knew Kelly had taken the news hard. 'Rest now,' he told her. 'We'll talk tomorrow.'

'Where is she?' Composing herself as best she could, Kelly was determined to know it all.

'Please, Kelly.' Getting out of her chair, Amy took hold of Kelly's hand. 'You have to rest. We shouldn't have told you. Not yet.'

'I'm glad you did,' Kelly answered warmly. 'Now I need to know . . . where is she?' Her gaze went to Luke. 'Please.'

'Fran was taken to the chapel of rest,' he revealed. 'She'll be buried on Thursday.'

'Thursday?' In five days' time. Kelly didn't yet know how long they planned to keep her in the Infirmary, but of one thing she was certain. 'I need to be there ... to say goodbye.'

When Luke and Amy glanced at each other, Kelly insisted, 'It's five days away, and the doctors say I'm improving by the day. I'll be well enough, really I will. Talk to Dr Benson. Tell him I have to be out of here by Thursday.' Her mouth set in a determined line. '*Tell him, Luke.* Come Thursday, I'll be there to see Fran laid to rest, whether I have their blessing or not.'

And, knowing Kelly, they did not doubt her word.

⟫━◦━⟪

T HANKFULLY, BY WEDNESDAY, Kelly had made such good progress that the doctor agreed to discharge her. 'You can take her home in the morning,' he told Luke.

All that night she hardly slept. Out of bed by six, she quietly washed and dressed and was ready and waiting by seven. For a full hour she sat by the window, her eyes glued to the street below, watching for Luke and praying he would arrive soon.

When, at five minutes to eight, the doctor came to speak with her, she thanked him for everything. 'Take care of yourself,' he warned. 'I'll see you in two weeks' time.' Just a check-up, he told her, and knowing how well he had cared for her, Kelly thanked him again.

At ten minutes past eight, Luke arrived to take her

home. In the cab on the way to Johnson Street, he told her how good it was to have her back, and Kelly said he couldn't know how much it meant to be going home at last; though, in her heart, she wished Fran could have been there to greet her.

Amy was there though, and Charlie and the children. The homecoming was a happy occasion, but the fact that they would soon be saying their goodbyes to Fran overshadowed their delight.

As always, Charlie served up the tea, and they sat round Kelly's old table in the parlour. They talked of Fran, and Stella, and Charlie said that if there was any justice, she would swing from the end of a rope for what she'd done.

Amy wanted Kelly to know how she had looked after the little house in her friend's absence. 'It didn't feel right,' she said, 'me moving in while you were lying in the Infirmary.'

Kelly told her it was all right. 'I *wanted* you to move in,' she said, 'or I wouldn't have asked.' The truth was, she couldn't bear the thought of this house being cold and empty for a second time. 'Thank you, Amy,' she said. 'You've done a wonderful job.'

Looking round the room at the familiar furniture, polished until it shone, and the gleaming hearth, and cheery fire throwing out a soothing warmth, Kelly saw it as it had always been, her mam's pride and joy. And suddenly she was so emotional she couldn't find words to express her feelings.

'We'll be off to get ready,' Charlie said, and everyone was amazed at how quickly the time had flown.

The two men left. 'I'll be back for you all in about twenty minutes,' Luke told Kelly. 'I've arranged for the cabs to pick us up at midday.'

On the way down the street, Charlie spoke to Luke about Kelly. 'Did you see how that poor lass were close to tears all the time? By! She's been through a lot . . . and now there's the church an' all. It's bound to be an ordeal.' For *all* of us, he thought bitterly. 'Are you sure Kelly's well enough to be there?'

Luke was honest. 'No, Dad, I'm not sure, but Kelly means to go, and there's no changing her mind.'

Charlie smiled. 'She's a stubborn little sod, ain't she?'

'You could say that.' She was one in a million, he thought fondly, and he didn't intend leaving it too long before he asked her to be his wife.

Up in Kelly's room, there was intense discussion about what Kelly would wear to cover up the bald patch where the wound on her head had been stitched. 'I don't want to wear that awful hat I wore home from the Infirmary,' Kelly decided. 'I'd rather tie a scarf round my head.'

'No need for a scarf!' Jubilant, Amy produced a brown paper parcel. 'Have a look in there.'

Curious, Kelly undid the parcel on the dressing-table. 'Oh Amy, it's just what I want!' Drawing out a big floppy beret in deepest blue, Kelly turned it over and over in her hands. 'Well, I never!'

Impatient, Amy gave her a little nudge. 'Well, gal! What d'you think to it? I got it from the market on Tuesday. I'm sorry it ain't black, but it's dark and I reckon it'll suit you down to the ground. Besides, I knew you'd want to look your best for Fran . . .'

'Oh Amy, it's lovely!' Kelly tried it on and, after tugging it into just the right position, everyone said how much they liked it.

'Why did the doctors cut off your hair?' Sally wanted to know, and Tom told her not to be silly. 'The hair would get all caught up in the stitches if they didn't cut it off.' Indignant, he marched her out of the room. 'Charlie says you're to go for a wee before we leave.'

Amy laughed. 'Little sod!' she declared. 'An old head on young shoulders, that's our Tom.'

'They're wonderful, that's what they are,' Kelly said. And back came the old regrets.

<hr />

AT MIDDAY, THE funeral cab turned up and they all climbed in; Luke looked splendid in his dark suit; Charlie too, with his hair slicked back and a grey tie so tight round his neck it made him go red in the face.

Amy wore a calf-length tweed skirt and a tight-fitting black jacket, and the children looked smart in their Sunday best.

Kelly's navy two-piece was an old one, but smart and suitable. Long straight skirt and hip-long jacket, and with the beret tipped naughtily to one side, she looked most attractive. But her face was pale, and her walk unsteady, and in her eyes was a desolate look that tore at everyone's heart. 'Stay close to her,' Charlie said, as he took Amy and the children into the second cab. Luke didn't need any reminding.

When they arrived at the church, there were several people already there; a few of Fran's old boarders, and certain neighbours with whom she'd passed the time of day. There were one or two women from Johnson Street, come to pay their respects, and as one remarked to the other, 'Thank the Lord it weren't *us* who were set on by that mad-woman.'

Fran's two brothers sat in the front row, their heads in their hands, their families beside them. There was no sign of Fran's own family. 'Fran told me she had childer!' Charlie was deep-down angry. 'Where are they now, eh? That's what I'd like to know.'

Luke pointed out that maybe they hadn't heard about what happened. 'Not heard!' Charlie would have none of it. 'How could they not have heard! It were splashed all over the front pages of every newspaper. And what about the authorities? They allus winkle out the relatives. No, they heard all right.' He believed that intensely. 'They just didn't have enough love in their hearts to come and see their own mam laid to her rest.'

Kelly couldn't ever recall seeing Charlie so upset. But then, he and Fran had had intentions of making a life together, she remembered. He had loved her, more even than her own flesh and blood. 'I loved her too, Charlie.' Slipping her hand in his she smiled up at him. 'Let them stay away if they want,' she murmured. '*We're* her family now.'

Subdued, he looked down on her, momentarily lost for words.

'Fran was a good woman,' Kelly whispered. 'None of us will ever forget her.'

When the tears began to flow down Charlie's face, Kelly was glad. She had learned from experience that bad, hurtful feelings were best let out.

When the service was over, Kelly leaned on Luke's arm as they walked to the graveside. Up until then, she had kept her composure, and even as they lowered Fran into the ground, she held back the burning tears.

Then, just as she stooped to throw earth on the coffin, a small robin settled on her hand and stared up at her, his head to one side and the brightest look in his beautiful brown eyes. In that moment she was reminded of Fran's bright brown eyes, how kind and honest they were. She recalled how contented she had looked when she confided in her about Charlie, and it all seemed such a terrible waste. 'Oh, Fran!' The grief swallowed her whole and for a time, she was inconsolable.

Later, when everyone else had gone, Kelly lingered by the graveside. She made her peace with that dear woman, and then she went to Luke, waiting a short distance away. 'Fran knows how you feel,' he said, and deep in her soul, Kelly believed it.

THE NEXT FEW days seemed to fly by.

Amy and the children had settled into the house, and Kelly thanked the good Lord they were there. 'I don't think I could have stayed here on my own,' she said. 'I'm so lucky to have you and the children.'

Amy told her *they* were the lucky ones. 'If it wasn't for you, Gawd only knows where we'd be by now.'

Luke was never far away, watching over her, making sure she was all right. 'It's good to see you getting stronger by the minute.' Neither of them mentioned the unforgettable moment in the cellar, when they kissed and fondled, and almost made love.

Yet it was never far from their minds.

The day after the funeral, the police had called at Kelly's house. 'I have nothing more to tell you,' she said. 'I've told you all I know.'

Inspector Macdonald was persistent. 'You say the woman might have been Stella Porter?'

'It was dark. I couldn't be certain.'

He consulted his notes. 'Assuming it *was* her, what reason do you think she would have to hurt you?'

'I hardly knew her.' Evading the question, Kelly knew that if she were to reveal what Stella had said, that would implicate Luke, and she had no wish to do that.

'Would she have any reason to hurt Mrs Docherty?'

'Not that I know of.' Kelly bristled slightly. 'Fran

Docherty was a kind, generous woman. I can't imagine *anyone* wanting to hurt her.'

'And did she say anything, the woman who attacked you?'

'Everything happened so quickly. She threatened to cut my face . . . Fran came to help, and . . .' She didn't want to talk any more. She wanted him to go.

'But it *was* a woman – you're sure of that?'

'Yes.'

'But you're not sure whether it was Stella Porter?'

'Like I said . . . I've told you all I know.'

'This is a murder enquiry, Miss Wilson. I'm sure you understand, we have to keep asking questions.'

Having sat through his barrage of questions, and seeing how Kelly was growing weary of them, Amy leaped to her feet. 'Anybody'd think *she* were the bleedin' murderer!' she cried. 'All these questions, over and over, and Kelly only just out of the Infirmary. Fran Docherty was a good friend and we only just buried her yesterday.' Shaking her fist in the air, she ranted on, 'You should be ashamed o' yerselves! Kelly's told you everything, so bugger off, why don't yer? Get off yer arses and find whoever did it. Find Stella Porter . . . ask *her* yer bloody questions!'

Surprised by her outburst, the Inspector turned to Kelly. 'Sometimes we forget everything but finding the culprit,' he apologised. 'You must believe we're doing all we can to find whoever did this. As for Stella Porter, we're told by her mother that she left the area some time *before* that night. As yet we haven't been able to prove it one way or the other, because we haven't been able to trace her. We've searched in all the likely places . . .' Hunching his shoulders, he paused, his brow furrowed in concentration. 'It's as if she's vanished off the face of the earth.'

Minutes later he thanked her for her time, and left.

'Bloody good shuts an' all!' Amy was up in arms. 'I'm sorry I lost me temper,' she told Kelly, 'but I'm not sorry I told him to bugger off!'

Kelly chuckled. 'I don't know about *him*, but you frightened the life out of me,' she teased. 'There were a minute there when I thought you were about to smack him one.'

'If he'd stayed any longer, I might have done an' all!'

'Remind me never to get on the wrong side of you.'

Crossing the room, Amy came and knelt down beside Kelly, her two hands on Kelly's lap, her gaze soft and loving. 'I'd never hurt you,' she said. 'Never in a million years.'

Reaching out to take her hand, Kelly smiled whimsically. 'Life's a funny thing, don't you think, Amy?'

'In what way d'yer mean?'

'You and me – our parents. Yours ran off with different partners, and mine . . .' She took a long deep sigh. 'Then Barney leaving and me coming back here after all these years.' The tears swam in her eyes. 'If none of that had happened, Fran would still be here. Don't you see, Amy. Fran was killed because of *me*.'

'No, yer mustn't think that. It weren't because of you. It were what happened and it were a terrible tragedy, but not your fault, and yer must never think it. Things happen in life that we don't understand . . . awful, shocking things . . . and there ain't no way we can know what's round the corner. You couldn't help what happened with your parents and I couldn't help what happened with mine. We're all caught up in summat not of our making, and we do the best we can with what we've been given. After Barney left and you were all alone . . . it were only natural you should come home.'

Kelly nodded. 'I know you're right,' she said, 'but it's so hard. About Fran . . . and that night.' A solitary tear slipped over her lashes and fell on to her knee. 'If I could turn the clock back, I don't think I would have come back here – not if I'd known.'

'But that's just it, gal, we *don't* know.' Amy's face broke into a smile. 'Anyway, if yer hadn't come back here, you'd never have met me, would yer, eh?'

It did the trick. Smiling through her tears, Kelly suggested, 'You'd best go and fetch the bairns. They'll be running rings round Charlie.' Glancing towards the scullery, she sniffed the air. 'I'll get the hot-pot out of the oven before it burns to a crisp. By the time you get back with the bairns, I'll have the fire up the chimney and dinner on the table.'

Amy sprang to her feet. 'Sounds good to me,' she

said, and went to get her coat. 'Charlie's been like a grandad to them childer,' she told Kelly. 'I've never known 'em take to any fella like they've taken to him.' As she went out the door, Kelly called her back. 'What's wrong, gal?' Amy asked.

Halfway to the scullery, Kelly looked at Amy's small, shining face. 'Thank you, Amy,' she murmured.

There was a brief span of silence while Amy tried to read the torture in Kelly's mind. Then in her usual, spontaneous way, she ran across the room and gave Kelly a peck on the cheek. 'The hot-pot's burning,' she said, and was gone, out the door and down the street before Kelly had time to open the oven door and remove the hot-pot.

———— ❖ ————

AMY WAS ON her way out of Charlie's parlour with the children when Luke arrived. 'How is she?' His first thought was for Kelly.

'Hmph!' Indignant, Amy told him about the Inspector's visit. 'Grilled her as though she were the criminal. I told him to bugger off. "Get off yer arses and find the real criminal", I told him.'

'You did right.' He loved Amy's forthright manner. 'And what did he say?'

'He kept on about whether Kelly could be certain it were Stella who came after her and Fran.'

Luke's mouth set in a thin, hard line. '*I'm* certain!' he growled. 'It was her, all right.'

'What makes yer say that?'

It was on the tip of his tongue to admit that Stella had threatened Kelly, but he saw Charlie looking at him and thought better of it. 'Just a feeling,' he said cautiously.

'I'd better be off,' Amy said, smiling up at him. 'You look like you've had a hard day . . . I expect you're ready for yer dinner an' all.'

'I'll be up to see Kelly when I've washed and changed,' he declared. 'Meanwhile, tell her to be careful who she opens the door to.'

'So, you think the Inspector will be back?'

'Or somebody else.'

Alarmed, Amy told the children, 'Help Charlie in the kitchen, you two, while I talk to Luke.' When they ran off, she asked him: 'Are you afraid this person . . . Stella, or whoever it was . . . are you afraid they might still come after Kelly? Is that what you're saying?'

'All I'm saying, Amy, is this. Somebody attacked Kelly and nearly killed her – *meant* to kill her, if you ask me. It was Stella, I'm sure of it. She's a wicked, devious devil, and she won't give up so easy. Keep the door locked. Don't let anybody in that you don't know.'

'If Stella, or anybody else comes near that house looking for trouble, they'll find it, I can promise yer that!'

'Think, Amy!' he urged. 'Think what happened to Fran. I don't want you or Kelly taking any risks.'

Growing nervous, Amy called the children. 'We'd best go,' she told them, then, addressing Luke quietly, she said, 'Mind you, after what she did to Fran and Kelly,

I wouldn't mind getting my hands round that murderin' devil's throat!'

In a swift movement that made her gasp, Luke thrust her down in the chair. 'You're staying here,' he declared. Leaning towards her, he looked her in the eye. 'Don't you understand what I've been trying to tell you? She's out there somewhere, and who knows what's going through her deranged mind?' He called out to Charlie, 'Dad, feed this little lot, will you? I'm going up to see Kelly.'

'Hey!' Scrambling up from the chair, Amy protested, 'What's going on!'

'I'm bringing Kelly back. I want you here, where I can keep an eye on you all.'

'What? For tonight, yer mean?'

'For as long as it takes. I'll be all right on the settee. You and the bairns can have the front room. Kelly can have mine. That way I'll know you're all safe. Until they catch her, we can't be too careful.'

'Kelly will never agree to it.'

'We'll see.' With that, he marched out of the house.

'He doesn't really mean to keep us all here, does he, Charlie?' Amy found Charlie dishing up helpings of meat pie and veg.

'I had an idea he might.' Charlie winked knowingly. 'That's why I cooked more than usual.' He plopped another dollop of mash on to Tom's plate and carried it to the parlour table. 'The lad's hungry,' he said, and judging by the way Sally scrambled up to the table, so was she.

At the sight of that succulent meat pie, with its juices running into the mashed potatoes and the aroma filling her nostrils, Amy sat down beside them. 'I wouldn't mind some crusty pastry,' she said, 'oh, and an extra carrot or two if they're going spare.' It seemed so long since she'd eaten, her stomach was singing a song.

⟶•◦•⟵

KELLY WAS ADAMANT. 'No, Luke, I won't be chased out of my own home.'

He pleaded and cajoled, and even threatened to carry her out bodily. 'You don't realise what you're up against,' he said angrily. 'Listen to me, Kelly.' His voice softened, his two hands on her shoulders in a loving gesture. 'I don't want you hurt.' Before he knew it, the words were out. 'I love you, Kelly. I've loved you from the minute I set eyes on you.' He dared to go further. 'I want to marry you . . . Oh, I know it can't be yet, but soon, God willing.' He paused, his fists clenching against her. 'When I've rid myself of *her*,' he said. 'There'll be nothing more I want in the world than for us to be together.'

'Don't, Luke. Please don't.'

Her soft brown eyes looked up at him, and she thought what a good, caring man he was; she remembered how vigilant and concerned he had been while she was lying in the Infirmary, and she recalled the joy on his face when he brought her home. Luke would make any woman a splendid husband, she thought. But he wasn't Barney and never could be.

Suddenly, she was in his arms. He held her there for what seemed an age, kissing her, softly at first, then more ardently. Lonely and afraid, though she would never admit it, Kelly clung to him, and all the time she told herself, 'Barney's gone away. Luke wants you. He's here and you're lonely. And what if Barney never comes back?'

The lovemaking that followed was meant to be. The feel of his naked body against hers was exciting and oddly comforting. She felt his hands roving her body, fingering the erect nipples, cupping her breasts and sliding down to her thighs. Eyes closed, she enjoyed the experience, loving him back, wanting him more than she could ever have imagined. Just for a time, a very special time, she was a woman again; cherished by this wonderful man who had been there when Barney wasn't.

'Marry me, Kelly,' he whispered. 'When I'm free . . . marry me.'

'Yes,' she answered. 'When you're free.'

They sealed the promise with a kiss, and afterwards lay in the warm glow of the fire, lost in the wonder of what had happened between them, content in each other's arms.

But the moment had to pass, and it was Kelly who broke the silence. 'You'd better go now,' she whispered. 'Amy and the children could walk in at any minute.' It shocked her to think they could have walked in before, when she and Luke . . . But they hadn't, thank God.

They dressed and talked, and Luke was even more determined. 'Stay with me and Charlie for a few days at least. God willing, by then she'll be safe behind bars.'

Kelly was adamant. 'I'm not being chased out of my own home,' she repeated. But there was one concession. 'Amy and the children must be kept safe,' she said. 'Let them stay with you and Charlie. I'll be all right here. The doors will be locked, and if I need you, I know where you are.'

Angry now, he paced the floor. 'If you won't stay at Charlie's, then I'll stay here. I'll kip on the settee. When I'm at work, Charlie will keep an eye on you.' Slamming one fist into the other, he raged, 'The police should have somebody outside watching the house. They must know she's crazy enough to try it again.'

Kelly wasn't convinced. 'I know you mean well, but I won't be kept a prisoner, either here or at Charlie's house,' she declared. 'And I don't want no policeman standing outside my front door neither.'

Whichever argument he put forward, she flatly rejected. 'No, Luke, I won't change my mind.'

Admiration coloured his concern for her. 'I don't think I've ever met anybody quite so stubborn.'

Striding across the room, he bent to one knee, his hands covering hers. 'All right, I can see I'm banging my head against a brick wall. But, look, and I won't take no for an answer on this! If you're intent on staying in this house, I mean to fit some heavy bolts on the doors.'

Kelly didn't argue with that, and even if she had, it would have made no difference. Kissing her again, he told her, 'Bolt the door when I leave.' And he made sure she did before he went away down the street.

⟶✦⟵

As he'd expected, Amy insisted on going back to be with Kelly. 'You're worrying over nothing,' she told Luke, but deep down, like Kelly, she wasn't so sure.

After rummaging about in the stair-cupboard, he dropped a few tools in a bag before escorting Amy and the children back. 'The pair of you are enough to drive a man to drink!' he groaned.

It took about twenty minutes to fit heavy bolts on all the doors, and small but equally strong bolts on the windows. 'That should hold out an earthquake.'

Kelly thanked him. For some inexplicable reason, she knew in her heart they would be safe in this house. It was a contradictory feeling, especially when she remembered how it had been all those years ago.

At the door he held her close. 'You've made me a happy man,' he said, not knowing that Kelly was already having second thoughts. Yet he was a fine man, she told herself. Any woman would be proud to be his wife.

But still doubts crept in and consumed her. Had she been right to promise herself to him? Had she done him a terrible wrong? Especially when Barney still lurked in the corners of her heart.

Only time would tell.

——→•◦•←——

Darkness closed in fast, shrouding the world in shadow. A rising breeze herded the grey clouds overhead; like hooded ghosts they lent an eerie mood to the night.

Hurrying home, Luke thought he saw something ... *someone* ... not too far away and acting shiftily. Slowing his steps, he peered through the darkness. It was a woman, and she was making her way towards his wife's house. 'Who the devil's that?' he thought to himself. Straightaway he imagined it to be Stella, creeping about in the shadows, biding her time. 'My God!' He'd suspected she wouldn't be so far away but now, realising it, his fear for Kelly was tenfold.

Pressing himself against the wall, he watched for a moment, thankful when, just then, the gas mantle in the street-lamp flickered and died.

The figure hurried up the steps to the front door, where she glanced furtively about. Anxious, she fumbled for her key, moving quickly to pick it up when it clattered to the ground.

Hoping she hadn't seen him, Luke made his move.

In a rush he went for her, shocked and surprised when he saw it wasn't Stella but her mother. 'Get your hands off me!' Visibly shaken, the old woman lashed out with her fists. 'What d'you want from me, eh? For Gawd's sake, leave me be. *All* of you, just leave me be!'

'Where is she?' Luke had to know.

Afraid and guilty, she pleaded, 'It weren't me as killed that woman!' Crying out, she pummelled Luke on the chest. 'I wouldn't do that. I wouldn't hurt nobody in that way!'

'All right, all right.' Taking her by the arms, Luke drew her up until she was facing him full on. 'I believe you!'

Her mouth fell open in astonishment. 'You believe me?' Eyeing him suspiciously, she drew back. 'Why should you believe me, eh?'

In the softest of whispers he told her, 'Because I know who really killed that poor woman, and almost killed Kelly Wilson into the bargain.'

'How do you know that?' Trembling uncontrollably, she dropped her own voice to a whisper. 'Who was it then?'

'It was Stella . . . wasn't it?'

Her eyes widening with fear, she put a finger to her lips, 'Ssh!' She warned, 'It's *dangerous* to talk like that.' Suddenly on the defensive again, she flattened her two hands against his chest and pushed him hard. 'Go away from here, you! Go on! Get away!' Now she was shouting, in fear for her own life. 'I'm just an old woman,' she begged. 'I don't want no part of it. Leave me be, why don't you?'

'Do you know where she is?'

'No!'

His gaze went beyond her to the house. 'Is she in there?'

'NO!' Swinging round, she flung open the door and ran inside. Slamming it shut behind her, she called out, 'Leave me be ... else I'll have the police on yer!' Then came the sound of her footsteps fleeing down the passage.

As he turned away, out of the corner of his eye Luke saw something that made him smile. Warped and changed by the passage of time, the doors of these old houses had shifted, sometimes leaving a gap between door and frame. When the old woman slammed the door, it had not wedged home. Instead it had sprung back and now it was open at least an inch. 'So, she's not in here, eh?' He thought different.

Inside the parlour, the old woman had just lit the lamp. Now, as Luke pushed his way in, she was frantic. 'GET OUT!' Picking up the heavy poker, she waved it at him threateningly. '*Get out of my house, Luke Porter!*'

'I'll go,' he promised, 'when you've told me where she is.' Glancing about, he expected to see his wife lurking in some dark corner.

Suddenly the old woman rushed forward. At first he thought she was going to hit him with the poker. Instead she ran past him and closed the door. When she turned to him, her eyes were sticking out like two hat-pins, and her voice was low, trembling with fright. 'She'll kill us both if she knows you're here!'

Excited, he grabbed her by the arms. 'Where is she?'

There was a moment's hesitation, before she answered, 'I don't know.'

'She did kill Fran Docherty, didn't she?'

The old woman nodded.

'Was it Kelly she wanted?'

She nodded again. 'She's out there now,' she warned. 'You'd better get back afore she finds her. She'll kill her for sure, mek no mistake about it.' Fear made her snigger – a terrible, pitiful sound. 'She's wrong in the 'ead – you didn't know that, did yer, eh? Years ago, afore we came to this street, she were in an asylum.' A look of pride came over her wizened old face. 'I got her out. We came here where they couldn't find us.' Gulping, she lowered her voice until it was almost inaudible. 'She'd kill me too, if she thought I were telling you all this.'

'Is she here . . . in this house?'

Flinging open the door, she yelled at him again, 'I WANT YOU OUT OF HERE!'

'All right.' Appeasing her, Luke went through the door, but instead of turning left to the front door, he turned right and ran up the stairs. Crazed with fear, the old woman went after him. 'I already told you . . . *she ain't here!*'

With the old woman not far behind, Luke went from room to room, throwing open the doors and looking inside. At last he had to admit, there was no sign of her.

'See!' Jubilant, his mother-in-law followed him downstairs. 'I told you she weren't here, didn't I? Now piss orf out of it. Go on, piss orf!'

Weary and disillusioned, she stood a moment at the parlour door, watching him go down the passage. 'And don't come back!'

Going into the parlour, she took a moment to gather her strength. 'I wish to Gawd I'd never had no bloody childer.' Passing through to the scullery, she put on the kettle. 'A drunk husband who wanted every other woman but me, and who left me with three childer to fetch up on me own.' Slamming the teapot down, she waited for the kettle to boil. 'Three childer. Hmph! First a lad gone to sea and never been seen again. Then another, who spends more time in prison than he does outside.' The deep, heavy sigh lifted her shoulders. 'And now *this* one. I allus wanted a lass,' she murmured. 'I didn't know it would be like a never-ending punishment.'

Busying herself preparing a tray, she had no idea Luke was still in the house.

Having opened and shut the front door, he had crept stealthily into the front room. Here he waited, listening, convinced that Stella was hiding in the house somewhere.

It wasn't long before he heard the old woman mounting the stairs, grunting and groaning with every step. Daring to peer out, he saw her rounding the landing at the top. Softly he followed, keeping his distance, making certain she had no idea he was behind her. If he was wrong, and all she was doing was going to her bed, he would leave and secure the door behind him. The old woman would never even know he'd been there.

At the top of the stairs, he pressed himself against the wall and waited. She had gone into the front room. He could hear her moaning and muttering, then all manner of noises he couldn't quite make out.

Suddenly, there were voices. A smile crept over his face. 'Thought you'd outfoxed me, did you?' But he had to wait, because they were speaking in whispers, and because he hadn't recognised the other voice. He crept forward, taking each step with great care. The floorboards in these old houses were prone to creaking at the drop of a pin.

As he got closer, he recognised the voice. It *was* Stella! He stood still, his heart pounding as he listened to the conversation. 'You old witch!' She wasn't whispering now. She was screaming like someone deranged. 'I heard you telling him about me! AND DON'T LIE, BECAUSE I KNOW! I came down and listened from the bottom of the stairs . . . you told him I were mad, didn't you? You told him I'd been in the asylum, and that it were me as killed that bloody Docherty woman. You told him everything. Couldn't keep your trap shut, could you? It's a wonder you didn't tell him I were hiding in the attic. Why didn't you tell him *that*, eh?'

'Please, Stella, don't be angry with me.' The old

woman's voice shook with fear. 'Don't hurt me.' Her pleas heightened to cries of terror. 'NO! Please, Stella . . . NO!'

Alarmed that she might do something crazy, Luke ran along the landing, and flinging open the door, he stood there, afraid to go any further. 'Come near me, and I swear to God I'll throw her out.' Standing by the open window, Stella had the old woman in her grasp. With one hand on her shoulder and the other pressing her down, she had her half in, half out of the window.

Beneath that window was the yard, a sea of hard, uneven flagstones that could smash a body to pieces. 'Let her go.' He didn't threaten. Realising she was completely out of her mind, he thought it best to reason with her. 'Can't you see, she's had enough. Your mam's just a frightened old woman. Let her loose and I'll leave. I won't come back. Just let your mam go, Stella. Please.' Now he was as frantic as the old woman, but he couldn't show it. He had to be the calm one – persuade her to reason, if it wasn't too late.

Stella stared at him, her wild, crazed eyes daring him to come into the room. 'She's done a bad thing,' she said, smiling. 'People who do bad things have to be punished.'

'*You've* done a bad thing too, Stella.' He suspected her shouting and screaming had brought the neighbours out. He hoped and prayed they would have the good sense to get help while he talked her down. 'You killed an innocent woman,' he tenderly reproached her. 'You hurt

Kelly . . . meant to kill her too. Didn't you?' He wanted to rush in and shake her until she confessed the truth, but holding himself in control, he went on, 'Why, Stella? Why did you do it? You knew it was all over between us a long time ago. Murdering Kelly would have made no difference.'

'I *should* have killed her, then she wouldn't have been able to come between us.' A sadistic grin swallowed her features. 'The other one got in the way. I'm glad she's dead. If it hadn't been for her, the job would be done now and you'd be mine again.'

'No, Stella, it's too late for all that.'

Bringing her head to one side, she stared at him pitifully. 'She's *nothing*!' The anger faded and in its place came a sorrowful whine. 'Oh Luke, how can you love her?'

Thinking it best to ignore her probing questions, he pleaded again, 'Let your mother go, Stella. You're frightening her.' Quietly whimpering, the old woman tried feebly to get away. A swift twist of the arm caused her enough pain to keep still.

Incensed, Luke took a step forward. '*Stay back, I'm warning you!*' Stella threatened, inching the old woman further out the window. She laughed, menacingly. 'I mean it, Luke. They'll hang me anyway, so I've got nothing to lose.'

The old woman's cries rent the air. 'Help me!' Seeing the neighbours gathering in the alley, she called to them, 'Get the police!' A hard smack on the side of her head reduced her cries to sobbing. 'Don't kill me, Stella,' she moaned. 'I've allus looked after you. I swear to Gawd, I didn't mean you no harm.'

'Shut up, you old cow. You told him all about me, and now they'll all know. You promised you'd never tell. Liar. LIAR!' When she raised her hand to strike again, Luke intervened.

'What do you want from me, Stella?'

Lowering her hand she focused her stricken eyes on him. 'I love you, Luke,' she murmured. 'More than *she'll* ever love you.'

'Did you really think if you killed someone I care for, that I'd have you back again?'

'You do still love me, don't you, Luke?'

'We have different ideas of love, Stella. But if you let your mother go now, we can talk, you and I.' Not about love though, he thought harshly; not about the kind of things she needed to hear from him.

She thought on that for a minute, but then remembered. 'She betrayed me.'

'I *made* her tell me.'

She glanced contemptuously at her mother's terrified face. 'If I let her go, will you promise to take me back as your wife?'

Luke was torn between the horns of a devil. If he *didn't* promise, then she might do something he would regret. On the other hand, if he *did* promise, he might well live to regret it even more.

In the end he had to make a choice. He had known this woman for some years now; married her, lived with her, and gone through hell because of her. Yet in spite of all her threats and anger, he could not really believe she would hurl her own mother out of the window.

'You bastard! I asked you a question!' she snapped. 'If I let her go, will you take me back? Can it be like before?'

'No, Stella,' he answered truthfully. 'I won't come back to you nor can it ever be like before. But we can talk, you and me . . . you have my word on that.'

Suddenly there were people at the front door. 'OPEN UP IN THERE!' The sound of hammering shook the house.

From the cheering down in the alley, the old woman thought her ordeal was over. 'You'll have to let me go now,' she told her daughter. 'Or they'll hang you twice over.'

Just then came an almighty sound as the front door was flung back on its hinges. 'They've broken in!' Panic-stricken, Stella edged nearer to the window, one hand between her mother's shoulder-blades, the other on the windowsill.

'Be calm.' Luke feared the worst. 'I'll tell them it isn't your fault – you're ill. You couldn't help what you did.' Preparing to lunge at her, he forced himself to hold back. With the old woman positioned so precariously over the window, and Stella leaning back over the ledge, he feared the consequences of his actions. 'They won't hurt you.' He held out his arms. 'I won't let them.' They were coming up the stairs now. 'It's over, Stella.'

As the door opened, there was a slight pause while the men took stock of the situation. In that fleeting span of time, Stella looked at Luke, the tears streaming down her face. 'I could have made you happy,' she said. In one swift, terrifying movement, she thrust downwards, and the old woman was gone, her cries pitiful to hear.

As the police lurched forward, Stella smiled, her lips mouthed the words, 'I love you.' Then she, too, was gone.

'Oh, Jesus!' Shattered by what he had witnessed, Luke ran to the window and looked out. Below him he could see the two figures – the daughter lying on her back; the mother close by, reaching out, her hand covering Stella's. Pouring into the back yard came the neighbours, who had watched in horror as the scene unfolded.

'There was nothing anyone could do,' they said. But it would haunt Luke for ever.

Chapter Nine

THE DEATHS OF Stella Porter and her mother had shocked everyone. The days that followed were wretched.

No one, least of all Luke, had anticipated the turn of events that took two more lives; one innocent, one guilty. The police stopped looking for Fran's murderer because the truth had at last emerged. Stella was the one, and the case was closed.

'You've got to stop torturing yourself, Luke.' Kelly was concerned for him. 'You can't blame yourself. The woman was out of her mind, we know that now.'

'I know.' All the same, Luke was finding it hard to come to terms with the fact that while he was in that room with Stella and her mother, he had had it in his power to save the old woman, and he had failed. 'I just wish things had been different, that's all.'

'Well, they're not.' Charlie had a thing or two to say. 'If you ask me, it's good shuts to both of 'em. All right, the old woman didn't *murder* anybody, not so far as we know anyway, but she were a wicked old witch, may God forgive me.' Making the sign of the cross on himself, he rolled his eyes to heaven. 'She deceived us about her daughter's insanity, and she was a born troublemaker. There's many a time she's spread her poison about. Most every week she were fighting with one or other of the neighbours. Widow Murdoch was the kindest soul imaginable, but even *she* got on the wrong side of that old bugger! It got so she were afraid to go outside her own front door.'

He had strong opinions, did Charlie, and he didn't mind expressing them. 'It's all in the blood,' he declared grandly. 'Badness begets badness, that's what I say.'

Luke couldn't deny that at least *some* of what he said was true. 'I expect you're right,' he conceded, 'but she didn't deserve to die like that – frightened half out her wits before the end came.' No matter what Charlie or anyone else said, Luke found it hard to understand how Stella could have done such a terrible thing.

Yet, even while they were discussing one traumatic event, there was another on the way. And it was to do with Amy.

<hr />

A MY AND KELLY spent days and nights pinning notices up in all kinds of places where folk might congregate; in certain shops that would have no cause to complain about the means of her trade; at the tram-stations and boulevards, and on any spare wall they could find. 'It's a good notice,' Amy complimented her. 'You've a way with words.'

'If it doesn't bring trade to the door, it might as well be on old fish and chip paper.' Kelly was growing increasingly anxious about her dwindling finances.

'Well, if that notice don't fetch the buggers to the door,' Amy retorted, 'I don't know what will.'

Stepping back to admire her handiwork, Kelly read the notice aloud:

EXPERIENCED DRESSMAKER

If you are a lady with good taste in clothes and linen, you will benefit from a visit to Kelly Wilson of 12, Johnson Street.

I offer all kinds of services, including re-make, binding, and hat repair. Dress fittings; new creation; refit and alterations; all at reasonable rates.

I pride myself on my good work and being able to satisfy your needs. I can supply fabrics, lace, design ideas, and make a garment to the customer's design. I also make bedspreads and curtains.

There is no charge for a visit. Come and see me soon. I know it will be worth your while.

Kelly Wilson. Needlecraft and design.
12, Johnson Street, Blackburn.

'Cor! It's bleedin' brilliant!' Amy was beside herself. 'The work will flood in, you'll see.'

Kelly laughed. 'Happen you won't be so thrilled when you're screwing up your eyes over a sewing needle at half-past one of a morning.'

'It won't bother me.' Amy would be glad of a chance to repay Kelly for what she'd given her. 'If I was up half the night working on bloomers that would fit twice round the gasworks, I could never repay you what you've done for me and the bairns.'

'Come on, it's getting dark. We'd best make our way back. You collect the young 'uns from Charlie, I'll stop off and get cod and chips four times, with mushy peas and a bag of crackling. How does that sound?'

Amy said it was 'just what the doctor ordered', and they headed for the tram-stop. 'What about Luke?' He was always on Amy's mind.

'What do you mean, Amy?'

'You said he proposed?'

'He did!'

'And you accepted?'

Kelly hesitated. 'You know I did.' If she could only turn back the clock, she would never have been so impulsive. Now it had gone too far and there was no way out without someone getting hurt.

A thought crossed her mind. 'Amy, has it upset you – me and Luke being engaged to be married?'

Amy was sorely tempted to confess how she had been devastated by the news but, loving Kelly like a sister, she hid her heartache. 'Don't be daft!' she lied. 'I'm looking forward to being Maid of Honour.'

Sneaking a glance out the corner of her eye, Kelly saw the sad expression on Amy's face, and her suspicions were confirmed. Amy was in love with Luke. It was a worrying thought.

———◦———

THE CHILDREN SCRAMBLED their coats on. 'I hope Kelly brings lots and lots of chips,' Tom said, rubbing his tummy. 'Me too.' Sally did the same, making Charlie laugh.

'Little sods,' he said. 'Anybody'd think they were starved, an' they've just polished off the rest of my apple-pie an' all.' Charlie told Amy to tell Kelly, 'Luke's got an emergency at work and he'll not be back till late. He said to tell Kelly he'll call round on his way to work in the morning.'

At the thought of cod, chips and mushy peas, the children danced all the way home. When Kelly arrived they were sat at the table, their plates before them and a fire in the chimney. 'By! This is cosy to come into.' Taking off her coat, Kelly began to dish up the food, while Amy cut the bread and buttered it, and brought the teapot to the table.

After the meal, Amy gave Kelly Luke's message. In a way, after discovering Amy's feelings, Kelly was relieved Luke wouldn't be coming round tonight.

They were not alone for long though. That evening, Kelly had two visitors, both ladies, both having seen the notice, and both seeking to change their dress-maker. 'She's never there,' they said in chorus. 'And she's always late with deliveries.'

Delighted, Kelly talked them through her wares, and how they need never concern themselves about her letting them down or never being there. 'Though I won't be open for business until next week. You see, I haven't quite got myself organised yet,' she explained. 'I've not long moved into the area and my fabrics and such are still in transit.' It was a small fib.

Excited to have found her, they revealed, 'We have friends who will no doubt be knocking on your door any day.' Kelly said they would be made very welcome, and bade them a most pleasant, 'Goodnight.'

When they were gone, Amy laughed aloud. 'You little divil!' she cried, mimicking her to perfection. '"My fabrics and such are in transit." Cor, bleedin' Nora, I never would 'ave believed you could lie so well.'

Beside herself with excitement, Kelly paced the floor. 'I've already been to see the bank manager. He's allowed me a small sum to tide me over, but we'll have to use it very carefully.' Glancing at the sewing box in the corner of the grate she assessed their wares. 'We already have the sewing threads, needles and pins, and binding tape for all occasions. Tomorrow, Amy, we'll go into town and call at the drapers. I think it's time I started looking at fabrics. Not expensive, mind. We'll go for the usual, practical stuff but in the softest, newest colours. There's always a need for that.'

The planning went on into the early hours. 'We'd best get off to bed,' Kelly suggested, and they climbed the stairs, still fired with enthusiasm.

'It's been an odd sort of day, ain't it, gal?' Amy yawned.

Kelly nodded. 'We could both do with a good night's sleep.'

—————

In the morning, the two women were up bright and early. Between them they did the housework, and afterwards Kelly made the porridge, while Amy got the children out of bed. The four of them sat round the table and ate breakfast, chatting like they usually did, and glad of a new day before them. 'Mr Earnshaw said I did my sums good yesterday.' Proudly, Tom puffed out his little chest. 'It's eight times table today.'

'Well, I've done sums, too.' Sally wasn't about to be outshone. 'I know what six and eight is.'

Tom tested her. 'What is it then?'

After counting on her fingers, Sally held up her hands. 'Look!' Frowning, she turned her hands around. 'I ain't got enough fingers.'

When they all laughed, she looked set to cry until Kelly dropped a fat spoonful of strawberry jam over her porridge.

With time to spare, the two women cleared away the breakfast things while the children got ready for school. At eight o'clock, they were all ready for off; the children in their smart navy outfits, Amy in a flouncing dark skirt and long coat, and Kelly smothered in scarves, long coat and boots. 'You don't mean to catch a cold, do you, gal?' Amy laughed.

As they turned the corner, the tram could be seen drawing in at the stop. There was no more time for talk, because they had to set off at a run. 'My legs are tired,' Sally complained so, much to the child's delight, Kelly picked her up and ran with her all the way to the tram, where she bundled her on board. 'Hurry up, you lot!' The conductor was in a bad mood. 'Else I'll have to leave you behind.'

'Miserable old sod!' Wending her way to the front, Amy grumbled under her breath, 'He'd better not get on the wrong side o' me. Not unless he wants my bag round 'is 'ead!'

Kelly glanced at Amy's heavy tapestry bag and thought the conductor might do well to steer clear.

Half an hour later, with the children deposited safely at school, Kelly and Amy went on a shopping spree. They bought yards of fabric from the indoor market, pins and needles from the man on the street selling from his barrow, and all manner of paraphernalia from the drapers. 'Now, I think we deserve a cup of tea,' Kelly announced. 'After that, we'll go and see the tatter about that sewing machine he offered us.' And before Amy could protest, she conceded, 'All right, I know you'd rather sew by hand and that's fine. But if we get really busy, I might decide to use a machine after all.'

'Have you used one afore?'

'No.'

'Then don't blame me if yer stitch yer fingers to the table.'

That made Kelly have second thoughts. 'Happen we'll wait a while before we decide on a machine.'

In the tea-room they enjoyed a reviving pot of tea and a scone before, loaded with shopping, they took the tram home.

As Kelly opened the door, she saw the letters lying at her feet. There were two – one in a white envelope, the other in a brown, official-looking envelope. Both of them were addressed to Amy. 'Who the divil are they from?' Turning them over and over in her hands, Amy grew more and more worried. 'I don't know nobody who could write to me,' she said. 'Besides, there ain't many folks who know where I am.'

Kelly had a suggestion. 'Do you think maybe it's one of your parents? Happen they had you traced and want to see the children.' Going to the scullery she put the kettle on. By the look on Amy's face she'd had quite a shock.

'It better not be from them!' Amy declared. 'If they think they're taking the bairns from me, they've got another thought coming!'

Returning to the parlour, Kelly found her pacing the floor, working herself up into a dreadful state. Making her sit down, she ordered, 'Drink that,' and handed her a cup of tea. 'Afterwards, you can open the letters and put us *both* out of our misery.'

The first official-looking letter was from Fran's solicitor, summoning Amy to his office to discuss the contents of Fran's will. It was a surprise and Amy thought it was unlikely she had been left anything other than a small keepsake but, nevertheless, she was pleased.

Not wanting to dim Amy's good news, Kelly made a supreme effort. 'Oh, Amy, it's what Fran wanted. She so loved you and the bairns. She told me herself, many a time, how she wished you were her own, and that she had grandchildren like Sally and Tom. When her own children deserted her, it was the worst day of her life, that's what she said.'

'How could they desert her like that?'

'Some people don't value families; others don't deserve them.' Kelly knew exactly how Fran felt, for didn't she feel the very same? 'What happened was terrible, and we'll always think of her with fondness, but she made her will with you and the bairns in mind, you must remember that.'

With the letter lying open between them, they sat a moment, reflecting on Fran's warm and wonderful person, and wishing she had not been taken from them. But she had, and now they must move on.

'Open the other letter now.'

With fumbling fingers, Amy did so. It was another shock.

Having read it silently, she handed it to Kelly. 'Now I don't know *what* to do.'

Kelly began to read. When she had finished she sat back in her chair, the letter in her hands and a look of disgust on her face. After a moment, she told Amy, 'I'll tell you what I think, shall I? I think you should tear it up and throw it on the fire.'

'I can't.'

'Why not?'

'Because it's Fran's daughter we're talking about. She says she knows I've been summoned to the lawyer's and that she'll fight me tooth and nail to get what's rightly hers, and to tell the truth, Kelly, I reckon she's right. Whatever Fran's left in her will, her children have more right to it than me.'

Kelly didn't agree and said so. 'Fran had four children, and none of them wanted anything to do with her . . . she told me that. For years they have kept their distance, and now, when their mam's dead and buried, they want to pick her bones. No, Amy. Fran wanted you and the bairns to have something, because in the short time she knew you, you were more family to her than her own.'

'So were you.' Amy voiced her thoughts. 'Why didn't she put *you* in her will an' all?'

'Because she knew I would be all right. She knew it was only a matter of time before I got the business off the ground. Besides, I remember telling her how I liked my independence . . . preferred to find my own way. And, though she loved me too, it was in a different way from how she loved you and the bairns. I was a friend, but she adopted you as her own.'

'I won't fight her daughter.' Amy shrank from the idea of such a confrontation. 'It wouldn't be right.'

'Amy, please. Go and see the lawyer. At least find out what he has to say.'

Amy lapsed into a deep silence, and for the rest of the day, however much Kelly tried to draw her out, she had nothing else to say.

Later that evening, a chubby, dark-haired girl knocked on Kelly's door. 'I've seen the notice, and I want to know if you've got any work going.'

'What kind of work?'

'Sewing and the like.' Before Kelly could dismiss her out of hand, she went on hurriedly, 'I'm a proper seamstress, miss. I used to work up at the Hall, until they closed it down. The beams were all rotten, you see, and they had to get the workmen in. It'll take months and months, they said. Well, my mam said she can't have me hanging round the place without fetching money in, so when I saw your notice I thought I'd come and ask.'

Kelly liked her straight off, but, 'I'm afraid I haven't got any work to offer you. Maybe later, when I've built up the business, I might have a mind to take somebody on then. But not now. I'm sorry.' She was such a clean, tidy young thing too.

Before the girl went, she gave Kelly a folded piece

of paper. 'It's my name and address,' she said. 'In case you change your mind.'

Kelly bade her goodnight. Inside the passage, she read the note: Lucy Drew of 10, Armitage Street. Refolding it, she put it in her pocket. 'Poor little thing,' she muttered. 'Pity I couldn't help her.'

<hr />

T HE FOLLOWING MORNING, Amy set off to take the children to school. 'I'll be going straight on to the lawyer's,' she told Kelly. 'Wish me luck, and I'll see you when I get back.'

'I wish you'd let me come with you, Amy.' Worried in case the daughter started trouble, Kelly didn't want Amy going on her own.

'No, Kelly, thanks all the same, but it's best if I go on my own.' Before Kelly could argue, Amy had ushered the children together and bundled them out the door.

'Don't make any rash decisions!' Kelly ran after her, but Amy was already halfway down the street.

'Morning, my dear.' Red-nosed and unkempt, Lily Trainer had been at the booze again.

'Morning, Lily.' Nodding acknowledgement, Kelly went back inside. 'Drunk again.' Cocking her ear she could just make out Lily's shrill voice, singing like a bird, all the way down the street. Once inside the parlour, however, Kelly soon forgot about Lily. I wonder if Amy will be all right, she thought. It sounds to me as if Fran's daughter is out for blood.

<hr />

K ELLY WASN'T FAR wrong.

Leading her to the office, the thin-faced clerk felt sorry for Amy. Minutes before, she had overheard a very heated conversation and thanked her lucky stars it wasn't *her* about to face them inside. 'You've an enemy in there,' she whispered, 'but don't tell them I said so or I'll lose my job.'

Amy's stomach was already leaping and turning. The clerk's warning did nothing to settle her nerves.

At the clerk's announcement that Amy had arrived, the kindly lawyer got up from his seat. 'Come in, my dear.' His face lifted in a smile. 'We've been waiting for you.'

Taking her by the elbow, he introduced her first to the two men. Amy was delighted to meet them. 'Fran's brothers,' she said delightedly. 'I saw you at the funeral. Kelly's told me all about you.'

Subdued by the occasion, both men nodded and asked for their regards to be passed back to Kelly. 'A respectable lady and a good friend to our Fran.' Ted was the eldest of the two, and spoke for both of them.

Next came the woman; a lank, sour-faced individual, who eyed Amy from top to bottom. 'This is Miss Miriam

Docherty,' the lawyer told Amy. 'Miss Docherty, this is Amy Slater.'

Amy greeted her with a nervous smile. There was something very regal about Fran's daughter; dressed all in black and wearing jewels at her throat, she gave Amy an uncomfortable feeling that she ought to curtsey. Instead, she held out her hand. 'Pleased to meet you, ma'am.'

Accepting Amy's gesture of friendship the other woman shook her hand warmly. 'This is all so unpleasant,' she said. 'I wrote to you in haste. I hope you can forgive my sharp remarks. I wasn't thinking straight . . . grief-stricken. My sisters and I were so terribly shocked. Losing our mother. The way it happened . . .' Dabbing at her eyes with a stark white handkerchief, she apologised and smiled weakly. 'I hope you don't think too badly of me?'

Amy didn't know *what* to think. This woman didn't sound at all like the one who had written that nasty letter. Yet, just now, the clerk had warned that she had an enemy. Who was it then? The lawyer or Fran's daughter? Certainly not Ted or Wilf!

'Sit down, my dear.' Ushering Amy to a seat, the lawyer returned to his desk and sat himself down. 'Now then.' Loudly clearing his throat he consulted the papers before him. 'Let's see what we've got.'

There followed a moment of absolute silence while he perused the papers. Meanwhile, the two women were acutely aware of each other, and when the other woman patted her on the hand, Amy was taken aback. She felt out of her depth amongst these people. Not for the first time since getting the letters, she wished herself a million miles away.

With everyone discreetly eyeing everyone else, the only sound being the rhythmic ticking of the clock, and the smell of stale snuff permeating the air, it seemed an alien environment to Amy.

'Very well.' Cracking his fingers, the lawyer locked them together, flexing and fidgeting, until Amy's nerves were at shrieking point. 'The will is quite specific.' In a sombre voice he proceeded to read its contents:

I, Fran Docherty . . . leave my two brothers my beautiful walnut dresser and the pianola, to keep or sell as they think fit. I am grateful for the love and support they have given me over the years . . .'

Here, the lawyer looked up. 'Now we come to the children.' Glancing at Amy, he gave her an encouraging smile before proceeding:

. . . to my only son Seamus, I leave my blue china mantelpiece clock; it was his father's, and his grandfather's before that.

Keeping his head down but peering over his spectacles, the lawyer explained, 'Due to illness, Mr Seamus Docherty could not be here today.' Roving his eyes from one to the other, he made sure they had understood, before going on:

On our wedding day, my husband and I exchanged gifts. I have kept the brooch he gave me safe in my jewellery box, along with my trinkets.

Apart from the brooch, there is nothing of any value, although they are dear to me. All of these, I leave to my daughters, Miriam, Eileen and Rosalyn, including my clothes and other bric-a-brac, but excluding all other articles mentioned here.

The only real thing of monetary value I own is the guest-house, which, thank God, has provided me with a modest income. This independence did not come easy, however. It was hard won. Left alone, with troubles not of my own making, there were times when I despaired. But through hard work and perseverance, I have survived a very cruel wrong done to me.

Lately, I have found precious friends in two very lovely ladies, and I thank God for them. I know in my heart that Kelly Wilson will do well. She has a good business head and the energy to make her dreams come true. Amy Slater, however, reminds me of myself when I was younger. Deserted and destitute, she has taken on a heavy burden in the shape of those two lovely bairns.

For her sake, and for the sake of those bairns, who have become the grandchildren I never had, I declare that my guest-house, the ongoing business, and my small bank balance (the details of which are here enclosed, along with the house deeds) are bequeathed to Amy Slater, with all my love and gratitude, for the pleasure and sunshine young Tom and Sally have brought into my life.

This being my only will and testament, witnessed and signed, I, Fran Docherty, have named all my benefactors herein.

On the last word, the lawyer took off his spectacles, placed them on the desk and leaned back in his chair. 'So there we have it,' he declared. 'Fran Docherty's will . . . signed, sealed and witnessed; and perfectly legal to all intents and purposes.'

The stunned silence was broken only by the ticking of the clock. The two brothers looked at each other and understood.

Fran's daughter was grey as death, the knuckles on her hands bled white where the long, sinewy fingers fiercely clutched her bag.

As for Amy, she sat on her chair, eyes staring at the lawyer, and her mind in a whirl. *Fran had left her everything she cherished!*

The lawyer had seen it all before. He knew it would take a moment. And it did.

Suddenly there was a shrill scream as Miriam sprang from her chair. 'NO!' Banging her fist on the table, she addressed herself to Amy, her voice broken and pleading. 'This isn't how it should be! That was our mother. Everything she left to you should rightfully belong to us her children – me, Seamus and the others!'

Now Ted was on his feet, his face red with anger as he confronted her. 'Your "mother" is it?' he demanded. 'And what the devil have you cared about her all these years, eh? Where were you when she needed you? She said a wrong were done her, but it were *more* than that . . . and you were part of it. Not only did your useless bugger of a father walk out on her, but you girls and your precious brother couldn't wait to do the same. First she were left to bring up four young 'uns, and then you kids turned round and stabbed her in the back. What she should have done was drown the lot of you at birth! And shame on that brother o' yours . . . who I dare say ain't "ill" at all, but scared to show his measly face, 'cause he'll know what I have to say. All four of you are greedy, grasping parasites. No wonder you've never wed, Miriam, 'cause nobody with any sense would have you! You didn't give a toss about your mother! Even afore she'd recovered from one shock, you delivered another blow. Her own children, who she adored, leaving her all alone the way you did . . .'

Taking a breath, he gestured to his own brother, who was quietly weeping. 'If it hadn't been for us two, she wouldn't have had a soul in the whole world.' Grabbing his cap from the chair he slammed it on his head. 'We're going,' he snarled. 'And if we never hear from you again, it'll be too bloody soon!'

When they were gone, Amy stood up to follow. 'NO!' Rushing across the room, Miriam grabbed her by the sleeve. 'Don't listen to him,' she pleaded, tears filling her eyes. 'They don't know how it was, how it *really* was. My brother and us were torn between the two of them. After Father left, Ma got so miserable. Sometimes she would hit us and then cry all day because she was sorry. We didn't know what to do. When Father insisted we go and live with him, it was a hard decision, but we were afraid. We weren't happy with her any more, don't you see?'

Amy glanced at the lawyer; he was staring at the desk, looking embarrassed and worried. 'I have to go,' she told them. 'I need to think.' Breaking away, she threw open the door.

Miriam's voice held her there a moment longer. 'Think about what I'm saying – you'll see it's the truth. Please, Amy!' White-faced and pleading, she was frantic. 'We were just children . . . probably the same age as your little brother and sister. We didn't realise . . . it was such a hard decision.'

Swinging round, Amy looked her in the eye. 'We *all* have to make those,' she murmured. 'Nothing is easy.'

The lawyer looked up. 'I'll be in touch,' she told him. Then, as quickly as she knew how, she ran from that place.

⟶⟩◈⟨⟵

SMILING, THE LAWYER came round the desk to where Fran's daughter stood. Calmly, she slid her arms round his neck. 'Do you think she'll fall for it?' she asked with a cunning smile.

'I think *anyone* would fall for a sob story like that,' he said, drawing her to him. 'You're a good actress. But don't try any tomfoolery with *me*, or you'll be sorry.'

'Why would I want to?' she purred. 'We have a good deal going, don't we?' Stroking the tips of her fingers over his neck, she kissed him full on the mouth. 'I'm told the guest-house will bring a tidy sum. Split between us all we should do very well out of it.'

'That's only *half* the deal,' he reminded her.

'I hadn't forgotten.' Slithering out of his grasp, she crossed the room and locked the door.

By the time she turned round again, he had already taken off his shirt . . .

Chapter Ten

OVER THE NEXT two days, Kelly grew increasingly concerned about Amy. Confiding as much to Luke, she said, 'It's ever since she went to see that lawyer.'

Luke gave a wry little smile. 'It was the reading of a will. When relations gather like vultures, there's bound to be blood spilled.'

Kelly knew it only too well. 'What am I to do if she won't talk about it?'

'Maybe you and Amy are *too* close.'

'In what way?'

'Sometimes, when you're feeling hurt, really deep down, it can be easier to talk with someone you don't know quite so well.'

'I hope you're not suggesting I wouldn't be sympathetic?'

'No, that's just it. You might be *too* sympathetic. Maybe what Amy needs right now is less sympathy and some good old-fashioned talking to.'

'Will *you* talk to her, Luke?' Kelly had tried everything else and Luke was such a kind, understanding man. 'See if you can find out what's playing on her mind. She's unhappy about something, I do know that much.' It wasn't like Amy to mope. Normally she was a bright, cheerful soul, but lately it was as though she had the weight of the world on her shoulders. 'I've got a sneaking suspicion that somebody's trying to talk her out of her inheritance.'

'If she won't discuss it with you, what makes you think she'll do so with me?'

Kelly smiled. 'Because you have a way with you.'

'Cunning, you mean?' Returning her smile, he thought how pretty she looked, with the firelight playing on her hair and lighting her eyes with a warm, fiery sparkle.

Laughing, Kelly tweaked his nose and let him kiss her. Then, at the sound of the front door opening and the chatter of children as they piled into the passage, she clambered up to straighten her skirt. Amidst all the hubbub, she could hear Amy telling Tom and Sally to take off their coats and hang them up.

Bringing a cold rush of night with him, Charlie came through the door. 'Brr!' Rubbing his hands together he made straight for the fire, where he turned his backside to the heat. 'I tell yer what, Kelly lass,' he said with a shiver, 'it's turned bitter out there. I reckon we're in for a frost.' Just then the children came running in and he pointed them out to her. 'Look at their red noses,' he laughed. 'We didn't need no street-lamps . . . we could see for miles!'

Kelly chuckled. 'They're not the only ones with a red nose,' she said. 'Look at your own.' Holding out her arms to the children, she greeted them with a smile. 'Hello, you two! Got a spare cuddle, have you?'

One by one the children threw themselves into her arms, and for a while she held them there, loving every minute. 'Right! Wash your hands,' she ordered. 'When you've done that, Tom, you sit next to Uncle Luke and keep him in order. Sally, you sit between me and Amy.'

Sally's inquisitive face looked up. 'Where will Uncle Charlie sit?'

Kelly said, 'He'll sit on the other side of me, where I can be sure he won't tease and torment you while you're eating your tea.'

'I *like* him teasen and menting,' she said, having difficulty wrapping her tongue round the big words.

Pointing to the kitchen, Kelly used her most authoritative voice: 'Hands . . . washed . . . *now!*' And off they ran, with Tom wanting to know what 'teasen and menting' were supposed to be. 'There's no such words,' he argued.

'Yes, there are,' she replied grandly. 'Kelly said so.'

Throughout the meal, Kelly kept a wary eye on Amy, who seemed deeply preoccupied; the only time she took an interest was when Sally wanted to know if she could 'wear a pretty frock when Kelly and Luke get married.'

'You'd best ask Kelly that, sweetheart.' Amy's lovely

smile seemed spontaneous, but inside she was breaking up.

Taken unawares, Kelly gave Luke a nervous glance. 'If Luke doesn't mind, I'm sure that would be just wonderful,' she said, and Luke agreed.

'It goes without saying,' he answered, 'but we'll have to get Kelly to name the day first.' Looking at Kelly, he seemed to be urging her to say it now.

Instead she stood up. 'We all seem to be finished,' she observed. 'I'll start clearing away.'

Charlie offered to help but was told, 'You're a guest, so behave yourself for once. Just make sure the children don't throttle each other.' Even as she looked, Kelly saw how they were already rolling about the rug in a mock fight. It made her pause; that was how she and Michael used to play, she thought. Even though he was ten years her senior, they had both thoroughly enjoyed tickling and tussling with each other.

Amy followed her to the scullery with a pile of dirty plates. 'Is it all right if I go and sit upstairs for a while?'

Brushing her hand over Amy's forehead, Kelly said, 'Are you all right, love?' Something was gnawing away at her friend, Kelly knew it. 'If there's anything on your mind, we can talk. We always have before.'

Amy thanked her, but said, 'I'm all right, Kelly, honest I am. It's just . . .' Lowering her gaze, she seemed lost for words.

'Amy, look at me.'

She lifted her gaze.

'It's to do with the lawyer, isn't it?' Kelly asked. 'Something was said in that office and it's upset you. I wish you'd tell me. Because if they're trying to bully you into signing away what Fran wanted you to have . . .'

'Nobody was bullying me.'

'What then?'

'I'm just not sure, that's all. Everything's changing, and I don't know what to do.'

Unsure herself, Kelly pursued what she believed to be the root cause of Amy's distress. 'Look, Amy. If Fran went to the trouble of writing you into her will . . . saying how much she loved the children, and how much pleasure they'd given her, then she knew *exactly* what she was doing. It isn't for us, or anyone else, to say it can't be the way Fran wanted it.' Bending her head so as to see Amy's downturned face, she asked tentatively, 'There's something you're *not* telling me, isn't there?'

'I just need time to think, that's all.'

'All right, Amy, but while you're at it, think on what I told you just now. Fran had a right to do with her things whatever she chose, and she wouldn't want you to feel guilty.'

'I know that.'

'Go on then.' Sliding an arm round Amy's shoulders, she walked with her to the door. 'You go and sit upstairs if that's what you want. I'll tell the others you've got a bit of a headache or something.'

She watched Amy walk across the room, and when Luke glanced her way, Kelly nodded towards the door, as if to say, 'Go after her, Luke, talk to her, because I can't.'

He gave a curt little nod, and leaving Charlie playing hide and seek with the children, he followed Amy up the stairs.

Seated on the bed with her back to the door, Amy gazed out of the window. Bathed in the glow from the lamp, with her shoulders hunched and her legs tucked beneath her, she looked like a lonely, lost child.

For what seemed an age Luke stood there, not sure why he had offered to talk to her, or how she would take his interference. For one uncomfortable minute he was tempted to turn away and leave her to her quiet thoughts. Then he remembered his promise to Kelly, and how sad Amy had been all through the meal.

Softly, he closed the door and went forward.

With all manner of things going through her mind, Amy didn't realise he was in her room until he said, 'Is it all right for me to come in, Amy?'

Jolted, she looked up to see who it was. A smile dimpled her face. 'Looks like you're already 'ere, don't it?' she answered.

'Mind if I sit down?'

'Yer might as well.' Suspecting Kelly had sent him, Amy expected him to sit in the stand-chair opposite. When he sat beside her, she asked pointedly, 'Kelly's sent yer to talk to me, is that it?'

He nodded. 'Something like that, yes.'

'There ain't nuthin' I can tell you that I ain't already told Kelly.'

'She's worried about you, Amy. She knows you're hurting, but she doesn't know why.'

Amy looked at him, her eyes already bright with tears. She didn't speak, but when the tears spilled over and her face crumpled with sadness, he took her in his arms. 'Oh Amy,' he whispered, 'if you don't tell me, I can't help. None of us can.'

She buried her face in his neck and the tears fell wet and warm on his skin. Something inside him turned over and he felt like he had never felt before. 'That woman, Fran's daughter, has she threatened to fight you over Fran's will – is that it?'

Amy gave a small laugh. If only it were *just* that, she thought. If only I didn't love you so much.

'Amy?'

'She thinks I'm a gold-digger.'

'Then she doesn't know you.'

'She said I was taking what was rightfully theirs. She said it wasn't her fault that Fran frightened them when they were little, and that they felt safer with their father. She pleaded with me to think about what I was doing, taking Fran's guest-house; that it belonged to them.'

'It sounds to me as if they're playing on your good nature.' With her small, warm body close to his, and her soft, persuasive voice invading his senses, Luke felt a certain danger in staying. But as much as he wanted to, he could not tear himself away.

Suddenly she was looking up at him, and his heart turned somersaults.

It happened so quickly that he couldn't recall the exact moment when he grabbed her to him. Almost without realising, they were in each other's arms, kissing with a fire he had never felt with Kelly. The kisses were long and sensuous; powerful, forbidden feelings rushed through him, of want, self-hatred, and an anger that he had not realised before now. It was emblazoned on his brain like a red-hot brand. *I've loved her all along, and didn't even know it.* Oh God, what now? What now?

Backing off, he took one last long look at her, cradled in his arms, her hair fanned out over his shoulder and her sorry eyes gazing up at him, and he loved her so much it was like a physical pain inside him. Without a word he hurried away, as though the very devil was after him.

When he had gone, Amy sat there, a lonely, solitary figure, eyes closed and her heart breaking. 'Oh Kelly, forgive me. How can I stay now, after what I've done?'

She realised that it wasn't just the business with Fran's will that had been playing on her mind. It was also about Kelly and Luke, and herself. Now, however painful, she knew she had to do the right thing by Kelly. 'Tonight,' she decided. 'I'll do it tonight.'

DOWNSTAIRS, KELLY WAS asking Luke, 'Did she tell you what was wrong?'

'She didn't tell me any more than she told you.' With Amy's kiss still tingling on his lips, he hardly dare look Kelly in the face.

'So we still don't know what was said in that office?' Kelly could think of no other reason for Amy to be so unhappy. 'I've a damned good mind to go round there and find out.' But then she chided herself. 'I can't do that,' she said. 'They would only tell me it's none of my business, and in a way they'd be right.'

'I'm sure Amy will tell you when she's ready.'

'I expect she will, yes.'

A short time later Charlie and Luke prepared to leave.

'See you tomorrow.' At the door Luke kissed Kelly good night. It was a warm, pleasant kiss. After the crippling experience with Stella, Kelly had given him hope for a new life, and he had leaped at the chance; though now he knew he hadn't taken the time to think it through.

Tonight had told him that there were many different kinds of love: the kind Stella knew – demanding and obsessive; the love he felt for Kelly – a kind of all-over love, a need to protect her for the good person she was. And just now, when he had kissed Amy, it was different again. Feeling her in his arms, cradling her to him, he knew a love that tore at his very soul.

He also knew that Amy felt the same way.

And now, God forgive him, he had wronged Kelly, a sweet, darling woman who knew nothing of what had gone on. But she would have to know. At some awful moment, when the truth got too unbearable, he would have to tell her.

❖

LATER THAT EVENING, when the children were in bed and all was quiet, Amy and Kelly sat either side of the fireplace; Amy worked on her pillowcase, while Kelly concentrated on a different, more painstaking task.

'I'm so excited, Amy.' Looking up from her work, Kelly told her, 'This bedspread is my first big order.'

'It's beautiful.' Amy observed the bedspread, with its colourful patchwork squares and pretty lace, and all she could see was Luke and herself, upstairs in that bedroom.

Unaware of Amy's guilty secret, Kelly chatted while she sewed. 'Once the work comes pouring in, and I know it will, we can start to make real plans.'

When Amy made no comment, Kelly glanced up. 'I had thought we might form a kind of partnership,' she confessed. 'You know, when the business was underway and everything. Now, though, what with being left the guest-house, I expect you'll have other plans?'

It would be strange in this house without Amy and the children, Kelly knew that for sure, but it was a wonderful legacy. 'You don't know how thrilled I am to see you set up, Amy,' she said. 'Your own front-door key . . . and a business into the bargain. Fran knew you would look after her little kingdom. It was the saving of her, she told me that time and again. Still, she's left it in safe hands with you.'

Contentedly sewing, she didn't look up. 'I expect you'll be wanting to decorate and such. It goes without saying I'll make your curtains and bed linen, when you've a mind to change them.'

Amy nodded, but she wasn't really listening. Her gaze was deep in the fire, and her mind down the street, with Luke. Then it was here with Kelly, and upstairs with the children, and every now and then the face and voice of Miriam Docherty would haunt her, and it would bring back all the pain of losing Fran. And then she would ask herself the question: was it true what Fran's daughter said, or had Fran been telling the truth when she claimed her children had deserted her in such a cruel way? How could Amy be sure? And who was *she* to judge? Must she believe the daughter to be a liar and a schemer? Or should she doubt Fran's word? It seemed like the worst betrayal.

With so much pulling at her heart-strings, she didn't know which way to turn. More than anything, she ached for Kelly. Tonight, upstairs in that room, she and Luke had betrayed the only friend she ever had.

Kelly sensed her torment and wanted so much to help, but for whatever reason, Amy would not let her near. So she sat and sewed, and turned the bedspread one way then the other. The clock ticked quietly in the background, and the fire grew dimmer, and still Amy sat, silently picking at her work, and never once looking Kelly in the eye.

At half-past nine, Kelly laid the bedspread over the chair and made up the fire. 'I expect I'll be down here for some time yet,' she told Amy. 'Mrs Donaghue is collecting the bedspread at ten tomorrow, and she's bringing that friend of hers for a dress-fitting.' She clapped her hands with delight. 'Oh Amy, it's all coming together at long last! I can't tell you how content I am.' Except for Barney not being here, she thought, and except for the fact that I can't marry Luke and daren't tell him. Kelly knew she would *have* to tell him at some time or another, but the thought of it made her miserable.

Then there was the other thing; Amy. Being as quiet and secretive as she was, she made Kelly nervous. What was she really fretting over, and why wouldn't she talk about it? Was it that she didn't want to live in Fran's house and couldn't bring herself to admit it? Did she intend selling Fran's property and moving away? There was something gnawing at her, about that Kelly had no doubt.

All these things were running through Kelly's mind, giving her some very anxious moments. She couldn't tell which way Amy would decide. Only Amy knew the answers, and for now she wasn't telling.

'Right!' Going to Amy, she stooped to look into her down-turned face. 'How about if I make us a brew?' She hated seeing Amy so quiet; it wasn't at all like her. 'If you're hungry, there's a scone in the larder too.'

Mentally shaking herself, Amy looked up. 'Oh Kelly, I'm sorry. I was miles away.'

Kelly sat on the edge of the chair, and putting her arm round Amy's shoulder, asked gently, 'Why don't you talk to me about what's troubling you? You never know, I might be able to help.'

Amy's smile was half-hearted. 'You're not to worry about me,' she said. 'It's just that, well, all the business with Fran's will and her daughter an' all.' She looked away. 'I need to decide what to do, that's all. Nobody else can do that for me.' The guilt was overwhelming.

Planting a kiss on the top of her head, Kelly gave her a hug. 'You're right,' she said, 'but if you need me, I'll be here. Will you keep that in mind?'

'Thanks, Kelly.' Oh, if she only knew, Amy thought. If Kelly knew what she and Luke had done . . .

'So? Is it tea and a scone, or what?'

'Kelly?'

Pausing on her way to the scullery, Kelly turned. 'What?'

'What would you do if Barney came back?'

Surprised at her question, Kelly answered it with honesty. 'He won't.'

'How can you tell?'

'I just know, that's all.' There was a feeling of loss, a feeling that never again would she find such happiness. 'Barney and I had some good times together, but I always knew he would go, and when he went, I knew just as surely that he wouldn't be back.'

'But what if he *did* come back?'

Kelly thought on that for a minute and a great wave of nostalgia flowed over her. 'He won't come back,' she answered again. 'Barney is a free soul. No woman on earth could keep him in one place for too long.' But *I* did, she thought. And it was heaven.

When her heart grew heavy, she turned away and went about her task. 'Anyway, what brought all this on . . . about Barney, I mean?' With a burst of humour, she chided Amy, 'Fancy dragging up my old boyfriends, when here I am, engaged to be wed. Whatever would Luke say?'

She was still smiling when she returned to the parlour with a tray of goodies; astonished to find Amy on her feet and with her work packed away. 'I'm going to bed,' she told Kelly. 'You don't mind, do you?'

''Course I don't mind.' Putting the tray on the table, Kelly was troubled. 'Amy, are you *sure* you wouldn't rather stay and talk? I'm worried about you.' Taking a deep sigh, she confessed, 'Though she meant well, I wonder if Fran did right in leaving you that guest-house. It seems to have turned your world upside down.'

'It isn't just that.'

'What then?' Thankful that Amy might now share her troubles, Kelly asked, 'Is it to do with your mother . . . your father? Have you an idea one of them might be coming for the children – is that it?'

For a long moment Amy was on the brink of confessing the truth to Kelly . . . that she and Luke had kissed and fondled, and that she loved him so much it was impossible to stay. 'I'm tired, Kelly.' Yet again her courage deserted her. 'Happen I'll feel different after a good night's sleep.'

A moment later she was gone, out of the room and on up the stairs, and Kelly was left standing there, feeling very lonely, 'Good night, God bless, Amy,' she called softly. Closing the door, she returned to her work, but she couldn't concentrate. All she could think of was Amy and how sad she seemed. Half an hour later, she folded away her work and went to bed; it wasn't long before she was fast and hard asleep.

In the next room, Amy was wide awake. Fully dressed, she sat by the window, her eyes on the night sky, her heart with Luke.

She heard Kelly come upstairs and waited until all was quiet again. Then she took out her portmanteau and packed a few things. When that was done, she found paper and pen and sat down at the dressing table to write:

Dearest Kelly,

I know when you read this letter you will find it as hard to understand as I find to write it.

No one was ever kinder to me than you, and I will always love you like the sister I never had. I want you always to remember that.

These last few days I've not felt happy, and you were

right when you thought it might be because Fran left me the guest-house. I feel as if I'm doing wrong in accepting her wonderful gift, especially when she had children of her own. I know they were not there when she needed them, and I'm not sure of the truth about all that. All I do know is that I have no right to take what isn't rightfully mine. I could never enjoy it.

You were right, too, when you thought there might be something else on my mind. There is. But you can't help me, Kelly, no one can. Like I said, it's something I have to work out myself.

Don't worry about me or the children. We'll be all right.

I wish you well with your business, and like Fran said, you'll do well with it. I worried about leaving you in the lurch, but when that young girl came to the door, I knew you would be all right.

God bless you, Kelly. I hope one day we'll meet again. Thank you for everything.

Have a wonderful wedding, and be happy.

Amy.

xxx

Amy also wrote another, much briefer letter. It was addressed to the lawyer. Dated and signed, it declared that she now declined her legacy, mainly because, 'If Fran had lived, I'm sure she would want to be reunited with her children. Then, there would be no question of her leaving the house to anyone but her own family, and that's how it should be.'

When the letter was written, Amy felt a great weight was lifted from her. Meaning to deliver it that very day, she slid it into her pocket.

Softly, she went through to the children's room. Gently waking them, she ssh'ed them to silence and got them dressed quickly. 'Where are we going?' Sally rubbed her sleepy eyes. 'Where's Kelly?'

'Kelly's asleep, that's why we have to be very, very quiet.'

'Isn't she coming with us?'

'No. Kelly's happy here, sweetheart.'

Tom was difficult. 'I want to stay here. Charlie's my friend.'

'Ssh!' Putting her finger to her lips, Amy played a bluff, praying it would work. 'All right. You get back into bed. Sally and I have to go now.'

It worked. 'NO! I'm coming too.'

'*Ssh!*'

Quickly, Tom pulled on his clothes and helped Amy stuff his spare things into the portmanteau. 'Mind that creaky stair halfway down.' Amy ushered them before her, intermittently glancing back to Kelly's room, her eyes wet with unshed tears, and her heart heavy as her boots.

Leaving them outside the parlour door with a warning to be 'quiet as mice', Amy propped the letter against the plant-pot in the centre of the table, where Kelly was bound to see it. 'Sorry, sweetheart,' she whispered. 'I can't see no other way.'

After making agonising progress on tiptoes, they emerged on to the street, where Amy softly closed the door. 'You weren't really going without me, were you, Amy?' Tom looked up at her with sorry eyes.

''Course not.' Stooping to take her little brother in her arms, Amy confessed, 'I would never leave you. *Never!*'

His smile enveloped her. 'I knew that all along,' he said bravely.

'I'm glad.'

Wagging a finger, he laughed. 'You tricked me!'

'Ssh! Quiet now, Tom.'

Turning towards the town, the little trio huddled together against the cold night air. 'When will we come back?' Tom wanted to know.

When Amy replied truthfully that she didn't know if they ever would, Sally began crying and Amy had to pacify her.

With Sally crying in her arms and Tom carrying the portmanteau like the little man he was, Amy knew there would never be a moment when she would hate herself more than she did right now.

———❦———

K ELLY WOKE WITH a bad feeling.

Outside, the postman whistled on his merry

way. The milkman's horse could be heard clopping along the cobbles, and through the morning came the hoot of a factory whistle. But there was something not right, Kelly thought; something in the house was not as it should be. The house was too quiet; there was no sound from the children's room, and no clattering of teacups downstairs.

'Tom! Sally!' Still in her nightie, Kelly came out of her room. Noticing Amy's door was wide open, she went along the landing at a quickening pace. A fleeting glance told her there was no one inside; the bedclothes were crumpled but not turned back. 'She didn't sleep after all,' Kelly groaned. 'Oh, Amy! Why ever didn't you wake me?'

'AMY!' Raising her voice, she ran along the landing. Coming to the children's room, she looked inside. Here, the evidence of bedclothes tossed to one side suggested that they, too, were up and about. 'TOM! SALLY! Where the devil *is* everyone?'

Barefoot and with only her nightie to keep out the biting cold, Kelly ran down the stairs. At the parlour door some kind of sixth sense made her pause. She glanced around. Everything was exactly as she had left it the night before. 'Amy?' She swallowed hard, a terrible suspicion creeping up on her.

Just then, her frantic eyes came to the letter tucked beside the plant-pot. 'Gone out, has she?' She plucked out the letter with trembling hands. 'I expect she's gone to see the lawyer.' Tearing open the letter, she began to read, and as she did so she felt the strength go from her legs. 'Oh, Amy!' Falling heavily into the chair, she clutched the letter to her, folding it into her fist and wondering at the state of Amy's mind for her to do such a thing.

When the shock of Amy's going sank in, she read the letter again. When she had finished, she laid it on the table before her, looking at it for what seemed an age. Then she laid her head on her arms and sobbed like a child. Amy had gone and taken the children with her, that was all she could think. Amy had not trusted her enough, and left. Just like Barney had left. Now all that remained was Luke, a fine man, who would stay long after everyone else had gone.

Half an hour later, Kelly was dressed and outside. First she walked the length of the street, up and down, and halfway round the block. She walked to the tram-stop, and asked every passerby: 'Have you seen a young woman with two children – a boy and a girl?' The answer was always the same. 'Sorry, miss. I ain't seen no one like that.'

She took the tram into Blackburn town and searched the boulevards. There was no sign of Amy anywhere. Weary and disheartened, she caught the tram back, her eager eyes looking through the window, searching every inch of the route. Still she could not understand it. 'Oh Amy, what made you leave like that? Why didn't you confide in me?' The tram was empty now; there was no one to hear her save for the conductor, who gave her a wary look.

Right now, Kelly was confused and hurting; hurting for Amy, hurting for herself. For the life of her she couldn't imagine what had taken hold of Amy to go off like that, so suddenly, like a thief in the night.

Later though, she would come to wonder about the real reason for Amy's leaving. When the truth began to dawn, as it surely would, she would vow to turn heaven and earth inside out to find her young friends and bring them home.

⟵⟶⊙⟵⟶

LUKE WAS SHOCKED. 'What do you mean she's gone?' 'Gone. Taken the children and *gone!*' Kelly had a mind to go and see the lawyer, but Charlie dissuaded her. 'You can't do that, lass. Amy's a grown woman. She can leave or stay as she pleases. She wouldn't thank you for tracing her through the lawyer, and anyway, if he's worth his salt, he wouldn't give out any information. It's against their policy.' He shook his head forlornly. 'Still an' all, I can't believe Amy would just up and go like that. It must have been something powerful worrying to make her do such a thing.'

Luke sat by the table, head in hands and saying very little. 'What do you think, Luke?' Kelly urged. 'Where might she go? Last night, when you tried to talk with her, did she give you any idea at all about what might be worrying her?'

Luke slowly shook his head from side to side, his

mind in turmoil at the news of Amy's going. 'She told me nothing,' he answered. He thought of the way she had looked at him, and he knew why she had left. Amy was as much in love with him as he was with her, and neither of them had the guts to tell Kelly the truth. That was why Amy had gone, and it made him doubly ashamed.

'I have to find her, Luke.' Kelly was beside herself. 'If only to satisfy myself that she's all right.'

'We'll find her,' he promised.

Because, God help him, he knew he would not rest until he had Amy back again.

PART THREE

BARNEY

Chapter Eleven

'I THINK IT´s time you went home, matey.' The barman had no quarrel with the customer. He paid good money and seemed an amiable enough sort, but right now he'd had too much to drink. 'You've had enough,' he told the man. 'You'd do well to go home and sleep it off.'

The man smiled, showing a beautiful set of straight white teeth. 'You could be right,' he said. 'Only, you see, it might be difficult for me to go home.'

'Oh, and why's that?'

''Cause I haven't *got* a home to go to.'

Sidling up alongside of him the young woman nudged his elbow. 'You mean to say a handsome fella like you hasn't got a woman to take care of him?' Tall and slim, with long dark hair, she was extraordinarily attractive.

The man turned, his kind eyes smiling. 'And have you got no man to take care of you?' he asked mischievously.

She shook her head. 'It seems we're on our own, you and me.'

'Seems that way.' Reaching out, he casually shifted a strand of dark hair from across her eye. 'What's your name?'

'Jackie. Short for Jacqueline.' Leaning forward, she pushed his pint of ale away. 'And what name do *you* go by?'

He held out his hand and she shook it. 'The name's Barney,' he said, 'and according to your barman, I'm too drunk to stand up.'

She gave him a naughty, knowing smile. 'You're not, are you,' she murmured, 'too drunk to "stand up"?' Her lewd meaning was all too clear.

He looked away. 'I'd best be going.' Digging into his pocket he drew out a collection of coins which he threw on the counter. 'Give this lovely lady a drink,' he told the barman, 'and don't show her the door because she's doing no harm.' He winked at her. 'She's just a bit lonely . . . like me.'

As he turned to go, she caught hold of his sleeve. 'You don't have to be lonely. We could go somewhere, get to know each other. What do you say?' Behind the smile was a sadness that tugged at his heart-strings.

'It's a tempting offer,' he told her, 'but I'll say no, and hope not to offend you.' Calling Kelly's face to mind, he smiled. 'Only, I've a way to go and someone to see. I've been away too long, and now I think it's time I made an honest woman of her.'

'She's a lucky woman.'

'No.' Taking out his wallet, he withdrew a crisp new note. '*I'm* the lucky one.' Shoving the note into her hand, he said, 'If she'll have me back, that is.'

The young woman gazed at him longingly. Here was a man she would have followed to the ends of the earth. 'What's her name?'

Her name fell to his lips, and when he spoke it his heart glowed. 'Her name is Kelly,' he said, 'the kindest, warmest soul on God's earth.'

Seeing the love in his eyes, she knew he was already lost to her. 'If *she* doesn't want you, there's always me.'

Grabbing her fist, he made sure she had the note tight. 'Don't do this.' Gesturing to the group of men in the corner he told her softly, 'You have it in you to do better for yourself.'

She watched him go, and suddenly she was lonelier than ever. When, a moment later, one of the men came over and offered to take her upstairs, she looked at him, at the sneer on his face and the hungry look in his eye, and suddenly she saw how sordid and empty her life was. 'You can do better for yourself', that's what he'd said, and he was right.

'Sorry,' she told him. 'I don't do that any more.'

Peeved, he made a grab for her. There was a scuffle and suddenly all hell was let loose. Two of his pals came rushing to help him; several customers threw their weight behind the young woman, and it took the barman to sort it out. 'And don't show your faces in here again!'

Slamming the door on them, he turned to the woman, who was shocked and bruised. 'You asked for that,' he told her. 'You can't lead a man on, then slap him down without there being trouble.'

'I'm sorry.' Trying to hold the top of her blouse from falling away, she walked to the door. 'I won't trouble you again.'

'Hey!'

'Oh, I expect you want me to pay for the broken glasses?' Holding out the note she had kept tight, she told him, 'This is all I have, but you're welcome to it.'

Taking a deep sigh he shook his head. 'Keep your money,' he told her. 'I dare say you need it more than I do.'

She looked at him in disbelief. 'I'm sorry about what happened,' she murmured, 'but I won't trouble you again.'

Observing her now, he thought what a beauty she was, and how she had demeaned herself. 'You haven't been on the streets long, have you?'

'How could you tell?'

'I've been a landlord long enough to know a scrubber when she walks in . . . and you don't fit the bill, that's all.'

'Family troubles,' she said. 'I had to leave, or kill somebody.'

'Who?'

'My stepmother.'

'And you've no other family?'

'No, but I'll manage. I'll find a job and a decent life. That man . . .' They both knew who she meant. 'He told me I could do better for myself, and he was right.'

He looked at her torn clothes and her bruised face and thought of his own daughter, happily wed, with a son and a home to be proud of. 'How old are you?'

'Nineteen.'

'There's a room back there if you want to tidy yourself.'

'I'd like that.'

'Through the bar, then first left.'

Thanking him, she made her way across the room. 'I won't be long,' she promised. 'As soon as I've made myself decent, I'll be on my way.'

'That would be a mean way to repay my generosity.'

Swinging round she stared at him. 'You bastard!'

Wagging a finger, he chided, 'There'll be no swearing, and no making eyes at the men.'

'What are you talking about?'

'You reckon you could do better than walking the streets and I'm offering you the chance. I need someone to help me behind the bar. Since I lost my wife last year it's been difficult. I've had a string of barmaids and none of 'em any good.'

'What!' As the truth dawned, she laughed out loud. 'You're asking *me* to be your barmaid?'

'If you're interested. You'll be paid a decent wage. There's a room above if you want it, or a room in the boarding-house across the street. Either way, it don't matter to me, as long as you're behind this bar when I open of a morning.'

For a long, wonderful moment she stood there, unable to believe he was really trying to help and not out for what he could get. Here was her chance, and she would take it with open arms. 'A decent wage,' he'd said, and a room of her own. It was the start she'd been looking for. *'Am I interested!'* Running across the room, she flung her arms round his podgy neck. 'Oh, thank you! Thank you!'

'None o' that!' Shoving her away he turned her in the direction of the wash-room. 'Go and make yourself look decent,' he said. 'Then I think we'd best find you a bob or two to go out and buy some decent clothes. I'm not having you dressed like a tart, not behind *my* bar.'

As she went to clean herself up, the man looked towards the window. In the distance he could see Barney climbing into a cab. 'You're a good man,' he muttered. 'I hope you find your woman, wherever she is.'

Chapter Twelve

'MARIE WILSON?' THE paper-boy shook his head. 'Never heard of her. But I've only been here a week, so I don't know everybody yet, and anyway, I only do half the village. Billy Ruff does the other half, an' he's gone fishing.' Pointing to the corner shop, he said, 'Jack Todd might know the lady you're after. He owns the shop and he's lived here all his life – so he tells me. He's a miserable old git, throw you out his shop soon as look at you. But if *he* don't know this Marie Wilson, nobody will.'

Barney thanked him for his time and gave him a sixpence. Looking towards the shop he could see a queue of customers waiting to be served by the sour-faced man behind the counter. 'I don't suppose you could ask him for me, could you? I was thinking I might have a bite to eat in that little café over there.' He gestured to a pretty bay-windowed café set by the edge of the river. 'I've come a long way and don't relish the idea of standing in a queue. Get me the information and it's worth another tanner.' His back ached, his feet ached, and there were blisters on his hands where he'd carried his belongings with him. He didn't mind admitting, if he didn't get to sit down soon, he'd *fall* down.

The boy was tempted, though in the end fear overcame greed. He knew the consequences if he was late delivering the papers yet again. 'Better not,' he said. 'You don't know old Toddy! I bet he's watching me right now, and thinking up some awful punishment for when I get back. No, it's more than my job's worth, mister.' Muttering how he was already late, and how Jack would have his guts for garters if he didn't get on, he mounted his bike and rode away.

Barney looked longingly at the café, then at the shop and its queue of customers. It wasn't hard to decide. With Kelly strong in his mind, he strode across the road and into the shop. 'Excuse me!' Going straight to the counter, he leaned over to the man serving. 'I wonder if you could help me? I've just arrived in West Bay, and I'm looking for—'

'I don't care *what* you're looking for!' Glaring at him, Jack Todd flicked his arm in the air. 'Get to the back of the queue and wait your turn.'

Barney thought he might get more civility from the customers, but when he turned to smile at them, fourteen pairs of eyes glared back. 'Shame on you!' One woman spoke for all. 'Do you think we're queuing for the fun of it? You'll have to wait like everyone else here.' It seemed the man's bad temper had rubbed off on his customers.

'Well, excuse me!' Thinking his best bet was to ask in the café, where they might be more inclined to help, Barney made his way there.

'Bacon, sausage, two eggs, fried bread and a mug of piping hot tea, if you please.' The smell of cooking filled his nostrils and revived him. 'A *large* mug of tea,' he emphasised, 'the largest you've got.' Settling himself in the chair, he set down his heavy bag and looked round; the place was small and pretty, with blue curtains at the window and vases filled with roses on the windowsill. Somehow it reminded him of Kelly.

'Not like the shop over the road, is it,' he commented when the girl brought his tea. 'Thank God, there's only me and you, and not one Jack Todd in sight.'

The girl laughed out loud. 'Oh! You've met him, have you?'

'You could say that, miss.' He couldn't help but laugh with her. 'Once met never forgotten, eh?'

'He's a bad-tempered old devil,' she apologised. 'The only one you'll find like that here,' she promised. 'The rest of us are friendly enough.'

'I'm looking for someone – a lady, late sixties maybe. Her name's Marie Wilson.'

'No good asking me. I live the winter in Bridport with my dad, and the summer in Weymouth with my mum. I work here weekends, and one day in the week, when Mrs Johnson has to go out on business.'

'Good grief! You *do* live an interesting life!'

The girl's smile vanished. 'Interesting or not, I'd give everything for my mam and dad to be together so I could get on with my own life.'

Barney nodded. 'I can see what you mean,' he said. 'I'm sorry.'

'It's all right, you weren't to know.' She took a liking to him. 'Anyway, this woman you're after . . .'

'Marie Wilson.'

'I'll ask the cook, but I don't think she'll be much help because she keeps herself to herself. The poor old thing hardly ever goes out. She spends her days in the kitchen and her nights up in her room.'

'I'd be grateful if you'd ask her all the same.'

'I will, and if *she* doesn't know her, Mrs Johnson will.'

'Why not ask her instead then?'

'Because she's out. Remember, I already told you . . . I only come here weekdays, when she's out on business.'

'Silly me.' He was beginning to think he might be going crazy. 'And when will she be back, do you think?'

'By the time you've finished your breakfast, I shouldn't wonder.'

'I'll tell you what.' Leaning forward, Barney dropped his voice to an intimate whisper. 'Let's *not* ask the poor old cook. Let's wait until the famous Mrs Johnson comes back. Meanwhile, I'll just enjoy my breakfast, then there'll be no time lost.'

'Good idea.'

When she went away, he covered his face with his hands to smother a rise of laughter. 'Oh, Kelly! Kelly!' he chuckled. 'I hope it won't be too long before I find you. But when I do, oh, I've many a tale that'll bring a smile to your pretty face.'

Just then his breakfast came; a feast of a meal for a starving man. 'And another mug of tea,' he requested. After trudging the road for many a long mile, he had a raging thirst on him.

He tucked into the meal with relish and, as he warmed his tummy, his heart was warmed too. Up until now, he had searched in so many corners for Kelly; at her old house in Bedford, then round the neighbourhood, but no one knew where she had gone.

Just when he thought he must give up, he searched his mind and came up with a name: 'West Bay' in Dorset. Kelly had told him it was her mother's favourite place, and though it was a slim chance, he had nothing else to go on. Now, for some inexplicable reason, he had a really good feeling that when Mrs Johnson returned, she would lead him straight to Kelly's mother and, God willing, she in turn might lead him to his darling Kelly. Then his arduous searching would not have been in vain.

❦

U NAWARE THAT SHE was being watched, Marie could hear the boy's excited chatter. He wasn't talking directly to her, but chatting about the fish and the sea, and how he and his grandad went out one day and came back with a whole bucketful of fish which lasted them a week. Marie nodded and smiled, but his chatter made no demands on her; which was just as well, because her attention was elsewhere.

Lost in her thoughts, she let her quiet gaze reach out over the sea; the gentle waves rose and dipped, lulling her into a nostalgic mood, and, as always, her thoughts turned to her daughter. What is she doing right now? she wondered. Is she thinking of me? Will she get in touch with me? Will I ever see her again? The idea of never seeing Kelly again was unbearable.

Suddenly aware of someone tugging at her sleeve, she looked up. 'What is it, sweetheart?' The boy had been talking to her and she hadn't even heard him.

'I had a fish on the end of my line, but it got away.'

'Never mind. I'm sure you'll catch another one soon.' She looked at the boy with his big eyes and innocent face and he reminded her of Kelly. 'You're not cold, are you?' Feeling his arm, she satisfied herself that he was comfortable.

'Were you thinking of your little girl again?'

'Was it that obvious?' She had a smile uncannily like Kelly's.

'You miss her, don't you?'

Marie nodded. 'Yes, Sammy,' she admitted, 'I miss her very much.'

'Marie?'

'Yes, sweetheart?'

'Your little girl's not dead, is she?'

'Oh, no!' Dear God! His innocent question turned her heart over. 'She's not so little any more either. She was little when I saw her last, but now she's a grown woman.'

He appeared not to be listening. With his next statement she knew why. 'My mummy and daddy . . . they're dead, aren't they?'

Taking his small hand into hers she answered truthfully as always. 'Yes, sweetheart, but their love is still alive . . . in you.'

'Grandad says they're in heaven, and only good people go to heaven.'

'Your grandad is right.'

'I want you to be my grandma.'

'I hope I am.'

'If you and Grandad got married, you'd be my *proper* grandma.'

Marie smiled. 'I'll bet your grandad told you that, did he?'

'He said it's a very serious matter when two people get married, and they have to love each other very much.'

'He's right again.'

'Do you love him very much?'

Feeling cornered, she hugged him to her. 'I love *you* very much,' she laughed. 'As for your grandad . . . I think I might have a word or two to say to him!'

From a short distance away, Bill watched her every move.

In a plain white shift and big straw hat, her slim, tanned figure belied her age. The only tell-tale sign that she was no longer in the first flush of youth was the long, greying plait peeping from beneath her hat and hanging down to her waist. Seated on the low bench, with her bare legs dangling over the end of the jetty and with fishing tackle scattered at her feet, Marie was like a young thing, carefree and happy. To those who did not know her, she might not have had a worry in the world.

The way she looked, the way she threw back her head when she laughed . . . that deep, warm smile in her brown eyes whenever she gazed on him. Ever since he first set eyes on her he had loved her. She and the boy meant everything in the world to him.

'I bet she was a good-looker in her time.'

Startled, Bill swung round. 'Arnold! I didn't see you there.'

Plump and balding, Arnold Hale had run the local Post Office for as long as most people could remember. 'I've lived here for twenty years,' he went on, 'and I know everything about everybody in West Bay, but not her.' He gestured to Marie. 'I don't mind telling you, she's got me baffled. She never receives a letter or a parcel, and as far as I can tell, never sends one away.'

Like most people here, Bill had no liking for the nosy fellow. 'I wouldn't know about that,' he said cuttingly. 'After all, it isn't my business, is it?'

Realising he was not welcome, the man hoisted his rucksack tighter to his shoulder and readied himself to move on. 'Mind you,' he confessed, 'this place has come alive since she moved in. Attractive lady, on her own, and wealthy too by the looks of it. Always bound to raise a few eyebrows, if you know what I mean.'

'No, I can't say I do.'

'Right, well.' Turning aside, the man made his way to the foot of the jetty. 'It's half-day,' he explained. 'I've shut up shop and I'm off to do a spot o' fishing.' Glancing up to where Marie and the boy were talking, he moaned, 'I hope them two chatterboxes don't frighten the fish away.'

As the postmaster negotiated his way to the end of the jetty, Bill frowned. 'Nosy bugger!'

He wasn't surprised at the curiosity surrounding Marie, however. Nobody but himself knew of her past and, God willing, nobody ever would. It was true, she *had* caused a stir when she moved into this small, tight-knit community and, being a private person who confided in no one, the locals soon grew inquisitive. Now, after almost three years of being amongst them, Marie remained a mystery. She smiled and passed the time of day; they watched her come and go, and brushed shoulders with her at every turn. But no one really knew her. Not even the boy who was her constant companion.

Bill knew her more than most, and though he didn't know the whole of it, she had confided in him as a friend. Though she rarely spoke of what had happened some thirty-three years ago, Bill suspected that even now, behind the laughter, her heart was quietly breaking.

Deep in thought, he hadn't realised Marie and the boy had made their way back. 'Penny for them?' Marie was surprised to see him there.

'Aw, I were just thinking about this damned heat.' Blowing out his cheeks, he took off his peaked cap and wiped the palm of his hand over his hair. 'It's more like August than November. Two weeks and no rain . . . it's not good.'

Marie had to agree. 'It's no wonder they're calling it a "freak June".' With a ready smile, she declared, 'Mustn't complain though. I expect the rains will come soon, and then we'll be moaning. There's no pleasing us, that's the trouble.' Looking from one to the other, she teased, 'I don't suppose anybody here would like an ice cream?'

Samuel hopped up and down. 'Me! I'd like an ice cream.'

Bill's throat was parched. 'I'll have a shandy if it's all the same to you . . . and it's my treat.' When she seemed about to protest, he gave her a narrowed glance. '*My* treat, or I don't come.' She was such an independent soul. He supposed that was the result of her hard background.

As they walked across the bridge to the café, Barney stood aside to let them pass. 'Thank you.' Each unaware of the other's identity, they exchanged smiles and went on their way.

'What were you really thinking about back there,

when Samuel and I surprised you?' She gave Bill a sideways glance. 'It looked to me like you had something serious on your mind.'

'Well, you were wrong,' he lied. It wouldn't do for her to know what he had been thinking. Feeling uncomfortable beneath her curious gaze, he turned his attention to Samuel. 'Well?' Ruffling the boy's hair he asked, 'Any luck with the fishing?'

The boy shook his head. 'Only a tiddler . . . but it got away.'

Inside the café, they ordered two strawberry ice creams and a shandy. 'No strawberry left.' The girl wetted the end of her pencil and poised to write. 'There's vanilla or raspberry, and that's all.'

Marie looked about. 'No Mrs Johnson today?'

'She's helping Cook in the kitchen. We've got a big party coming for dinner and she's panicking a bit.'

'I'll have vanilla. What do you want, Samuel?'

'Raspberry, please, with a wafer.'

They had been in there ten minutes and were just starting to enjoy their treat when a red-faced Mrs Johnson came out looking for the girl. 'I thought I asked you to get the best wine glasses out of the cupboard. And see if you can remember where you put the red table-cloths.' Casting an eye round the room she saw there were only six customers and all served. 'We're not too busy now,' she observed. 'Run along and see to it while you've a chance.'

Making faces behind the older woman's back, the girl

scurried away. 'Good afternoon, Mrs Wilson.' Having caught sight of Marie and her friends, Mrs Johnson came over. 'There was a man asking after you earlier,' she explained. 'He seemed an honest sort, so I told him where you lived. I hope I did right?'

Marie sat up. 'A man . . . asking after *me*?' Fear rippled through her. Who could it be? She didn't know of anyone who might be looking for her. 'What was he like?'

'Good-looking in a quiet sort of way, I suppose. Late thirties, early forties. He was carrying a large bag of the kind sailors use.'

While Marie tried to think who it might be, Bill addressed Mrs Johnson in a severe tone. 'You should never give people's addresses away without their knowledge,' he said. 'It was very wrong of you.'

When she began fussing and apologising, Marie took charge of the situation. 'It's all right, don't worry,' she told the woman. In truth she agreed with Bill, but thought Mrs Johnson had enough to worry about for now.

Regretting her hasty action in sending the man to where Marie lived, Mrs Johnson said she would have the girl bring the bill.

Marie was troubled. As far as she could tell, it could only be one of two people . . . the private investigator she had used to keep a track on Kelly and Michael, or Michael himself. But how could he have found her? The lawyer was under strict instructions never to give her whereabouts to anyone.

As they made their way up the hill, with Samuel skipping ahead, she confided all of this to Bill. 'The lawyer was to send me information on anyone wanting to know where I am. That way, I would be in control.'

'Do you *want* it to be Michael?'

'I'm not sure.' Memories flooded back.

Michael had protected her when she was in danger of being beaten to within an inch of her life. 'I had hoped he might have had the courage to answer my letter through the lawyer, but he didn't, and I suppose I'm not surprised. What he did put me in prison for a very long time, but if he hadn't done it, I probably wouldn't be here now.' A kind of quietness came over her. 'I'm never sure what to think about Michael, but I do owe him that much.'

'You don't owe anyone anything.' Bill had never met Michael, but from what Marie had told him over these past years, he felt the boy had killed his father in a rage; not only for his mother's sake, but for his own too. 'Michael freed you, yes, but he freed himself too. He also let you be imprisoned for something he did.' To Bill that was the worst thing of all.

'*I* made him keep silent about what happened.' Torn two ways, she spoke her mind. 'There have been times when I've wondered about him. He took a life, you see, and I find that hard to come to terms with. Oh, I know he was driven by fear and hatred, but somehow that only makes it worse. All those years when I was locked away, I kept asking myself, why didn't I take the children away? Why didn't I kill that monster myself? Why did I let it go on to such a terrible end?'

She looked at him, her face a picture of suffering. '*That's* why it was right for me to be locked away. I deserved to be punished. And Michael? I don't know what to think. He has a cowardly streak – I saw that in him when he was tiny. But a mother overlooks that in her child, don't you think?' She smiled wistfully. 'Even if somewhere deep down she wishes it wasn't like that. She might not respect him, but she can't stop loving him.'

The guilt would never leave her. 'Maybe it wasn't his father who did that to him. Maybe, in some way, it was me, for putting up with the beatings and staying too long.'

As they pushed on up the hill, he glanced at her, thinking what a courageous and wonderful woman she was. She had been through so much, and yet found it within herself to forgive those who had put her through it. To his mind, a man should face the consequences of his actions. Michael was wrong not to take the blame and pay the price. He should never have let his mother be put in prison, however willing she was to do it. But he respected her feelings and her love for her children. Because of that, and his own love for her, he would never tell Marie how he really felt about Michael.

Marie lived right at the top of the hill; from here she could see the whole of West Bay. The house had been derelict when she found it. Now, after spending a respectable part of the money left her by the wealthy late husband she had married shortly after coming out of prison, she had restored the house to its former glory. Surrounded by vast gardens, it was like her own little paradise.

Barney thought it the most beautiful place he had ever seen. 'By! Whoever would have thought Kelly's mother lived in a grand place like this?' For a time he had wondered if he'd come to the wrong house, but on asking a neighbour he was curtly told, 'Mrs Wilson is a very private woman.' He knew then that he was in the right place. Kelly's mother, like Kelly herself, had never changed her surname. In fact, she had reverted to it after her second husband's death, as a way of feeling closer to her children.

So he sat on the step and waited.

When, a short time later, she came through the gate, he stood up to greet her, his curious gaze searching for a likeness to Kelly. What he saw was Kelly in years to come; a woman of quiet beauty, with a smile that would never age, and the eyes . . . oh yes, she had a look of Kelly.

As she came closer, his heart yearned for the woman he loved. 'I'm Barney,' he told her. 'I've been searching for Kelly. A man called Jack Denby delivered her belongings from Bedford town, where she had been living, to some other place, but I couldn't find him. A neighbour told me his uncle had died and left him a farm and property. Nobody knew exactly where it was.' With stricken eyes he searched her face. 'I have to find Kelly,' he murmured. 'You're my only hope.'

Contented, she smiled. 'Barney . . . Oh yes, I should have known. But how did you find me?'

'I remembered Kelly speaking of your love for West Bay.'

Turning, Marie gestured to Bill that it was all right for him to take the boy home. 'It's a friend of Kelly's,' she said. 'We'll talk later.' Then, addressing Barney, she said, 'You'd best come inside. Before I can help you, if at all, I need to be sure of you.'

'I know what you mean and I understand.' Suspecting she knew more about him than he knew himself, Barney told her truthfully, 'I've learned my lesson. My wandering days are over. Now all I want is to find Kelly and ask her to be my wife.'

Brushing past him, Marie gestured for him to follow.

Sure in his heart that he would find Kelly, he followed her inside the house. 'I know I should never have left,' he said regretfully.

And, for Kelly's sake, Marie agreed.

Chapter Thirteen

FOR KELLY, EVERY day was like a year. She got up in the morning, went to bed at night, and in between worked her fingers to the bone. She searched her memory constantly, desperately trying to recall every word Amy had said, so she might discover where she'd gone, and who Amy had known before she came to live with her.

Nothing came to mind, and now several weeks had passed, a lonely Christmas, too, and there was still no sign of Amy and the children.

'Ouch!' the fat lady squealed. 'That's twice you've pricked me with your needle!'

Apologising, Kelly helped her down from the stool. 'I'm sorry, Mrs Kenyon,' she said. 'It's this new thimble . . . it keeps slipping off my finger.' That was a lie. It was Amy in her thoughts that made her lose concentration.

'For goodness sakes, get yourself another thimble then, before you do somebody an injury.' Stooping, she rubbed the offended ankle. 'How much longer before the dress is finished?'

Kelly helped her slip out of the dress; a long, swishing creation in crimson, it made Mrs Kenyon look very stout indeed. 'I still think a straighter skirt would suit you better,' Kelly suggested for the umpteenth time. 'And slimmer sleeves, down to the wrist, instead of just below the elbow. It would be so much more flattering to your figure.' Mrs Kenyon's 'figure' was already ample enough, without exaggerating it.

A good-natured soul, Mrs Kenyon saw through Kelly's discreet suggestion. 'I know I'm fat,' she acknowledged, 'and I know you could disguise the fact if I wanted you to, but the truth is, I don't see being fat as being ugly. My late husband always used to say he liked to feel he had a real armful of woman. Besides, this dress is so beautiful, how could I not want to wear it?' Touching the crimson dress, she sighed, 'I've got more money than I know what to do with, and a circle of people I call friends, but none of that is important. I'd change it all tomorrow for what you have here . . . this little house which you've made so pretty, it's a pleasure coming here. And you have *real* friends . . . neighbours who come into your home and care for you like family.'

Kelly smiled. 'You mean Charlie and Luke?'

'*Everyone* I know who's met you has a good word to say about you. You're a kind young woman, and you have such talent.' Sighing wistfully, she went on, 'I've tried dress-makers who charge the earth and produce rubbish. None of them can hold a candle to you, my dear. Look at this beautiful dress, for instance . . . every stitch lovingly done, and when it's finished there won't be a dress in the whole of Blackburn to match it.'

Flattered, Kelly thanked her. 'I do my best.'

'Oh, don't be so modest! If I had talent like yours, I'd shout it from the rooftops!' Lifting her purse from her bag, she took out a florin and placed it on the table.

'You don't have to do that,' Kelly protested. 'The dress won't be ready for another week. I won't be asking you for any money until then.'

'Oh, it's not towards payment on the dress.' Mrs Kenyon pulled on her blouse and did the front buttons up. 'It's a little thank you.' Putting on her jacket she prepared to leave. 'When I attend the charity ball in that dress, I know every woman in the room will envy me. That's worth a florin or two, don't you think?'

Kelly thanked her. 'I'll see you the same time next Friday.'

'I have a mid-afternoon appointment. Could we make it four-thirty, instead of five?'

Kelly checked her appointment book. 'Yes, that'll be fine. See you then.' Walking her to the front door, Kelly bade her goodbye.

'Goodbye, my dear, and don't work too hard. I noticed you're looking a little tired.' And before Kelly could answer, she was in her carriage and away.

'I wish they were all like you,' Kelly murmured as she waved her off. 'Sometimes I'd like to chuck the buggers in the canal. Moaning and complaining, whatever you do to please.'

Inside the parlour, she took a few minutes to clear away. Glancing at the clock, she groaned, 'Quarter-past six.' With no other customers due, it promised to be another long evening.

When the tidying up was done, she reached up to the mantelpiece and took down a long brass jar. Going to the table, she took off the lid and poured the contents on to the table-cloth; a cascade of florins and shillings flowed out. 'Look at that, Amy,' she whispered. 'There's four guineas in there, hard-earned little thank yous from grateful clients. *And* there's money in the bank account that's not already owed.' It was such a shame Amy wasn't part of it all. 'At long last it's coming good, but you're not here to share it.'

Dropping the florin into the jar, she then replaced it on the mantelpiece. 'It's yours, Amy,' she said. 'Yours and the children's. I'll keep it safe for when you get back.'

'You're so sure she's coming back, aren't you?'

Swinging round, Kelly chided him. 'Luke! You startled me. I didn't hear you come in.'

Striding across the room, he put his hands on her shoulders and kissed her gently on the cheek. 'It could have been *anybody* coming in,' he chided. 'You left the door open.'

Surprised, Kelly told him, 'I was sure I'd closed it.'

'Happen I'll check the lock before I leave.'

Leading her to a chair, he suggested, 'You sit down while I put the kettle on.' Fondly stroking her face, he observed, 'You look tired, my love. You're working too hard.'

Kelly couldn't deny it. 'I can't stop wondering where she's gone.' Amy's wellbeing was beginning to haunt her. 'Oh, Luke! How has she managed . . . with two children and no money?'

'Just now, when you put the jar back on the mantel-piece, you said you were saving it for her. In your heart you know she'll come back. Just keep thinking that. Meanwhile, I'll go on searching and asking, and one day soon, like you, I know we'll have her back again.'

Now, as she looked up, Kelly's face betrayed the haunting fears. 'I still can't understand it, Luke. Why would she go like that? It *can't* have been the business with Fran's will – not altogether. I mean, she could have made a decision about that and still stayed with us. I know she lived in fear of her parents tracking her down and taking her brother and sister away from her, but I think it's much more than that.'

'Kelly! You've got to stop torturing yourself.'

He knew why Amy had gone, and the shame never left him. There had been moments these past weeks when he had come close to confessing the truth to Kelly. But she was already so distressed, he didn't have the heart. Guilty as he was, he would not hurt her more than necessary.

There would be time enough to tell her how it was; that he loved Amy, and without her his life seemed empty.

It didn't take long for him to brew the tea. Finding a scone he put that on a plate with a helping of jam and came back into the parlour to find her lying back in the chair with her eyes closed. Realising she was sleeping, he set the tray on the table and sat in the chair opposite, watching her, and thinking how pale she looked. 'No sleep, and probably little food,' he muttered. 'It's bound to tell on you.'

He wondered if he might have been neglecting her in his search for Amy. 'I'll have to keep a closer eye on you, I can see that.'

He stayed with her then; sitting there, watching her gently sleeping, he wondered how he might tell her when the time came, and how she would take such treachery by two people she had trusted and loved. When the evening grew cooler, he went to the door and took down her long-coat, which he laid over her. 'Rest now,' he murmured, thinking how pretty she was. 'I won't leave you.'

Good as his word, he sat quiet in the chair, drinking more tea and wondering what his next move might be. And the more he thought, the more he realised he had left out one very important avenue of enquiry.

K ELLY SLEPT FOR an hour, and when she woke, she was horrified. 'Oh, Luke! Why didn't you wake me?'

'Because you needed to rest,' he told her. 'You're up before I go to work at six in the morning. I see your light on, so don't deny it. You start work early, and don't even stop for a break in the daytime. I know, because Charlie's told me all about it. Oh Kelly, you must know we're both concerned about you. I dare say it'll be midnight before you go to bed, and then you won't sleep because you're worrying about Amy and the children.' Coming across the room, he enfolded Kelly in his arms. 'It's no wonder you're exhausted. You'll make yourself ill, that's what you'll do. Please, Kelly, slow down . . . give yourself time to breathe. I'm doing all I can to find her, you must know that.'

'I know, and I'm grateful.' Smiling up at him, Kelly had no idea he was looking for Amy, not just for her, but for himself. 'You're a good man, Luke,' she whispered. 'I don't know what I'd do without you.' How could she know her praise tore him in two.

Making her a fresh brew he sat down beside her. 'While you were sleeping, I had time to think,' he said. 'I went over everyone I've asked to keep an eye out for Amy – anyone who might have seen her or had the slightest inkling of where she might be.' His voice trembled. 'But there's one person I never gave a thought to. He might know something. It's worth a try. I can't imagine why I didn't think of him before.'

Kelly sat up in the chair, eyes wide with anticipation. 'Tell me!' Enthused by his excitement, she demanded, 'Luke, who is he? What makes you think this person might know where Amy is?'

'Because he's got a finger in every pie. He owns every little filthy room that's rented out at exorbitant rates. He took Amy's house from her and threw her out on the street. You *know* who he is, Kelly. Think about it!'

'My God!' Realisation dawned. 'Of course! The monster who sold me this house. You mean John Harvey, don't you? And you're right! If Amy was desperate for cheap accommodation, he's the one she'd have to go to.'

They talked it through, and the more they talked, the more they hoped he might lead them to Amy. 'We can't do anything tonight,' Luke reminded her. 'We don't know where he lives, or how to root him out.'

'No, but we can go there tomorrow.'

'Tomorrow then. We'll be there, waiting.'

All fired up and raring to go, Kelly offered up a prayer. But then the doubts resurfaced. 'Oh Luke, what if he doesn't know where she is?'

'We'll find that out tomorrow.'

Like Kelly, he hoped this was the lead they had prayed for.

Chapter Fourteen

AMY HAD BEEN away for several weeks now, and her heart became heavier with every day that passed. Moreover, she'd been wrong when she thought she'd be able to find work and a room in a matter of days. 'I can't let you stay any longer, I'm sorry.' The manager was adamant.

These past weeks Amy had been helping out on a fruit-stall at Darwen indoor market. The manager's wife had let her and the children sleep in the back storeroom, but now the big boss had sent notice that he was on his way. 'It's more than my job's worth to let him find you here.' Sweating profusely, the manager kept saying how sorry he was, but, 'I ain't got no choice. You must see that?'

Amy had no choice either, so she packed her meagre things and got the children ready for the road. 'Where will we go, Amy?' Sally was bone-tired, and Tom hadn't said two words all morning.

Amy hugged them. 'I'll look after you,' she promised. 'We'll look after each other, like we've allus done.'

Before they went, the manager gave her the wages she'd earned that week. 'I don't know if it'll do any good, because rooms round here go almost afore they're empty, but you might do well to make your way down to the Sun public house tonight. You'll find a certain gent there who might be able to help you.'

Suspicious, Amy gave him a wary look. 'What do you mean, help me? He doesn't run a whorehouse or anything like that, I hope, 'cause I've never done anything of that kind in my life and never will!' Outraged, she was about to land him one when he raised his voice to make himself heard.

'For Gawd's sake, stop carrying on, woman! It's nowt like that!'

'So what d'you mean by saying he can help me?'

'He's a business gent. Knows how to make a shilling turn into a guinea, if you know what I mean.'

'In what way?' Against her deeper instincts, Amy was intrigued.

'He's got what you want, I dare say. Providing o' course you've got the cash to pay for it, 'cause he ain't the kind to give owt for nowt.'

Cupping his two hands beneath his huge stomach he heaved himself on to a stool. 'Comes from out Liverpool way, or so they tell me. According to one of our regulars, he's bought up most of the rundown houses in Darwen and lets them out in rooms. I dare say it ain't the

Ritz, but it's a place to call your own till you find summat better.'

'I expect his rents are too high for me.'

'You won't know if you don't ask.' He tapped his nose in a knowing gesture. 'Don't kid me that you're penniles, 'cause I know better. You should have a tidy sum put by. I've paid you good wages – and I'm not saying you haven't earned 'em because you have . . . twice over. I've never had a lass who'll fetch and carry crates of oranges and such and not moan about it. I've even had you barrowing sacks o' coal and still you've had a smile on that lovely, cheeky face.'

'I've been glad of the work, Mr Potter.'

'And I've been glad of your labour. The wife's been good to you an' all, feeding you and the bairns for an hour's washing time.' He laughed. 'Gawd knows what she'll do now you're going. She'll not take kindly to doing her own washing again, that's for sure.'

'I appreciate what you've both done for us,' Amy conceded, 'but whatever money I've earned won't last long if I don't soon find work.'

'Oh, you'll manage, I'm sure. Besides, I know you've been putting away a bob or two every week since you've been here. *And* you've just got your wages. So you're not destitute, are you?'

Amy gave a wry little smile. 'Not yet I'm not, but don't forget that from now on I'll have to feed three of us, and I'm not sleeping under no flea-ridden blanket, so I might have to shell out for new bedclothes, although

I dare say I could pick out some material at the market and make my own at half the price.'

'There you are then!' Sliding off the stool he plopped to the floor like a red jelly. 'I said you'd manage, didn't I?'

'I'll need his name if I'm to go looking for him.'

'I don't know his name.'

'What time does he turn up at the public house?'

'Don't know that neither. All I know is, he turns up twice a week, Fridays and Saturdays, or so I've heard.'

Amy thought she had nothing to lose. 'It might be worth a try,' she said. 'Anything's better than walking the street.' Since living with Kelly and knowing a decent life, it was hard settling for less; harder still for the children.

It was half-past seven when Amy turned up at the Sun public house. Standing by the door she could hear the rowdy lot inside. 'I hope this is worthwhile,' she told the children.

'I don't like it here.' Sally was tired.

Tom didn't like it either. 'Can't we go back to Kelly's?' That was the one question both children asked, time and again.

'Hello, darlin', fancy me, d'yer?' A long thin fella with a droopy tash and too much drink inside him fell against her. 'I've a spare bob or two in me pocket if yer want it.' He winked meaningfully. 'Yer don't get it for nothing though.'

Amy pushed him away. 'I was told a man comes here on a Friday, and Saturday. He's got rooms to let.'

'*I've* got a room, darlin'. You're welcome to share it, for a few hours.' He laughed, wobbled, and fell at her feet. 'I'm drunk!' he giggled and hiccuped all at the same time.

'Drunk?' Holding back the laughter, Amy left him where he lay. 'More like paralytic, I'd say!'

'I'm sorry. No women allowed in here.' The landlord had seen her come in and was across the room in seconds. 'There's other public houses where they don't mind women drinking, but I have strict rules, so I'll be glad if you'll turn round and go out that door. Now!' He glanced at the children cowering behind her. 'You ought to be ashamed. Them kids should be at home in bed.'

'Nobody knows that more than I do!' Amy stood her ground. 'I'm not here to drink. I'm here because I were told there's a fella who rents out rooms.'

'You're still in the wrong place.' Jerking a thumb towards the door, he told her, 'Go back the way you came, then round the back by way of the side alley. When you come to a door, you'll see a room to the left. That's his office.'

'What time does he come?'

'He's there now.'

Pointing to the rear of the room, she asked, 'Can't I just go through here?' She didn't relish the idea of taking the children down some dark alley.

Gripping her by the shoulders, he propelled her towards the front door. '*He* might own the place, but in this bar *I* make the rules. I want you out . . . the same way you came in!' With that he pushed her through the door and on to the pavement. 'Down the alley, to the back door,' he growled. 'You'll see his light on.'

With no choice but to follow his instructions, Amy turned into the alley.

Pitch black, with only a speck of light from the rear to guide her, it was a scary place. Groping her way through all manner of dirt and dung, Amy held her nose. The stench was sickening. When a rat ran across her foot she snatched Sally into her arms and told Tom to, 'Stay close, we're almost there.' She had half a mind to turn back, but it was getting late and she knew from past experience that there were few, if any, rooms available in the town.

She got a shock when a man came out of nowhere. Realising the danger, she pressed the children against the wall and bade them be quiet until, so close she could smell the stale tobacco on him, he passed without knowing they were there.

An even bigger shock awaited her when she opened the door to the office, because sitting there behind his desk was none other than John Harvey; the man who had thrown her out of house and home in Blackburn.

The shock was mutual. 'Well, I never!' Taken aback, he stared at her in disbelief. 'Amy Slater no less! To what do I owe this pleasure?' Leaning back in his chair he sucked on a cigar while eyeing her up and down; and thinking how she was every bit as lovely as he remembered.

'I don't like him.' Sally clung to her, while Tom sullenly peered out from behind Amy's skirt.

For a moment Amy didn't quite know what to do. She could either turn and leave, back through the alley and into the dark beyond, or she could brazen it out and test him.

In those few minutes while she turned it over in her mind, he left his desk and came to escort her inside. 'Close the door,' he said, urging her to sit down. 'We don't want all and sundry to invite themselves in now, do we?'

Glad to relieve herself of Sally's considerable weight, Amy sat down, with one child either side and her arms protectively round them. 'I need a room,' she said curtly. 'I have money.'

Coming back to his desk he smiled at her. 'Oh? You have money, do you?'

Like a mouse before a cat she watched his face for any sign of danger. 'It's *my* money!' she said. 'And it's hard-earned.'

'You've caused me a certain amount of bother, did you know that?'

'What do you mean?'

'I mean, you're a wanted woman. If I was vindictive, which I'm not, I could turn you in and make myself a pretty penny.'

'You're lying. I've done nothing wrong.' Except to come between Kelly and Luke, she thought sadly. Except for ruining all their lives.

'Oh, I'm not talking about the police. I'm talking about certain friends of yours – Kelly Wilson and her manfriend. Those two have turned Blackburn upside down looking for you. They came to me, thinking I might know where you were, but of course I didn't, and why should I?'

He grinned, showing a row of teeth yellowed by cigar smoke. 'I do *now* though, don't I? Those two seemed very anxious to find you. I'm sure they would pay for any information.' Studying her at length he dropped his voice to a more intimate level. 'I wonder why they're so desperate to find you? Steal the family silver, did you?'

Amy's heart went cold. Kelly and Luke were looking for her. Oh, how she would love to go back and put it all right. Fighting back the tears, she said coolly, 'I need a room. Either you have one or you don't.'

'Oh, but I do! Yes indeed, I have the very room for you, but not here I'm afraid. There isn't a single room to let in Darwen, and I should know, since I own most of them.' His greasy smile slid away. 'You don't seem very impressed. Oh yes, I've done very well since you and I last met. Gone from strength to strength, you might say. I've bought property all over Lancashire, and made a great deal of money into the bargain.'

'I'm not interested in what you've achieved – on the backs of other poor unfortunates, I expect. I'm here for a room, in Darwen, like I said.'

'You won't find one.'

'Then I'm wasting your time and mine.' Rising to leave, she paused when he told her, 'I can give you a place of your own, *and* paid work into the bargain. If you can afford to turn it down, then I'll say good night to you.'

When she sat down and listened, he explained, 'I have no quarrel with you. Throwing you out of your home was unfortunate, but I'm a businessman, not a charity.'

'Work and a room?' It seemed too good to be true.

'Yes, but not here.'

'Where then?'

He smiled. 'You're a hard little bitch, aren't you?'

'No harder than you.'

'I think we understand each other.' Leaning over the desk, he went on, 'I've just acquired my first property in another area; spreading my wings as I told you.'

'Where is this property?' For all she knew it could be on the other side of the world.

Ignoring her question, he continued, 'It's a big house, with three storeys. The first and third floor are split into six rooms. The second-floor area was the owner's accommodation, so was never split. It will give you two bedrooms and everything you need to be comfortable. The rooms are all let to respectable people. I need someone I can rely on to caretake the house. As yet, I've not been able to find anyone who can do the job properly. If you want it, the job's yours. Keep the house clean and tidy, keep an eye on the tenants, and you can have the accommodation rent-free.'

'What's the catch?' Amy didn't trust him.

'No catch. I've got decent tenants paying good money in that house, and it needs someone there who'll keep it up. What do you say?'

'You still haven't told me where it is.'

'Liverpool.'

Amy's eyes opened wide. '*Liverpool!* But that's miles away!' Something else occurred to her. If he knew her whereabouts, he might not think twice about charging Kelly for the information.

She said as much to him now.

'What? Give away your whereabouts and rob myself of a reliable person to take care of my property? I was most impressed by the state of the house in Blackburn after I had to repossess it . . . most unfortunate, I'm sorry about that. Most people would have rubbished it before they left, but not you. The house was impeccable – every room lovingly taken care of. That's what I want for my new house in Liverpool; someone who takes a pride. So why would I betray your whereabouts? Please, don't take me for a fool.'

Amy still wasn't sure. 'After what you did to me and the children, how can I trust you?'

'Because it's a straightforward deal, with no frills; you work for me, I pay you a basic wage, and you get a roof over your head. I can tell you now – you won't get a better offer anywhere else.'

What he said was true enough. 'Is it furnished?'

'Yes, but nothing fancy.'

'I'll give it a try – say a month. After that, if I'm not happy, I'm free to go, without argument.'

Amused, he laughed. 'Anybody would think you didn't trust me.'

'I don't.'

'A month's trial then.'

'I want it in writing.'

'Whatever you say.' Already he was devising a wicked plan. 'There's a room at the top of the pub here – you can stay there tonight. Tomorrow you catch the train into Liverpool.'

Scribbling on a piece of paper, he handed it to her. 'Here's the address – it's easy enough to find. I have early business to attend to, so I'll meet you there at two p.m.'

'I'm not using my own money on the train fare.' Amy was adamant about that.

Taking two coins from his purse, Harvey threw them to her. 'That should take care of it.'

Looking down at the coins, she taunted him, 'Aren't you afraid I might run off with your money?'

'Oh, I don't think so. You see, if you run off with my money, I'll just have to come looking for you.'

Amy might have given him a smart reply, but the door opened and a burly fellow strode in. 'Evening, guv.' Big as he was, he seemed amiable enough. 'I'm told you got rooms to let?'

'Come in, my good man, sit down.' Greeting the fellow with a smile, he then turned to Amy. 'Tell the landlord I said you were to stay here the night. I'll see you tomorrow.'

'I still haven't made up my mind about the job and everything.' She felt nervous. Unsure of him.

Shrugging his shoulders, he seemed not to care. 'Up to you,' he said. 'Sleep on it, why don't you? When I get back in the morning, you'll either have gone to catch the Liverpool train, or you'll have given the landlord my money. Either way, it's for you to decide.'

Feigning a casual attitude, he addressed the man with a smile. 'Now then, sir, what can I do for you?'

Bemused, Amy left the office. 'Come on, you two.' She led Jack and Sally back down the alley. 'It looks like we'll have a proper bed, for tonight at least.'

If Amy had heard the conversation in the office she had just left, her deeper suspicions would have been confirmed.

'I've got work in Darwen and I'm looking for a room,' the man said.

Glancing at the door to make sure Amy was long gone, John Harvey smiled greasily. 'You're in luck,' he said. 'I've got a room in one of my best houses, near to the town centre *and* it's a very reasonable rent.'

'I'll take it!' Mutually delighted, they shook hands on it. Terms were agreed and the deal was done in the time it took Amy to get to the far end of the alley.

THE LANDLORD'S HOSTILE attitude remained unchanged when Amy passed on the message from John Harvey. 'I've been offered a job working in one of his new properties,' she said, not feeling too proud about it, but knowing, as John Harvey claimed, that she would not get a better offer anywhere else. 'We're to stay here tonight.' Drawing the children closer, she gestured up the stairs. 'John Harvey said you have a room at the top?'

The landlord started muttering under his breath about 'Men who think they've a right to boss other folk around! I run his pub and make him money and here he is, parking women and brats on me without so much as a by your leave!'

When Tom began to snigger, Amy chided him with a finger to her lips. But when the landlord muttered and complained all the way to the attic room, she couldn't help smiling herself.

'There you are then.' Placing his lamp on the table, he told her, 'If it gets chilly in the night, there's extra blankets in that cupboard.' Pointing to the alcove cupboard, he assured her, 'There's no fleas on 'em neither. My wife takes a pride in her housekeeping chores.'

Looking about, Amy could believe it. 'I can see that,' she observed, and got a frown for her trouble.

'Right then! I'll leave you to it.'

'What about . . . ?' Amy began, but was interrupted by an increasingly irate landlord.

'What now? I suppose John Harvey said I were to give you food and drink an' all, did he?'

Before Amy could answer, he'd closed the door and gone, with the promise of 'Cheese sandwiches and coffee, it's the best I can do at short notice.'

Turning to the children, she chuckled. 'I was only going to ask where the wash-room is, but if he means to feed us, who are we to complain?'

'Not me.' It was the first time all day that Tom had laughed out loud.

'Not me neither.' Sally was always hungry.

'Right then.' Swinging her heavy bag on to the bed, Amy blew out a long weary sigh. 'First I'll sort out us baggage, then we'll go and find the wash-room. It's high time you two were in bed.' Me too, she thought. For some reason she felt dog-tired.

'Will you work for that man?' Tom was anxious again.

'I'm not sure. We'll have to see.'

'Why can't we stay here?'

'Well, because I haven't got work to pay the rent, and secondly, the room is only lent to us for one night.' Longingly, she looked round. 'It's a shame,' she said, 'because it is a lovely room.'

Though riddled with the faint aroma of booze and stale tobacco, the room was surprisingly pleasant. The window looked down on to a well-lit street, and the lamp cast a soft, warm glow. 'And look here!' Turning back the bedlothes, Amy declared, 'We've got a room, and food with a waiter to bring it, and clean sheets too. Whatever next?'

But she couldn't help feeling there would be a price to pay.

A SHORT TIME later, she and the children found the washroom, where they took it in turns to scrub down. 'Oh! Ouch! I've got soap in my eyes!' Sally had a few minutes of tears and tribulation. Tom made it worse when he told her she was a 'big baby'.

Afterwards, they tucked into food and drink, grudgingly delivered by the landlord, and when their tummies were full the children scrambled into bed and fell into a deep, contented sleep. 'Goodnight, God bless.' Amy covered them up, with a kiss. 'Let's hope tomorrow brings us better fortune.' She prayed, too, that when morning came, she would make the right decision; for the children's sake more than her own.

Ten o'clock came and went. Then eleven, and still she made no move to climb into bed beside the children. Instead she sat in the chair, mulling it all over until her mind was in a whirl. 'He's after summat, I *know* he is.'

Amy had seen both sides of John Harvey, and she didn't care for either. In the pit of her stomach she knew he was up to no good, and yet what he offered seemed genuine enough.

Her thoughts turned to Luke and Kelly. 'I miss them

so much,' she whispered aloud. But there was no going back, she knew that, and for the rest of her life she would regret it.

After a while she fell asleep, hunched in the chair, her head lolling over the arm and her feet curled beneath her. For three hours she slept and woke, then slept again, and when the morning dawned she ached from her head to her toes. 'Oh, my Gawd!' Getting out of the chair she stretched and groaned. 'I feel like I'll never walk upright again.'

First she satisfied herself that the children were all right. Then she glanced at the clock and saw that it was already half-past eight. 'There's a lot to do,' she murmured. 'And I want a word with that landlord before I go.'

'Come on . . . wakey, wakey!' Gently rocking the children she told them, 'It's time to get up.'

It took a few minutes, but they were soon out of bed, yawning and stretching, and asking awkward questions. 'Are we going to Liverpool?' Tom wanted to know. 'Will we have a proper house to live in?'

Sally seemed to have got used to the idea, and besides, 'I've never been on a train.'

Amy still hadn't made up her mind. She didn't trust John Harvey, but maybe she was still hurting from losing their home, and putting the blame on him when it was as much her parents' fault as his.

Like a little troop, they marched to the wash-room and took turns in freshening themselves up. Amy combed the young ones' hair and made sure they were fit to be presented to the world. Then she gathered their belongings together and led them downstairs. 'My Gawd!' The landlord was up and about, preparing for a busy day. 'I didn't reckon to see you lot till much later.'

Feeling much braver, Sally piped up, 'We've a train to catch.' When Tom dug her in the ribs, she pushed him back and fell into a sulk.

Amy thought the landlord seemed more amiable this morning and said so. 'Aye well, Friday night's a nightmare,' he confessed. 'You get the workers in, wanting to go through their money in five minutes and getting so bloody drunk they start fighting. Saturday's busier, but quieter, if you know what I mean?' He looked at the children and made a suggestion. 'If you want to sit down over there, I'll get the wife to make you a bit of breakfast.'

Amy thanked him. 'Can you tell me something?'

'I won't know till you've asked.'

'John Harvey. How long have you known him?'

The landlord pursed his lips and cast his mind back. 'About six months, I suppose. Before that, the pub was owned by Thwaites Brewery. When they got rid of half a dozen of their properties, John Harvey snapped this one up.' Tutting, he shook his head. 'If I'd have had the money he wouldn't have got his hands on it, I can tell you.'

'You don't like him, do you?'

The landlord seemed surprised by her remark. 'I

resent him getting the pub from under my feet, but I can't really grumble. I couldn't buy it, and he's kept me on, with the same wages I got from Thwaites. Anybody else might have got rid of me, but he didn't, did he?'

'Hmph! That's because he knows you're a damned good landlord!' The voice was that of a large, round-faced woman with a smile that lit the room. 'How d'you do?' Holding out her hand, she almost crushed Amy's within it. 'And what about you two, eh?' Tweaking Sally's cheek, she laughed when Tom came between her and his sister. 'You do right to protect her from monsters like me,' she said.

Resuming the conversation between her husband and Amy, she said, 'It's Len here who makes this place what it is. He works hard and brings in the customers, and the till rings a damned sight more than it would if there were somebody else behind it. John Harvey knows it, and that's why he keeps him on.'

The landlord brought her attention to the children. 'Can't you see these young 'uns are starving,' he chided. 'Away and get them some breakfast, woman. We'll have ours with them, an' all.'

Looking at Amy, she smiled. 'Bossy bugger, ain't he?' But she went all the same.

'You sit yourselves down over there.' Pointing to the far table, the landlord told Amy, 'When she comes back, we'll have a chat. For now, I've to get down the cellar and clean them pipes or the beer will be bloody awful. Go on,' he urged, 'she'll not be long.'

And she wasn't.

Toing and froing, she let Amy help. 'I ain't got enough arms, that's the trouble,' the older woman laughed. Amy thought she was wonderful.

They all sat down to eat. 'It looks so tempting.' Amy's stomach was rumbling a tune. The table groaned with five huge plates, all filled to the brim with eggs, bacon, sausage and fried tomatoes. In the centre was another plate heaped with chunks of bread, and beside it a jug of sarsaparilla for the children, and a pot of tea for the adults. 'Get that down you!' the landlord grinned at the children, and they didn't need telling twice.

'Now then.' With half a sausage hanging out of his mouth, he addressed Amy. 'What were we saying before . . . about John Harvey?'

'I just wondered what you thought of him.'

'In what way?'

'Can he be trusted, do you think?'

'As much as *any* businessman can be trusted. He's a sharp fella, I'll give you that . . . knows how to buy and sell, and make money hand over fist.'

The landlady had a question for Amy. 'Why are you asking about John Harvey?' Taking up her cup, she slurped her tea so loudly that it made the children giggle.

'He's offered me a job.'

'Oh aye? What sort of job?' Wiping a trail of tea from her chin, she put the cup down again.

Amy explained, 'He's bought this big house in

Liverpool and he wants a caretaker. I'll get a wage and rentfree accommodation, and a month to see if I'm happy there.'

The landlord thought it was a good offer. 'I might have taken it meself if I'd known it were going begging.'

'Don't be daft!' His wife knew better. 'You'd be lost if you didn't have a bar to stand behind.' She turned to Amy. 'You're worried, aren't you?'

'A bit. I knew John Harvey before, you see.'

'Ah! I thought as much.' The landlady prided herself on knowing everything. 'What happened then, if you don't mind me asking?'

Amy told her everything, 'So you can understand how I'm not sure whether to trust him or not.'

'Ah well, I don't know about that. As far as I can tell, this is a straightforward business offer. A job and a home, and a month to see if you like it. I don't see how you can lose.'

Having eaten his fill, her husband had a word or two to say. 'I know it sounds harsh, but the fella is a businessman after all, and we know they ain't got no heart, especially when it comes to losing money. It's a matter of course to send in the bailiffs when the rent ain't being paid, we all know that. Oh, I know it were bad, 'cause you had these two young 'uns to think of, and it must have made you hate his bloody guts . . . but when you think about it in the cold light of day, what else could he do? He couldn't let you stay in the house without paying rent, could he?'

Amy had been telling herself the very same thing, but still there was a feeling about John Harvey that she couldn't shake off. 'So, if you were me, and he'd thrown you out on the streets, would you be able to trust him?'

'I don't know about trust him, 'cause I don't trust any o' the buggers and nor should you. But I reckon I'd get on the train to Liverpool and give his place the once-over. If you don't like the look of it, you can always get on the train and come back.'

His wife thought so too. 'The trouble is, if you're looking for a place to stay and work alongside, it's not much use coming back to Darwen 'cause there's not much going in that way, nor likely to be for some long time, I reckon.' Patting Amy on the hand she urged, 'Go on, luv. It really won't hurt to have a look.'

Amy could see how, in a way, she might have blamed John Harvey for troubles of her parents' making, and now she was ready to think again. Her mind was made up, when just then Sally piped up, 'Me and Tom want to go on a train, don't we Tom?' And Tom's eyes lit up.

Twenty minutes later, Amy thanked the couple for their kindness. 'Like you say, it won't hurt to go and have a look.' And that was exactly what she meant to do; have a look, and move on if it didn't feel right.

Like the woman said, what did she have to lose?

Chapter Fifteen

THE TRAIN JOURNEY was an adventure the children would never forget. Entranced, they sat by the window, watching the landmarks that appeared then disappeared, and the rhythmic throbbing of the engine was like a lullaby to their ears. 'I'm going to be a train-driver when I grow up.' Loud and clear, to the amusement of other travellers, Tom announced his avowed intention.

'Not *me!*' Indignant, Sally declared how she wouldn't like to be covered in soot and smoke all day, because, 'How would I see where I was going?'

While they delighted in the train ride, Amy let her thoughts wander; first to John Harvey and his new enterprise then, inevitably, to Luke and Kelly. The longer she was away from those lovely people, and the more miles she put between them, the sadder she felt. 'I wonder if I'll ever see you again?' Her voice was the merest murmur, but the woman in front heard it and turned to look at her. Embarrassed, Amy smiled and the woman looked away.

'Amy! Amy!' Jumping with excitement, Sally tugged at her sleeve. 'There's an animal in the grass . . . look!'

Amy looked and saw a huge hare leaping across the field. 'It's a *rabbit*, silly!' Tom had seen pictures at school, and thought he knew the difference.

Amy didn't correct him. There were other, more important things on her mind. Instead she just smiled and told Sally, 'Keep your eyes open, sweetheart, and you'll see all kinds of animals.'

Going back to her thoughts of Luke and Kelly, she recalled two wise old sayings: 'Absence makes the heart grow fonder', and 'Out of sight, out of mind'. She wondered which one applied, to Luke in particular. Did he still hold dear the kiss between them? Did he regret it as much as she did? Like her, did he wish they had told Kelly right from the start? Was it too late now? Had too much water passed under the bridge for it all to be put right?

So many questions. So much heartache. And yet, though she loathed the idea of betraying Kelly, she could not regret the love she felt for Luke. It was too real, too powerful to be denied. But he wasn't hers and she had no right to feel that way.

Her thoughts were shattered by Tom's shrill cry. 'We're here! The train's stopping! Look, Amy, it says "Liverpool"!'

And there it was, a big black sign raised above the barrel of flowers and bathed in smoke; Amy read the big letters: LIVERPOOL. What did it hold for them, she wondered.

'Come on you two, get ready.'

Steadying them as they went down the corridor, gently bumping and swaying from side to side, Amy led them to the door. 'Keep hold of me,' she warned, but it wasn't easy, not with everyone pushing and shoving to get to the front.

When they finally reached the door, Amy held them tight in case they should get too close to the open window. 'The man told me that somebody looked out last week and had her head taken off at the shoulders,' Tom declared proudly. Sally burst out crying and Amy told him that was a very cruel thing to say. At which point he went into a sulk that lasted a whole minute; at least until they climbed off the train and were immediately shrouded in smoke. 'It's like a mystery!' he said.

Neither Sally nor Amy knew what he meant, though Amy had a sly little chuckle to herself. Even when she was feeling low, these two could always bring a smile to her heart.

'Victoria Street, eh?' The porter scratched his chin. 'Hmph! It's a fair walk from here. Your best bet is to take a cab. It won't but cost you a tanner, if that.' Pointing to the main gates he told her, 'You'll find the cab waiting out there.'

With that he was gone, eager to help a man who showed him a florin. 'More money than sense!' Knowing the value of a penny, Amy was not impressed.

The cabbie knew the street. 'Not far from the docks,' he told her. 'Big houses, mostly well-to-do folk – seafaring captains and tradesmen with a bob or two in their pocket. Lately, one or two have been snapped up by outsiders who don't care a bugger! My old mam, God rest her soul, she used to wait on in one o' them big houses.' He regarded Amy with interest. 'By! The way things change, tut, tut. She'd turn in her grave so she would.' That said, he sang all the way to Victoria Street. 'That'll be ninepence,' he said, helping Amy down from the cab.

Amy was surprised. 'The porter said it wouldn't be more than sixpence.'

'Well, the porter was wrong.' Spitting in his hand he held it out. 'Ninepence, if you please.'

Begrudgingly, Amy paid up.

'Good night then.' Climbing into the seat, he clicked the horse on its way. 'Wup, me old beauty, let's have you!' With a gentle slap of the rein on its rump, the horse moved on.

'Right then.' Amy observed the area. 'Not bad,' she murmured. 'Better than I'd feared.'

The street was short and wide, with houses on either side; they were of a grand old sort, with wrought-iron railings round the cellar steps, and stained-glass fanlights above the doors. 'Proud houses at one time,' Amy said. 'They've seen their best though.' On at least two of the houses, signs of age were already creeping in. The timber on the windowsill was beginning to rot, and there was a sad look about the heavy wooden doors. 'Still an' all, they're a cut above what we're used to.'

'Which one is ours?' Tom never stopped asking questions.

Consulting her piece of paper, Amy took note of the number. 'Number fourteen.' Looking up, she saw that they were standing outside number six. 'The houses on this side go up in even numbers of two,' she observed. 'So it's on this side . . . four doors up.' She started walking and the children followed, full of questions yet anxious, just like her. 'Here we are.'

They stood for a moment, looking up at the house, and wondering what to do next. 'I thought Mr Harvey was meant to meet us here?' That was Tom again.

Amy glanced at the church clock in the distance. 'Two o' clock, that's what he said, and it's five to now.' She ran her gaze up and down the street. 'He's not here . . . happen he won't come at all.' It would be just like him, she thought, to send her on a wild-goose chase. But surely he wouldn't risk losing his money?

Just then, the door of the house opened and there he was. 'You're five minutes early, I like that.' Throwing open the door he invited, 'Come inside.'

When Amy hesitated, he got impatient. 'Be quick, I haven't got all day.'

As she brushed by him, Amy felt like a fly caught in a spider's web.

He took them straight to the second floor. 'Nice, eh?' As he had promised, the rooms were furnished; not the kind of furniture Amy might have chosen, but practical and solid, and not too damaged. The rooms were too big, too cold, and not much like 'home'. Unloved and filthy, it was. 'I don't think much to the people who were here before me,' Amy told him. 'They weren't too particular, by the look of this place!'

The beds had torn sheets and the blankets were dirty. There was stale food in the kitchen, spills on the floor, and a choking smell that permeated the air. 'An old sea-captain and his woman,' John Harvey explained. 'What do they care . . . here one minute, gone the next, and no time to put down roots.'

'Is the rest of the house like this?' Amy was beginning to see she'd have her work cut out.

'You'll see soon enough,' he answered cagily. 'Now then, I've a business appointment in half an hour and won't be back till later on tonight, to see how you've got on.'

'Hang on! I'll want to see the rest of the house. Remember, I haven't taken on the job proper yet. If I do, I'll need keys to the rooms, and if they're all as dirty as this, I'll need a mountain of cleaning stuff, too.'

'There'll be time enough for that tomorrow,' he replied. 'I'll be in Liverpool for a few days yet. For now, you just make yourself at home, and like I say, I'll be back later to see how you've got on.'

Digging into his pocket he drew out a handful of coins, which he proceeded to count on to the table. 'There's more than enough there to put this place to rights. You'll want food in the cupboard and fresh sheets – the blankets want washing, as you can see. There's a laundry room just a few streets away from here – Dock Lane, bottom of Victoria Street, turn left and straight on, it's easy enough to find. You'll get all you need down there. By the time you've found what you want, the blankets will be washed and ready to collect.'

Taking her hand, he thrust the money into it. 'If you're careful, there should be enough left over for you to buy yourself a new frock.' Glancing at the children, he told her, 'Them poor little buggers look tired. I should get 'em to bed early if I were you.'

Amy bristled. 'What time the children go to bed is *my* business!' But he was right. They did look worn out.

'Stroppy little thing, aren't you.' He stared at her for a minute, then flung two keys on to the table. 'You'll need that to get back in.' He did up his coat and strode to the door with one last instruction: 'I'll be back tonight. You think on what I've said.' Then he was gone, and the room was cheerier for it.

'Hmph!' Amy's back was up and she was ready for a fight. 'If he thinks he can boss me about, he's got another thought coming!'

'I'm hungry.' Sally didn't care where she was, as long as she was with Amy and Tom.

'This place smells!' Tom wrinkled his nose.

'*Stinks*, you mean.' Amy felt dirty just being there. 'I tell you what. You two search for a bag or summat, and I'll strip the beds. Afterwards we'll take the blankets to the laundry and find ourselves summat to eat.'

'Summat to eat'; magic words. Excited, the children

scurried off. From the bedroom, Amy could hear them opening and shutting cupboard doors. 'Little loves,' she murmured. 'They ain't had much of a life.' Except when they were with Kelly, she thought, and was suddenly close to tears. The moment quickly passed. Hard though it was, she daren't let herself break down.

Ten minutes later, they were stuffing blankets and sheets into two old bolster cases. 'We found them in the wardrobe,' Sally told her. 'There was a mouse there and it ran away.'

'It wasn't a mouse,' Tom corrected. 'It was a *rat*. Like the one Kelly found in the cellar.'

Amy was horrified. 'We'd best get a few rat-traps while we're out.'

Sally objected. 'It was ever so pretty, with little pink ears and a moustache.'

'Was it now?' Amy pretended to be interested, but made a mental note *not* to forget the traps. There was a place for people and a place for rats. And it wasn't all in the same bed!

With the children carrying one bolster case between them, Amy carried the other. As they made their way to Dock Street, Amy recalled the instructions: 'Down to the bottom of Victoria Street, turn left and straight on.'

A few minutes later they arrived at the laundry. 'I need them back soon,' Amy told the little Oriental man. 'They're the only ones we've got.'

He bowed and smiled and told her they would be 'ready in two hour.'

'How much?' Amy had to make sure she kept the money back.

Again, the little man smiled and bowed. 'How many blankets, Missy?'

Amy mentally calculated. There were two from each bed. 'Two double, four single – oh, and six sheets.' There weren't any spares for changing. She would need to mention that to John Harvey when he came back tonight.

'Two shillings and sixpence, please. You pay when finish.'

Amy told him she would be about two hours.

In fact it was nearly *four* hours, because they got caught up in the excitement of dockland, and before they knew it the time was running away with them.

They wandered about the docks and found all manner of quaint, well-hidden little shops; they had fish and chips at Jimmy's café; walked along the dock edge and were amazed by the big sailing ships and the sight of sailors running up and down the rigging, as sure-footed as a cat on a wire. 'I want to be a sailor when I grow up.' Tom changed his mind at the drop of a hat.

Liverpool Docks was an exciting place to be; the smell of fish and old rope; the chatter and rush of busy men. And oh, those wonderful, majestic sailing ships and the soothing sound of water splashing against their hulls. It was a memory they would carry with them for ever.

Lost in it all, they shopped and browsed and shopped again, and when darkness began to draw in, Amy decided they had better make their way back. Though she hated to admit it, John Harvey was right. 'You two are ready for your beds.' And so am I, she thought. So am I.

'Thought you don't come back, Missy.' The little Oriental man greeted her with a big, wide smile. 'All done, two shilling and sixpence, thank you.'

For some strange reason, the bed-linen seemed lighter to carry. Distributing it between herself and the children, Amy casually remarked on it. 'I expect that's because it's all folded neatly,' she said.

'No, it ain't.' Tom had a theory as usual. 'It's because all the dirt's been washed off.'

Amy laughed. 'Why didn't *I* think of that,' she chuckled. A simple theory, but probably true.

'Where's it all gone?' Sally wanted to know.

'Where's all *what* gone?' Tom slung the bag round his neck. It was easier to carry that way.

'All that dirt . . . where's it gone?'

'Down his drains, I expect.'

'Won't they get all . . . er . . .' She couldn't think of the word.

'Clogged up?'

'Yes.'

'I don't know.' He lapsed into silence while he thought about that one.

Suddenly it began to rain; not soft rain that might have cooled them, but a relentless, heavy downpour. 'Run!' As they were only a few doors away from the house, Amy thought it best to keep going.

Gasping but not yet soaked, they ran up the steps. 'Here we are.' Taking the key from her skirt pocket, Amy unlocked the door. Pushing it open she was startled when a dark-haired man of middle age rushed in behind them, almost knocking her over. As he ran up the stairs, Amy called out to him, 'Rude bugger!' She had no time for ill manners. 'You might have let *us* get in first!' Her reply was a dark, sinister scowl that turned her stomach over.

Ushering the children inside she told them, 'You're never to open that door for *anybody!*'

'Not even for Mr Harvey?'

'No. Not even for him. If anybody at all knocks on that door, you're to fetch me, do you understand?' Deliberately keeping calm, she tried not to frighten them.

Entering her own quarters on the second floor, she closed the door thankfully, with relief. Taking a towel from her bag she set about drying the children's hair. 'Who wants to help me clean up this place?'

They both did, so she set them a task each; Tom cleaning out the ashes from the fire-grate, and Sally wiping down all the surfaces with a wet cloth. While they got on with that, she took up the rugs and shook them out the window, then she swept and scrubbed, and before too long there wasn't a speck of dirt anywhere. 'There!' With her back aching, her skirt hung with cobwebs and her face covered in a film of dust, she looked like the chimney-sweep. 'Time to re-make the beds.' She couldn't rest until it was all done.

A short time later, with the beds made and the whole

place sparkling, it began to look more like home. 'I think we might be comfortable here after all,' Amy surmised. 'As long as I'm allowed to get on with my work and no aggravation.'

Unbeknown to her, the aggravation was already on its way; in the unwelcome form of John Harvey.

It was half-past nine when she tucked the children up in bed. Ten minutes later they were fast asleep. 'I'm not surprised you're out on your feet,' she murmured, stroking their sleepy heads. 'Dragged from one end of Lancashire to the other, and never knowing where we'll end up next.'

Gazing down on them, she marvelled at their resilience. 'You've not had much of a start in life, have you?' she sighed again. 'First your mam and dad desert you, then you're thrown out of the only home you've ever known. Dear God! The things I've put you through, and still you give your love without condition.'

Sitting on the edge of the bed, she continued to gaze on them, wondering how it would all end. She didn't mean to fall in love with Luke, but she had, and what she felt for him would never go away, she knew that. And how would she ever dare to look Kelly in the face again? The answer was, she couldn't. And that made her a coward, when she had never been afraid of anything in her whole life. 'Oh Kelly, I wish I could see you . . . talk to you and explain.' She smiled wryly. 'But then, you don't know, do you? Unless Luke told you, after I'd gone.'

Not for the first time, she wondered about that. 'In

a way, I hope he *has* told you. I hope he's man enough not to make you his wife, when all the time he loves someone else.' But Luke wasn't a coward, she thought. Not like her.

Softly leaving the children's bedroom, she went into the kitchen where she made herself a mug of steaming hot cocoa. Taking it into the sitting-room, she curled up in a chair and drank every last drop. A few minutes later she was in a deep, dreamless sleep, worn out by a long, hard day, and the worry of a friendship lost for ever.

So deep in sleep was she that Amy didn't hear him come in.

Sure-footed and having done it so many times before, John Harvey crept towards her. There was a stranger in his wake who, like John Harvey, had bad things on his mind. He was the same man who had rushed past Amy and the children at the front door; he knew then that she was being set up for his enjoyment.

'Wake her up.' Whispering, the other man touched him on the shoulder. 'I like my women to look me in the eye when I'm having fun.' Leering at Amy with avaricious eyes, he reached out and tremblingly lifted her skirt. 'Oh yes, she'll do!' He liked the cut of her shapely legs, and now, as he traced the pertness of her breasts with the tip of his finger, he was positively drooling. 'Leave us!' he told John Harvey excitedly. 'Get out, man . . . here.' Reaching into his wallet he drew out a handful of notes and thrust them in John

Harvey's face. 'Two hours, no less, then you can have her back.'

John Harvey was none too pleased. 'The deal was *one* hour!' he hissed. 'I've got somebody else waiting.'

'Then let 'em wait,' the man snapped. 'She's mine for two hours, or I'll have my money back and go elsewhere.'

Seeing the colour of the other man's money, John Harvey reluctantly agreed. 'I'll be back in two hours, but you'd better be finished. Like I say, I've got somebody else waiting.'

'Don't worry, I'll be finished.' He grinned. 'Now clear off!'

Clutching his money, John Harvey went softly out of the room, silently closing the door behind him.

'Now then, my lovely . . . it's just me and you.'

Leaning forward, the stranger took hold of the hem on Amy's skirt and very gently raised it to her knees. Her legs were bared before him, and his appetite was tenfold. With his every limb shaking, he clumsily wiped the saliva from his open mouth and got down on bended knees. Ever so carefully he undid the buttons on her blouse, delighting in the half-exposure of her breasts; small, pink mounds, so soft and perfect, the sight of which set him trembling uncontrollably. 'Ohh . . . Oh.' He could hardly contain himself.

Reaching down he opened his mouth, intent on teasing out the nipples with his tongue. He even closed his eyes in anticipation of pleasure.

In her sleep, Amy grew cold. She blinked and saw him there; in her waking state, she opened her mouth to scream but he was too quick. Flattening one huge hand over her mouth he held her still with the other. 'Ssh!' Like a mother quieting a child, he told her softly, 'It's all right. I won't hurt you.'

Amy's only defence was to sink her teeth into his hand; when he fell away in pain she leaped to her feet with him in pursuit. At first she instinctively fled towards the children's room, her intention to keep them safe. Then, realising he might hurt them, she ran for the door, praying he would follow.

Clumsy and caught unawares, it took him a minute to gather his wits, by which time she was running along the landing, shouting for help. At the top of the stairs he caught hold of her skirt and swung her round. 'You little bitch, I'll teach you to turn on me!' Raising his hand he went to strike her, but she dodged away and was about to run down the stairs when he swiped out with the whole force of his arm.

Losing her balance, Amy felt herself toppling over the banisters. She screamed, a shrill, seemingly endless scream that faded as she fell, and stopped when she hit the ground below.

The scream brought Tom and Sally from their beds. Tom saw Amy fall, but it was too late; dashing forward he beat the man with his fists. 'AMY! YOU'VE HURT AMY!' Tears of anguish ran down his face; in all his life he had never been so afraid.

Crouched in the corner, Sally stared through the banister rails, her wide, stricken eyes fixed on the seemingly lifeless form of her sister. She didn't say anything. She couldn't think. It was all too much to bear.

Kicking Tom aside the man made his getaway.

Hearing the commotion neighbours stayed hidden behind closed doors. They had heard it all before and were afraid. This time though, a sense of horror permeated the air.

So they sat very still, hardly daring to breathe. What they didn't know couldn't hurt them.

❦

OUTSIDE, A WOMAN of the streets was plying her trade. Strolling up and down Dock Street, she often pulled in a client with money, but not tonight. 'Looks like there's nothing doing.' The evening had grown oddly chilly. Drawing her coat tight about her, she crossed the road. It was then that she saw the man run out of the big house. 'Hmph! Got his arse on fire by the looks of it,' she sniggered. 'Some woman sent him packing, I expect. Serves the bugger right!'

Still laughing, she crossed to the other side of the road and, glancing through the open door thought she saw something. But she didn't get a chance to have a closer look because suddenly she was viciously kicked from behind. 'Bugger off, you old slag, we don't want your kind round here!' John Harvey didn't want any competition for Amy in the neighbourhood. 'Go on! Get away from here, I told you!' He gave her an almighty push and sent her sprawling.

By the time she got up and steadied herself, she had seen it all. She saw Harvey and the man go in, and before the door swung shut, saw Amy's twisted, bleeding body lying there. 'God Almighty!' Before she could put it all together in her mind, the door was flung open again and two small children came running out. The boy had hold of the girl and the two of them were being chased by the man who had just kicked her aside.

As he ran past, she put out her foot and sent him sprawling. Before he could gather himself together, she went after the children. Catching up, she swung Tom round. 'What's wrong, young 'un?' she demanded. 'What the devil's been going on? It's all right . . . you can tell me. I'm a friend.'

Sally was sobbing. 'They've hurt Amy,' she whimpered. 'I want my Amy.'

Looking down the street, the prostitute saw Harvey heading towards them. Realising she'd be killed for what she'd seen, and the children too, she started yelling at the top of her voice: 'MURDER! HELP, POLICE!' She thanked God when her cries brought the sound of a police whistle, followed by the thud of running feet.

Within minutes, help arrived. While the woman hid herself and the children in a doorway, Harvey was arrested and the house was put under surveillance.

'You don't want to get caught up with the rozzers,' she told Tom. 'You'd best come with me.'

'No.' Tom wanted to go back. 'I have to be with Amy. We have to help her.'

The woman shook her head. 'I'm sorry, darlin',' she told him gruffly, 'but it looks to me like your Amy is past help.'

At this, Sally cried out, 'NO! Amy! I want Amy!'

Alerted by Sally's cry, the policeman came running. 'Hey! What's going on there?'

'Quick!' Shoving them aside, the woman warned Tom, 'If they get hold of you they'll lock you up.' Suddenly, the policeman had her by the arm; a fierce struggle ensued, with the woman screaming for the children to, 'RUN! Get away from here!'

Terrified when the policeman made a grab for them, the children took her advice and ran like the wind, as far away from there as they could get.

They had no idea of the streets or which way to go, but Tom realised there was one person who could help. *'Kelly!'* Suddenly there was hope. 'She'll help us, Sally, don't worry!'

With that in mind, they were soon swallowed up by the darkness. But there *was* hope. In all the terror and uncertainty, there was one tiny chink of hope.

Chapter Sixteen

THE SPRING SUNSHINE was pleasantly warm.

From the land-berth where the boat was secured, Barney looked out across the harbour. It was so different from anything he'd ever known . . . so uniquely pretty, with the boats bobbing up and down in the gentlest swell, while above them in the bluest sky, the seagulls dipped and dived for pure enjoyment.

Stripped to the waist and soaked in sweat, Barney let the beauty invade his senses; there was nothing to compare with the salty tang of sea-air and the blue skies and bright sunshine, the sound of screeching birds and that vast expanse of sea stretching to God only knew where. It was incredible.

'You like it here, don't you, Barney?' Bill had been working alongside him, painting the boat and making it good for another year. 'These past few days I've seen you change. You seem more content, not as frantic as you were.'

'Ah, well, that's because I don't talk about it too much any more,' he answered cagily. 'It doesn't mean to say I'm not as determined as ever to find Kelly.'

'I understand, but you do know Marie won't give away her whereabouts. She's been keeping tags on Kelly and knows where she is. But until she's sure it's right for Kelly, she won't be giving anything away. I mean, you said yourself it was you who walked out on her.'

'One of the biggest mistakes of my life, I know that now.'

'All the same, until Marie gets the full picture from her investigator, she won't let you near her daughter.' He smiled. 'She's protected her, you know, all these years.'

'I can see that.' Knowing the family history made it easier to discuss. 'Neither of us ever imagined her mother would appoint a guardian angel to watch over her.'

'Oh, there was a time when she couldn't afford it, but her late husband, the man she met and married on her release from prison, left her well off. She doesn't spend anything on herself; "I'm keeping it safe for the children," she says.'

'They're hardly children any more, are they?'

'They are to her. She may have kept them at bay, but she loves them the same as she always has.' He smiled wistfully. 'Even Michael, the one who let her go to prison for what *he* did.' The smile fell away. 'I have mixed feelings about that fellow.'

Barney had often talked with Kelly about Michael, and what he said to Bill now was, 'Thank God we've neither of us ever been in that situation. He was a frightened young man who never had the nerve to stand up to his father, then one day he saw his mother being beaten half to death and acted on impulse, that's how I see it. And when he finally stood up for her, he went too far and killed the bastard.'

'His mother will protect him to the very end. Kelly too.'

'I can understand why Marie is trying to protect Kelly from me. Like you say, I did up and leave. But I never deceived her. It was always on the cards that I would go one day.' He looked out to sea. 'There's a big world out there and I needed to find my own place in it.'

'And have you?'

'Yes, I've found the place I want to be.' He thought of Kelly and smiled from the heart. 'It's with Kelly, that's where my place is, and for as long as I live – *if* she'll have me.'

'Ah! But *will* she have you?' They knew each other well enough now to speak openly. 'Kelly's moved away and made a new life. Don't forget that.'

'I've thought about nothing else,' Barney answered reflectively. 'It's for that reason and that reason only that I've given Marie the time she asked for . . . because I, too, need to know the way of things with Kelly. If Marie finds out that Kelly is happier without me, I'll go away and never come back.' Though it would break his heart to do it.

'Maybe it won't come to that.'

'When will Marie tell me where she is?' he asked. 'I wouldn't hurt Kelly. I love her too much for that.'

All the same, he was riddled with doubt. What if the news was bad? What if Kelly had shut him out of her life for ever? He wouldn't blame her if she had; though the thought of not being with her again was too unbearable for words. 'Ask her, Bill,' he pleaded. 'Ask Marie how much longer she means to keep me here.'

Just then, Bill noticed Marie coming along the beach. 'Here she is now,' he told Barney. 'Ask her yourself.' In a loose blue dress and familiar sun-hat, Marie looked a picture.

She had brought enough food for an army. 'Time for lunch.' Lifting the wicker basket to Bill, she gripped Barney's outstretched hand and clambered on deck. 'Ham and cheese sandwiches, a selection of fruit pies, four juicy oranges and a big jug of cider; that should keep you lads going.' There were plates, drinking mugs and napkins too.

Setting the basket on deck, Bill opened it up and there before him lay a feast for anyone's eyes. 'Look at that!' He laughed. 'Enough to feed the five thousand.'

'I don't know about that, but Samuel's on his way,' Marie explained. 'He's gone to the shop for a fishing hook, then he'll be here as fast as his little legs will carry him.'

As she spoke, the lad appeared, running along the beach like the wind. 'Isn't youth a wonderful thing,'

Bill sighed. 'I've forgotten the last time I could run like that.'

Marie laughed. 'I can't imagine you *ever* being able to run like that.'

'Don't be cruel, woman!'

While Samuel and his grandfather examined the fishing hook, Barney used the opportunity to take Marie aside. 'I know you have your man checking everything out, but it's been going on for quite a while now, and still you haven't told me where she is. For God's sake, can't you see, I'm going quietly mad.' Running his hands through his hair, he dropped his gaze to the ground. 'I can't wait much longer. To tell you the truth, I'm beginning to think you're running rings round me for some reason.'

'That's not true.' In fact, Marie had long thought Barney was the man for Kelly. 'I'm doing the best I can – you have to believe that.'

'How *can* I believe it? What's taking so long, for God's sake? You know where she is. For pity's sake, tell me and let me go to her!'

'I can't. Not yet.'

'Why not?' A terrible thought came into his head. 'My God! She's all right, isn't she?'

'Yes. It's not that.'

'What then?'

'Look, Barney . . . I just need you to leave it a bit longer, that's all.'

'No!' His patience had finally snapped. 'You've led

me on long enough already.' He issued an ultimatum. 'I promised Samuel a new fishing-rod for his birthday tomorrow. It should take me half an hour to check whether it's come in. I hope by the time I get back you'll have decided to tell me where Kelly is. If not, I'll have to find her *without* your help – even if I have to turn the whole world upside down!'

Still fuming, he strode away, leaving Bill open-mouthed. 'You've tried his patience too far,' he said. 'All he wants is for you to tell him where he can find Kelly. Good God, Marie, without your help he could be searching for ever, and might never find her. That's why he stayed here so long.' Like Barney, he didn't understand her reasons. 'It's not like you to be so cruel,' he commented. 'Day after day, you've led him on, like a carrot to a donkey. Oh, Marie! Can't you see what it's doing to him?'

'You don't understand.'

'Then *help me* to understand.'

'There's a man.' She took a deep breath. 'It's difficult.'

'Why difficult? All right, Kelly has a manfriend. What's so difficult about that? I don't suppose for one minute Barney hasn't had his share of flings while he's been away. It doesn't mean to say anything will come of it.'

'His name is Luke Porter and, from what I'm told, they plan to marry.'

'I see.' Bill was taken aback. Certainly it seemed to

put a different complexion on things. 'Why didn't you tell Barney? Don't you think he has a right to know something as important as that?'

'Not if it spoils her chances of happiness, no.'

'You said you thought Barney was the perfect man for Kelly. Kind and thoughtful, hard-working and head-over-heels in love with her, that's what you said. Have you changed your mind about him, is that it?'

'No, of course I haven't. But Kelly obviously has.' She hoped he could understand her dilemma. 'I *can't* tell him where she is, Bill! It wouldn't be fair of me to push them together. What if Kelly didn't want that?'

He began to see, but: 'Why don't you just tell Barney that she's planning to marry?'

She smiled, that lovely enigmatic smile that had drawn him to her in the first place. 'Because, deep down, I suppose I'm hoping Kelly might change her mind and decide she doesn't want Luke after all. Then I could send Barney to her with a clear conscience.'

Taking hold of her hand, Bill pressed it to his lips. 'You're just a hopeless romantic, that's the trouble.'

She shook her head. 'No, Bill. The trouble is, I just know Barney is so right for her. But it's for Kelly to decide, not me.'

'Well, all I can say is, it's a pity Kelly ever went back to Johnson Street, then she would never have met Luke, and Barney would have found her right where he left her.' His brow furrowed. 'I still can't understand what made her go back to Blackburn.'

'Oh, *I* can.'

Marie had given it a great deal of thought. 'Sometime in the future, I would like to go back myself,' she murmured. 'Terrible things happened in that house . . . good things, too. It's a strange thing, Bill; it's as if you're suddenly jolted out of everything you've ever known, and you feel hopelessly lost; because however bad it was, it was still your life. It's an odd feeling, one you can never really come to terms with. Until you know it's really over, you can never stop being afraid.'

'And you think that's why Kelly went back? To come to terms with what happened . . . to stop being afraid?'

'Perhaps.'

'And what about Michael? Do you think he feels the same way?'

'Ah, Michael.' Marie's eyes clouded over, her heart heavy inside her. 'I think he suffered more than any of us,' she tapped her chest, 'in here, if you know what I mean. I never did know what made him tick. He was such a quiet, secretive little boy.'

'A coward, that's what you said.'

'And you think that's too harsh?'

'I don't know him, so it isn't right for me to say.'

'All I ever wanted was for Michael and Kelly to be happy . . . not afraid or sad, the way I was.' Now, almost without her knowing it, a tear slipped down her face. 'Sometimes, when I'm thinking about . . . everything . . . the way it was then, it's Michael I feel for most of all. You see, Kelly is strong. She'll always come through, but not

Michael. He's so easily hurt. I'm afraid he'll let people use him, and there's nothing I can do about it.'

Suddenly she was crying; all the pain and sorrow she had kept shut away came pouring out.

'Ssh!' Taking her into his arms, he kept her safe.

Neither of them noticed the boy. Softly, Sammy dropped over the side of the boat and ran along the beach the way he had come. Remembering how the fishing-rod was supposed to come today, he went into the shop. 'Did Barney just come in here?'

'Sorry. He's been and gone.'

Rushing to his grandfather's cottage where Barney had been staying, Samuel ran round to the back door. 'Barney! Where are you? *Barney!*'

There was no answer. He burst inside, going up the stairs two at a time to Barney's room. Once there he flung open the door. There was no sign of his friend. Desperate, the boy threw open the cupboards and drawers; all emptied.

Lying across the bed was the new fishing-rod, and a card beside it. Seeing his name written there, the boy opened it: *Happy Birthday, Samuel* it read. *Be good . . . Barney*.

By the time he got back to the boat his lungs were almost bursting. 'He's gone!' Angry tears ran down his face as he stared at Marie. 'It's *your* fault. You made him leave, and now he'll never come back!'

Marie was stunned. When she turned to Bill her manner was calm and dignified. 'Go after him, Bill,' she said. 'He must have gone on foot along the main road. Tell him where she is. Ask him to go to her.'

'I'm glad,' he said quietly. 'It'll be all right, you'll see.'

She watched them go, the boy running ahead as they made for the main road. 'I did wrong,' she whispered. 'Find him, Bill. Tell him I'm sorry.'

<hr />

AN HOUR LATER, unaware that they had been looking for him, Barney jumped down from the wagon. 'Sorry, mate,' the driver apologised, 'but this is as far as I go.'

'No matter.' Barney thanked him all the same. 'I'll pick up another ride in no time at all.'

Walking on, he thought of his purpose and smiled confidently. 'I'm on my way, Kelly,' he murmured. 'I don't know how long it will take to find you. But I'm on my way.'

PART FOUR

HOMECOMING

Chapter Seventeen

I T HAD PROMISED rain all day, and now, in the first flush of evening, it poured down with a vengeance.

Drenched to the skin, Michael stood at the church doors for what seemed an age, not daring to go in, not wanting to stay out. 'This is your chance to put things right,' he told himself. 'Don't lose it for the sake of that first difficult step.'

Summoning every last ounce of courage, he stepped forward; the next step was easier, and before he knew it he was inside the church, looking down the aisle towards the altar.

He made no move for several minutes. Instead he stood quite still, his gaze focused on that heavenly cross above the altar, and his heart uplifted by the peace and quiet in God's beautiful house.

Tentatively, he made his way to the front, where he knelt before the cross, his eyes raised upward, and his lips moving in prayer. 'I don't know if You've deserted me, or if You doubt that I even deserve Your love. I know I've done wrong, and I mean to make amends.' Though he whispered, his voice seemed to echo to the rafters. 'I need Your forgiveness, Lord, or I can't go on.'

Out of nowhere a priest appeared by his side. 'He *does* hear you.'

Surprised by the voice at his side, Michael quietly observed the priest – his contentment and aura of well-being – and envied him. 'Will He *help* me though?'

'If you're troubled, He will always help you.'

Disillusioned, Michael turned away.

Persistent, the priest came and knelt beside him. 'Do you think you could tell *me* about it?'

Hesitating, Michael took a deep, regretful sigh that lifted his shoulders and bowed his head. 'It's haunted me for so many years,' he answered softly. 'Oh Father, it's such a burden.'

'Then it's high time you let someone else share it with you.'

There was a hush while Michael sought the way to begin. How could he tell this man of God what he had done? It was hard. Harder than the first step that brought him here.

At first the words wouldn't come and then, when he believed his courage had failed, he found himself confessing. 'I killed my own father.' Saying it like that, hearing it with his own ears, was a shocking thing. 'My mother took the blame. God forgive me, I let them lock away an innocent, and did nothing to stop it.'

He gulped the sorrow back. 'Every day with him was a living nightmare. She was a victim of his brutality. In the end, I was no better than him because I made her a victim too. She never told, and I was glad of that . . . *then.*' He paused, unable for a time to go on. With his head down and his eyes closed, no one could imagine the pain he was going through.

Blinded by his tears, he looked up at the priest. Sensing his anguish, the priest nodded. 'It's all right,' he said. 'I'm here.'

Michael told it all. He told about his vicious father and his wonderful, gentle mother, and he told about how he took Kelly away from it all. 'She was such a lovely, happy little thing,' he said, 'but after they put our mother away, Kelly went very quiet. She didn't laugh any more, and she didn't speak of it . . . *neither* of us did. She knew, you see. I made her a part of the conspiracy. That darling little girl saw it all. She saw me kill our own father, and was sworn to secrecy. She never spoke of it. She kept it all inside, and when she was old enough she went away.'

His voice broke. 'She even told me where she was. I wrote just once, but she didn't answer. We haven't seen each other since she left.'

'You could have gone to her.'

'No.' The priest didn't understand after all. 'I couldn't do that to her.'

'What about your mother?'

'I went to see her in prison.' He gave a half-smile. 'She forgave me, you know. She was the one who said

I mustn't tell. She wrote to me . . . I know she wrote to Kelly, but I haven't seen her. I haven't seen either of them.'

'Do you love them?'

'Oh, yes. So much it hurts.'

'Then search them out. Go to them.'

'I'm too much of a coward.'

The priest shook his head. 'It took great courage for you to tell me all these things.'

'What can I do, Father?'

'Only you can decide that. But you have a family. Don't be afraid to let them know how much you love them.'

They stayed there, kneeling before God, quiet and reflective. Some while later, knowing what he must do, Michael thanked the priest, and left the sanctuary of the holy place for the several duties that awaited him outside. It was time to put things right.

⟶≫•≪⟶

STRIDING PURPOSEFULLY DOWN the street, he set out his plan. First he must make amends with his wife. Things had not been good between them, and he blamed himself. With this in mind he quickened his steps.

Going in the front door, he took off his jacket and hung it on the peg. Still deep in thought, he didn't hear the sound at first. Then he wondered what it was: a rhythmic, grating sound coming from the front room.

Intrigued, he made his way there. Softly opening the door, he peered in, and was sickened by what he saw.

With her back supported by numerous cushions, his wife Joyce lay sprawled across the sofa; on top of her was a man, also naked, both too involved in what they were doing to care who might be watching. The rhythmic grunting noise he had heard was the man as he drove into her time and again, his head arched up in blissful agony. The woman beneath was curled round him, eyes closed, enjoying it to the full.

The anger began like a growl in the base of his throat, rising to a crescendo as he ran across the room. 'SLUT!' Already they were scrambling to get free. The man was desperately trying to put on his clothes. But not the woman. She stood before Michael, naked, brazen and defiant.

Taking the man first, Michael ran him across the room and through the house. Opening the door he threw him, half-dressed, on to the street, his clothes sailing through the air behind him. Thankful to be out of there, the fellow quickly dressed and ran. He had been afraid for his life, but not for hers. He didn't care what happened to Joyce Wills. After all, it was the stupid bitch's fault.

Inside the house, casually dressing, she taunted Michael beyond endurance. 'He's a *real* man and you're not!' she screamed. 'You never have been. Oh yes, you've kept me well provided for, and that's the only reason I've stayed. I hate you . . . I've hated you for a long time.'

She went on and on, until he could take it no more. 'I'd better go,' he said, turning away, 'before I do something I might regret.'

He had gone only two steps when she was on him. 'You bastard! I don't want you – can't you understand that? I hate the sight of you! Can't bear you to be in the same room!'

Shocked, he stared at her. 'Why did you stay, then?'

'To use you! And don't look at me like that, with big innocent eyes, because we both know the truth, don't we?' When she screamed, her saliva sprayed over his face. He had always thought her attractive in a strong sort of way, but now he had seen her in a truer light. 'I don't love you,' she yelled. 'I never have, and I never will. But you'd better not leave me. Who'll take care of me? What about my clothes – I'm used to the best now. If you go, I swear I'll tell the world about you . . . what you did. MURDERER!'

With her fists pummelling his shoulders and her voice screeching in his ear, he had taken her punishment because he felt he deserved it. But when she called him a murderer and threatened to tell the world, it was too much.

Swinging round he made a grab for her, but she fell backwards, on to that same sofa where she had opened herself to another man. This time, though, there was fear in her eyes. Still, her tongue didn't stop with its wickedness. 'What are you going to do? Kill me – like you killed your own father?'

His hands were on her throat, tightening with her every word. Suddenly, he cast her aside and stood over her, shame filling his soul. 'You're not worth it.' He saw her for what she was, and knew he was well rid. 'You're just like he was – taking everything and giving nothing . . . stripping away a person's soul. You like to hurt people. You want to reduce them to nothing so you can grind them into the ground. I see that now. I see you as I should have seen you before. But I was blind . . . blind to so many things.'

Calmer now, he looked about him, at this place he had called home. 'I'll take nothing with me,' he told her. 'I want nothing that has been tainted by you.' One more long searching glance at her, and he walked away.

Relentless, she followed him. 'Go on then! I'll be all right. There are others who'll take care of me. Get out of here . . . and don't come back. I hate the sight of you! DO YOU HEAR ME?'

Then she was sobbing. But he knew about that, for hadn't he heard his mother sobbing – oh so many times. And every one etched forever in his memory.

Outside, Michael took a deep, refreshing breath. He felt reborn. For the first time in many long years, he knew what he must do.

First, though, he had a call to make.

I N THE DRAWING-ROOM of the big house, Kathleen was restless. 'Are you all right, ma'am?' The maid was concerned. 'Can I bring you anything?'

'No, thank you all the same. I'm fine. I won't need you for the rest of the evening. Why don't you go and see that young man of yours?'

The girl blushed pink. 'Oh, ma'am, I didn't think anybody knew.'

Smiling, Kathleen promised, '*I* won't tell if you don't.'

'Oh, it's not that I'm ashamed, ma'am,' the maid told her, 'Only, I thought if you knew, you might think I'm about to get wed and then you'd be rid of me.'

Kathleen was horrified. 'Shame on you! I would never do that.'

The girl gave a great sigh of relief. 'Even if I *did* get wed, ma'am, I would never want to leave you.'

'Where does he work, this young man of yours?'

'At Pardey Grange. But he's not very happy there.'

'Well then, if the two of you get wed, we shall have to find him work *here*. And maybe we'll build you a little cottage in the grounds.'

'Oh, ma'am, that would be wonderful.' She couldn't believe her ears.

'You run along then . . . take the evening off. Tell him what I said.'

'Oh, I will, ma'am, I will!' She ran off, excitement

making her forget her manners. Returning a minute later, red in the face, she was full of apology. 'Thank you, ma'am,' she muttered, and left in a more dignified manner.

With the girl gone, Kathleen took up her vigil by the window. 'Where are you now, Michael?' she murmured. 'Are you lonely, like me?'

———⇒•⇐———

OUTSIDE, MICHAEL COULD see her at the window. It was all he could do to stop himself from going to her and declaring his love. There was so much at stake, and he didn't want to hurt anyone else the way he had hurt his mother and sister. But oh, he *did* love Kathleen . . . in a way that he had never loved any other woman. All he wanted was to be with her. But he knew it was not to be.

He stepped back into the shadows, the rain from the trees dripping down his neck, and the darkness closing in around him. He stood there for a long time, watching her, loving her . . . needing to leave but loath to go.

At long last he turned away. In that split second, the light from the house caught his figure as he moved, and suddenly she was at the door. 'MICHAEL!' She had seen him and there was laughter in her voice.

He turned to see her running towards him, her hair loose about her shoulders as she ran, and her arms open wide. With a cry of joy, he caught her to him. 'Oh,

Kathleen! Kathleen, what will I do without you?' He kissed her then, a kiss that betrayed how very much he loved her, and she him.

Wrapping his jacket round her shoulders, he walked with her to the shelter of the trees. 'I have to go,' he said. 'And I won't be back.' It broke his heart, but it had to be said. 'There is no place for you in my life, because I won't have a life for a very long time to come.'

'Please, Michael – don't shut me out.'

He knew what she meant and told her everything. 'I'll never be free of it,' he said brokenly, 'until I face the punishment.'

'We'll face it together,' she murmured. And her sincerity brought a tear to his eye.

'Why couldn't I have met you long ago?' he wondered aloud.

'There's a time for everything,' she said. 'It just wasn't our time, that's all. But it is now, and, oh, Michael, I'm so happy we've found each other.'

They embraced for a long time; they talked and planned, and when all that was left was their abiding love, he walked her to the house. 'Wait for me.' He held her tight. 'The day you see me walking towards you will be the first day of our lives together.'

Kathleen was crying when he left, but they were tears of joy, for now she knew he wanted her she would wait for ever. 'I love you,' she called.

He turned and smiled, then walked on, eager now to be done with it.

PAUSING BY THE river, he took out his wallet and dropped it into the murky waters; next came his jacket and tie, and finally the wedding ring Joyce had put on his finger. He smiled as it all disappeared in an ever-growing arc of ripples. 'It's nearly over,' he murmured.

It was as though the burden he carried was part of his life, and his life was there, in the things he wore and owned, and until now had put a value on. As he dropped them into the water one by one, he felt he was purging himself of things that were of no value. And he could feel the weight being lifted from his soul.

WHEN, A SHORT time later, he walked into the local police station, the Constable on duty stared at him in amazement. With his hair wet and dank from the rain, and with no jacket or tie, Michael presented a very strange picture.

'What can I do for you, sir?' Curious, the officer moved forward to the desk.

'I've come to give myself up,' Michael told him. 'I killed someone. A long time ago.'

Chapter Eighteen

K ELLY WAS LIKE a cat on hot bricks.

With the onset of May, the weather had turned so warm she had to throw every window open; the front door, too, in order to let a breeze through. The heavy tapestry curtains she was working on hung across her legs and arms like a dead weight, smothering her so she could hardly breathe. Twice she got up and poured herself a glass of lemonade, but even that was warm to the taste.

At half-past four, Mrs Arkwright came to collect her curtains. 'There's an extra sixpence,' she said, counting out the coins. 'You've done a wonderful job, as always.' These were the last of the four pairs of curtains commissioned for her boarding house. 'I wonder if you could make me four cushions to match?' she asked. 'They would just give that finishing touch, and my boarders do like to be comfortable.'

Kelly told her she would be delighted to do so, but couldn't fit them in for at least another two weeks. 'I'm that busy I'll be meeting myself coming back, if I'm not careful,' she teased.

Mrs Arkwright was disappointed, and not used to being turned down. 'Can't you get straight on to them,' she pleaded. 'I'd so like to set them out when Mr Arkwright puts up the curtains.'

Kelly shook her head. 'I'm sorry, I can't.'

'Not even for an extra shilling?'

'Not even then.' Already Kelly had so much work she was rising at six and going to bed at midnight . . . and that was even with the capable girl she had started on.

Seeing she would get no change from Kelly, Mrs Arkwright shrugged her bony shoulders. 'Well, if you can't, you can't,' she grumbled. 'But you *will* get on to them as soon as possible, won't you?' When Kelly promised to do that, she thanked her with an extra shilling and a wink. 'Don't leave it too long though, eh,' she cooed. Straightening both her back and her expression, she called her husband in from the carriage. 'The curtains!' she snapped. 'Surely you don't expect *me* to carry them out?' She clicked her fingers and like a little dog, Mr Arkwright gathered up the curtains and toddled out.

At six o'clock Kelly called Lucy Drew in from the front parlour; she was the girl who had knocked at the door the day before Amy had gone to hear Fran's will being read. Kelly was very pleased with her, and often told her so. Lucy was a bright young thing with quick fingers and a sense of pride in what she did. She didn't say much, but then there was little time for chat when they got down to the day's work, so it was just as well.

'Time to pack up,' Kelly told her. 'I'll see you in the morning.' As it was Friday, she handed the girl a small brown packet; wages well earned. 'There's an extra sixpence in there,' she winked. 'A present from Mrs Arkwright.'

Pleased to have done another day's work, the girl packed her sewing away. 'Good night, Miss Wilson.'

'Goodnight, Lucy. Don't forget, you'll only be working till twelve tomorrow. Like I said, we both deserve a Saturday afternoon off.'

Kelly and the girl usually worked all day Saturday, but not tomorrow. She had things on her mind, and they were to do with Amy.

At seven o'clock she had packed away her own sewing, and was watching out the window for Luke to come home. Impatient, she began drumming her fingers on the windowsill. 'Come on, Luke,' she urged, 'I have an idea.'

In the moment she went to pour herself a drink, Luke appeared round the corner; worn and weary, he looked like he'd had a hard day.

Returning to the front parlour, Kelly pulled up a chair and sat there for some time, sipping her drink and keeping a wary eye on the corner of the street. When the mantelpiece clock chimed eight, she knew she must have missed him. 'He must have gone by when I went to the scullery.' She decided to go down the street to Charlie's house and talk with him there.

First she took her glass into the scullery, splashed her face under the big old tap, then brushed her hair. 'Can't go down the street looking like a scarecrow,' she muttered. 'A woman has her pride, after all.'

After passing the time of evening with several neighbours, Kelly climbed the three steps to Charlie's house; like herself on this close May evening, Charlie had left the door open to allow a breeze through.

As always, when the door was open, it was the habit not to knock until you got to the parlour door – and then only as a matter of politeness. So she went blithely down the passage and on towards the far door at the foot of the stairs.

Raising her fist to knock, she paused at the sound of voices. There was nothing untoward about that, because of an evening when Luke came home, the conversation always turned to Charlie's day and Luke's work in that order; it was even known for them to have a bit of an argument over dinner.

This time though, it was different, because they were discussing *her!*

Curious, Kelly dropped her hand to her side and listened; a thing she would never have done if it hadn't been for Luke saying, 'No, Dad! Kelly *has* to be told! I've kept it from her long enough, and she doesn't deserve that.'

Charlie sounded frantic. 'Listen to me, son. She's already worried sick for Amy. Going out of her mind she is, wondering what's happened to her and them childer. Telling her now would be selfish. I won't have you hurting her just to ease your own conscience. I won't have it, do you hear?'

'Look, Dad, be sensible. Kelly believes I mean to marry her.'

'Then let her go on believing it – at least until we know whether Amy's coming back, and then this whole bloody sorry mess can be sorted out! Kelly's a good woman. She'll make you a fine wife, mebbe even manage a grandchild for me afore it's too late. Oh Luke, don't throw all that away. Don't break her heart. I love that lass like my own.'

Luke was distressed and it showed in his voice. 'Do you think *I* don't love her? Of course I do, but not in the way I love Amy. I didn't mean for it to happen, but it did, and now I'm trying to do the best thing for Kelly. And yes, for me and Amy if it should ever come about.' There was a pause, before he could be heard scraping the chair back and striding across the room. 'I'm going to Kelly now. I won't deceive her any longer . . . and Amy *will* be back, I know she will.'

He flung open the door and was stopped in his tracks by the sight of Kelly standing there. 'Kelly!' He gasped as though recovering from a blow. 'I didn't hear you come in. Oh Kelly, I'm so sorry.' Running his hands through his hair the way he did when agitated, he looked at Charlie, then at Kelly, and didn't quite know what to do. 'You'd best come in,' he said, and stepped back for her to pass.

'Sit down, lass.' Charlie drew out a chair. 'Do you want me to go?'

Kelly shook her head. 'Where would you go, Charlie?' she smiled. So he sat down opposite, his head in his hands and a sorry look on his homely old face.

Luke remained where he was, shifting uncomfortably from one foot to the other. 'I suppose you heard it all?' He hated himself.

'Tell me one thing,' Kelly murmured. When he turned to look at her, she asked, 'Does Amy feel the same way about you?'

'Yes.'

'Is that why she ran away?'

'I think so. I can't be certain.'

'Please, Luke, come here. Sit beside me.'

With his heart in his boots he went to her. 'We didn't mean to deceive you,' he said. 'It was just once . . . a kiss, that's all. And then we both knew.'

'Shall I tell you something?'

Reaching out, he took hold of her hand.

Kelly held it tight, reassuring him. 'You love Amy,' she murmured, 'and from what you tell me, she feels the same way. It's ironic, isn't it?'

He didn't know quite what she meant. 'None of us can help who we love, Kelly. I was about to tell you tonight. I couldn't keep you in the dark much longer.'

'If it hadn't been you telling me,' she smiled a secret smile, 'it would have been *me* telling *you*. The truth is,

Luke, I couldn't marry you any more than you could marry me. You see, I still love Barney.' She chuckled. 'That's why it's so ironic . . . both of us loving someone else and too afraid to say.'

Her news had taken him aback. It took a moment to realise what she was saying. When he did, he gave the greatest sigh. 'I'm glad,' he said. 'Oh, Kelly! You'll never know how much.'

The sound of Charlie laughing made them look up. 'Well, I never!' His old face was creased with happiness. 'Now we've got that all sorted, we'd best find the lass and make an honest woman of her.'

Squeezing Luke's hand affectionately, Kelly told him, 'That's why I came here tonight. I've been thinking about Amy and that time we asked John Harvey if he knew anything. I can't help feeling he was lying. I'm *sure* he knows where she is.'

'You're right!' Luke was already putting on his jacket. 'We let him off the hook too lightly.'

Charlie, too, had his say. 'I told yer afore, didn't I? If the lass wanted somewhere to live, she'd *have* to go to this Harvey 'cause there ain't nobody else got property in this town.'

Kelly had a suggestion. 'Happen he uses the alehouses near his office. We could try there?'

'Aye, an' if he's not there, we'll search every bloody alehouse in Blackburn till we find him!' Loath to be left out, Charlie dashed through the door after them. 'Watch him though, son. He's a cunning fox.'

W HEN THEY GOT to Ainsworth Street, they were delighted to see a light burning in Harvey's office. 'Well, I'm buggered!' When the other two quickened their steps, Charlie was almost running to keep up. 'That's a stroke o' luck, ain't it?'

Inside the office, John Harvey had his clerical assistant in tears. 'You're nothing but useless!' he told the girl, Helen. 'I wanted them contracts ready to take home, and here you are only halfway finished.'

'I'm sorry, Mr Harvey, really I am.'

There was no appeasing him. 'Sorry is not good enough! I should have been gone home half an hour since, and now I'm having to wait for you. I've a damned good mind to send you packing here and now.' Every few words, he shook her by the arms and made her squeal. 'Useless!' With a final cruel jerk, he spat out: 'I'm going across the street for a jar, and I'll be gone twenty minutes. If those contracts are not done by the time I get back, you can take your cards and clear off for good.'

Suddenly the door burst open, startling them both. At the sight of two men and Kelly, all looking ready to take on the world, the girl cowered behind the counter, while Harvey, bold as ever, coolly confronted them. 'What the devil do you want? What right have you to come bursting in here like that?'

Luke stepped forward. 'We've come for the whereabouts of Amy Slater.'

Guilt coloured Harvey's features. 'I've already told you. I don't know where she is.'

Kelly had suggested that Luke should bluff the truth out of him. 'You're a liar, Harvey! We *know* she came to you looking for a room.'

'Whoever told you that is the liar. She never came anywhere near here – ask my assistant. She'll tell you.' Ever since the fiasco in Liverpool, the agent had been living on his nerves. His guilt showed now, in the expression on his face and the tremor in his voice. 'Get out of here or I'll call the police.'

'Where is she?' They could almost smell his guilt.

'Honest to God, I don't know where she is.' His eyes were big with fear, and the sweat was running down his temples.

Luke advanced on him. 'You *do* know where she is. I want the address, Harvey. I'll stay here all night until you tell me.'

'GET OUT!' Fear made the other man bold. Dashing forward he hit out at Luke, catching him hard on the shoulder. 'Don't you come here threatening me. I've done nothing wrong, do you hear? Nothing at all.'

Catching him by the lapels, Luke stared him in the eye. 'Nobody said you'd done anything wrong,' he told him in a soft, accusing voice. 'Why would you say a thing like that, unless you had a guilty conscience?' Holding him tight, he leaned forward, his face almost touching the other man's. 'I'll ask you once again, Harvey. *Where is she?*'

Harvey knew it was more than his life was worth to reveal the truth about Amy. 'Take your hands off me, you bastard!' Breaking away, he hit out again, this time catching Luke on the mouth and splitting the skin.

The fight that followed was fierce. Charlie wanted to get involved, but Kelly held him back. 'Leave them,' she said. 'He knows where Amy is, I saw it in his eyes.' Not for one minute did she believe Harvey would get the better of Luke.

Each man had the strength of his convictions; Luke because he was desperate to find Amy, and Harvey because he knew what had happened and daren't let it be forced from him. So they fought, hard and long, and in the struggle furniture went flying, blood was spilled, and still Harvey kept his mouth shut. 'Where is she?' Over and over Luke asked, but still it was the same answer . . . 'I don't know.'

Luke had him pinned aganst the wall, fist raised. 'You're a liar! You'd best tell me, Harvey, or I won't be responsible for my actions.' He raised his fist higher.

Seeing how it had all gone too far, Kelly ran across the room. 'Tell him,' she begged the other man. 'Tell him, or I can't save you.'

Weary and afraid, Harvey pleaded with her. 'I don't know where she is,' he lied. 'If I did, don't you think I'd tell you?' Close to tears he glanced at Luke. 'You'd best take him away from here. He's gone crazy.'

When Kelly saw how Luke was about to bring down his fist against the other man's face, she put up her arm and stopped him. 'No, Luke. Even if he does know where she is, this isn't the way. It's gone too far. We'll find her. There are other ways.' Staring at Harvey with a measure of hatred, she told him quietly, 'We *will* find her, and when we do, if it turns out that you knew where she was all along, we'll be back.' She hoped it would be enough to keep him sweating.

There was a moment when she thought Luke would hit him anyway. But then he lowered his arm and, giving the other man a look that made him tremble, he went with the others into the night, looking for Amy.

Behind them, the clerk ran about fetching water and trying to help. Cleaning the blood from Harvey's nose she foolishly let her feelings run away with her. 'I'll look after you, Mr Harvey,' she babbled. 'I love you. I won't let anybody hurt you again.'

Shocked by her revelation, he stared her in the face. '"Love me!"' The disgust on his face was like a knife to her heart. One minute he was laughing out loud; the next he had swiped out to send her careering across the room. 'Get out of here!' he growled. 'You're finished.'

For a painful moment she lay there, dazed and hurt.

Lolling forward in the chair, he mumbled to himself, 'Bloody fools! I wonder what they'd say if they knew she'd been lying in the Infirmary for weeks . . . and her brats in the hands of the authorities.' The idea that he'd got away with it put a smile on his face. 'I hope the lot of 'em rot in hell.'

Struggling up, the girl appealed to him. 'Don't sack me, Mr Harvey. Please don't send me away.'

His answer was to smack her hard across the mouth. 'I thought you'd gone. Piss off!'

Sobbing, she grabbed her bag and ran off, the sound of his cruel laughter following her down the street. 'Silly cow,' he bawled after her. 'I wouldn't give you the time of day, not even if you were naked and offering yourself on a plate.'

Chapter Nineteen

'A JAR OF ale and a meat pie, if you will, landlord.'
'Coming up, sir.' The landlord was not the usual kind; thin and pale, and immaculately dressed he looked more like an undertaker than a publican. 'That'll be ninepence-halfpenny.'

Barney paid up. 'I'll be over there.' Pointing to the far corner, he made his way towards it and sat down at a table. It was about that time, when the day's work was done and men crowded in for one quick drink before going home to their evening meal.

Choosing the far corner gave Barney a chance to sit away from the noise and bustle, where he could think, and assess his own situation.

Curious to see a stranger, one of the men sauntered out of the crowd. 'Looks like you've been doing some travelling, mate?' he said in the characteristic Liverpudlian accent.

Right now, Barney didn't want company. 'That's

right.' Taking a pen and map from his rucksack, he picked up the last point of contact, Manchester, and drew a line to Liverpool, where he was now.

Persistent, the man sat down beside him; reaching over, he stole a look at the map. 'You've had a long journey . . . all the way from the South to Manchester, and now here. What's your business, if you don't mind me asking?'

'No, I don't mind you asking.' Barney closed the map and put it away. 'So, I hope *you* don't mind if I choose not to answer.' It was always the same. Just when you wanted peace and quiet, somebody always wanted to chat. But the fellow was harmless enough, so he didn't mind too much.

Chuckling, the man offered his hand in friendship. 'In other words, mind me own business.'

Shaking him by the hand, Barney grinned. 'Sorry about that. Like you say, I've travelled a long way, and I'm not feeling very sociable at the minute.'

'I can understand that.' He nodded. 'The name's Alf, by the way.'

'Mine's Barney.'

'Well, Barney . . . you're a lucky man.'

'Why's that?' He didn't feel very lucky at the minute.

The man glanced at Barney's rucksack. 'Seems to me you're footloose and fancy-free, with not a worry in the world.'

'Not quite true, old mate.'

Just then the landlord came with his order. Thanking him, Barney lifted the jar of ale and took a deep swig. Wiping the froth from his mouth he told the other man, 'You should never be fooled by what you see.'

'Aye, but what I see is a man without ties ... travelling from one end of the country to the other.' He sighed noisily. 'It's what I'd do if I got the chance – travel. Just take off and let my feet go where they will. What I wouldn't do for that!'

'Why don't you do it, then?'

'Hmph! I've got a wife and four kids and a job that I hate. But it brings in the money and keeps the roof over our heads.'

'What kind of work is that then?' Taking a chunk out of his meat pie, Barney waited for an answer. Now that he'd got into a conversation, he found it pleasant. So often on the road you didn't get to converse with honest men.

'I'm a porter.' Raising his glass he downed half the liquid. Watching the juice trickle from that succulent pie on to the plate, he licked his lips. 'Landlord! I'll have one of those meat pies, please.'

'Oh, so you work on the railways.' Leaning back in his chair, Barney observed the man; big and stout with hands like shovels he was surprised at his gentle manner.

'Oh no!' The man tutted forlornly. 'I'm not so fortunate. No, I porter at the Infirmary. I fetch and carry, that sort of thing, run the patients to the operations room, and take out the dirty linen. I clean a bit and chat a bit and take out the empties when I'm told.'

'Empties?' Barney was intrigued.

'Them as ain't with us no more, if you know what I mean?' He tapped his nose meaningfully.

Wishing he hadn't asked, Barney put down his knife. 'I see what you mean. But surely there must be a brighter side to your work?'

The man shook his head. 'Can't think of one if there is,' he answered solemnly. Suddenly his face lit up. 'Well, yes, I tell a lie. It allus does me heart good to see somebody come in at death's door, and then a few weeks later they walk out on their own two feet. It gives a body hope, if you understand my meaning.'

Another swig of ale and he was all the merrier. 'The old ones are the funniest,' he said. 'Last week I had to fetch this old boy back and put him to bed. He'd only gone to the ladies' ward, hadn't he? Had delusions about having his wicked way with somebody. Well, I caught him climbing in with an old dear of about ninety. "You'll not get much change there," I told him. "She's forgot where she put it".'

Even Barney spluttered and laughed into his ale.

'But there are some sad sights, I can tell yer.' His mood darkened. 'There's this lovely little thing – been with us some weeks now. Fell down a staircase or summat. Anyway, she's in a bad way. The doctors don't think she'll make it, and I tend to think they might be right.'

'That *is* sad.'

'Her name's Amy. Got two kids with her an' all, by all accounts. Well, o' course, the poor little beggars are in the hands of the authorities, so there's no telling *where* they'll end up ... working for some bully of a tradesman, I dare say. She keeps asking after 'em, but the authorities, in their bloody wisdom, won't let the kids go to her, in case it upsets 'em too much. Drifts in and out of consciousness, she does, crying for the bairns and calling out for somebody by the name of Kelly.'

'KELLY!' Slamming his drink down on the table, Barney sat up. 'Kelly *who?*'

Startled by Barney's reaction, the other man snapped back, 'How would *I* know?'

'Can I see her, this Amy?'

Blowing out his cheeks in frustration, the man shook his head. 'I'm not sure. Somebody as poorly as she is – well, they're bound to be a bit careful, aren't they?'

Taking out his purse, Barney dug out a florin. 'Would *this* get me in to see her?'

The man's eyes glittered greedily. 'Happen *two* might.'

'All right. Two florins it is then.' That said, Barney was on his feet and throwing his rucksack over his shoulder. 'One now and one after I've talked to her.'

A moment later, they left the alehouse.

As they hurried along, Barney prayed this would be the lead he had been looking for.

———❖———

THE MATRON REGARDED Barney through suspicious eyes. 'Her *brother*, you say?'

'That's right.' Barney soon had her wrapped round his little finger. 'I had no idea she'd been hurt,' he said. 'I've only just today got back from the sea.'

'A sailor, eh?' She observed his weathered features and the rucksack on his back. 'My father was a sailor . . . the finest man who ever lived.'

'I'm sure, ma'am. But I'd like to see my sister now, if it's all right with you?'

Addressing the porter who had lingered, she told him, 'Take the gentleman down.' Warning Barney she said, 'Sailor or not, I'll be along in ten minutes to see you out. She's very poorly, and I don't want her tired out.'

'Come on. Quick.' The porter led him towards the ward. 'Before the old battleaxe changes her mind.'

Even though the porter had warned him how ill Amy was, Barney was shocked at the sight of her small grey face, and the deep dark hollows under her eyes. 'My God!' He looked down on her sleeping face with compassion. 'She's just a girl.'

'Twenty – twenty-one, summat like that.' Stooping, the porter took hold of her hand with a tenderness that surprised Barney. 'Amy?' He gave her the gentlest shake. 'Amy, lass. Here's a visitor for you.'

Slowly, Amy opened her eyes. 'The children?'

'No, it ain't the children, but it's a friend. He reckons he knows your Kelly, the one you keep calling after?'

Now, when she looked up at Barney, the eyes seemed large as saucers in that tiny, sick face.

'It's all right,' he told her, leaning forward. 'I really am a friend.' He smiled. 'I told the matron I was your brother or she wouldn't have let me in.'

She managed the tiniest of smiles. 'Who are you?'

'I know someone called Kelly. I need to know if it's the same one.'

'What's your name?'

'Barney.'

She nodded. Kelly had spoken of this man she loved so many times. Tears rose in her eyes; weakness prevented her from speaking.

'I'm not sure if it's the same Kelly I know,' Barney confessed. 'Only I've been searching for her, and I have an idea she might be in the North. Her family came from here, though I'm not sure exactly where.' He squeezed her hand. 'The matron will be here in a few minutes, Amy. Please, listen carefully. This Kelly, what other name does she go by?'

Amy closed her eyes. She could see Kelly's bright face, oh so clearly, and beside her, Luke. Always Luke.

'Amy, *please!*' Glancing up the ward, Barney could see the matron heading their way. 'What other name?'

Opening her eyes she looked up. 'Kelly . . .' He could hardly hear her. 'Kelly . . . Wil . . .' When she hesitated he finished it for her, his heart in his mouth. '*Wilson!* Amy, was it Kelly *Wilson?*'

When she nodded, the relief was like a tidal wave gushing through him. 'Oh, dear God!' Burying his head in his hands he fought back the tears. 'Where is she, Amy?'

The matron was on them before Amy could answer. 'The ten minutes are up and you're out,' she said, and without any more ado, she ushered him from the ward and into the corridor. 'Come back tomorrow,' she said. 'When your sister is rested.'

Distraught yet exhilarated all at the same time, Barney began his slow journey along the corridor. Maybe when the matron had gone he could sneak back to Amy and she would tell him where Kelly was.

As though reading his mind, the matron stood like a sentry at the door of the ward, her beady eyes on him until he was out of sight. When he peeped back a moment later he saw her going into the ward, and the porter coming out.

'Quick, mate.' Grabbing Barney by the arm, he ushered him to a corner. 'This woman you're looking for . . . is she worth another florin?'

Without asking questions, Barney dug out another coin, but withheld it until he got what he was after. 'She lives in Johnson Street, Blackburn,' the porter revealed. 'Amy told me. She said you're to fetch her quick. "Kelly will help get my bairns", that's what she said.'

On impulse and much to the other fellow's astonishment, Barney hugged him. 'Tell her I'll fetch Kelly back,' he promised. 'And we'll get the bairns. You tell her that!'

While the porter went back to tell Amy what he'd promised, Barney ran into the street to hail a cab. 'Take me to the railway station,' he said. 'I've a train to catch . . . and a woman to see.' As they went along he scribbled down her address: 'Johnson Street, Blackburn.'

After all this time, he couldn't wait to get there.

PART FIVE

TOGETHER

Chapter Twenty

I T WAS LATE evening when the knock came on the door.

Covered in flour while baking a cake for Charlie's birthday, it took Kelly a while to get down the passage; meantime the knocking became frantic. 'For goodness' sake! Wait a minute, will you!' Wiping her hands on her apron she flung open the door. 'Who the devil . . .' The words stuck in her throat. Too choked to go on, she stood there staring at Barney, unable to believe her eyes.

His grin was as wickedly charming as ever. 'You're a hard woman to track down.' Throwing open his arms he leaped the three steps to the door, grabbed her by the waist and swung her round and round, until she cried out for him to stop.

'Oh, Barney!' Her heart was going thirteen to the dozen. 'However did you find me?'

'It wasn't easy.' Wiping the tears from her face he told her, 'But you always knew I'd find you, didn't you?'

'I hoped you would,' she answered truthfully. 'I didn't leave any forwarding address, because I didn't want you to come back and feel obliged to come after me.'

Holding her to him, he gazed down into those wonderful, familiar eyes. 'I had to go away,' he murmured. 'Then I had to come back. I thought about you every day, until one morning I woke up and realised I must have been crazy wanting to go out and see the world, when all the time *you* were my world.'

Bending to kiss her, he pressed her to him and held her there, and for a moment Kelly thought she must be dreaming. 'I missed you so much,' she whispered.

He smiled on her, teasing. 'So you *do* want me back then?'

Rolling her eyes to heaven, she pretended to consider it. 'Well, I suppose I could give you a trial run . . . say a week, and if you're not suitable then I'll have to show you the door.' Holding out her hand, she laughed. 'Is it a deal?'

'I'll think about it,' he answered with a devil-may-care attitude, and the two of them went into the house arm-in-arm, laughing together just like they used to.

All too soon, the laughter stopped when he told her about Amy. 'She's in a bad way,' he said. 'She's asking for you . . . They've taken the bairns and she thinks you can get them back.'

Until he saw her sobbing, he had no idea how close she and Amy had been. 'It's all right,' he murmured.

'I'll take you to her. She'll buck up once she knows you're there.'

In a minute she was on her feet and running for the door. 'I must tell Luke!' She ran down the street with Barney in pursuit. Pummelling her fists on the door, she called out: 'Luke, it's Amy! BARNEY FOUND AMY!'

Suddenly the door opened and Luke appeared, still in hs working clothes, still unwashed. 'Amy's in Liverpool Infirmary,' Kelly told him. 'She's asking for me . . . they've taken Tom and Sally away.'

Only taking a minute to grab his coat and enough money, Luke shouted to Charlie, 'I'm off to Liverpool! Amy's in the hospital there.'

'Is she all right?' Charlie came to the door, visibly shocked.

'I'll be back as soon as I can, Dad. Don't worry now.' Nodding at Barney, Luke suggested that Kelly should tell him everything on the way.

The moment Kelly had fetched her coat and bag, the three made straight for the railway station, and Liverpool.

⟫•❮

ADAMANT THAT THEY should not disturb Amy, the matron sent for the doctor, who called the three of them into his office. He told them how Amy had been found lying injured at the foot of the stairs. 'The boy saw her fall but couldn't say how it happened. But then the boy and his sister were distraught . . . they're in the care of the authorities now,' he informed them. 'I'm sure they'll be well looked after.'

'What about Amy?' Luke's first thought was for her.

'I'm afraid she's very ill. The broken bones are healing, and so too are the superficial wounds, but she has no fighting spirit, and without that I can't hold out much hope.'

'You don't know anything about her!' Kelly rounded on him. 'Amy was always *full* of fighting spirit!' she argued. 'They've taken the children. I can imagine they're fretting for her, and she's worried sick. From what I can gather they're not allowed to see each other, in case it upsets Amy. Whose stupid idea was that?'

'My duty is to put the patient first.'

'Oh! For pity's sake, Doctor, don't you know how much those three need each other? You've taken away every good thing she ever had. Don't you understand? *That's* why she's got no fighting spirit.'

'I think you had better leave.' He took umbrage at having his methods questioned.

Up until now, Barney had stood back, but then he stepped forward. 'Please, Doctor, don't be too hasty. What Kelly says might just be right. If your first duty is to your patient, then why not ask Amy if she needs to see the children. And don't send away these good people. These are her friends. Like you, they only have Amy's interests at heart. Please, Doctor. Let them go to her, if only for a minute.'

Something in the timbre of Barney's voice, or the honesty in his eyes, made the doctor consider his position. 'All right then,' he conceded. 'But if I see she's disturbed, I'll ask you to leave and I *don't* expect an argument.' He directed his gaze to Kelly.

Contrite, she nodded acknowledgement. He crossed the room and opened the door. 'One at a time,' he said. 'Or not at all.'

Neither Kelly nor Luke could argue with that.

Outside the ward, Luke suggested that Kelly should go first. 'She asked for you,' he reminded her. 'Besides, you know how things are between me and Amy, so it might be best if you broke the news to her.'

Barney had no idea what they were talking about, but he knew that whatever it was, Kelly would deal with it in the best way.

Following the doctor, Kelly was taken to Amy's bedside.

Amy was sleeping. 'Oh, she looks so small.' Putting her hand to her face, Kelly smothered a heartfelt sob. 'Oh, Amy!' Sitting beside her, she continued to gaze down on her dearest friend. 'I'm here, Amy, I'm right beside you, sweetheart.'

It was a few minutes before Amy opened her eyes, and while she waited, Kelly prayed. 'Let her get better, Lord,' she whispered. 'Don't let her die.'

When she felt Amy's eyes on her, she put out her

hands and took both of Amy's small hands into her grasp. 'You've got to get better,' she whispered, and this time she couldn't hold back the tears. 'You've got to get strong, Amy, for the children.'

Seeing Kelly there was too much to take in all at once. Softly crying, Amy couldn't speak. Instead she held out her arms and Kelly went to her, and for a long time they stayed like that, two dear friends and a wealth of love between them. 'I'll bring the children,' Kelly promised. 'You know I'll find a way.'

While they embraced, the doctor stole away; but the matron stayed, and though she tried to keep a stiff upper lip, she found a tear trickling down her face.

'Luke's come to see you.' Easng away, Kelly quickly assured her: 'I know how you two feel about each other, and it's all right. I could never have married Luke and it was wrong of me to promise. I never stopped loving Barney, but he's back now . . . he found me, Amy! Barney found me, and everything's going to be fine.'

A short time later, Kelly came out and Luke went in. 'I've told her,' Kelly said. 'Go to her . . . make her see that she has to come home to us, Luke.'

Curious, Barney saved his questions until later. For now Kelly needed his reassurance.

Together they watched Luke go to her. They saw how he held her in his arms, and how Amy clung to him. 'She'll get better now,' Kelly whispered. 'She has so much to look forward to.'

Chapter Twenty-one

BARNEY LAY AWAKE for what seemed an age, propped up on one elbow and gazing at Kelly's sleeping face. How could he have left her? he wondered. One thing he did know, he would never leave her again.

Kelly stirred, and he slid his arm round her. 'Morning, sleepyhead.'

Nestling in his arms, she ran her hand over his chest, playfully tweaking his nipples until he couldn't stand it any longer. Laughing, she slipped out of bed and threw open the curtains. 'It's such a beautiful day,' she said, blinking in the morning sunshine. 'After we've been to see Amy, happen we'll go to the park and stroll about.'

Getting out of bed he came to the window, and putting his arms about her, curved her into him. 'Last night was wonderful,' he murmured in her ear. 'I hadn't forgotten. Every minute I was away, I hadn't forgotten.'

She turned to him, her soft eyes looking up, holding his gaze. When he pressed her to him, she said, 'If you ever want to wander, I won't hold you.' Even though she would dread the day, more than ever she did before.

'My wandering days are over,' he vowed.

Kelly gave no answer. Time will tell, she thought, and left it at that.

After breakfast, Barney told her he would have to look for work. 'Luke said there might be something going where he is.' He glanced at the clock. 'There's time enough for me to go down there before we leave for Liverpool.'

Kelly asked him to leave it until the morrow. 'Give yourself time to breathe,' she said. 'You've only just got here. Besides, I want you to myself for another day at least.'

'One more day,' he conceded. 'Then I have to get work.' From his seat at the table he glanced round the room. 'I never dreamed you'd come back here.'

'It was something I had to do.'

'And are you happy?'

Kelly thought about her mother's torment in this house; now it seemed so far away it was as though it had never happened. 'It's a lovely house,' she murmured. 'Now that you're back, and Amy's on the mend, I couldn't be happier.'

As he passed to take his plate to the kitchen, he stroked her hair and kissed the top of her head. 'That goes for me too,' he said.

⇒⊶०⊷⇐

A SHORT TIME after Barney and Kelly went to catch the train to Liverpool, a carriage drew up outside the house in Johnson Street. For a moment it seemed as though whoever was inside had changed their mind and was not getting out after all.

A little later, however, the door opened and a man stepped down. Holding open the door, he reached inside the carriage and guided the woman out. 'Are you sure you don't want me to come with you?'

Marie thanked him, but said, 'No, Bill. This is something I have to do by myself.'

Going up the steps, she knocked softly at first, then more firmly. When it became clear there was no one in, she went back to the carriage. 'Do you want to leave?' Bill asked.

'Not yet.' Standing there, with her back to the carriage and the house directly in front of her, Marie suffered all manner of emotions. 'It's just the same,' she said wondrously. 'The street, the lamps and cobbles, and this house, although . . .' she studied the house more closely '. . . it seems, I don't know, more contented.'

Bill stood beside her. 'Could that be because *you're* more contented, do you think?'

Marie didn't hear. Her mind was way back then, in a time when she dreaded being in that house, and feared every step outside. Even now, as she gazed on it, there was the tiniest flurry of fear inside her. She supposed it would never really go away.

After a time, they returned to the carriage and sat inside, looking out. Marie didn't speak, and though he desperately wanted to, Bill had no way of understanding what was going on in her mind.

'We'll go into town,' she said after a while. 'I don't know about you, but I'm peckish. We'll give it an hour, then come back.'

Bill issued the directive to the driver and they went at a sedate pace down the street towards Blackburn town. 'I wonder if it's changed,' Marie said.

Nothing *else* had.

———————◆———————

I T WAS LATE afternoon when Kelly and Barney got off the tram. They walked the few hundred yards to Johnson Street, chatting all the way. 'Did you see how much better Amy looked already?' Kelly remarked. 'Oh, and her face when the doctor said that if she kept on mending, he wouldn't be at all surprised if the children were to come and see her.'

'You're right,' Barney agreed. 'It's just the tonic she needed.'

Kelly recalled the children's faces when she and Luke had found them. 'If all goes well, Luke means to take the children to see Amy a week from now.'

'It'll all work out, sweetheart, you'll see.'

'The children so much wanted to come home,' she sighed. 'Oh, Barney, won't it be wonderful when they're back and we can all begin to plan our lives?'

'*My* plans are already made.'

'Oh, are they now?' She looked up at him with mischievous eyes. 'And am *I* part of these secret plans?'

'You might be.'

'Go on. I'm listening.'

'Right, well, first I'll get work, then we'll be wed, and some time in the near future you'll make me a daddy. I know neither of us is young, but I believe there's still time.'

'Is that all?'

'It's enough to be going on with.'

Kelly lapsed into deep thought. She had never dared to imagine this day would ever come.

'Penny for them?'

'I was just thinking,' she sighed. 'I can't wait to get Amy and the children home.'

Barney smiled. 'It will happen,' he replied. 'All in good time.'

And somewhere deep inside, Kelly knew that it would.

⇒➳∘⋲⇐

WHEN THEY TURNED the corner into Johnson Street, Kelly was laughing at something Barney had said, but then she saw the carriage, and the woman sitting on her doorstep, and her heart almost leaped from her chest. 'My God!'

When she stopped, Barney looked at her face, so white and shocked, he feared she might keel over. 'Kelly . . . what's wrong with you?' he asked urgently.

Too shaken to answer, Kelly couldn't take her eyes off the woman. In her mind's eye she conjured up a familiar picture of her mother, sitting on that same step, watching her and Michael playing on the cobbles with the other children. When she saw them looking, Marie would smile, and when she thought the children weren't watching, she would bow her head and look so sad it would break Kelly's young heart.

Now, seeing her mother there, head bowed and thoughts miles away, it was more than she could bear. 'It's my *mother*!' Her voice trembled. 'Look . . . on the step, Barney! My mother.' Barney looked and recognised Marie and, for some inexplicable reason, a sense of panic ran through him.

Kelly didn't know whether to run towards her or run away. In the event, it was Marie who came to her.

Watching her as she came down the street, Kelly's heart turned somersaults. She saw how lovely and elegant her mother had grown, and though time had slowed her step and etched its mark into her face, it was still the same face, the same proud, dignified woman.

'Hello, my darling.' As she looked at Kelly, the love shone out of her eyes. 'I've been waiting for you,' she said. Just like she had always waited, when Kelly was a bairn, and ever since. 'I'll go away if you like?' As she spoke, her eyes glittered and her lips trembled. The heartache was never far away.

Kelly looked at this woman who was her mother, and softly shaking her head, let her emotions run free. All these years . . . this street . . . how strange it all seemed. She was that same little girl who had played in the street and seen her mother on that very step, hunched and broken, just as she had seemed when Kelly saw her a moment ago.

A moment. A lifetime. One and the same.

Suddenly they were in each other's arms, and the years fled away. There were tears, and afterwards recriminations, and then a great and wonderful reservoir of love that had never flowed away and never could.

Watching the two together was a fine and humbling experience for the men in their lives. This was something very special. Something they knew nothing of and would never be a part of. And so they stayed away, and wondered.

LATER, MARIE WANTED to go all over the house. Leaving her to her memories, Kelly followed a short distance behind.

Finally, she watched her go, hesitantly, into that front bedroom; Kelly wondered what effect it would have on her mother, and when Marie seemed to be in there a long time, Kelly ventured forward.

At first she couldn't see her mother, but then she heard, and realised. Marie was sitting on the floor, in front of where *he* used to lock her in the cupboard. Sobbing and distressed, she begged Kelly to, 'Leave me, please.'

Returning downstairs, Kelly drank the tea Barney made for her. For the next ten minutes her eyes were focused on the door, waiting for her mother to appear. When at last she came down, her face was slightly puffed where she had been crying, and there was a sad look in her eyes; at the same time she seemed incredibly calm, as though she had been haunted and now she was not.

Meeting Kelly's worried gaze, she said softly, 'It's not so bad, not now.' She had cried over her husband for the last time.

Kelly gestured for her to sit down.

'I have something to tell you,' Marie said. 'It's about Michael. That's why I came.'

'*Michael*?' Kelly felt a rush of fear. 'He's all right, isn't he?'

'He's in trouble,' she answered. 'He needs us.'

Marie retold the whole story, of how Michael had given himself up and was now charged with the murder of his father. 'It doesn't seem to matter that I already paid the price,' she said. 'He still has to answer the charges.'

'But *why* would he give himself up?' Kelly feared for him.

That had been Marie's first question, too. 'I asked him that,' she said. 'Reading between the lines, it would seem your brother gave himself up for the same reason you came back here, to this street – the same reason I felt the need to go all over this house. All these years, Michael has carried the very same burden, and more besides.'

She took a moment to compose herself. 'One thing I do know,' she murmured. 'I did him wrong all these years.' Looking at Kelly through regretful eyes, she said, 'Michael is *not* a coward. He never was.' She tapped her heart. 'Not in here. In here, he was just Michael, your brother. My son.'

She sighed. 'I wonder now if it wasn't *me* who was the greatest coward of all.'

Chapter Twenty-two

O N THE DAY of the trial, they were all there to lend support: Kelly and Barney, Marie and Bill. Michael saw them there and drew strength from them.

Widely publicised, the trial generated a great deal of interest. The courtroom was packed to the rafters, and when Marie gave evidence, the people grew silent; the only sound that could be heard was her clear, honest account of all that had happened.

She told how Michael had pleaded with her not to take the blame. 'He even confessed to one officer that *he* was the guilty one, and not me. I said he was lying to protect me, and they believed me; a son trying to protect his mother . . . and in a way they were right, because that was exactly how it happened.'

She went into the detail of their lives at the hands of the man who had fathered her children and tormented them every living day afterwards. She praised Michael for the son he was, and the man he had become, and now she pleaded for their mercy on his behalf. 'He has suffered every minute of every day since it happened, and long before that. Punishment has already been demanded and given, in exchange for his father's life. I know, because I paid the price. And that is as it should be, because I was the one who brought my children into the world, to a place where terror reigned. As long as I live, I will regret that.'

The barrister summed up his defence by echoing Marie's sentiments. 'Justice demands a price to pay,' he told them. 'The price has been paid tenfold, by Marie Wilson and, in different ways, by each of her children.

'This was no premeditated plan. It was the impulsive and desperate act of a young man on seeing his mother being beaten to within an inch of her life. He heard her screams and had to act . . . If any one of us had been in that same situation, how can we be sure we would not have done the same?'

Searching each of their faces in turn, he pleaded, 'I ask you to find it in your hearts to send this man home to his family.'

⋙•◆•⋘

AFTER A LONG, nerve-racking wait, the verdict of Not Guilty was returned, and the court erupted in loud cheers and whistling. Alarmed at the scale of reaction, the judge threatened to clear the court but no one heard him.

Some short time later, Michael was hurried through the crowds to the waiting carriage; all around him people cheered and wished him well. 'You did right!' One woman pushed her way forward. 'I'd have killed the bastard myself!'

But Michael was not celebrating. It was a bad thing to take a man's life, especially his own father's, and he would never forget.

'Let's go home, son.' Marie was reunited with her children at long last. It was all she had hoped for.

Chapter Twenty-three

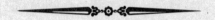

O N A GLORIOUS day in July, they all came together at Kathleen's beautiful home near Harrow. 'I'm that excited.' Amy climbed out of the carriage and couldn't believe her eyes. 'By! It's a bleedin' mansion!'

Mansion or not, it was home to Kathleen, and now Michael, and they had something to tell everyone. With his arm about the woman he loved, Michael said, 'Kathleen and I are getting wed. There are some things to be settled yet, but once that's out of the way, I mean to make this lovely woman my wife.'

Everybody cheered, and Kathleen blushed, and they settled down to the most wonderful tea out in the garden, served by people brought in from outside, and on china plates of the very best quality.

Amy was like a child let loose in a toy shop. 'It's the first time I've ever been to a garden party.' Making a face and rolling her eyes in feigned astonishment, she had them all laughing, and when she danced on the lawn with

Tom and Sally running rings round her, it was, as Tom kept saying, 'Like magic!'

Dazed with happiness, Kelly looked about her – at Amy and Luke, and the children between them; then at Barney, who never left her side and nor did she want him to. At Michael, so happy with his Kathleen, a lovely, gentle soul, who hit it off staight away with everyone . . . especially with Marie, who took to her as if she'd known her all her life.

Somebody wound up the gramophone and Charlie danced with Kelly on the lawn. 'I've never been happier,' he said. 'I've had a wonderful wife, and I had the privilege of knowing a lady by the name of Fran. I lost her, but I've got a family any man would be proud of.' There was the smallest glint of a tear in his eye when he said, 'Remember how we talked on that first day when you came back to the street?'

'We talked a lot,' Kelly remembered.

'And I told you how – somewhere, someday – we all get our own little share of paradise.'

'And you were right,' she answered, with a grateful kiss, and he swung her round like a man half his age.

Later, Bill's delightful grandson Samuel told Kelly how Marie would soon be his 'real' grandma. When Kelly mentioned it to her mother, she blushed, confiding, 'Bill asked me to marry him, and I said yes, but we didn't want to steal Michael's special day, so we'll keep our news until later.'

Kelly looked at Barney, who was smiling, and when

Marie looked puzzled, Kelly held out her hand. 'My news won't wait,' she laughed, proudly showing the narrow gold ring on her finger. 'We didn't want a big fuss, Mam, so we went to the Register Office and got wed quietly.'

While Marie was taking that in, she had another piece of wonderful news. 'And the baby's due early next year.'

Marie's mouth fell open, and soon she was gathering them all round. 'Kelly and Barney are wed and they're having a baby,' she cried, the tears rolling down her face. 'And I'll be a grandma twice over, with young Sammy here, when Bill and I tie the knot!'

To celebrate, Michael broke open a bottle of champagne, and the party went on into the small hours.

***

AFTER EVERYONE BUT themselves had gone to bed, Kelly and Barney sat under the trees in the warm evening air. 'You've made me such a happy man,' Barney said, holding his new wife close.

Kelly gazed at him with eyes full of love. She looked at the house and thought of all the people inside, and her heart was bursting. 'It all came right in the end, didn't it, my darling?' she murmured.

Together, as they would be for the rest of their long lives, they strolled to the house. Just an ordinary couple, in love, under the moonlight.

Headline hopes you have enjoyed reading SOMEWHERE, SOMEDAY and invites you to sample the beginning of Josephine Cox's compelling new saga, RAINBOW DAYS, out now in Headline hardback . . .

Chapter One

'WHAT'S TROUBLING YOU, Jessie?' All week, he had noticed how the old woman seemed preoccupied, as if there was something weighing heavy on her mind. Always independent, too concerned about hurting others to unburden her troubles on them, Jessie had a way of keeping her thoughts to herself.

Not today though. Today, she had a feeling that things were coming to a head and she needed to talk to someone, before it was too late. 'It's our Cathleen.' Her soft Irish voice was lost against his mutterings.

'Look at that!' Irritated and impatient he gave the nail another hammering. 'Can't get the damned thing to hold!'

Jessie looked up from her sewing, watching Tom at work and as always wondering what would happen to this lovely man after she'd gone. Moreover, what would happen to Cathleen? Young Robert too. Oh, but he was heading for a fall, that one.

Tom glanced at her. 'Sorry, Jessie. What did you say?'

'Nothing important. It can wait.' But not for much longer, she fretted. The matter of Cathleen would have to be addressed and soon.

'Damn it!' Plucking the nail out he moved it further up, to where the oak beam had sunk level with the wall; one swing with the hammer and it bit hard. 'That's better.'

Jessie followed his every movement: the hammer coming down, his eye intent on driving the nail home; the smile on his face as he wiggled the nail to satisfy himself it would hold.

Despairing, Jessie shook her head. She knew him all too well. When that task was finished he would start another. He never stopped. Rising at five to travel into Blackburn town and light the big ovens at the bakery, he never arrived home until the streets were shrouded in darkness. Even then he would find all manner of jobs to do about the house.

'What's that about our Cathleen?' Taking the picture, he hung it skilfully on the nail and stepped back to see how it looked.

Jessie didn't answer straight away. Instead she continued to observe him, noting how the long hard hours shovelling bread in and out of ovens had gently stooped his shoulders and weathered his face with a deep, warm glow. Tom was in his mid-forties, but seemed older. Yet even now he would have been a catch for any woman. Long of limb and dark of eye, he was still an easy-looking man. With no life outside of his work and his children, he was often lonely. He could have found himself a wife without too much bother, but Jessie knew he never would. The plain truth was that Tom still loved the woman he had wed all those years ago. And though she was gone now, he wanted no other.

'What about our Cathleen?' he repeated. Turning from his task, Tom's dark eyes sought her face.

'I didn't think you were listening.'

'Sorry about that, Jessie. The damned nail wouldn't take hold.'

'I don't want you worrying, but . . .' Having started, Jessie had to go on, 'I've been meaning to have a word with yer, so I have.'

Sensing trouble, Tom put down the hammer and came to sit opposite her. 'Why? What's she done?'

'Nothing wrong, as I know of . . .' she answered. 'It's just that . . .' She shrugged her shoulders, trying to make light of it; already regretting being the cause of the anxiety on his face. 'Aw, sure it doesn't matter. It's just an old woman's ramblings.'

'Huh! I've yet to see the day when *you* take to "rambling",' he declared. 'Come on, Jessie. It's obvious you're concerned about our Cathleen. You'd best out with it!'

'I never said I were concerned,' she chided. 'I were just thinking . . . now that she's eighteen, and with not having a Mam an' all . . . well, I reckon yer might need to have a talk with the lass.' Feeling uncomfortable beneath his curious gaze, she began to wish she had kept her worries to herself.

Frowning, he asked, 'What kind of talk?' Cathleen was the joy of his life. If there was a problem he needed to know. 'Jessie! What are you getting at?'

Changing her mind, the old woman shook her head, 'Aw, sure, it's summat and nothing,' she replied with a shrug.

'Let *me* be the judge of that, Jessie.'

'I were just wondering if you'd said anything to the lass . . .' Her mind raced ahead, thinking that the best thing was to change tack, at least for now. '. . . about the business, that kind o' thing?'

Crossing her fingers under her pinny, she asked the good Lord not to strike her dead for telling lies.

Reassured, Tom gave a sigh of relief. 'By! I thought for a minute you were saying she'd got herself in trouble, with some young fella. That bugger Lou Matheson comes to mind straightaway.'

She laughed. 'Lou Matheson might fancy his chances, but our Cathleen's never had eyes for him.'

Unsure, he searched her eyes looking for the truth then, suddenly leaning forward, he took hold of her hand. 'Look here, Jessie,' he said, 'I know you love the lass, and you've never been one for telling tales, but, if ever there was anything worrying you, about Cathleen in particular, I wouldn't want you to keep it from me.'

Shame and guilt filled her kind old heart, and now

she was in a dilemma. 'I understand what yer saying, so I do.'

He kept his gaze locked with hers, a fond smile creeping over his manly features. 'That doesn't mean to say I don't trust you or anything, and I'd never want to hurt your feelings, Jessie. I love you like you were my own mother.'

Casting his mind back to the past, he thought of how it used to be. 'You've been an absolute godsend to me,' he told her kindly. 'You were there the day our Cathleen was born . . . then three years later when young Robert came along.' His eyes clouded over. 'You stood by us when their Mam fell ill and were taken only days after.'

Swallowing his grief, he confessed, 'I fell apart after that, I let things go, God help me. I lost my work and my senses. But you were always there, for all of us. You saved my sanity.'

Jessie was special, he knew that. And he owed her more than he could ever repay. 'The day you persuaded us to come and live here with you in Pleasington, oh, Jessie!' He bowed his head. 'Throwing open your home to the three of us, well, it was a grand thing you did. Not many women would have done the same.'

'Aw, I'm sure they would,' Jessie answered. 'Where family is involved, a woman will always give that little bit extra.' A cheeky grin lifted her features. 'Besides, I didn't do it just for you!' she declared craftily. 'We've helped each *other*, so we have.'

Jessie had her own painful memories. 'When my

Thomas died, he left behind a rundown bakery and a pile of debts. You took it on, and in no time at all the bakery was making more money than ever, and all the debts long ago paid off.' She chuckled. 'I've even managed to save a shilling or two for me old age, so I have.'

Smiling, Tom shook his head, 'However much you might dismiss it, you still saved my life, Jessie . . . mine *and* the children's. I know this much . . . if it hadn't been for you, I don't think I would ever have come through it.'

Remembering, Jessie nodded. 'Mebbe . . . mebbe not.' A great sigh rippled through her. 'There's no denying, it were a bad time,' she recalled. 'You lost a wife and I lost a daughter, but we were blessed with two little souls. We've a lot to be thankful for Tom, you must always remember that.'

Taking a deep breath, he leaned back in the chair. 'I know,' he agreed. 'Sometimes though, I wish young Robert was more like Cathleen.' He shook his head. 'I swear he drives me to despair.'

Jessie knew what he meant and agreed, but would never say so. Instead, against her own instincts she always found herself defending the lad. 'I'll not deny Robert is headstrong and rebellious, but sometimes that's the way it is . . . no two bairns are ever the same, any mother will tell yer that. He'll grow out of it, so he will. Sure, the lad's only fifteen, and o' course' – a familiar sense of sadness filled her old heart – 'from the day he was born the poor wee soul never had the love of a mother.'

She paused, thinking how Tom's only son did seem to have a streak of wickedness in him, but went on, 'For all his wild ways, he's still his mother's child, and his mother was goodness itself. So we mustn't despair.'

Suddenly, in that appealing way she had of turning a situation round, she began to chuckle. 'Matter o' fact, I were quite a handful meself in me young days.' Rolling her speckled brown eyes, she confided, 'I don't mind telling yer, *I* were a little divil, so I was!'

Tom couldn't help but throw back his head with laughter. 'I don't doubt that for a minute, Jessie Butler!'

Jessie's old eyes twinkled. 'I've allus loved the dancing.' She wasn't telling him anything he didn't already know. 'I reckon when I were born the good Lord gave me feet that wouldn't keep still. Me Daddy told me I danced at the drop of a hat . . . soon as ever the gramophone was wound up, sure I'd be off like a spinning top . . . dancing all over the place, and making everybody laugh. It's allus been the same so it has, the music starts and my feet begin to itch. When I were old enough to be allowed on the dance floor, I'd be the first one on and the last one off.' As she spoke, her feet tapped a gentle rhythm on the rug. 'I were never short o' partners neither, though I wore the buggers out one after the other, so I did.'

Chuckling at the memory, she added mischievously, 'Sure, them other bonny lasses didn't like it at all, but that didn't bother me none. As long as I could dance, I was in me glory, so I was.'

'Sounds to me like you were a bit of a handful, Jessie

Butler,' he laughed, 'I should think you drove your Mam and Dad to distraction.'

'Aye, that's what *they* said an' all.' She laughed with him, her heart happy at the memory.

Tom could imagine how she might have caused a stir as a young woman. With those beautiful hazel eyes and that long, thick hair she must have turned many a young man's head. Now, at sixty-nine years old, she still carried a haunting kind of beauty; though the hair was plaited and streaked with grey, there was a mischievousness about her that gladdened the heart.

'You dance as if you were born to it,' he told her. 'Your daughter always said you should have made a career out of it.' He smiled wistfully. 'I wonder what she'd say if she'd been here on Cathleen's birthday, and seen you dancing round the garden like some little pixie . . . wearing out everybody who was brave enough to try and keep up with you.'

'Oh, *Cathleen* kept up. She were still dancing when I sat meself down, so she were.'

'Aye, well, that's not surprising is it? 'Cause we all know, our Cathleen is her grannie in the making.'

Feeling his loneliness, Jessie took hold of his hand, saying softly, 'you wondered what her Mammy might have said if she'd seen us? Well, I'll tell yer . . . she'd have said how *you* should try dancing more often. She'd have said you needed to find yerself a woman, someone to spend the rest of your days with.'

Nodding thoughtfully, he conceded, 'Happen you're

right, Jessie, but it's not likely I'll ever find a woman like my Mary, even if I wanted to.' Before the memories came flooding back, he shrugged off Jessie's suggestion with a smile. 'Besides, I'm not a dancing man,' he said. 'So, I'll leave all that to you, and Cathleen, for you're two of a kind, and that's a fact.'

'Now you could be right about that,' the old woman agreed. 'She's got the feet for dancing, so she has, and a heart the same. And doesn't she love the outdoors an' all? Sure she'd spend her life like a gypsy on the road if she had half a chance.'

'She's a good girl isn't she, Jessie?' It wasn't that he needed reassuring. It was just that, lately, Cathleen had seemed to grow up so quickly. She wasn't his little girl any more. She was a young woman and very beautiful at that.

'Aye, she's a good girl, Tom. Our Cathleen will always make you a proud man, I'm sure of it.'

'And Robert?' He always felt anxious thinking about his son.

'Aw, the lad's young and headstrong. But so is every other lad at his age. So stop yer worrying, why don't yer?' Though to her mind, Robert was a lost cause. 'Robert will come right in the end, mark my words. Besides, Cathleen keeps a wary eye on him, so he won't go far wrong, I'm thinking.' She prayed she was right.

'Oh, Jessie, I do hope so.'

Momentarily closing his eyes he pictured Cathleen's mother; slim and pretty, with vivid blue eyes and flowing fair hair, she might have been Cathleen herself.

Suppressing the image, he looked at the old woman. 'We seem to have got off the subject,' he chided. 'You were saying . . . about Cathleen?'

Having lied once, she did not want to do so a second time. Tom was a good man and deserved better. Besides, there was nothing to be gained by worrying him with her suspicions, so she quickly shifted her thinking. 'I were just wondering about her future.'

'Go on,' he urged, 'Tell me what's really on your mind.'

Jessie found herself edging towards the real issue, 'I've taught Cathleen all I know. She can read and write; she has a quick grasp of numbers, and a natural love for music and nature, but, now that she's eighteen, you need to be thinking about her future.'

Tom sat up, suddenly aware that he had been neglecting his parental duties. 'By! It never even crossed me mind,' he admitted. 'She grew up when me back was turned and now I'm not sure what I'm supposed to do.' An idea struck him. 'Look, Jessie! If the lass is good at figures, like you say . . . happen we should take her into the business? She's already doing deliveries, and folk think the world of her.' His face darkened. 'I had thought our Robert might take over some day, but I don't think he has the spirit for hard work.'

'It's not a bad idea, Tom,' Jessie conceded. 'But I wouldn't want her weighed down with too many responsibilities, not yet anyway. She's of an age when her whole world is opening up. Many a lass of eighteen is already wed, with bairns running at her feet. For all we know, Cathleen could be setting her cap at some young man right now. If yer ask me, we should be guiding her in the right direction.'

'In what way d'you mean, Jessie?'

'I mean . . . if she were to fall for somebody not of her own station, it might cause the lass, and us, no end of grief!'

Alarmed, Tom sensed Jessie's veiled warning. He finally understood what she had been leading up to. 'My God! That's what's been playing on your mind, isn't it . . . Cathleen and Silas Fenshaw.' He toyed with the possibility and rejected it out of hand, but when he looked up, neither his smile nor his voice was convincing. 'Surely to God, she's got more sense than to entertain such an idea? They're *friends*, Jessie! They've *allus* been friends, and no more.'

Now that she'd stirred his suspicions, Jessie kept at it, like a dog with a bone. 'Think about it, Tom,' she pleaded. 'They spend every waking minute together. Yes, to be sure, they've been friends since they were children and that's innocent enough. But friendship can change.'

'Not in *that* way.'

'*Yes*, Tom!' Forcing him to look at the possibility, she urged, 'Love can take a hold and before you know it, they're seeing each other through the eyes of grown-ups. 'Cause that's what they are. What's more, they've already got a head start on many another young couple who have fallen in love and found themselves in a tangle.'

'I still can't see that happening, Jessie.' To him Cathleen was still a baby.

'Then you'd best put yer mind to it, because she's *not* a bairn any more. She's a young woman with time on her hands, and you know what they say . . . the devil will surely find mischief for idle hands.'

'Silas Fenshaw has always been earmarked to wed the Turner girl, everybody knows that. Our Cathleen doesn't even come into the picture. It's all to do with business, and power.'

Jessie shook her head, 'There's nothing more powerful than love, and besides, no matter how desperately his father might want Silas to slip a wedding ring on Helen Turner's finger, it will never happen. Young Silas has no liking for her. You know it, I know it, and the whole of Lancashire knows it.'

'I think you're barking up the wrong tree, Jessie.' All the same, Tom's mind was made up. 'First thing Monday morning, I'd best make a start on teaching Cathleen the ins and outs of the bakery business. With your blessing o' course . . . seeing as we're partners.'

Jessie smiled, 'It don't mek no difference to me, son,' she answered. 'My half will come to her anyway, one o' these fine days.' Though she hoped that day was far off yet. 'But yer must ask *her* first, and see if that's what she wants.'

With that they each resumed their tasks, but their

thoughts were of one mind; could Cathleen really have stepped out of line and fallen in love with Silas Fenshaw?

If she had, then she had already taken the first step down a painful road; for while Edward Fenshaw might have accepted the baker's child as a playmate for his only son, he would never entertain the idea of her being one of the family. Never in a million years!

Despite the hot sun beating down on her head, Helen Turner made no move to find shade. Instead, she stayed by the verandah steps, hidden from sight and secretly observing the two figures below; her devious eyes following their every move.

Unable to tear herself away, she continued to watch them, hating their innocence, their obvious joy in each other. Oh, how she longed to run and tell them what she had discovered, and how because of it, she held both their futures in the palm of her hand. But, however much she wanted to, she could not tell them yet. Tomorrow would be soon enough, she thought bitterly.

Her hard features lifted in a smile. 'Enjoy each other while you can,' she murmured softly. 'It won't be long now, not if I have my way.' The smile gave way to a low, rumbling laugh. 'And, as you should know by now, I *always* get my way.'

Bad Boy Jack

Josephine Cox

Deserted by the two women in his life, Robert Sullivan is left to raise three-year-old Nancy and her seven-year-old brother Jack. Unable to cope, Robert is driven to abandon his children to those who he believes can provide them with a better life. However, he quickly has a change of heart and decides to go back for them. But on the way there, he is involved in a horrific accident.

Unbeknownst to him, Jack and Nancy are placed in the brutal regime of the Galloway Children's Home, where Jack's fierce devotion to his sister and fiery temper land him in more trouble. Clinging together, the two children find themselves at the mercy of the corrupt Clive Ennington, who splits them up and sells Nancy off to the highest bidder.

When Robert begins to recover in hospital he is determined to find and reunite his family. But he soon begins to realise the terrible consequences of his own cowardly actions.

Praise for Josephine Cox's writing:

'Cox's talent as a storyteller never lets you escape' *Daily Mail*

'Driven and passionate' *The Sunday Times*

Bad Boy Jack is also available in an audio edition.

0 7472 6640 9

headline

Now you can buy any of these other bestselling books by **Josephine Cox** from your bookshop or *direct from the publisher*.

FREE P&P AND UK DELIVERY
(Overseas and Ireland £3.50 per book)

Bad Boy Jack	£6.99
Jinnie	£6.99
The Woman Who Left	£6.99
Let It Shine	£6.99
Looking Back	£6.99
Rainbow Days	£6.99
The Gilded Cage	£6.99
Tomorrow The World	£6.99
Love Me Or Leave Me	£6.99
Miss You Forever	£6.99
Cradle of Thorns	£6.99
A Time for Us	£6.99
The Devil You Know	£6.99
Living A Lie	£6.99
A Little Badness	£6.99
More Than Riches	£6.99
Born To Serve	£6.99

TO ORDER SIMPLY CALL THIS NUMBER

01235 400 414

or visit our website: www.madaboutbooks.com

Prices and availability subject to change without notice.